The Roar

of the Crowd

other Ravenstone mysteries by Janice MacDonald

Sticks and Stones
The Monitor
Hang Down Your Head
Condemned to Repeat

For my darling Masani so glad to get some time with you!

The Roar

of the Crowd

love

A Randy Craig Mystery

By

Janice MacDonald

RaveN
STONE

Roar of the Crowd
copyright © Janice MacDonald 2014

Published by Ravenstone
an imprint of Turnstone Press
Artspace Building
206-100 Arthur Street
Winnipeg, MB
R3B 1H3 Canada
www.TurnstonePress.com

Turnstone Press gratefully acknowledges the assistance of the Canada
Council for the Arts, the Manitoba Arts Council, the Government of
Canada through the Canada Book Fund, and the Province of Mani-
toba through the Book Publishing Tax Credit and the Book Publisher
Marketing Assistance Program.

This novel is a work of fiction. Names, characters, places and incidents
are either the product of the author's imagination or are used fictitiously,
and any resemblance to actual persons living or dead, events or locales, is
entirely coincidental.

Printed and bound in Canada by Friesens for Turnstone Press.

Library and Archives Canada Cataloguing in Publication

MacDonald, Janice E. (Janice Elva), 1959–, author
    The roar of the crowd / Janice MacDonald.

(A Randy Craig mystery)
ISBN 978-0-88801-470-2 (pbk.)

    I. Title. II. Series: MacDonald, Janice E. (Janice Elva), 1959-
Randy Craig mystery.

PS8575.D6325R63 2014   C813'.54   C2014-903011-8

This book is dedicated to my wonderful friend
Barbara Reese:
extraordinary actress, wife, mother, world traveller,
Edmonton arts maven, and voracious reader.
Your generosity of spirit and your love are so appreciated.

The Roar

of the Crowd

1.

Even dead, Oren Gentry could fill a theatre. That is what it seemed like, anyway. The memorial was supposed to begin in five minutes and people were still streaming in, finding a place to sit in Zeidler Hall, the smallest of the three theatre spaces in the Citadel Theatre complex.

"They'll wait till 2:08, mark my words. Theatre tradition," hissed Sarah Arnold, who was sitting on the other side of Denise from me. "They probably already planned it that way." She fluttered back into her seat, arranging her layers of black in a seemly fashion.

I wasn't sure full hat and veil were required of non-family mourners, but Sarah didn't seem to be taking any chances. I felt a slight tremor from Denise's shoulder. I didn't dare catch her eye, for fear both of us would begin to giggle.

Denise Wolff, my best friend, was a Shakespeare professor at the University of Alberta, one of the very few U of A–minted PhDs they had ever hired into their ranks, I might add. That was

3

true for most universities. They preferred to hire from outside their student body, possibly to create more cross-pollination. Or maybe it was just one of those "grass is greener" concepts. Luckily, they had realized you don't get lusher than Denise when it comes to her love and understanding of the Bard, and her ability to get that enthusiasm across to undergrads.

She had brought a lot of new ideas to the department once she received tenure, and this event was the result of one of them.

Not Oren Gentry's death, of course. Edmonton's most famous son had died all on his own, no thanks to Denise. She was the reason the two of us were here at his memorial service, though. If it hadn't been for her cross-departmental initiative with the Drama department to create an Elizabethan rendition of Shakespeare in the outdoor rotunda between the Fine Arts and Law buildings, the likelihood of our being surrounded by Edmonton's theatrical community to mourn one of their own would be slim to nil.

The concept of having Shakespeare classes in the English department mix and mingle with acting classes in the Drama department must have occurred to someone before Denise, but if so, no one else had been able to create the fusion necessary. I had been roped in to help her tote and lift, as I was "between engagements" as a freelancer. It helped, of course, that Denise was utterly irresistible to men while at the same time exuding some sort of unthreatening air to women. Everyone wanted to be connected to her, and judging by her string of friendly ex-boyfriends, everyone was just happy to have had some time in the sunlight with her.

She was my closest pal in Edmonton. We had met in the English department, while I was working as a teaching assistant and writing up my Master's thesis and she was in the throes of her PhD dissertation. We'd both had offices in a university-owned house across the street from the Humanities building, and the connection had continued through the ensuing years. Denise had kept her eye on the brass ring, a professorship within the university. I, who had hoped to spend the rest of my days teaching introductory English literature courses to freshmen students, had found it impossible to maintain a lifestyle filled with luxuries like groceries and electricity on the two to three courses a year a sessional lecturer could often nab, but never count on. I had to admit, as Denise grew more and more confident and alive in her secure and permanent position, little tendrils of envy grew in my heart. Still, she was my friend, and since I had no other pressing deadlines this spring, I had figured I might as well help with the inaugural Spring Session Courtyard Shakespeare 284. Denise had a budget for printing and publicity, and had hired me for a nominal amount to create handbills and tickets.

She and Sarah, the sessional lecturer hired to teach acting, who was also quite well known as an actress around town, had been the masterminds behind the project. With the blessing of several of the local bigwigs in the theatre community, like Alex Karras, Jim de Felice, and Oren Gentry, the three daytime productions of *Romeo and Juliet* had been very well received. The three-week spring session English class had all been Montagues and the Drama class Capulets and the line in the sand had been obvious. University students, curious theatre folks, and a lot of retired people who could afford to spend two-and-a-half hours standing or perched on railway-tied landscaping steps, provided an appreciative audience, and the project was written up in the *Edmonton Journal*, *Avenue Magazine* and featured on the Sunday arts program on the CBC. Denise and Sarah were the flavour of the month.

It had worked out rather well for me, as well. The artistic director of the summer Shakespeare in the Park festival had been really taken with the whole idea of springboarding the interest in Shakespeare with first- and second-year students. His company was made up of professionals, but they had a mandate to hire two or three freshly graduated students, as well, in an effort to help them on their way to their Equity cards, and to provide some essential training in the classics. They also ran a Shakespeare camp for junior high and high school students, who met during the day down at the site and learned about Shakespeare and acting, along with stage fencing, makeup, costuming, and repertory work. The junior high program was well developed and run by an actress with a teaching degree, who had been part of the company since its inception. The high school program was waning, though.

Kieran Frayne had approached both Denise and Sarah to see if they would be interested in creating some sort of bridging class for the summer high school students who self-identified as wanting to spend three weeks studying Shakespeare and acting. Neither woman had the time or inclination, but Denise had loyally offered up my name to him. I had met with him twice, providing a syllabus of what I thought would provide insight, background, hands-on work, and fun. I was hired, gratefully, I had the feeling. The course was set to begin at the end of June, giving me just under a month to get ready, once I was through with the marking I'd signed on to do for a couple of profs. Of course, it didn't hurt that Kieran had begun seeing Denise socially. Ah well, if you can't make nepotism work for you once in a while, why bother making friends?

In the meantime, the best-known actor/director/television personality to have ever come out of Edmonton, Oren Gentry, had died. Although he was only in his fifties, Gentry had lived hard and fast and bright, very much in the public eye. No one was overly surprised by his sudden heart attack. Sad, yes. Messages of condolence were coming in from all over Canada. The prime minister had been filmed saying that Gentry was his favourite actor, calling him the patron saint of Alberta. Flags flew at half-mast at the Legislature, City Hall, the university, and the Victoria School for the Arts, where Gentry had once attended school.

And here we were, the theatre community of Edmonton, come to mourn one of our own.

The lights began to dim, causing a slight flurry to our right, as Sarah flipped back her dark veil in order to see. I checked my watch, pushing the glow button in the dark. 2:08. Showtime.

2.

The curtains drew back to reveal one empty spotlight on the stage. It stayed lit for a full minute, which seemed interminable, and then was abruptly shut off, leaving the stage entirely dark for another minute. Slowly, so that I couldn't even say for sure when it had begun, a low orchestral piece, relying heavily on strings, built in the background, providing a fuzzy warm sound in the wings.

The stage slowly relit, and this time there was a podium to the left, a long table in the middle of the stage, draped with a purple cloth and holding a photo of Oren Gentry, next to a brass urn that caught the overhead spotlights and seemed to glow. Coming from the wings stage right, dressed in an off-white, homespun cassock and a purple alb, was Bill Oakes. I smiled in spite of the sad occasion. What a perfect choice of cleric to lead the funeral of such a larger-than-life and vibrant Edmontonian. Oakes, a former moderator of the United Church of Canada, had run for provincial office after his time in the synod and won his seat handily. Totally at ease with people, and mildly charismatic to boot, Oakes had held his seat through three premiers and was an always pleasant thorn in the side of the reigning Conservative Cabinet.

He held his hands up, in a way I associated with Evita Perón, and I am sure you could have heard a pin drop. The music stopped, then swelled into its final cadenza. As the silence fell, Oakes tilted his head forward in classic indication and said simply, "Let us pray."

The rest of the funeral was the usual blur. Oakes gave a very personalized homily, as he and Gentry had been acquainted for years and had served on various community committees. A cousin got up to speak, as did Tom Wood, the lead actor-in-residence at the Citadel, and former Edmontonian Brad Fraser, who had flown in from Toronto to attend the funeral of the man who had first produced his plays. A beautifully edited short film of Oren Gentry receiving an award from the City, striding onto the stage as a startlingly beautiful young Hamlet, working with student actors, and walking his poodle in the river valley, ran while Cathy Derkash sang "If Ever I Should Leave You" from *Camelot*.

I doubt there was a dry eye in the house. I could hear several people weeping, but I wasn't close enough to the front of the house to determine how those in Gentry's inner circle, his closest friends and confidants, were affected. Denise looked stoic, but there was no colour in her face, and I knew she was moved. I now understood why Sarah had opted for the dark veil.

We sat as the rows in front of us emptied, and by the time it was our turn to reach the lobby, the party was in full swing.

It was like stepping through Aunty Em's front door into Oz, the difference in temperament and tone. While we were in the service, catering staff had set up shop in the lobby of the Citadel. Finger foods and glasses of white and red wine were set out on tables at the sides, and waiters abounded, circulating with trays of hors d'oeuvres and open bottles to top up glasses. A klezmer band was playing gypsy oompah music in front of the staircase to the Shoctor Theatre upper lobby, probably to keep the crowd from wandering all over the complex. Even so, since the lobby to the theatre was open to the public, and attached by pedways to a couple of other buildings, businesspeople and several folk who looked more homeless than theatrically bohemian in their clothing choices were also in evidence.

"This was what Kieran was talking about," Denise laughed. "A note on top of the papers they found with Oren's will stipulated he wanted a party thrown for his funeral. Apparently he had made loose arrangements for this long ago, the way some people buy a graveyard plot."

"He hired caterers and booked a band?" I was skeptical. After all, how would he know the date?

Denise shook her head. "Not that specific, no. But Kieran was saying that folks were scrambling to find a dance band, because the note specified he didn't want a string quartet. Talk about directing your own sendoff, eh? This is perfect," she smiled as she nodded to the waiter wanting to refill her wineglass.

I was impressed. The whole event had been orchestrated to maximum effect. People were not going to forget Oren Gentry. And of course, that was as it should be. He had been a strong force in the Edmonton theatre community. Without the vision and gumption of him and his cohort who had burst out of the U of A Drama department in the late 1970s, founding theatres and starting festivals, we likely wouldn't have half the live theatrical events the city was famous for. It was said that Edmonton had more theatres per capita than any other city in North America. When you couple that sort of statistic with the knowledge that our roads are icy and snow-clogged for a good five months of the year, and that our population, besides government and university workers, was predominantly blue-collar rather than the more homogenized mix in other burgs, it just had to make you proud.

We had a strong sense of drama in the schools, which bred students to enjoy live theatre. Our Fringe Theatre Festival in the late summer was the first of its kind in North America and still considered the best of the rest, which had sprung up in cities from Orlando to Victoria in its wake. The Freewill Shakespeare Festival produced two plays in repertory every summer in Hawrelak Park, one comedy, one tragedy. The Citadel's Shoctor Theatre did the big-budget season of a Shaw, a Shakespeare, a Tony Award–winner and a Broadway-styled musical; the Maclab Theatre was where they put on their extravagantly wonderful Christmas Carol every December.

Edgier plays could be seen at the Roxy, at the other end of the downtown on 124th Street, in a former movie theatre, or across the river in Old Strathcona, where the Fringe took hold in the summer. Two former fire halls and the previous site of the public transit bus barns were now year-round theatre spaces for three or four theatre companies to share. Black Box Theatre, Taryn Creighton's baby, moved around the city, finding empty spaces in which to perform.

There had been a lovely little theatre built in the basement of the Northern Alberta Jubilee Auditorium, the huge hall where operas and touring musicals were booked and university convocations took place, but it had mysteriously closed. Some said it had to be used for furnace space in a subsequent remodelling. Some said it was still perfect, but locked away for unknown reasons.

And Oren Gentry had been part of it all. He had started as a BFA actor, dazzling everyone in his fourth-year performance of Sebastian Venables in *Suddenly Last Summer*. A few summers at Stratford later, he was back in Edmonton, honing his directing chops in the MFA program and starting his own theatre company in a former movie theatre down from the west-end Grant MacEwan College arts campus. Chautauqua Theatre had juggled classics that most people only studied in play analysis classes, Canadian plays past their first blush, and new works. He ran spoken-word evenings and was always to be seen on site during the Fringe, laughing with a crowd in the beer tent, bouncing into a seat on the aisle at performances of popular winners and sophomoric one-man efforts alike. If Colin MacLean was the "dean of Edmonton theatre" due to his years of supportive reviews and journalistic coverage, Oren Gentry had been the "soul of Edmonton theatre." It was probably scaring more than one person drinking mid-priced wine at this party to think what everyone was going to do without him.

"The show must go on," I muttered, and Denise turned from

chatting with Sarah about her running and stair-climbing exercise routine to look at me.

"What's that?"

"I was just wondering, who is going to be able to fill the gap he's left?" I said.

Denise nodded grimly. "Yes, it's going to be very interesting to see how it plays out. After all, there's an artistic director position up for grabs. There is a senior statesman role to fill. And boy, if you think nature abhors a vacuum, just wait and see what artifice thinks of it." She motioned her head questioningly toward the doors leading to the Clifford E. Lee Pavilion of trees and benches under glass, which we'd have to traverse to get to the parkade stairs leading to her car. I nodded back gratefully; it was time to go.

We said our goodbyes to Sarah and several other people Denise ran into along the way to the car. The party had spilled into the atrium, and several beautiful young actresses in black were conversing near a bench on which an old woman with bags at her feet was sitting, not paying them or the rest of the world any mind.

I held the door for Denise and we made our way into the underground parkade shared by the Citadel Theatre, Winspear Concert Hall, and Edmonton Public Library.

"Do you really think Oren's death is going to shake things up?"

"Oh, I think we have just seen the prologue, Randy. This is a five-act succession drama just waiting to unfold. Let's just hope it's *Henry V* and not *Richard III.*"

"Really?"

"It's like English department politics, the knives are so sharp because the stakes are so small."

We had reached Denise's convertible cream-coloured Bug by this time, and the sudden blasting of a Joel Plaskett in mid-song, the CD that had been playing when we'd pulled up, smothered my burst of pent-up laughter.

3.

Being even tangentially involved with theatre people sort of felt to me like coming home. Long before I decided to return to academe to do my master's and teach freshmen, a dream that seemed to have fizzled out while I wasn't looking, I was a freelance writer, working mostly in radio. And how I had got into radio was through a senior-level course in my undergrad days on writing and acting for radio.

Back in the days when I first went to university, there wasn't yet the unholy push to determine what career you would pursue the day after you stepped off the convocation stage. I had dabbled in writing for the student newspaper, acting in various MFA directors' productions, and DJ-ing a late-night folk music program on the campus radio. In between, I had learned enough about geology and peak oil to be firmly on the side of David Suzuki, poked around in classics and philosophy classes with enthusiasm but little skill, polished up my rusty French in order to ascertain that Camus had been clinically depressed, and skimmed through a survey in psychology that helped with the aforementioned diagnosis. Radio was what had stuck.

Some of the student actors I knew in those days were very talented and had gone the distance. I saw their names in the credits of CTV shows and in movies funded by Telefilm Canada. One or two of them were even in Hollywood movies and on the Disney Channel, living down in California. Sandra Foyle, who had shone like a diamond in every student production, now reigned in Stratford; I had seen a spread of her two-hundred-year-old house filled with beautiful antiques, Dora Awards, and pretty children in *Canadian Living* just a month or so ago.

I wasn't one of those success stories. There was something about the transience of theatre, or maybe the messy collaboration of it all, that never sat right with me. I was so much more at ease tackling my own work, moving to my own rhythms, and heading for my own deadlines. Factoring in the egos and vulnerabilities of five to twelve other people while at the same time remaining on good terms with the stage manager was just not my style.

When I moved back to Edmonton to do my MA, I noted a few familiar names in the theatre scene here, probably drawn to the city for the Fringe and then charmed into staying, and met a few others. I doubted the old acquaintances would recall my name, unless they'd been insomniac folk music fans. Even then, I hadn't used my real name on the campus airwaves. I'd been Miranda Lang, using my mother's maiden name, for reasons I could no longer remember but seemed important at the time. I played about a bit, doing small roles in MFA directors' works, and then hunkered down, got my thesis written, and drifted away from theatre entirely.

Now here I was, sliding back into the orbit of the theatre crowd. Denise saw it as repayment for my doing her a favour, and of course I was very grateful she had put in a word to the Shakespeare folks, since the rent did have to be paid and all that. But something was waking up in me, the more time I spent with the actors and directors. It was as if deep inside, a little Mickey Rooney was conspiring with a miniature Judy Garland, whispering, "Mom can make the curtains—let's put on a show!"

I had met with Kieran Frayne, the artistic director of the Freewill Players, and Amanda Sparrow, one of the original artistic partners of the company, who was also in charge of the Camp Shakespeare arm of the festival. Amanda had dreams of expanding her successful two-week camp into a solid high school program as well. She had a tried-and-true week for Grades 4-6, and then another for the junior high kids, but had never completely cracked the Grades 10-12 set. High school was the time when they had to knuckle under and study Shakespeare in English classes, and various schools in the area had strong drama departments, producing some first-rate year-end plays. Of course, high school was also when kids wanted to be working summer jobs to fund any extras their parents weren't going to provide. Amanda was sure that, with a bit of thoughtful planning and strong marketing, we could provide a useful fortnight of training in acting with classical scripts, stage fighting, repertory work, and dialects. I wasn't so sure it would compete with a retail job in the mall, but I was willing to try.

While I had the feeling she would rather have had a Drama department sessional roped in for the work, Denise had sung my praises to Kieran, who was predisposed to be interested in anything my beautiful friend said. And so it went. Amanda was stuck with me.

I wasn't sorry to get the gig. There is a touch of messianic zeal that is fostered by teaching freshman English, and the thought of bringing even younger teens to Shakespeare, self-selected teens who chose to come down to the park every day for two weeks instead of selling Orange Juliuses, sleeping in, or watching You-Tube videos, was invigorating. With Amanda's blessing, I had crafted the camp into four modules a day, with short breaks and lunch in between. The first section of each day involved exercise. The festival's choreographer ran dance and movement classes that alternated daily with stage fighting run by the fight director on the stage itself, and both had a warm-up exercise component leading off. After the break, the kids would gather in the area up the hill equipped with picnic tables and box stools from a previous production to discuss aspects of Shakespeare's works, world view, writing style, and history. If it rained, we would move into the tent set up nearby for pizza and barbecue dinners prior to the shows.

We would set aside three-quarters of an hour for lunch, followed by vocal work. This would be a smorgasbord of activities, as we had access to a dialect coach, a singing coach, and the festival's musical director, who enjoyed extemporizing on Shakespeare's various lyrics with found instruments and student tunes. Each student would be responsible for a monologue to work on in this section. After the afternoon break, the kids would move into their assigned scene groups to rehearse their segment of a highly truncated version of one of the plays. This would eventually be put together and performed for an invited audience on the last afternoon of the camp. Everyone who came to the student production was given a ticket to that evening's performance, which made for a guaranteed spike in the audience. The food trucks that trolled the park had been made aware of these dates, when hungry theatre patrons would be sitting ducks, and so it looked to be a win-win-win situation.

So far, Amanda and Kieran were happy with my outlined plans. Now it was up to me to make it all happen. I was alternating my days with putting together lesson plans for the morning lectures, which I would be fielding, and cold calling high school drama and English teachers to see about promoting the camp. This was the worst bit, since I knew they were up to their armpits in getting their own classes wrapped up. But we had a cool poster that could be downloaded and printed on a piece of legal paper for their bulletin boards, and application forms right on the festival's website. Very little extra effort was needed.

According to the *Farmers' Almanac,* something I rarely followed, summer this year was supposed to be mild and spectacularly dry. This might not be what farmers were hoping to hear, but I would take it. The last thing you wanted was damp, whiny teenagers swatting off mosquitoes while you were trying to extol the wonders of the Bard of Avon.

I had plenty of time to get my work done, as well, since Steve Browning, one of Edmonton's Finest, and certainly best in my books, had set off the day before Oren's funeral with the officially titled delegation of Western Canadian Police Service and Peace Officers to Scandinavia, studying their process and safety procedures on their public transit. There had been a steady rise in attacks and minor crime on the public transit here, and the forward-thinking Chief had cast a net looking for places in the world similar to ours where people weren't scared to ride the bus after dark. Several cities in Sweden and Norway with similar weather, demographics, and percentage of citizens relying on public transit, didn't have the problems we were facing. Steve and nine other representatives had gone to see if they could figure out what they were doing right that we had not yet tried.

I wasn't all that scared on the bus. Of course, I didn't normally ride it through the shadier areas of town and rarely took the train or bus after dark, except, of course in winter, when to go out anywhere before 9:00 a.m. or after 4:00 p.m. was to go out in the dark. I was pleased for Steve, since this month-long junket was sort of a promotion for him; he was ostensibly leading it and would be the face of the group when they reported back to the chiefs and city councils of four or five major western cities. But I missed having him around.

We had been really working on defining our relationship just before he'd left, too. My choice not to move in with him the year before, after my apartment had been ransacked, had been taken by him as some sort of lack of confidence in our future together. I hadn't seen it that way. To me, it was just a matter of feeling strong enough to be on my own, unafraid. I had to test myself against that sense of violation, not just cower and fold the minute I was attacked.

But maybe I had made too much of buying new furniture and replacing ruined CDs. Maybe it was true that I needed my own space and autonomy. What I didn't understand from Steve's argument was how my requiring autonomy in any way infringed on our future together. Still, it had been a bit prickly for a while. This break was probably a good thing for both of us. We could shake out and reboot ourselves without having to worry about the other for an entire month. Then, when he got back, we could explore the ways we naturally came back together.

That is what I thought in the daytime, when I had my mature businesslike face on. At night, when I was alone with the television and a bowl of ice cream, I just missed him.

This was one of those nights, though I hadn't bothered with the ice cream and my choice of escape was a mystery novel. Eventually I pulled myself away from Laurie R. King's glorious revisioning of Sherlock Holmes, uncurled myself from the contortions I had to undergo in order to lie on my loveseat, and tried to reassemble myself into a functionally upright human being. Denise had urged me to buy the loveseat rather than replace the lovely overstuffed chesterfield that had ruled the room until it was slashed to pieces last autumn in an attempt to frighten me away from a research job. The loveseat admittedly did make the room seem more spacious and balanced. However, I had not yet shifted my habits, and my attempts to get maximum relaxation out of my new furniture was probably akin to a Great Dane trying to get comfortable on a pillow bed designed for a terrier. I would snuggle down so my head was propped on a pillow against the padded armrest and bend my knees so that my ankles were grazing my butt. Eventually my legs would end up hanging over the other armrest, negotiating space with the side table. I was going to have to learn to take my books to bed earlier in the evening.

I set about to do just that, taking time to tidy up the living room and brush my teeth and hair before crawling into bed. I splashed water on my face and then leaned toward the mirror, examining the crow's feet near my eyes and the slight laxness of the skin at my neck. Being around actors these days was making me far more self-conscious about my looks and body. While I had never been particularly athletic, I was quietly pleased that my body was navigating middle age without letting me down too severely. I walked pretty much everywhere and tried to be mindful of what I ate. My biggest vice, other than books, was coffee, and the general swing these days seemed to be back toward its being a natural booster. I have always worn sunglasses to keep from squinting and sunscreen to keep from burning, so my skin tended to make people peg me about ten years younger than my chronological age. Either that or they just thought I was immature.

It didn't bother me one way or the other. I was perfectly fine with being in my forties, and had no qualms about turning fifty up ahead. I knew from past decade-shifting experience, though, that forty-nine might prove to be a problem.

It had happened in my late thirties, too. When I hit thirty-nine and realized I had only one year left to fulfill all the dreams of that decade, I found myself fretting about my lack of career, dearth of anything but some magazine articles and a paltry MA to show for my efforts to that point, my being so slow to get around to doing my MA, my lack of an abiding relationship. It was a hell of a year. By then I was forty, and I calmed down to be once more on the cusp of possibilities. Calendars of any kind are so good for that. Of course, it was also around that time that I met Steve, which made things doubly cheerful.

So, I had been sailing through my forties, feeling fulfilled and gypsy-like, moving from one academic morsel to another. While my dreams of teaching English literature and puttering about researching and writing for academic periodicals while wearing tweed jumper dresses and fashionable footwear had never really materialized, I had managed to pretty much stay on campus. I had been a sessional lecturer, delivered distance courses via the Internet, worked for the Centre of Ethnomusicology, helped create a virtual museum site for Rutherford House at the edge of the university, and spotted for overworked profs as a marker from time to time.

This job setting up the high school camp sessions for the Shakespeare festival was tangentially connected to the university, too. The festival board had applied for various grants, and the one under which I had been hired specified that the work should be done by a post-graduate degree holder from the U of A. I am sure the granting officials had been thinking of someone in the performing or fine arts, given that it was so specifically geared to summer festivals and had funded several Fringe plays in the past. However, Kieran checked and I did fit the qualifications, so he had his grant, Amanda had her high school program, and I had a job till August. At which point I could begin to worry about turning old with no pension.

Ah heck, I would worry about that when the calendar told me to. I turned the bathroom light off and went to bed.

4.

The drama department had a longtime understanding with the Shakespeare Festival, given that so many of their artistic partners on the board were graduates of either the BFA or MFA programs. The theatre lab was offered as rehearsal space, and Kieran and the actors were there for the full Equity-allotted time each day. He also seemed to be constantly online, keeping in touch with the managing director of the festival in the office upstairs in the downtown library, and cc'ing everyone including me on every email. I had never felt so popular, with my notification pinging at least three times on the hour all day long.

I was alternating time between my dining room office, which was my desk wedged under the window next to my smallish kitchen table, and an equally tight and measurably more claustrophobic setting in the corner of the downtown office. I wasn't sure how they'd managed to fit three desks into this space, along with boxes of promotional materials, banners, old scripts, framed posters from previous runs, and a huge grey exercise ball which Kieran insisted on using as an office chair. I had the use of the back desk and could look up and out the long slit of a window to a southern view of the Westin Hotel across the small, under-utilized square behind the library. This city was full of spaces like this, ideas that had been given full throttle only to somehow run out of gas.

If I craned my eyes to the left, I could glimpse a corner of glass and orange metal: the Citadel Theatre, where we'd recently gathered for Oren Gentry's funeral. I wondered if Denise had heard anything about who was going to fill the gap Gentry had left as the head of Chautauqua Theatre. While it didn't do to rush in and declare a new artistic director the minute the obituary ink was dry, theatre was such a precarious profession that not to have someone strong at the helm for any length of time could capsize a company. I was pretty sure there would be one or two bright sparks vying for the position, and their board might be thinking about casting further afield, bringing in someone from Vancouver or Toronto. Several theatres across the country had gone dark in recent times; it would be easy to attract big-name talent.

If Kieran knew anything about it, he wasn't divulging it in any of his myriad emails. While he was very free with every idea for production enhancements or top-of-the-hill refreshment tent improvements or the camp program, he didn't gossip or speculate on anything outside his own immediate purview. I had to admire that, but it was a grudging admiration. Here I was, for once on the inside of a professional theatre of sorts, and I wasn't getting any of the dirt.

Micheline, the managing director, responsible for the running of the festival and cleaning up after Kieran, was far less discreet. I couldn't help listening in on her end of her phone calls, piecing together the gist of the conversations speculating about who would take over Chautauqua, whether Kieran would throw his hat in the ring for the job, whether the City was going to spray for mosquitoes early or only for the weekend of the triathlon, whether the printer we'd always worked with was ripping us off for the cost of the programmes, whether the bathrooms down at the amphitheatre would be cleaned daily or only every second day, who had the bigger ass—Georgia Dranchuk or Cara Sampson, who had the bigger ego—Christian Norgaard or Mervyn Forrest. I eventually brought my noise-cancelling headphones to work and plugged in a playlist of Alison Brown and Tony Trischka, interspersed with a little Oscar Peterson, to get me through the day.

When I need to concentrate, I require instrumental music. Anything with words will yank me out of my thoughts and take me along another path entirely. So, if I was trying to escape "Days of Our Edmonton Theatre Lives" at the next desk, sinking into Ian Thomas or Hawksley Workman wasn't going to do much good.

Not that I wasn't curious, of course. If Kieran were to jump ship, I wasn't sure what that would do to this summer's festival. While it probably wouldn't have an impact on my work for the high school camp, it might put the kibosh on my netting a return engagement the following summer. If Kieran left, the whole focus of the festival might shift with the new artistic director. After all, though it was run by a board with artistic partners who had a say in the way things operated, there was no doubt that the vision of the artistic director in any theatre or festival would steer things a certain way.

I was almost finished putting together a crossword puzzle made entirely out of words either coined by Shakespeare or first appearing in print in his plays when the phone rang for me. I pressed my little flashing button, miming shock to Micheline, and answered.

"Randy Craig!"

"Hey Randy," chirped Denise. "I am so glad I caught you there. I tried your cellphone, but wasn't sure you'd see my texts before leaving."

I reached into the side drawer of the desk to retrieve my phone from my bag. Sure enough, there was a little envelope lit up with the number 5 in it. The phone itself was on silent.

Denise went on. "I was wondering if you wanted to catch a bite to eat? I can swing by and pick you up in front of the library in, say, ten minutes?"

"Sounds great," I said, checking my wristwatch and noticing that it was already past five. That is the trouble with summer in Edmonton. You really have to keep an eye on the time or you will clock in way more hours than anyone is ever going to pay you for. The sun doesn't even think about setting till around ten o'clock, so all your workaday signals are shot. I looked over my shoulder and noted Micheline was packing up as well. "See you then."

I slid my work into a folder marked Puzzles and pulled out

the left drawer of the desk. I was chalking up the files already. I had colour-coded them, too. Games were green, puzzles were purple, research was red, scenes were blue, and soliloquies were yellow. I was hoping to develop enough material so that every day had different elements to it. These kids wouldn't leave the camp as Shakespeare scholars or Stratford-ready actors, but they should be able to wow their English teachers come September and have some fun along the way.

There was no need to lock the desk, since the entire office was bolted. The sixth floor of the library was full of offices devoted to arts and other non-profit organizations. Litfest, Opera in the Schools, the Richard Eaton Singers, all sorts of diverse groups housed their managers and business files here. There were also meeting rooms you could book for board meetings and such, but this had to be okayed with security, because at a certain point the elevator doors were locked so that the general public couldn't wander the upper halls.

That was the glory and the trouble with public buildings like libraries. Open to all, they collected a strange assortment of lonely singletons, homeless folks, crazy people, old-fashioned researchers, youngsters on cheap dates, families with more children than literary budgets, and civic-minded folks who cling to the concept of the public library as the panacea of all things civilized.

I said goodbye to Micheline and headed for the elevator. While it had been quiet on the sixth floor (the Narcotics Anonymous crowd usually arrived for their meetings at six-thirty), the main floor of the library was still buzzing with activity. Two security guards stood near the entrance, which otherwise was deceptively open plan. There were gates that set off alarms if you went through them with unchecked materials, but there was a distinct lack of librarians here. They were seated further back, at the reference desk or in the video area. It felt to me as if all the technology that made self-checkouts possible might be making the position of librarian, to my mind an essential role in society, a trifle redundant. I sure hoped not. Feeling budgetary pinches, a lot of schools had cut back on having teacher-librarians, and the system was poorer for it. There was no way a harried teacher, responsible for more than thirty children day to day, was going to be up-to-date on all the new literature coming down the pike, let alone the lovely augmenting materials like films, biographies, histories. Instead, lesson plans focused on the same thing as last year, because it was known to work and at hand. From experience, though, I knew that the spark of joy in the teacher's mind could be so easily extinguished in the retelling of the same old stories, anecdotes, and lectures. And when it came right down to it, in this world where information was only a few keyboard strokes from anywhere on the planet, it was that spark of joy that made classroom education worthwhile.

The front of the Stanley Milner Library faced Sir Winston Churchill Square and was a gathering point for buses heading into the northeast quadrant of the city. It also seemed to be a gathering place for teenaged boys bristling for something to erupt. This was the demographic that had sent Steve to Scandinavia. These were the riders who looked menacing, spoke in loud and profane bursts, and revelled in intimidating the older women who waited tiredly, standing as far from the sidewalk-spitting strutters as they could get and still catch the bus before it pulled away from the curb.

Lucky for me, it was a sunny spring afternoon and Denise was crazy punctual, one of the many things I loved about her. A bus to Beverly pulled away from the curb and Denise and her little car slid in. I dropped my bag into the footwell behind the passenger seat and opened the side door. She pulled away as I was buckling up, yielding space to another impatient bus. Her hand went up in the cheery wave that mitigated against road rage everywhere, and we were soon turned toward Jasper Avenue and rolling past the Citadel.

"Do you feel like Indian food?" Denise asked and as she said it, my stomach grumbled. I had nibbled cheese and cucumber slices at my desk for lunch and breakfast had been a long time before that. The thought of butter chicken and curry made me salivate, like Pavlov's bell.

"Oh gosh, yes."

"Great, because I have to go grocery shopping after, anyhow, so I thought I would aim us in that direction. Have you been to the Masala Wok?"

We were on the tail end of the evening rush hour, but everything is lighter in the springtime, it seems, and Denise was a firm, just this side of aggressive, driver. We were soon whipping down 99 Street toward 34 Avenue, the region of sari and spice shops and some of the best Indian restaurants, all tucked into little strip malls between car dealerships.

The restaurant was just starting to fill up, so we got a table for two near the wall and were soon in line at the steaming buffet table. I tried to moderate my choices, the way Denise did, but couldn't help myself, and soon my plate was heaped high with various meats and vegetables in colourful sauces. By the time we got back to our table, a basket of naan bread was waiting for us. Denise must have been just as hungry as me, because neither of us spoke for at least ten minutes, we just ate steadily from one rim of the plate to the other side.

Eventually, Denise sat back, dabbed at her mouth with her napkin, and began to converse between bites.

"Oh glory, this is good. Shall I go back for more curries, or is it better to save room for that carrot halwa dessert? Dilemmas, decisions!"

I smiled. Denise began to shift her syntax to mirror the plays she was teaching when she was right into things. This had the tone of *As You Like It,* and I was betting she was concentrating on the comedies for her second half spring session intensive.

"How is your class going?" I asked. Denise finished chewing a piece of naan before replying.

"Not bad at all. There are only twenty-three of them, which is a dream when you think of the marking. Several of them seem to be teachers on sabbatical, so the class discussion is a bit more satisfying intellectually than I am used to. We'll see how they unbend to do scene readings, though, which is the group component of the course."

"Oh, god save me from group projects," I growled, and stabbed a piece of butter chicken. "I hate being in them and I especially hated having to teach them."

"I know." Denise nodded. "There are always one or two people who do nothing and coast on the drive of others, usually one other member of the group. And that person, who is usually a young woman with aspirations and glasses, ends up coming to see me in office hours, incensed and exhausted, and desperately wanting me to punish the lollygaggers."

"Or you get stuck in a group that all want to do different things, and nothing gets done properly as a result. Or they all want to be the speaker. Or they all want to create a video, dreaming it will win a short film festival award but ends up looking like the Blair Witch Redux."

Denise laughed. "God knows why they make us incorporate group work. If you wanted to really acclimate students to the eventual real world, you would teach them about chain of command and hierarchies. Nothing actually gets done by a committee until the committee assigns roles and breaks away to do things."

"Exactly. There is a baseline concept that common respect will only come out of group work and team dynamics, but I think that is actually some conspiracy on the part of gym teachers and varsity coaches to keep team sports funded."

"Absolutely! Up the racketball court. Down with arenas!" Denise raised her water glass in mock toast. I saluted her with mine, and then took a long slug, having just bit into a pepper.

"What about you? How is the prep for the high school group going?"

Denise was being careful with her words, I knew. While it was nothing to sneeze at and I was certainly grateful to her for helping me land the job, this gig was really nothing compared to teaching a course or two at the university or college. Of course, that ship had sailed.

There were too many grad students, both MAs and PhDs, who needed the income a teaching assistantship could bring, for me to break back into teaching at the university, and they had cut back on the number of courses sessionals could teach at Grant MacEwan, so everyone there was jealously guarding their numbers. A few weeks back, I had run into a friend of mine who taught there. Valerie had seemed apologetic and almost ashamed to look me in the eye when I asked what the work possibilities might be. It's never an easy life for a gypsy academic, and the further we got into the twenty-first century, the tighter it was getting.

I wasn't totally sure why, either. Well, I realized that costs were going up and there were incentives being offered to students to move toward more practical training in the trades, but it seemed as if everywhere you turned anymore, they were requiring a degree. You now needed a BA for things that had previously required college diplomas and an MA for jobs completely within the purview of a Bachelor's level of education. It was an employer's market, so they could ask what they wanted.

But that trickled down to include lecturers and professors, too. Colleges no longer hired MAs to teach freshman English, not with all the surplus PhDs hanging about.

Not that Denise was surplus. She was one of those gifted and driven people who had been born for the ivory tower. I didn't begrudge her the successes she had achieved, because not only was she always one of the brightest people in any room, she was also the most accessible. I had seen Denise teach, and her mix of logic, grace, and utter belief in her topic opened up even the most recalcitrant students, previously unwilling to see the need for compulsory English courses in their timetable.

I, on the other hand, had wooed my various classes with enthusiasm for the works we were studying, and while it worked for most of the students, there were always a few skeptics lurking in the back rows, folks who watched me with the same detached amusement they would bring to seeing a golden retriever walking on its hind legs balancing a ball on its nose.

Maybe I was lucky to be out of it.

"I think I'm on target. I just have a recollection of my own sense of high school, and my detachment, that worries me. What if they all just loll in their seats snapping their gum and ridiculing me?"

"I think you're mixing up your real high school experience with old episodes of *Welcome Back, Kotter*. Besides, this isn't high school, it's camp! It's summertime and they'll be outdoors frolicking and having a good time and learning about theatre. What's not to love?"

"You're right; after all, it's not like they didn't want to come, right? Otherwise they wouldn't be signing up for it. It's not like these will be kids that parents had to find a place for, as a baby-sitting service. They could be left at home alone if they wanted, to watch DVDs and eat Kraft Dinner." I scooped some chickpeas on to my fork. "What is wrong with these kids? Why don't they want to stay home and watch DVDs and eat Kraft Dinner?"

Denise laughed. "They're drama nerds, and they'll be wonderful. They will imprint on you and adore you and work their tails off." She mopped up her plate with another bit of torn-off naan. "I've heard it said you could power New York City for a year if you could harness the energy of a high school drama class."

"Yes, but will they use that energy for good or evil? Who comes to Shakespeare Camp? Spiderman or the Green Goblin?"

"Probably they'll both be there. Relax, Randy. They're going to love you, and you them."

I smiled. Denise was right. It was going to be a great gig. To show my appreciation for her support in getting the job, I cheerfully picked up the tab. We spent the next couple of hours grocery shopping at the H & W for fresh produce and Costco for toilet paper.

Denise dropped me and my provisions at the back door of my apartment, and drove off waving down the back alley. I wrestled with my keys, finding the new locks on the outer doors a useful nuisance, since I didn't ever want a repeat of a break-in to my apartment.

Once inside, I dropped my bags in the doorway to the kitchen and made a point of filling the kettle and setting it to boil on the stove. A cup of tea once the groceries were unpacked would be a just reward for the effort.

I was just pouring the hot water into the teapot as my phone rang. I popped the lid on the pot quickly to let it steep before racing back to the dining area to answer the phone.

It was Micheline from the Shakespeare festival.

"Randy? Can you come in tomorrow morning to the university rehearsal hall? Kieran has called an emergency meeting for the whole cast and company."

"Sure, but why?"

"Well, I'm not supposed to say, but—" I could sense Micheline leaning into the handset as she whispered to me what she had probably told every single person on her list to phone— "Eleanor's been killed!"

5.

Eleanor Durant was western Canada's answer to Sarah Polley. She had grown up before our eyes, starring as a young Emily Carr in the long-running series about the reclusive painter who embraced the land of Haida Gwaii and became one of the greatest Canadian artists. Eleanor had then appeared on a comedy series conceived and written by Paul Mather, as the youngest mayor in Alberta, presiding over the fortunes of a small town trying to keep its town status. *Gopher Broke* had won countless Geminis, the Canadian television awards, and Eleanor was a well-recognized face all across Canada, but especially in Alberta.

She had been living in Toronto, but rumour had it she was back in Edmonton taking care of a failing grandmother, and that was the reason Kieran had been able to nab her for this year's festival. She was playing Hero in *Much Ado About Nothing*, the comedy, and Desdemona in *Othello* for the season. I guessed that offering Eleanor the lesser role in the comedy was a sop to Louise, one of the resident actresses normally cast as the main female, but Louise was getting a little long in the tooth to pull off a seventeen-year-old Venetian maiden.

Eleanor, of course, was quite a way past seventeen as well, but she skewed young and would likely be playing teenagers well into her forties.

From what I had seen of the ensemble which, granted, was just at the opening party that took place after the first reading of the comedy and once or twice when I had dropped by to get Kieran's signature on something or other, the group had welcomed Eleanor into their circle and things were fine. She and Louise had apparently hit it off right away, which may have been something Kieran engineered for the sake of harmony in the rehearsal hall.

Micheline had said *killed*, too, not *died*. Unless she was overly dramatic, which obviously couldn't be discounted, this was not a case of a sudden allergy or aneurysm. Of course, Eleanor could have been hit by a bus, for all I knew. People were described as being killed in car accidents.

The trouble was, when I heard the word *killed*, it usually meant murder.

You would think that, given the low rate of gun deaths in Canada and the relatively low rate of crime in Edmonton, an average (okay, slightly above-average) citizen wouldn't have been exposed to much murder and mayhem in the course of her life. But in my case, you would lose that bet. For some reason, crimes of passion seemed to be attracted to me like iron filings to a magnet.

I couldn't deny that part of it was likely due to my own makeup and personality. Academics are curious by nature and very loath to leave questions unanswered (unless, of course, they are in philosophy, in which case academics just stockpile and toss them about underfoot to trip everyone else up). Circumstances had unfolded to connect me to several criminal investigations, but I couldn't quibble about that, since it was how I'd met Steve, the love of my life.

And now it seemed here we were again.

I had awoken at the usual time, and for a minute or two had forgotten about Eleanor, but it was as if there was a cloud above my bed. As I stood up, it engulfed me, and I made my morning ablutions with a sadness I couldn't shake.

I had really enjoyed *Gopher Broke* and had bought all four seasons on DVD. It had been filmed in southern Alberta, and there were even tours of the town and brown tourism signs on the main highways pointing to it now. I was looking forward to getting to know Eleanor over the course of the run and rubbing shoulders with one of those rare creatures, a Canadian star.

We are funny in Canada about our celebrities. We don't seem to afford them the same glamour that our cousins to the south do theirs. Instead of wondering about the relative torridness of their love lives, we are given photoplays of their Toronto townhouses or seaside places near Peggy's Cove. We tune in to hear them discuss their recipes for Thanksgiving cranberry butter, rather than whether their father beat them as a child. We nudge each other and smile shyly when we see Graham Greene or Paul Gross stroll by, and we buy tickets to hear Mary Walsh talk when she's in town, but on the whole, we tend to treat our well-known personalities as we would "Harold's girl who went to the city and made good."

I was among the first to arrive at the Fine Arts Building. Micheline was helping Tracey, the stage manager, set up the coffee she'd ordered, and two of the junior actors, who were hired to fill ranks, learn the ropes, and earn points toward their Equity cards, were setting up chairs in a wide semi-circle. A few of the regular actors were huddled off to the side, and when Amanda and Louise entered the hall together, they made a beeline for that group.

I tried to chat with Micheline, but she was less forthcoming under the watchful eye of Tracey, who was the consummate professional. Or maybe she didn't know any more than what she had said on the phone. Kieran could be very closemouthed.

Taking a cup of coffee, I went to sit on one of the chairs. Soon I was joined by Amanda, which was kind of her, as I knew her better than any of the rest of the company. Kieran walked into the hall, and all eyes went to him immediately. The man knew how to make an entrance, that was for sure. He walked over to Micheline, put a hand on her shoulder, nodded at something Tracey said, and then with a subtle movement of his arm, suggested everyone take a seat. We did.

"Thank you all for coming in early. As I am sure most of you have been told, we have lost a great actress and compatriot: Eleanor Durant is dead."

There was a low buzz, which Kieran silenced by a slight raising of his voice.

"I have been in touch with the police, who are coming to speak with all of us today. I would request that you give them your full cooperation. It seems that there is some question as to how Eleanor died, and an investigation will ensue. I've been assured this should not affect our production dates in any way. It will, however, make life a bit more hectic for Thalia, who will have to rejig Eleanor's costumes to fit Louise, who will be playing Hero, and Stacey, who will take on the role of Desdemona."

The buzz was stronger now. Stacey, one of the student actors, looked as if she was going to burst into tears. Louise was sitting on the other side of Amanda from me, so I couldn't gauge her reaction.

So, we were going to be questioned by the police. I wondered what the investigators would make of this gang. There was a self-aggrandizing mode that many actors popped into when speaking to strangers, as if they were auditioning and needed to be the centre of attention. I hoped they realized that being the focus in a police investigation was exactly what they didn't want to be.

I also wondered who would be leading the investigation. If he had been in town, it probably would have been Steve. He worked out of the southside precinct and somehow drew the majority of university details. His take on it was that, having a sociology degree and an ease with the campus made him the likeliest for the role.

I didn't have to wait and wonder long. There was a knock at the door, and in came Steve's partner, Iain McCorquodale. With him was a striking woman with long dark hair pulled back into a clip, highlighting the business cut of her pinstriped pantsuit.

This must be the new detective Steve had spoken of, Jennifer Gladue. I noted that he hadn't mentioned to me how attractive she was. Perhaps he just didn't think that would be something that would interest me, and it likely shouldn't have. Most times it wouldn't. It was probably just because I was missing him and feeling a bit edgy about how we'd left things before he had gone to Sweden.

Iain conferred with Kieran and commandeered a table in a corner of the hall. Detective Gladue introduced herself to us and asked us all to print our names on a clipboard she handed us. From it, she read and checked off names as each of us was sent to the corner to give our statements.

I was completely in the dark as to times and circumstances relating to Eleanor's death, but I didn't want to appear ghoulish by asking Amanda if she knew any more than I did. Instead, I sat there, trying to subtly listen in on conversations to my right and left.

"I heard she was found in her hotel suite."

"Really? I heard she was killed in the river valley, on one of the running trails."

"Who found her?"

"Kieran, I think, but it might have been the manager of the hotel."

"Some joggers spotted her body."

"The hotel manager was called in about some noise."

"Noise? Like a fight?"

"No, the television was on all night, way too loud. It was disturbing folks on either side of her room."

"There was blood everywhere, is what I heard."

"Blood? Was she shot? Or stabbed to death?"

"No one is saying."

"Has Kieran said anything to you?"

"He just told me to round everybody up for this morning."

Just then, Detective Gladue stepped into the centre of the group and called my name. As I stood up, I could sense she was eyeing me curiously. So she knew who I was, in that I was connected to Steve Browning. I wondered if she had been contemplating how easy Detective Browning was on the eyes and seeing me as a potential rival. I hoped not. My sense of our relationship was not sturdy enough at the moment to withstand that sort of energy coming at me.

I smiled what probably looked like rictus to her, in an attempt to mask my own sense of discomfort, and followed her over to the table where Iain was set up with double-paged statement sheets and a small voice recorder.

"Hey, Randy, fancy meeting you here," he drawled drily. Iain and I had an odd relationship. He had been Steve's partner almost as long as I had, and had been at times leery of how much Steve shared with me about the general workings of their job. He had also seen me get embroiled in various situations that he felt were unseemly for an amateur. On the other side of the coin, we had been through a lot together and had shared more than one of the weird adrenalin rushes that come when you realize you may be about to die. And that was a bond of sorts, undeniably.

So Iain and I tolerated each other, in that great Canadian

understanding of the word. I smiled wearily at him, and he motioned for me to sit down. Detective Gladue sat at the end of the table, taking notes. I could almost see her invisible antennae, bobbing between us, trying to gauge the relationship.

"I am going to be asking you a few questions to establish where you fit in this situation. Please take your time and be as clear as possible in your answers. Answer all questions verbally, please, as I am recording our conversation for transcription purposes." Iain pointed to the recorder. "Please state your name, telephone number, and the position you hold with the theatre company."

"My name is Miranda Craig, and I go by Randy, in case anyone mentions me." I tried to get a smile out of Iain, but it was no go, so I just recited my telephone number dutifully and continued with my role. "I have been hired by a grant to the Freewill Shakespeare Festival to run a high school camp experience for a three-week session during the course of the run."

"You're going to be a camp counsellor?"

I wasn't sure I didn't detect a sneer in Iain's question. I would have loved to hear a replay of the recording.

"Not so much a counsellor as a facilitator. I've been working from the main office of the Festival to create materials to augment the teenagers' experience. They will be learning about the times, focusing on one of the plays, doing some acting exercises, learning a bit of stage fighting and fencing, and putting on a truncated, one-hour version of *Much Ado About Nothing* on the last day of the camp, as a matinee performance for their families and invited guests."

Iain shrugged. To him, it probably sounded like what I did in English courses for my college students, all wedged into a three-week outdoor experience. He wasn't far off base, really.

"And you got this job how?" Detective Gladue looked over her clipboard at me.

"Do you mean what are my qualifications to teach Shakespeare to fifteen-year-olds, or who pulled strings to get me hired?" Okay, so that came out a little bit more belligerently than I'd intended.

"Just wondering how you ended up in this company, Ms. Craig." She was glacial, and I had to admire that. What I wouldn't give for a bit of that poise. I could feel the heat sliding up my neck toward my jawline. Soon the telltale flush would creep onto my cheeks and she'd know she'd got to me.

I shrugged. "Well, my friend Denise Wolff recommended that I apply for the job, which she had heard about through her work with the artistic director and other folks in the Department of Drama. I was probably in a better position to take it on than some people, since I didn't have any spring or summer sessional work lined up. Being as I come from the English end of things, I wasn't enmeshed in getting ready for a Fringe show. And I needed the money."

"Why would connections to a Fringe show matter?" Detective Gladue sounded more curious than interrogatory.

"Well, to get a slot in the Edmonton Fringe Theatre Festival, you have to put your name and a bond of something like $500 in around November of the previous year and hope that your name is drawn in the lottery. You are informed by the end of

December whether or not you have been allotted a time in one of the eleven venues, and that is when the fire hits the belly. Most Fringe performers are either in school till May or holding down one or two other jobs, and so early planning and rehearsals all take place in and around some really wacky schedule adjustments." I shrugged. "Chances are Kieran was turned down by two or three of his first choices for this gig, if they found out they'd got Fringe slots."

"How many shows take place at the Fringe?" asked Iain, interested in spite of himself.

"There are eleven venues, each showing somewhere between eight and ten shows in rotation. Then there are more than forty 'Bring Your Own Venue' sites, featuring one to four shows, so it's hard to gauge. Those get added to the mix after February, and I'm not totally sure what sort of bond is required in order to get into the programming."

"So you are saying that the possibility of doing a Fringe play, depending on whether or not you get a slot, which is totally random and up to chance, are how actors in this city organize their year's commitments?" Detective Gladue sounded incredulous.

"Actors, directors, designers—and they run the risk of their play being panned by a critic who normally writes car columns in the newspaper, or having no one come to their show because they are scheduled in at eleven o'clock every night. Fringing is a phenomenon. It's a chance to be experimental and edgy, and you take away 100% of the box office and create a larger audience for yourself, because more than just the theatre set come to the Fringe. The Fringe is big."

Iain jumped in, probably sensing the edginess between me and his new consort. "So, back to the situation at hand. You have mostly been downtown, not here in the rehearsal hall?"

I nodded. "There was a first-day reading for each play, and we were invited to come to that. I did, because I thought it would be useful to make notes about which actors might be able to help the kids with soliloquies, and I also wanted to check how Kieran had cut *Much Ado*. I have to take out more than half of it, and I figured I would start from his cut and then go further." I was oversharing. I always seemed to do this when being questioned by the police. "I went to the party that Kieran held after the first week of rehearsal, too. But aside from that, I've been mostly downtown or working from home."

"So, tell me what your experiences with Eleanor Durant were, if any."

I had been thinking about that ever since Micheline had called. When you are told that someone has died, I suppose it is only natural to flick through all your memories of that person, polishing them in your mind.

It's not as if Eleanor Durant was the only celebrity I had ever met. I had volunteered at a lecture for Roberta Bondar, shaken hands with Béla Fleck, and once, when I was eleven, been kissed on the cheek by Prime Minister Pierre Elliot Trudeau on a campaign visit. Eleanor was probably the only one I'd talked to for more than two minutes, though.

She and I had exchanged pleasantries at the first reading. I had remarked how much I had enjoyed her television show, and we had shared a laugh or two about favourite episodes. Then we had started talking about places near her apartment hotel and I had steered her to various places, including Audreys Books, only three blocks from her.

At Kieran's party, she had sought me out to tell me how much she had enjoyed shopping at Audreys and at the Alberta Craft Council's shop down the street from the bookstore. Denise and she had started talking about running and the various trails and stairs through the city. That had morphed into talk about running shoes and shoes in general. We had also connected over the shared need for shoe stores that carried half-sizes and shops that carried long-length trousers. These weren't actually things I wanted to share with Detective Gladue listening in; it would make me sound so materialistic to admit that all we had spoken of was where to shop for what.

"We spoke about pretty mundane things, really. She had never stayed in Edmonton for any length of time, so it was mostly filling in with where to shop, what to see while she was here, where to eat, that sort of thing." I shrugged.

Iain was writing something down and seemed happy to move on, but Jennifer Gladue seemed skeptical. I guess I didn't look like the sort who might give shopping tips to a television star.

"Did you meet with Eleanor Durant at other times than scheduled festival events?"

I had to stop and think about that one. There had been a couple of smiles and nods on the street, one of them on the High Level Bridge. I was walking home to my apartment just a block south of the bridge and she was jogging north toward her downtown apartment. That time she had just nodded and smiled and didn't even slow down to take out her earbuds and talk. I had been grateful, since all I wanted was to get into my apartment and relax after a long day, and the last place I could think of to unwind and visit would be in the middle of a half-mile-long bridge high above the North Saskatchewan River. Not that I am afraid of heights or water. It's bridges that make me nervous. After all, everything made by humans eventually wears out or breaks. Maybe I'm afraid of engineers.

I must have been drifting for a bit, because Detective Gladue brought me back to her question by tapping on the side of the table twice, the way Chinese people do to ask for more tea.

"We ran into each other a few times on the street, and she was probably at Oren Gentry's funeral, though I don't remember seeing her there. We didn't socialize, though, if that's what you mean."

I had no idea what Detective Gladue meant. She was giving me a look as if she couldn't imagine what someone like Steve Browning, or Eleanor Durant, either, could see in me. While I was not usually prone to making snap judgments about people, I really didn't like her. And I had the idea the feeling was mutual.

Iain McCorquodale must have been picking up on the tension between us, because he took over the conversation, asking me a few more general questions about the way the Festival camp program was coordinated, and pretty soon I was back in the circle of chairs, picking up my satchel and sweater. I'd been told we could leave, but I wanted to talk to Micheline or Amanda before I headed home, to let them know I would be putting in some hours from my apartment. There was no point in heading downtown if Micheline was here all day, and I could just as easily cut Shakespeare cards at home.

I was planning a Shakespeare game, a modified version of Happy Families, where in order to win, you had to complete sets of characters in the plays. I was going to need at least five decks of cards for the run of the camp. I had to cut out card stock, then print the character onto one side. I was still experimenting with tracing the design onto the card versus glue-sticking a printed image onto the card and then sending all the cards through a laminator at the library. Micheline had suggested printing them directly onto manila stock on an oversized printer, but I had been put off by the costs of that approach, which would still leave me cutting out each separate card, as well as having to find my way out to the wilds of the west end of town and back. So I was back to trying to tough it out with my original plans.

Micheline nodded distractedly when I approached her with my farewells, and Kieran saluted from where he was sitting nearby. I let myself out of the darkened rehearsal hall and wandered out into the sunlight between the Fine Arts building and the Timms Centre for the Arts. I was two blocks west of my apartment. I was also approximately one block north of the best salad in Edmonton, and my stomach was rumbling. I headed south, with no recriminations, and was happily ensconced at a table at the Greenhouse with a quinoa and jerk chicken salad and a frothy latte, when my phone buzzed.

I dug in my bag for my phone and monkeyed with the

easy-lock action for a minute before I could access the text message. It was Denise, wanting to know how I was. The news must have hit the airwaves, or maybe Kieran had let her know.

I texted back my whereabouts and she told me to sit tight, as she could meet me in ten minutes. I figured that free time would give me a very good excuse to cap off my meal with a frozen yoghurt concoction and call this my big meal of the day. The bowl, covered in sunflower seeds and shaved coconut, was just being delivered as Denise strode in. She followed the waiter to the counter, put in an order for a small-sized steak salad, and then joined me.

"I am eating away my grief," I said in response to her raised eyebrows to the fulsome bowl of sweet excess in front of me.

"Grief? Really? How well did you know Eleanor Durant?"

"Don't you start in on me. I've already had it up to here with that new detective grilling me over my actions and interactions. I have no idea what Steve sees in people. He said she was a good fit with the team, but as far as I can tell, she is going to rub people the wrong way and he and Iain will be having to run behind mopping up after her."

Denise beamed one of her megawatt smiles at the fellow bringing her salad and cutlery, which I supposed was as good as the tip I had given him before. He seemed to think so, and I was sure I detected a lilt in his walk away from the table.

Denise was too busy digging into her salad and quizzing me to notice the effect she had on him. Or maybe she was so used to having that effect on people that she no longer paid it any attention.

"So, the police were at the Festival rehearsal this morning?"

"I think they're likely still there. I was lucky enough to be processed early, probably because of Iain. Or more likely because he figured I would know nothing anyhow. There were still twelve actors and the design team waiting when I left."

"Was Kieran still there?" Denise was fiddling with the black olives in the bottom of her bowl, spearing them carefully on the tines of her fork and not meeting my eye.

"Yeah, he was still there. Denise, how serious is it with you two? Are you being exclusive, as it were?"

"You know me, Randy, serial monogamy all the way." She smiled, a bit ruefully.

What have we done in the twenty-first century that makes us ashamed of values our forebears held sacrosanct? It's as if we're all supposed to be too cool for school. Well, since school was my world, that term never applied to me. Of course, I had never been given the option of dating more than one person simultaneously. Maybe if I had Denise's ability to attract every male on the planet, it would be more than an academic theorem.

"Well, yes, I get that. What I meant to say was, is it serious? I wasn't sure how much you were seeing him, that was all."

Denise pushed away her bowl, which still had a few tidbits of goodness in the bottom, but I restrained myself from reaching over with my fork to nab a neglected piece of steak.

"I thought we were keeping it light and easy, but as the spring rolled on, Kieran has been seeming more and more intense. I honestly started to think he might be trying on the emotions as he was working through the staging notes in his book for the shows. I was a bit cautious, because after all, it's me I want him to be kissing, not some amalgam of Beatrice and Desdemona. But then, when the rehearsals began, things got a bit more normal, and I thought we were moving into a deeper phase."

"The toothbrushes in each other's cups?"

Denise smiled. "Exactly. So things have been pretty easy for the last few weeks. Kieran's been a bit less intense, and I've been having a pretty good time co-authoring this paper with Sarah about our theatre experiment. We have the evaluations back from the students, and the metrics are fantastic in terms of retention, understanding, enthusiasm and focus. We want to get the paper whipped into shape in time to present it in New Orleans in January. The *Shakespeare Quarterly* folks may be interested in publishing something like this, too." Denise beamed at me, and I got a hint of why so many waiters did her bidding happily. "It would be amazing to have cross-discipline interest happening, with both the teaching focus and the scholarship ends appreciating the same work."

I noted that Denise's conversation had segued from talk about Kieran, where she seemed uncomfortable and hesitant, over to her research area, where she was more at ease. It didn't take a degree in psychology (thankfully) to figure out she was avoiding the topic of Kieran.

I wasn't sure why. While we were far from schoolgirls, Denise had never shied away from discussing her relationships with me, as I had with her from time to time. Of course, mine tended to be variations on the same theme, Steve, while Denise flitted from man to man, like a butterfly that had yet to find the right garden. She and Kieran seeing each other since early May of this year was probably the longest stretch of dating she had done in quite a while.

I had a sense she didn't want me prying into it any further, and since I had just been through my own inquisition this morning, I was in no mood to inflict that feeling on anyone else. We finished our lunch with less problematic conversational gambits, like whether it would be a good thing if the City sprayed the parks with insecticide and what we would haul in front of the cameras if the Antiques Roadshow ever came through Edmonton.

We left the restaurant together but parted at the doors, because Denise had parked in the lot behind the building and I was on foot. She offered to drop me at home, but I waved her off. She would have an easier route to her place if she left the parking lot and kept going south, rather than twisting through the labyrinth of one-ways that kept traffic slow and reasonable through the residential student neighbourhoods bordering the university. Besides, I had frozen yoghurt to walk off.

By the time I got to my apartment, I had two things sorted out in my mind. I would definitely want my grandmother's purple vase evaluated by antique experts, and Denise was worried about Kieran.

6.

I cleared off the table in my dining room/office area and spread three sheets of manila board out for grid measurement. My best bet was to get 28 cards a sheet. Since I was figuring on 12 groups of five characters each, 60 cards per deck, and factoring in wreckage and error, the job was still going to require more patience than I was born with.

I drew light pencil lines marking the grid and set the sheets on a pile of newspapers. Using a small X-acto knife, I scored the sheet along the long lines first. Wiggling the paper back and forth where I'd sliced, I managed to create a pile of long thin strips without much trouble. Bored with the repetitive nature of the task, and feeling my back begin to protest at leaning over the table for so long, I moved my industry to the front room. I could use scissors to cut the long strips into four-inch cards, and it seemed an easy enough job that I wouldn't be ruining anything by multitasking. I reached for the remote control to the television, telling myself it was good to stay current with world events and secretly hoping for an Ingrid Bergman movie on TCM. I didn't watch television in the daytime much, unless I was weathering a flu, so I wasn't certain what was on offer. I flicked through the channels, trying to avoid the more abrasive talk shows, but stalled on what seemed to be a news channel. The camera was focused on a familiar outdoor scene, one of the wooden staircases dotted along our river valley.

Used by joggers, commuters, and dogwalkers, the stairs that connected the deep river valley to the upper roads presented an aerobic challenge to one and all. I usually had to stop at the small decks every 65 steps or so, to catch my breath and step aside to let the athletic stair runners get by me. Denise had tried to get Steve and me to join her in a stair challenge one summer, whereby you had to head down the Kinsmen stairs on the south side of the river by the High Level Bridge, cross the LRT bridge, run up the stairs by Enzio Farrone Park, cut through the Legislature grounds to 104th Street and the stairs just east of McKay Avenue School, down again into the river valley and across the Walterdale Bridge and up the stairs in Queen Elizabeth Park. I tried to point out to her that this route would land you a mile away from where you had begun, necessitating a needless walk along Saskatchewan Drive, but she dismissed this inconvenience as bonus toning.

Steve and I had joined her once or twice before I flaked out on intentionally raising a sweat. She herself had done the route religiously for three months, and while I had to admit her legs looked great that fall, I hadn't been aware of a time when Denise's legs didn't look great. I had made my way through three Russian novels during the same time. My accomplishment couldn't be gauged by a superficial look, of course, though I had taken to drinking strong coffee and pining for Moscow. I still think I came out ahead.

The reporter's voice was saying "the body was discovered under the stairs" and that police were not releasing any information, though they had confirmed the identity of the woman who had died of knife wounds.

This had to be Eleanor they were describing. It occurred to me that I hadn't learned anything from the police this morning about how and where she had been killed. If this report was connected, then Eleanor had been stabbed on or near the stairs in Queen Elizabeth Park and shoved under the stairs, to be discovered by an early-morning jogger. It was a very good thing the jogger likely had a strong heart from all that aerobic exercise.

Denise had made me do those steps, too, and while I couldn't bring them clearly to mind, I had a hazy recollection of two or three stretches of wooden stairs with a wooden gutter on either side for people to push their bicycles up or down. Landings every 40 or more steps occurred, but unlike the steps near the Macdonald Hotel, there were no clever little benches built into the banisters. You could see through to the hill beneath as you trudged up, though that sort of readjustment of focus between the tread and the further depth usually made me nauseous. On the way down, you just had to rely on faith that no ghoulish arm would dart out to grab your ankle and send you tumbling to your certain death, or at least a bad sprain. Now that I knew it was also a place to wedge murder victims, the lure of the step circuit was even more unlikely as a means of exercising my way to living forever.

I clicked through a few more channels before settling on a western marathon. It was easy to keep track of the action when it was measured in wagon wheel rotations, and I could concentrate on cutting the cards evenly.

By the time I had four sets of cards piled up in front of me, *High Noon* had given way to *Bad Day at Blackrock*, and my reverence for Spencer Tracey led me to curl up on the loveseat and watch it through to the end before I tidied things up and moved on to decorating the cards with their specific characters. That part was going to take concentration, anyhow. I had found a few cartoonish versions of Shakespeare's plays in the Edmonton Public Library and thought I could cobble together a set of suitable caricatures based on those models.

Finally the movie was over. I turned off the television, tossed the scraps of paper I'd accrued into the blue bag, and put the kettle on. While it simmered, I dug through my desk drawers for my sketchbook and a 2B pencil. I needed to practise a bit before committing to card stock.

I was hoping for some strong-lined cartoons that would give a nod to each character's idiosyncrasies. Malvolio, with his cross-gartered legs, would be simple, as would Juliet leaning over a balcony or Lady Macbeth cupping her hands full of imaginary blood. And of course, I would be printing their names below their portraits, just in case they all came out looking like versions of the wooden top family. On the whole, though, I figured I was up to the task. I'd been sketching and painting from an early age and enjoyed art classes down at the City Arts Centre every now and then. Nowadays, it amounted to so much doodling, but I occasionally pulled out the stops and created an original Christmas card. In fact, my rough designs and drawings in page after page of my notebook had been translated by a pair of amazing IT designers into the virtual museum Rutherford House was now proudly displaying on the Internet.

I stopped to heat up some soup around six and tilted the Venetian blinds around the same time I was turning on the lights, but went right back to sketching my groups. I was fairly pleased with Falstaff and quite proud of Mistress Quickly, but couldn't for the life of me figure out how to distinguish Prince Hal from Mercutio or Sebastian. I was also having a hard time drawing leeks that didn't look like scallions, so I wasn't certain that Fluellen would stand out from his Irish and Scottish compatriots. Ophelia looked like Betty Cooper drowned in the bath. I struck a line through that sketch.

I was tweaking the books that Ferdinand of Navarre was sitting on when the burbly sound of a Skype call sounded from my desk, where my laptop was sitting. At one time, I had owned a desktop computer and a laptop, but after a break-in during which most everything of value had been broken or stolen, I refurbished minimally and decided to work completely from a laptop with an auxiliary hard drive.

I moved to the desk chair and lifted the lid of my laptop. Punching in my password, I stole a quick look at my reflection in the glass cover of a print on the wall beside me. I had a pretty good idea who was calling me at 10:30 p.m., and if I was correct,

I didn't want to scare him into the arms of some Scandinavian fjord maiden.

Pushing my eyebrows into place and checking my teeth for parsley, I pressed the little green phone button and Steve's face bounced into place. He looked way too chipper for what would be 6:30 a.m., but he had always been a morning person.

"Hey doll! How are you?"

"Hey yourself! You're wide awake. Nice to see you."

We then, as all Albertans seem to, descended into a convoluted discussion of the weather there, here, in the past at this time of year, what it was predicted to be, and how different it had been last year. Steve was the first to segue out into real conversation, which was his right, as the initiator of the call. There are rules, after all.

"I read the news about a body being found."

"Bullshit. You've been talking to Iain."

"Guilty." He laughed again. "So sue me. I wanted to know how you're doing."

I shrugged. "It took over the rehearsal this morning, and I spent the afternoon and evening working from home, but that was probably just as well, since I think I've been really productive." I hauled my sketchbook from behind me at the table and tried to position it so that the camera could capture some of my drawings to show Steve. He was suitably impressed and made nice noises as he slurped his coffee. "I am not sure, though, that this is going to affect me at all. I have no real connection to the actors, after all. It's made Kieran have to rejig his casting, but I'm not certain he'll be able to hire anyone else, given the tight strictures of the grants they play with, and the timing. I think he's moving actresses around and making do, rather than starting over with someone from outside."

"Iain said he was going to be talking with Denise tomorrow," Steve remarked. "I couldn't quite follow his reasoning for that."

"Oh, I can. They're an item these days."

"Really? Denise and Kieran Frayne?" Steve smiled, and as he did, the picture of him froze for a bit, making me miss him even more. I hit screen capture, just to grab the moment. "Why doesn't that surprise me?"

I laughed. "Well, she is really enjoying the connections between the Drama and English departments at the moment. She and Sarah intend to present their paper about the joint production at the International Symposium for the Teaching of Humanities in New Orleans this coming year. I heard all about it at lunch today."

"Sounds intriguing. Well, I guess if I could swing a trip to New Orleans out of it, I could come up with any number of paper topics." Steve was animated again, and looking as if he was getting ready to be off.

"How is your work coming along?" What I really wanted to ask was when he was coming home, but I didn't feel right about it somehow. The last thing I ever wanted to be was whiny when it came to our relationship. It seemed to me that Steve had put up with a lot from being associated with me over the years, and I wanted him to have this time without any worries that I was pining for him. The trouble was trying to ride that fine line between sounding okay and making sure he knew I was missing him.

Steve filled me in on his itinerary, which seemed to be full of interviews with station minders, chiefs of police, training officers, and city councilors whose portfolios included pubic safety. One of the most interesting things he'd learned was the correlation they were making between the relative cleanliness and brightness of the station and the lowering of crime levels. Apparently, instilling a sense of pride in the locals was enough to dissuade petty criminals from working that particular beat.

"The problem lies in the more urban central stations, where there is a lack of ownership of the site. No one actually lives in the centres where we have the biggest problems, so we have to start to figure out ways to create more civic connections there. Possibly shops and businesses in the concourse levels, maybe some school art displays." I could tell he was thinking out loud, but it was fun to be in on the way his brain worked. "Anyhow, the stats are amazing here. Honestly, pretty much everything is amazing. It is sort of tough to see some of the stuff they can do here, with citizen buy-in and strong government support. It's not the nanny state that libertarians and neo-cons would have you believe it is when they talk about how much taxation takes place. It's more as if everyone in the country is invested in how the country operates. You get way more political debate and far more community interest in anything that city hall proposes than what we are used to at home."

We talked for another ten minutes, winding down into general pleasantries and promises on my part to water his plants and make use of his washer and dryer if I wanted, since he was going to be in Scandahoovia for at least another two weeks.

I was the first to click off as we said our goodbyes. I hated being the one hung up on, I always had.

I considered going back to my sketching but decided against it. I could start up again in the morning. I left my kitchen table covered in books and sketches, and my coffee table piled with cardboard card sets, and went to bed.

It was probably the events of the day working themselves into bizarre patterns, but my dreams were wild and disturbing. At one point, Steve was wandering through, dressed in a doublet and hose, saying, "Everyone has to be invested." And the next thing I knew, I was looking down on a body in the weeds. I knew it was going to be Eleanor, but I was scared to turn her over. All of a sudden, Detective Jennifer Gladue was there, officiously telling me not to touch anything, and reaching out a long hook, like the ones they used to pull bad performers off the vaudeville stage, she turned over the drowned body. My dream scream woke me up and I found myself sitting up in bed, shivering. The body in my nightmare hadn't belonged to Eleanor Durant. The drowned girl in my dream was my best friend, Denise.

7.

There is nothing like a police investigation to make any sort of schedule turn into chaos. While I was feeling pretty secure in the work I had completed and what I still had to do, I could tell that tensions were running pretty high among the cast and crew. Kieran was exhorting people to run their lines and continue to develop their characters in between the times everyone could be together. He and Detective Gladue had been through the rehearsal schedule and come up with a compromise for how to keep scene rehearsals flowing while various actors were invited to the police station to formalize their interviews and sign off on their statements.

I had a feeling Detective Gladue was hoping that pulling them away from their comfort zone in the rehearsal hall would give her the advantage, but I wasn't sure. Meanwhile, Kieran and his crew worked like crazy to rehearse in a patchwork fashion. I'd been told that movie actors had to do this sort of thing all the time, shooting out of sequence and sometimes being utterly surprised by the final product, stitched together and edited into a much different whole, but theatre actors seemed to work in a more holistic manner, building one scene into the next. That made sense to me. After all, when the audience was out front and the pressure was on, they would be called upon to bring that audience on a complete journey from beginning to end.

That offbeat rehearsal process, more than anything, was likely causing the tension. The additional element of being suspected of murder was just icing. I knew how that felt, from past experience. I was more than grateful that Detectives McCorquodale and Gladue hadn't decided I was worth another interrogation.

On the other hand, Denise was on my mind. Her first interview with the police had been relatively painless, as far as I could tell from her subsequent description, just questions about where she had been at various times, who she knew in the cast, what her relationship was with Kieran Frayne, that sort of thing.

It was the fact that they had called her in two more times for questioning that had me worried, and though I tried not to overreact and cause her to worry, she was no dummy. Somehow, they were seeing her as a suspect; if not the prime suspect, certainly one in the Fibonacci sequence. I really wished Steve was around. As much as I liked Iain McCorquodale, I knew that he was my friend only because I was Steve's girlfriend, and that my word and opinion had no actual sway with him. From what I could sense of Detective Gladue, my relationship with Steve Browning was likely a hindrance, since I could imagine her making a real play for my man if I was out of the picture.

Denise had called and asked if she could come over. I put on the tea and put her to work printing names carefully under the caricatures I had painstakingly drawn on the decks of cards I was creating.

"This really is a clever game, Randy. You could market it to some educational company." Denise was admiring my Puck, who looked a bit like Alfred E. Newman from Mad magazine, only dressed all in leaves.

"That would take entirely too much effort on my part," I laughed.

"I'm serious. Why don't you take a photo of some of these, write up the rules to your game, and pitch it to a publisher? What could it hurt? You never know, royalties on this sort of thing could add up. Games sell in the twenty-to-thirty-dollar range. That would be three dollars a deck. Even if every high school in the city bought only one deck each, you could at least take me out for dinner for helping you!" She tilted her head and grinned at me and I laughed.

"Okay, you're on. I will make one pitch, after the kids in the camps have played with them, and if they're a success. Satisfied?"

"Totally. But you know, wheedling a stake in your upcoming royalties isn't actually why I wanted to come and talk to you."

"I didn't think so, but you have come in very handy."

"Thank you." Denise bowed her head to acknowledge my appreciation. "The thing is, I came to get some advice from you. Or maybe some help."

"Sure. Anything; what do you need me to do?"

"I think the police are going to arrest me, Randy."

"What?"

"Don't bother going there. I know you've been worried about the number of times they've called me in for questioning." A pained look crossed her face. "They think I had a reason to kill Eleanor Durant, because it seems Kieran was having an affair with her."

"Oh god."

"That's what I said." Denise took a swig from her teacup and coughed a bit. "Honestly, I had no idea it was happening. I just assumed that the requirements of getting two shows simultaneously into rehearsal were eating up his spare time, and I was trying to be good about giving him room for that. Lord knows I wouldn't want to be considered a cloying girlfriend."

Denise as a cloying girlfriend was the last thing I could imagine. Usually it was a matter of men lining up to bask in her presence.

"Are they positive he was having an affair with Eleanor?"

"Apparently so. At any rate, he's not denying it." A tear welled up and spilled over Denise's lower lid and splashed onto the table. She moved her hand to wipe at the table, not her cheek. "Randy, I'm not sure what to think. The police say I had a motive and the opportunity, since I am known to run those stairs. Kieran doesn't seem to be sticking up for me, in that he makes it sound as if a blind person would know he was stepping out with Eleanor. And I honestly had no idea. I didn't know I was supposed to be hating her, so how could I have killed her?"

"Have they said whether they have anything more than that to put you on their list of suspects? Surely they can't just be saying this was all to do with jealousy on your part?"

"They aren't really telling me anything. Any time I ask a question, that Detective Gladue just gets this Medusa look in her eye, as if I've somehow transgressed some unwritten rule. But what am I supposed to do? How do you prove a negative?"

There was the million-dollar question. If you were an innocent bystander, how on earth did you prove to people shining their flashlights on you that you had nothing to do with the crime? Innocent people don't go around collecting alibis, as I had learned once when a man who wielded the power to lose me a dream job was murdered. Now Denise seemed to be in the same boat.

My thoughtful silence must have scared her.

"Randy? You do believe I'm innocent, don't you?"

I looked across the table at my beautiful friend, who had never been rejected in her life, who had never had to worry if she was good enough. Things always came easily to Denise, though she, to her credit, worked hard to be worthy of her academic honours. How would she react if thwarted or bested, she who had never had to deal with that sort of thing? Would she strike out against someone who deigned to come between her and her prize? Would she lash out? Could she murder someone? Could I imagine her doing so? Did I believe her?

"Of course I do."

8.

Ordinarily, if I had an issue with the law, I would just call Steve, who always could ride in with support, information, or a calming word. But here I was with a best friend about to go to jail, where I could just imagine a flinty-eyed convict, played in my mind by Margo Martindale, claiming her as some sort of orange-jeaned servant-concubine. And where was Steve? On the other side of the planet, learning how socialists ride the bus.

I was going to have to determine a new road into the sort of information I required, and I was pretty sure it wasn't going to come from Jennifer Gladue. On the other hand, I probably didn't have a hope of getting Iain McCorquodale to unbend from his official persona without Steve around. He tolerated me for the sake of his partner, but on the whole, his idea of wives and girlfriends was that they created the dishes brought to potlucks and spent the rest of the time cleaning the house and doing charity work. At any rate, that is what he seemed to think his wife Myra did.

I wasn't being fair. Iain and Myra had what seemed like a lovely relationship, whenever I saw them together. He obviously worshipped her, and she was completely supportive of her man. I really liked Myra, too. She was funny and clever, and had brought up two lovely daughters and seen to Iain's comfort while also continuing a steady career as an optometrist. She had her own shop along Whyte Avenue, employed two other opticians and pretty much funded all their fancy vacations to a variety of Caribbean islands that they loved so much.

The more I thought about it, the more sensible it seemed to go get my eyes checked.

It hadn't been an easy sleep, worrying about Denise, so after my shower I carefully applied the cream that was supposed to counter dark circles under my eyes. I figured it would be stupid to wear mascara to smear all over the machinery, so I ended up looking pretty wan and weary in the mirror even with my magic cream. I pulled my hair back into a ponytail and shrugged. You couldn't spend your whole life worrying about what you saw in the mirror, or you'd live your whole life in reverse image.

I pulled on a light jacket. Late spring, or early summer mornings—depending on how optimistic you are—can be deceptively cool in Edmonton. In fact, there are only two times of year you can be secure in how to dress to step outside: a three-week period in late July, early August; and a multiple-week period between December and March. The rest of the time, we practise the layered look, peeling accordingly as the sun warms the air.

By eleven, I would be unbuttoning my jacket and by two o'clock it would be tied around my waist by the sleeves, but right now, I did up the buttons against the cool breeze and shoved my hands into my pockets, wishing I had a pair of light gloves.

The walk to Whyte Avenue took about ten minutes, mostly because I went cross country, cutting through the parking lot by the dance school/Pilates studio building, and through the neighbourhood made up of three-storey walk-up apartment buildings and old veranda-fronted houses interspersed every so often with a new monster house. This was the land of students and associate professors, and the rates were high to live here. The irony was that what had long been a pleasant neighbourhood of mature, leafy trees and academic types was becoming an edgy area where transients roamed and late-night noise from the pubs and clubs on Whyte Avenue drowned out the quiet pleasures. During the morning it retained some of its old grace, though I scanned the road ahead of me, to be certain I wasn't going to be surprised by anyone sleeping rough on the side of the street I had chosen.

One bulky person pushing a laden shopping cart two blocks ahead was all I could see, and I zigged onto the next street, bringing me alongside Old Strathcona High School, a century-old brick school that housed the academic cream of the crop. Students wrote placement tests to get in there, and only 100 were chosen each year. I used to get two or three of these grads in my introductory English courses, and they were all overachievers, either first-generation Canadians with something to prove, or from families who still privileged education and academic standards as a means to get ahead in the world. Other schools in Edmonton had good teachers, and there were probably some driven students in them as well, but Old Scona was where you went if you wanted to check out the next generation of doctors, political pundits, and professors.

I didn't cut across their courtyard, as a strenuous game of pick-up basketball seemed to be occurring. I turned at the corner and walked up the two short blocks to Whyte Avenue, coming out right in front of When Pigs Fly, my favourite store for browsing in when I had all the time in the world and no idea what to buy someone as a gift. Myra's shop was three doors down and up a set of stairs. She had cunningly lit display boxes placed in the stairwell, so that people were lured up from the street level. Her shop was beautifully apportioned, with tall cones covered in various shades of velvet standing on polished wooden flooring. The walls were stripped down to their original brick, and cases of the pricier frames were along one side. Large windows looked out onto the greenery of one of the budding trees that lined the avenue, so it seemed as if you were standing in a bower, rather than on one of the busiest roads in Edmonton.

Myra's optician/salesperson was sitting at a small desk, which was flanked by two comfortable chairs. Behind her was the door that led to Myra's inner chamber of machines and gizmos that determined just how blind you were. I smiled at the woman and gave her my name. In turn, she gave me a dazzling smile and told me it wouldn't be long and that I was welcome to either sit or browse.

I chose to browse. I love looking at glasses, which probably stems from the fact that I have always wanted and never needed them. My mother had glasses, which she had worn from childhood, but my dad had fantastic vision, and even now only wore reading glasses for close work. I had picked up the habit of wearing drugstore reading glasses at night, but usually tested out with 20/20 vision. I had ocular testing done every couple of years, though, because my grandmother had suffered from glaucoma and I had a paranoid fear of that disease ever since reading a biography of Annie Sullivan back in grade school.

This visit to Myra McCorquodale was in line with my checkup times, but the real reason I was visiting was to get an inroad into Iain. I was trying on a pair of navy cat's eye frames when Myra appeared in her now open doorway.

"Randy, they're you! Or maybe your mom. I'm not quite used to the return of all these retro frames yet, are you? Come on in!"

I put the frames back on their little Lucite nosepiece and followed her into the dim suite.

She sat me in a comfy chair and pulled my file toward her. "Last time you were in was about nineteen months ago and I had you on a two-year checklist. Have you noticed any changes or headaches? Not that it's not great to see you," she added, smiling, "but normally, people only come to us when there is an awkward shift in their vision. We're like the dentist, only vaguer."

"You mean people usually know what tooth pain feels like?"

"Exactly. But they will head off to the physician or to a massage therapist when they feel eye strain, because it often presents as headaches or neck tension. Eventually, they find their way to us, but on the whole, we catch things when people break their glasses or need to order new contact lenses."

"Well, I am here on a dual-purpose checkup. I figured I was close enough to needing a checkup that I wouldn't waste your time just popping in to ask you some things."

"Okay, then, let's get started, and aside from a couple of points where I need you to either be quiet or answer some questions for me, you can ask away." She pulled the table beside us in a clockwise motion and a large piece of equipment swung into sight. Soon I had my chin on a little plastic rest and was gazing into a very expensive ViewFinder. Once I saw a little red house at the end of a long road, Myra blew air at my eyeballs and had me sit back so she could heave another piece of equipment into place. Before she had me look through it, though, she handed me a little black paddle and had me cover one eye and try to read the chart a long way across the room. To my surprise, I could no longer read the bottom line with either eye. I was pretty clear halfway down on my right eye, and my left eye could see everything on the second-last line. Myra made some *hmm*ing sounds and wrote a few things into my chart.

She next had me sit with my head up against her last big machine. She punched numbers from my chart into the machine and then had me tell her which view seemed clearer as she moved lenses back and forth. We finally seemed to agree, and she pushed the machine to the side and looked at me.

"No glaucoma in evidence, but you know, you need glasses, especially if you intend to drive safely. Your close reading is fine, which is probably just because there is a point in our forties where problems correct themselves, on their way to the great decline, but you have probably sacrificed long distance for close work, training your muscles to lock in, and now they are reluctant to stretch."

Myra offered me a pamphlet on exercises to reduce eye strain and wrote me out a prescription for glasses, should I want to wander around seeing what life really looked like on the other side of the street. It was not what I had expected to get out of this meeting.

Myra sat back with a sympathetic look on her face. She had probably handed out this sort of news to people who saw it as a sentence of horror, but truth to tell, I'd always liked wearing sunglasses and didn't think having to wear glasses would be much different. I might get less grit in my eyes on windy days. I pocketed the prescription and nodded at her suggestion that I look around her showroom for frames I liked, but not to feel obliged.

Having got the business end of the meeting out of the way, I decided I'd better get to the meat of the matter, the reason I had hurried my date with optometry.

"Myra, as you know, Steve is out of town for a while, and something has come up where I would normally go to him for advice. Thing is, I'm not certain Iain would be open to me approaching him in the same way, so I thought I would ask you what you thought and how you think I should tackle things."

Myra's open sunny face looked a bit puzzled and concerned.

"I'm not quite sure what you're getting at, Randy. You want Iain to do something for you? Something police-oriented?"

"Sort of. Did you hear about the murder of Eleanor Durant this week?"

"Oh gosh, yes, the girl from *Gopher Broke*. Wasn't that dreadful? She was found under one of the stairs in the river valley, wasn't she?"

It sounded as if Myra had no idea Iain was even attached to the case, let alone about any of his thoughts. This might be harder than I had imagined.

"She was, and I was questioned about it, because she was here rehearsing for the Shakespeare festival shows, and I've been working for the festival revamping the senior high camp. The thing is, it's even more convoluted than that." I took a deep breath. "You've met my friend Denise, right?"

Myra nodded.

"Well, Denise has been dating the director of the festival, a fellow named Kieran Frayne. And it seems that Kieran was messing around with Eleanor."

Myra leaned forward. "It's like a TV show!"

I nodded, thinking she wasn't far off the mark. This had all the arcane trappings of a soap opera. If only my friend wasn't mixed up in it, it might even be somewhat entertaining.

"Yeah, it is. Denise thinks that she might be on the list of prime suspects, because jealousy seems like a good motive. And so I was wondering if you could ask Iain if she has anything to worry about, or to let him know that she didn't even know Kieran was stepping out."

Myra was shaking her head slowly. I had a bad feeling I had overstepped an invisible line. I had a habit of doing that sort of thing.

"Iain and I have an agreement. He doesn't bring the strain of his day into the house, and I don't ask. I know that sounds a bit antediluvian, but it works for us. You know what a cop's life is like, Randy. I try to give him some space where he doesn't have to deal with the underbelly of society, where he can come home to a semblance of happiness. There is just no way I could bring that up to him."

"Well, do you think I could? I have never discussed things with Iain, but Steve and I have been able to talk about things within certain boundaries. I know it's not easy, but I have a great deal of respect for the police force, and the limits there are on what we can and cannot discuss. If I could call Iain at home tonight, just to talk to him…"

"No." Myra looked firm now. Nothing was going to get past the parapets of the sanctuary she had built for Iain. This had been a wasted visit.

Aside from the new knowledge that I needed glasses. Perfect.

9.

No one had come by to arrest Denise by the time I got back to my apartment. I knew this because there were three messages from her on my voicemail. There was also a voicemail from Steve, who sounded a bit wistful, which I took to be a good thing. I had seen pictures of Swedish girls. I didn't need him enjoying his time away too much.

I called Denise back to let her know I had got her messages and to fill her in on my trip to the optometrist. While she was slightly amazed at Myra McCorquodale's fierce insistence on not being a part of her husband's work life, she understood the theory.

"It's a stressful life, I can see that. Iain's lucky to have a partner who has his back that way."

"So do you think I should be providing that sort of safe haven for Steve? Is that what you're saying?"

"Randy, you and Steve have a completely different sort of relationship."

"How so?" I was being a bit sensitive on this score, probably a combination of not having him near and being so recently Stepforded by Myra.

"For one thing, you're not married. You don't share accommodation, and you haven't built a family together. Where Iain goes to Myra for calmness and respite, Steve goes to you for inspiration and challenge. It's a completely different dynamic."

"Yeah, but what if he needs to find calm respite somewhere? And it's not with me?"

"You do know you're talking crazy, right? Steve adores you."

I recalled that I was talking to my friend who had just discovered her own boyfriend was cheating on her. This might not be the best conversation at the moment.

"Anyhow, I don't see any way of pussyfooting around Iain to talk to him about your situation. We either meet him head on, or just leave it lie."

"If I call him, the chances are just as good that I get Detective Gladue, and I know for a fact that woman dislikes me. I'm not sure why, but she has already made up her mind about me. I have a feeling she would love to find me guilty of murder so she could justify her feelings."

I couldn't dispute it. Detective Gladue did emit bad vibes. It might be that woman-in-a-man's-world sort of jockeying for power that sometimes happened; it could be the attitude one received from a woman who tallies up relative attractiveness and feels challenged. I had the uneasy feeling, though, that she was interested in Steve and saw me as a stumbling block on the road to her success with him.

However, if Denise was also sensing that sort of disdain from Detective Gladue, perhaps I didn't have anything to worry about. We were both just picking up a weird vibe in the way she presented herself. Or maybe we were both in all kinds of trouble.

I promised to keep in contact with Denise, who was feeling very edgy, especially as she hadn't heard from anyone that day. Neither the police nor Kieran had called her, and from the sound of her voice she had been keeping herself hydrated with caffeine. I told her to text me if she needed me and that I would always have my cellphone on.

As soon as I hung up, I went hunting for my cellphone. It was in the bottom of my satchel, battery totally dead. I set it to charge on the little umbilical cord near my desk and turned to making a pot of tea. I figured I would email Steve once I'd got myself a cup and ask him if he would continue to make passes at me, now that I'd be a girl wearing glasses.

Glasses. Was this the first sign on the slippery slope to middle age? Or was this merely a new accessory to be played with? Denise had warned against metal frames because the nose guards could be irritating if they pressed on a nerve. I figured I would take her with me to shop for plastic frames. I trusted Denise's concept of style. Maybe not her taste in men, though.

I set my big Jasper the Bear mug on a coaster and pulled my laptop to me on the loveseat. When I opened it up, the email icon told me I had fifteen messages. Eight of them were from Steve, but only one was an actual message. The rest were filled with photos from his adventures. He had been spending the majority of his time in Stockholm and was planning to head to Oslo with half the delegation while the rest went to Malmo. Steve's focus was crime on public transit within a major city, and Malmo's focus was on smuggling, so the Vancouver folks were more interested in that end of things.

This whole Canadian police contingent to Scandinavia was interesting. Aside from the fact that we too were northern people, we shared other elements with the Swedes, Norse, and Finns. A bent toward socialism and a strong welfare system begat its own type of crime and social involvement.

For instance, we didn't tend to see much vigilantism in Canada, but the police did have to deal with groups of concerned citizens righteously wading into situations where levels of violence fuelled by alcohol or drugs could transform the participating bystanders into victims in the blink of an eye. There were similar situations in Norway and Sweden. That similarity was the initial impulse for this contingent of police to head over, with the blessings of the federal government, which was underwriting the excursion. Even with Oslo gaining the moniker of crime capital of the north, there were fewer cases of violence on the trains or platforms of public transit, those sanctuaries of warmth that bring together the shivering underbelly and commuting middle class to mix in uncomfortable union.

Steve's pictures of Stockholm were breathtaking. Somehow, they were a month ahead of us in terms of flowers and trees, and the juxtaposition of ancient cobblestones with modern fashion and cars was exotic.

For the fifty-seventh time, I wished I'd managed to find a way to go with Steve on this trip. A few of the other detectives had brought their spouses along, who apparently were welcome to tour various elements if they wished or were allowed to head off on their own tours of folk museums and shopping plazas. It would have been expensive, though. Steve was rooming with an officer from Calgary, and we'd have had to spring for my airline tickets and the cost of a room to ourselves, since the delegation wasn't going to allow for our just paying half the hotel room costs. We had crunched the numbers, but my going along, paired with my not making any money for the month of June, just didn't compute.

So here I was, and there was Steve. I sent him back a quick email responding to his comments on Swedish streetlights, and considered adding in my worries about Denise. In the end, I deleted three lines of my email. There was no point in burdening him with worries. He was so far away, and there was nothing he'd be able to do except fret that I was getting myself into hot water.

Which there was no doubt I would be doing.

10.

Edmonton really is a theatre town, and has been for as long as I can remember, which is somewhere around the early 1980s. And when you consider the local situation, you can sort of see why it occurred.

First you take a city that grew as the capital of a province, even though it is twice as far north as any other major metropolis in North America. The closest city of comparable size is three hours away, if you drive on the naughty side of the speed limit and don't stop for a doughnut halfway. The winters are long and dark, and while the summer is a glorious secret, it's never long enough.

Since you cannot commute easily to another centre for fine art or culture, you have to grow it yourself. And boy, had we ever. The Edmonton Symphony Orchestra, which was the first to record with rock bands, tour the north and embed members into schools, now resided in the amazing Winspear Centre and had recently celebrated their sixtieth anniversary. The

Edmonton Public Library had been around for a century. The Opera was fifty. Alberta Ballet was more than sixty years old, the Citadel Theatre was closing in on fifty and the Walterdale Playhouse, home of amateur theatre at a high level, had celebrated their fifty-fifth birthday recently. Interspersed with all these stalwarts were smaller, edgier theatres, and even they were becoming august in their own right. The Shakespeare Festival in the Park Board had been mentioning their preliminary considerations for their thirtieth celebrations in a couple of years.

Both the University of Alberta and Grant MacEwan University had strong theatre departments, with separate focuses. While U of A's Bachelor of Fine Arts program was considered one of the best in the country, and had turned out some phenomenal actors in its time, the Musical Theatre program at Grant MacEwan had its own roster of triple-threat folks who could act, sing, dance, and likely juggle on unicycles.

Every two years or so, a new theatre would spring up, with a base of new graduates and a shared dream. The older theatres had been started by MFA directing students wanting political, local, Canadian, or noon-hour platforms, but now it was actors, realizing they needed work to tide them over between Fringe seasons, who were pushing the envelope.

You'd think all this energy coming from the performing arts would make Edmonton an easy place for the arts to exist, but it still seemed like an uphill battle. I guess people just don't take the long view on a day-to-day basis. Whereas I had spent much of my life immersed in literature and the study of the culture of civilizations, it didn't strike most people that their time on this planet would be remembered by the songs they sang and the art they made, not the roads they paved or the wells they dug. Those might be essential activities, but they weren't what defined us. If we wanted to consider our lives to be purposeful, surely it was to help create and sustain a civilization that questioned, enlightened, and illuminated the human story.

Tell that to the crowd in Oilers jerseys on the platform of the LRT on a Tuesday night.

I had been seeing more theatre this year than ever before, mostly because of my connection to Denise. Not only was she tied to the community through Sarah and Kieran, she had been tagged as a Sterling judge this year, which meant she had a responsibility to see everything on offer so that she could realistically vote on the best of the theatrical offerings for the year.

The Sterlings had been named for Elizabeth Sterling Haynes, the visionary woman who had been the driving force that began it all: Edmonton Little Theatre, The Banff School of Fine Arts, Studio Theatre at the U of A. Whenever Denise tired of going out to yet another play, usually with me in tow, she confided that she drew on thoughts of Mrs. Haynes, who had promoted theatre all over the province, riding trains and driving rutted roads, bringing her vision of a "theatre built not with bricks, but with people" to the prairies.

The big evening of awards was held at the end of June. It encapsulated two distinct seasons in its view, the regular September-to-May season of most theatres, and the June-through-August season of festivals and Teatro la Quindicina, which had several years ago determined that it was more fruitful to go against the grain and deliver evenings of entertainment to people who were looking for places to go that were air-conditioned and delightful on our long summer nights.

I wasn't going to the awards dinner, of course. As far as I knew, Denise was planning to attend with Kieran, but perhaps all that had recently happened had changed that. A press conference was being held this week to announce the nominees, five in each category, broken down between musicals, dramas, and Fringe productions, which was only fair, given the relative amount of cash thrown at those three formats.

I was interested to know whether or not any of the plays and actors Denise and I had seen and discussed over post-performance cocktails would make the short list. I wasn't quite sure how many Sterling judges there were, so the short list could be a completely different animal than the roster of plays Denise had submitted as being worthy of consideration. As she had explained to me, each judge submitted his or her list, and through some sort of crazy algorithm, a list of nominees was created, which the judges then met to vote on. Technically, a play one hadn't nominated might be on the final list, but at least all the judges would have seen the works and so could have an informed vote.

One thing was for sure. Oren Gentry would likely be featured as the Outstanding Contribution to Edmonton Theatre, since he had died this year. I always thought it was such a shame that they didn't smarten up and give lifetime achievements to people who were still around to receive them. If it were up to me, I would look around and celebrate a still-kicking member of the community. After all, Gentry would still be dead next year.

Of course, next year they might be celebrating Eleanor Durant, though she was only nominally an Edmonton actress. She had moved to Toronto as soon as the ink was dry on her BFA, or even sooner, according to some apocryphal stories.

First Oren, now Eleanor. It really wasn't a great year to be in the arts in Edmonton. I wondered if there was going to be a hat trick any time soon. After all, this was such a hockey town.

Denise had asked me along to the new Stewart Lemoine play, which had opened earlier in the week, and I had been looking forward to it. His plays, performed as usual by the Teatro la Quindicina, the theatre he had founded years ago, were a complex layering of froth, arch observations of human frailty, and devastatingly funny pronouncements given at a breakneck pace. It was as if Noel Coward had met up with Woody Allan and decided to collaborate on a parody of George Bernard Shaw. I loved them all and looked forward to the annual remounting of a classic along with a brand new offering and, on occasion, a musical written in tandem with some of the other members of the collective.

Denise and I were standing in line outside along the front of the former fire hall. Steve had once joked that, in an Edmonton twist, you shouldn't yell "theatre" in a crowded fire hall, since in Old Strathcona, two fire halls had been converted to theatres. The theatre itself in the Varscona was quite a nice space, but the lobby was the size of a shoebox and twice as claustrophobic, even with the windows. On pleasant days, it was easier to create a facsimile of the Fringe lines, with ropes designating where to wait.

Denise flashed her Sterling pass discreetly to the woman at the door, who nodded as the two of us passed through. I was secretly delighted to be part of this inner circle, and to try to be worthy of the free shows, I made a point of taking Denise for a drink or a coffee after each show to discuss our reactions. I hoped in some small way to be making the process of deciding who to nominate and who to vote for easier in her mind.

Later, after the show had whirled its way into a dizzying con-clusion, Denise and I perched on high chairs in Naanolicious, helping ourselves to amazing concoctions of garlic and tama-rind-flavoured naan bread and sipping mango lasses. We were agreeing on the sublime casting of Kendra Connor in the role of Daisy when several of the cast members entered the restaurant, burbling with post-show energy.

Jeff Haslam, the star of the show and artistic director of the theatre, spotted Denise and waved. After the group had divested itself of scarves and bags and settled in to order food, Jeff slipped off his stool and popped over to talk to us.

"It was a great show, Jeff, we were there this evening," said Denise with a smile, proffering our basket of naan. Jeff waved it off.

"I have more than enough coming, I won't gobble yours. I thought I spotted you; did you really enjoy it? I'm so glad."

"The part where you were attempting to translate the *Rubai-yat* into Esperanto was hysterical. Was all of that authentic?"

"As much as possible. I think Stewart put that section in there just to get back at me for beating him in a board game marathon. I am the king of *Ticket to Ride*. Ha!"

Jeff was as charming off stage as on, and having him speak directly to me made me laugh with him, even if I wasn't sure what the heck he was talking about.

He seemed to be intent on speaking to Denise, though, so I excused myself to use the washroom, just to give them a moment or two. When I got back to the table, she was drinking water from the pounded brass cup and looking weary.

"You okay?"

She didn't look it, frankly. What to anyone else would be a vision of serenity was to my experienced eye a very untranquil Denise.

"Jeff wanted me to know that there is a story circulating that I caught Kieran and Eleanor in flagrante, and murdered her as a result."

"Really? Among the theatre community? That's not going to bode well for when Detective Gladue goes asking questions. Does he have any idea where that rumour started?"

"He doesn't, but I do." Denise sucked up the last of her Indian version of a fruit smoothie and plunked it down on the table. "Would it be okay with you if we left now?"

I had half a lasse to go, but I quickly drank three big gulps of it, causing a minor brain freeze of mangoey goodness. She shoved two twenties in the puffy leatherette folder, even though I had planned on picking up the cheque, and we made our way out of the long, narrow restaurant.

Night life on Whyte Avenue was beginning to pick up, and

we passed gaggles of smokers congregated on the sidewalks near nightclub, pub, and restaurant doors on the way to the small parkade where Denise had left her car. This spilling out into the street of partying humanity had a tendency to make Whyte a bit louder and edgier than it had been in my grad school days, and most people who came down here on a Saturday morning to avail themselves of the Farmers' Market wouldn't recognize it on a Thursday evening after 10:00 p.m.

I felt safe enough walking in tandem, though, and we were soon at the car. Denise hadn't said another thing since the restaurant, and while we were navigating the sidewalk crowds, I hadn't particularly wanted to ask her anything more. Once we were in her Bug, though, I turned and picked up the thread of the dropped conversation.

"Who do you think has started the gossip?"

Denise looked grim as she turned the ignition key.

"I'm pretty certain it's Sarah."

11.

Sarah?" I squeaked. If I'd been asked to place a bet on who might have it in for Denise, Sarah Arnold would have been the last person on my list. Sarah had been instrumental in getting Denise connected to the theatre scene, and she and Denise had been inseparable while putting together the *Romeo and Juliet* spring course. It was Sarah who had introduced Denise to Kieran in the first place. "What makes you think that? Surely Sarah would be on your side in all of this?"

Denise shook her head slowly. "I'm not so sure. I have always had the sense that she vaguely resents sharing the credit for the Shakespeare project. I wouldn't put it past her trying to discredit me this way, so that I would be all tied up in police investigations while she went to New Orleans to present our findings at the conference in September."

"I wonder if that gossip has already found its way to Detective Gladue, and that is why she is focused on you?"

"That would be a relief, in a way. Because I can only imagine how much she is going to ramp things up once she hears it, if she hasn't heard it already."

We were at my apartment. Denise had pulled in directly in front, by some miracle. The Garneau Cinema around the corner must not have been playing an 11:00 p.m. showing.

"Well, let's not worry about anything. They haven't arrested you yet, and they can't actually find any evidence proving it was you, because it wasn't you."

The look Denise turned on me was so raw in its gratitude that I felt a bit embarrassed for her.

"You have no idea how good it is to hear you say that. Right now, it feels like I've fallen down a rabbit hole."

I nodded. I'd been there. There is nothing quite like being suspected of murder to let you know who your real friends are.

"Just keep on trucking. We will get through this. And you know, the Edmonton Police Service are fantastic. They are going to find the killer, the real killer." I leaned in and gave her an awkward side hug. Luckily I had already undone my seat belt, or it would have been really ungainly. "Meanwhile, go home and have a bath. Relax. And don't let it get to you."

"*Non illegitimi carborundum.*" Denise saluted and smiled. I got out of the car and watched her shoulder check and pull away from the curb. I wouldn't have wanted to be in her fancy shoes or perfect car for all the tea in China.

Although it was late, I pulled open my laptop when I got into my apartment and hit the icon for my email. Steve had sent another missive with seventeen thumbnail photos of his travels. I scrolled through, marvelling at how clean everything looked in Scandinavia, and then hit the return arrow. I needed to unload on someone and it might as well be someone with big, gorgeous shoulders.

I gave him a quick overview of the situation, how Denise was being isolated as the prime suspect and the way in which the community was staking her out as a scapegoat. I asked him if he could write a quick note to Iain McCorquodale to test the waters and find out how things were going. I stressed how brittle Denise was, knowing that Steve thought the world of my friend, too.

I was probably overstepping my bounds as the girlfriend of a cop, something we usually tiptoed around semi-gracefully when Steve was right next to me. From halfway around the world, it felt as if things were slightly different, and that I could maximize my connection to the police in return for my lack of physical proximity. I thought about what I was doing for about five seconds, and then hit Send.

Then I went to bed.

The next morning I got up early and spent a little extra time getting ready for the day. I had plans to work all day in the festival office in the library, and was supposed to meet up with Micheline and Kieran for lunch at Kids in the Hall, the restaurant in City Hall, so we could check in on each other's schedules and be sure nothing was being missed. I felt I was putting on armour as I buttoned up an off-white sleeveless cotton blouse and tucked it into my brown slub linen trousers. A peach-coloured cardigan, my hair drawn back into a tidy braid, and little gold hoops in my ears, and that was the best I could do.

Still, it was more professional looking than my usual tee-shirt and cords, my mainstay outfit since grad school.

I shoved my laptop, the file of Shakespeare word games, and three of the four decks of Shakespeare family cards I'd been working on. I was rather proud of how they'd turned out and intended to show them off to Kieran at lunchtime.

I checked the apartment over, making sure I'd turned everything off in the kitchen, and then locked up and headed to the bus. Since I'd replaced my lost and broken essentials with brand new items, I tended to look things over and commit them to memory each time I left, just in case. On the whole, though, losing everything can be a freeing experience. While I was possessive and appreciative of the nice things I owned, I had fewer ties to anything, since there wasn't much history attached to any of it.

Still, it wasn't as if I wanted to lose it again. There were bars on the windows and a massive deadbolt on the door now, and I took my locks seriously. Steve would have flayed me if I hadn't. For the most part, I felt pretty safe. The home invasion hadn't been random, after all. It was a targeted situation, which had been resolved. Anyone who had it in for me was either dead or behind bars.

That wasn't the case for Denise, though. And from past experience, I knew exactly how unnerving that could be. As I waited at the bus stop for the 9 to trundle along, it occurred to me that it might be more useful to think of who had it in for Eleanor Durant, rather than Denise. After all, Eleanor was the one who was dead.

The articulated bus arrived at that moment, and I stepped up through the door and showed the driver my bus pass. Making my way haltingly down the aisle as the bus took off and headed immediately down a forty-five-degree hill into the river valley, I grabbed at the hand grips along the way. No one watched me, although I felt all eyes on me as I almost toppled over into the lap of an old woman who was spitefully taking up two seats by placing her enormous tote bag made out of tapestry kittens on the seat closest to the window. She glared at me, and I hastily excused myself and slid into a seat past the accordioned twisty middle of the bus.

There are a few lengthy bus runs that cover the city from one end to the other. The 9 was one of these, going from the Southgate terminal to way past the Northgate one and making every single stop along the way. Express buses that picked up in two or three neighbourhoods and then zipped along downtown or to an LRT station tended to be quicker and somehow filled with more purposeful people. When you got downtown on the 9, though, you had the feeling half the riders would just sit there and traverse the city a few times until the driver noticed their ninety-minute transfer time was up. I approved wholeheartedly of buses in the abstract, as public transportation made so much sense economically, environmentally, and sociologically. Practically speaking, though, I tended to use a lot of hand sanitizer to get me through.

I got off the bus at City Centre, a Felliniesque stop under a pedway between two parts of the upscale shopping mall in the centre of town. Here you had to watch where you stepped amid sputum and suspicious puddles. It wasn't entirely obvious whether the people huddled outside here were actually waiting for a bus or a drug score or just hoping to panhandle out of the wind.

I bustled through, pretending to be deaf, which fooled no one, and pushed open the door to the mall. Inside, patrolled by vigilant security, far fewer indigent people roamed. In fact, the marble and mirrors and shiny central core of escalators were a startling change from what you passed through outside to get there. Two office towers and a four-star hotel were accessed from here, and another fancy hotel was built right into the west part of the mall. The CBC broadcast from one corner, where the Bay had stood in the '80s, and three floors of mid-level chain stores and high-end boutiques, two food courts, several doctors' offices, an eight-screen movie theatre, three or four nice restaurants, a large Winners and the new Bay made up the scope of City Centre Mall, which advertised itself by means of edgy black and white banners featuring moody models and sentence fragments. Still, the people in the shops tended to be cheerful and pleasant, and the different parts of the mall were connected by enough pedways that you could navigate them in the winter from two different subway stops at least four blocks away.

I walked the length of the east portion of the mall and exited through the corner doors kitty corner from the Stanley Milner Library. While I was aware of Vitamin D deficiencies and the need for sunlight, walking the streets of downtown Edmonton in some areas was akin to walking through a wind tunnel. This was especially true of 102 Avenue, which I had avoided by going the indoor route. My braided hair would survive the wind, but grit from the road always aimed for my eyes when I walked downtown. Though they were swept diligently in the spring, Edmonton roads were sanded so thoroughly throughout the winter that you couldn't help but still have it slipping into cracks and potholes, to be churned up in the winds through the concrete canyons.

I waited for the light, smiled and shook my head at a panhandler, and crossed toward my destination. The elevators to the sixth floor were running during the day, since there was enough traffic to keep people in the upstairs areas safe.

Micheline was already in the office and smiled as I walked in.

"Hey Randy, it's been forever. How are you?" I was glad she seemed to be in a good mood. I quite liked her, but when she was annoyed about something, it turned into everyone's problem.

"Micheline! I am well, on the whole. I managed to get quite a bit done, and I think I might just survive this summer. How about you? How are things going, what with having to work around a police investigation?" I had learned that you had to deal head on with Micheline. She didn't understand tact. Or maybe she just liked screwing with people's minds.

"You would not believe it. They have wanted to see everything, as if looking at contracts or cuebooks was going to help them figure out who killed Eleanor. They even took Kieran's directing binder away and photocopied it. They've taken statements from everyone and have an officer sitting in on rehearsals over at the Fine Arts Building."

"Why is that, do you think?"

"Well, I think they have the idea that Kieran might have killed Eleanor, because they were having an affair, but Sherry thinks they are watching David, who has a police record and was dating Stacey, the girl who now is playing Desdemona."

"David has a police record?" I tried to imagine what sort of trouble the shambling, amiable fellow hired to play Don Pedro and Iago could have got into that would warrant a warrant, and grinned at my own internal wordplay.

"Well, apparently he did community volunteer hours to work off being caught with marijuana at a peace rally a few years back." That sounded easier to believe than seeing David as some Napoleon of crime or gangland hood. Of course, he was a pretty good actor and could be fooling me right now with his genial granola goodness.

"So why does his dating Stacey have anything to do with it?"

"Well, Sherry thinks he could have got rid of Eleanor to clear the way for Stacey to have her big break."

Like Alice, I could believe seven impossible things before breakfast, but this wasn't one of them. Not only was David incapable of presenting as a killer in my mind, the thought of killing to help someone make it big in a secondary role in a tent in a park was a little too much to swallow. I snorted and Micheline cracked a bit of a grin as well. The next thing I knew we were wiping tears from our eyes as we laughed. All the tension of the past few days were likely requiring the catharsis our laughter provided.

"Somehow that seems sacrilegious, after Eleanor dying and all, but oh man, I needed that," wheezed Micheline. I sat down at the desk across from her and grinned with that drunken haze that comes from near-hysteria. I hauled out my laptop, signed into the network, and logged into my email. While I was waiting for the connection, I pulled out my decks of cards and tossed one set over to Micheline. She was appropriately fawning, and it was with utter contentment that I turned my attention to my computer screen.

That was a short-lived feeling. There was a return email from Steve. Curt and businesslike, all it said was: "Keep out of Iain and Jennifer's way. See you when I get home. Love, Steve."

12.

Now I felt entirely adrift and for all I knew, Micheline could have been talking to me for quite some time before she finally tapped me on the shoulder. Startled, I turned toward her. She pointed to the phone.

"Kieran wants to talk to you."

I got up and moved around her desk to reach for the receiver. I hoped whatever he had to say wasn't terrifically private, because there was no sanctuary from Micheline's eagle ears.

"Hello? Kieran?" The curt email from Steve was still stinging; my reaction to chastisement was always to close down. I could hear the bruised tone in my voice and hoped it didn't translate as such across the fibre optic line. I didn't need my boss thinking I sounded whiny.

"Hey Randy. I just thought I would check in with the two of you because I'm not going to make it downtown today for lunch. Rehearsals are a zoo, and I need to devote more time here at the moment."

"Oh, no problem."

"Was there anything you particularly needed to go over with me? Or are you feeling on track still? I take it you and Amanda have kept each other up to speed on things?"

"Pretty much, though I sort of need to know whether any of your actors will be available to my students, and when and how long I could expect them. Micheline says there is some sort of proviso in the contracts of several of them, but not all?"

"We only wrote it into four or five contracts, thinking it would be a particular specialty we'd tap for the campers. Let me get back to you on that. I know David has worked with the younger kids in past years and I am sure he'd be up for a soliloquy talk, or some such. Not totally sure about the others, but you are right, there is an expectation in a few of the contracts."

"Well, that's all I really had to talk about. I did want to show you my Shakespeare card game, but that can wait." Micheline gave me a smiling thumbs-up, confirming for me that she was listening to every word and probably extrapolating the entire conversation.

"Well, good then. Keep on keeping on, and remember, we move down to the park in another two weeks. That's when the fun really starts."

I was about to answer, then realized he had hung up on me without a farewell. I replaced the receiver and moved back to my desk.

"It's the murder that's changed everything," Micheline said, which to me was stating the bloody obvious but might have seemed profound to her.

"Guess so," I agreed. "Oh well, gives us a chance to go shopping at lunch instead of meeting. Want to hit Winners?"

Lucky for me, Micheline had no more desire to hang out with me than I did to spend my off hours with her. She muttered some excuse about needing to pay some bills, and I grabbed my laptop and shoved it into my bag.

I was out on the street in front of the library before I had decided in which direction I was headed. All I knew was I needed to clear my head from Steve's email and figure out my next move.

I had tried, for Denise's sake, to get closer to Iain McCorquodale, but Myra wasn't having any of that. I doubted I would be able to win over Jennifer Gladue, so Steve needn't have been quite so explicit in his directives. There had to be some other way I could help Denise. Maybe what she needed was more support from the theatre community as a whole. After all, she was a generally likeable person. If more people knew she was in trouble, surely there would be a groundswell of support for her.

Who was I kidding? The long view was more likely that the community would far rather have unpleasantness pinned on a relative outsider, or at least outlier, so they could then pick themselves up and go back to pretending everything was rosy in their little world. Denise was a very convenient person on whom to hang everything unseemly.

I found myself walking along 104 Street, heading toward Grant MacEwan University, where I had worked when it was still Grant MacEwan College, having only recently shucked off its "Community" designation. Although they could now grant degrees in some choice areas, I was in agreement with Shakespeare and Gertrude Stein, and like the rose in question, MacEwan was still the second-string institution in town.

I loved its campuses, though, especially the downtown one with its striking postmodern take on spires and the bold clock face over the main doors. The classrooms were on the whole smaller than the U of A's, and I'd enjoyed the group dynamics that had formed in the classes I'd taught there. On an impulse, I veered across the lawn to the doors nearest the campus bookstore and popped in to browse.

A bright assortment of insignia-emblazoned backpacks and binders was on display, ready to beckon the new students who would arrive in town shortly, or perhaps to attract the summer students who descended from all over the world to learn English while taking courses like calculus, the international language of numbers. I glanced over the small fiction section not tied to course selections and then poked about in the stationery section, coveting a few small booklets and a pen that looked like a red crayon.

"Randy?"

I looked up to see my friend Valerie Bock smiling at me from over the bank of animal-shaped paper clips. "What are you doing here? It's been ages!"

"It has. How are you doing? It's good to see you, Val."

"Do you have time for coffee? It's not overly busy in the cafeteria area this time of year. We could grab a seat and catch up."

I agreed, and after lining up to fill cups from coffee dispensers and pay at the central till, we were soon sitting near a window and trying to fill in the blanks since we'd last seen each other.

Val still looked great. She ran half-marathons, had a black belt in karate, and fairly radiated good health. Her springy dark hair framed her face in short, whimsically behaved curls, and while there was just a touch of silver creeping in at her brow, it was a spectacular silver, shining like intentional jewellery and just adding to the fun.

Val was a full professor in the English department and had been very nice to me when I was maintaining several online courses for the college. She also had a family of three or four high-achieving kids and a doctor husband, so we hadn't ever moved further than campus colleagues in the friendship spectrum. It was nice to see her now, though, especially as worried as I was feeling about Denise. Somehow, the tangible knowledge that there were other people I could connect with in this city besides Denise made me feel strong enough to be able to help her.

I filled Val in on my latest project with the Shakespeare festival, and she was kind enough not to sound condescending about what sounded more and more like being a glorified camp counsellor as I spoke.

"I love the idea of the Shakespeare cards! You could probably market those, don't you think? I know my Connor could have used something like that last year in high school."

"He's not as into English as his mother?"

Val let out a hoot of laughter that drew the attention of two young men at the next table. "You could say that! I have no idea where the interests of my children came from. You would think at least one of them would consider medicine or English literature, but David is studying entomology, Susan is bound for Wall Street, and Connor's back-up plan in case the NHL doesn't draft him is to become a massage therapist and travel the world." Valerie sipped her coffee thoughtfully. "I hope they aren't really meant to be literary critics and are caught in the net of rebellion against parental authority. That would be sad, wouldn't it?"

I laughed. "I can't imagine your kids having all that much to rebel against, to be honest."

Valerie wagged her finger at me. "Oh, you should never assume you know how people play out their home patterns from seeing their public displays. Isn't that what literature really teaches us? That subtext and backstory is where everything really happens?"

She had a point, and I conceded it as gracefully as I could. A lull fell over the conversation; it would have been comfortable if we'd been colleagues, but as we were just visiting, it seemed to herald the end of the visit. Val and I stood at the same time and walked our detritus to the wall of specified disposal bins: glass, paper, compost, recyclable, trash. I was half surprised there wasn't a radioactive waste label on one of them.

"I hear Denise Wolff may be in trouble," Val tossed off as she discarded her Styrofoam cup, not looking me quite in the eye.

I was caught a bit off guard. I hadn't known that Valerie and Denise even knew each other, but I suppose English literature is a small enough world that you'd be aware of faculty in the institution across the river from you. Perhaps they met at conferences. Maybe they'd been in the same undergrad classes, for all I knew.

"What did you hear?" I countered. It might be of use to know what the rumour mill was churning out.

"People are saying she killed Eleanor Durant because she caught her cheating with her boyfriend, that director."

"Kieran Frayne."

"That's the one. You're working there, what do you think?"

"Well, I may not be the best person to ask. When you're right in the thick of things, it's difficult to remain objective. However, I've known Denise a long time and I don't believe for a moment that she had anything to do with Eleanor's death."

"But the police were questioning her, right?"

"The police have been questioning all of us, Valerie."

I excused myself as quickly as I could, and while it had been nice to reconnect, it felt as if it had been a mistake to wander into Grant MacEwan. I didn't want to break my tenuous connection to Valerie, as I liked her a lot, but it was going to be difficult to reconcile people's natural curiosity and desire to gossip with my own worries about my best friend's predicament. While I didn't mind nosing about, asking questions of folks in the cast or the Drama department about their sense of what was up with Kieran and Eleanor, I somehow felt as if connections in Denise's circles were off limits. Maybe it was because I just couldn't face the thought of assuming for even one moment that she could be guilty.

Denise was my north star. Even though I could never hope to match her in terms of taste or willpower or vision, just knowing her and knowing that sort of strength existed somehow made me a better person and more capable of achieving my own small goals.

Denise could not be tarnished. And with that noble, if selfish, thought, I headed back down 107 Street toward the LRT. I had to get home and actually get to work on making all of this go away if I was going to get anything done.

Not to mention, I had to figure out at least three more activities to absorb and captivate teenagers for a fifteen-day stretch. I knew I had to over-prepare for that or they'd eat me alive. I had no delusions that I'd be dealing with "sweet gentles all" just because they were attending a Shakespeare camp. They were between the ages of fourteen and seventeen. I could just as likely have off-leash "dogs of war" on my hands. The only security I had was in over-preparing.

I wished Steve were not in Sweden.

13.

I threw myself single-mindedly into intricate plans for the camp after I got home and nibbled mindlessly on rice cakes instead of stopping for supper. By eleven, I had most everything worked out, including handouts of some kick-ass soliloquies, two good scenes for cold readings, a section for them to try their hand at editing down for modern audiences, the card game, a crossword puzzle, several action games, and a scavenger hunt that would take them quite a lot of time searching through the complete works in order to finish.

Add to that their times with the fight instructor, one of the actors, a Q and A with Kieran, and rehearsal time for their short end-of-camp production, and they wouldn't have time to find a conch shell and break the fat kid's glasses. Or at least I was hoping for a better outcome.

My sleep was ragged, and I woke up with the nagging feeling I had been dreaming about running all night. I wasn't sure whether it had been for exercise or escape, though. Whatever the case, I didn't feel rested.

A long shower woke me up a bit more. Dressed in jean capris and a long-sleeved striped tee-shirt, I made my way to the coffee pot.

I was turning the tap to fill the carafe with water when the phone rang, and the weird timing made me think for a moment that the sound was coming from my action at the tap. That brought to mind the movie *All of Me,* where the swami equated the flushing of the toilet with the ringing of the phone, and I must have had a laugh in my voice as I answered.

"Randy? Is that you? You sound pretty cheery for this time of the morning." It was Denise.

"Hey. Well, I guess so, though I didn't sleep all that well."

"You and me both. I'm not sure whether to blame it on the stars or the stress I'm feeling. It's probably a bit of both. The reason I called was to see if you're up for breakfast today. I could swing by and pick you up in ten minutes."

I looked at the half-filled carafe in my other hand. "Sure. I'd love it."

I poured the water I'd intended for coffee into my umbrella plant in the corner of the dining room/office, and returned the carafe to its alcove in the coffeemaker. My satchel, as usual, was hanging off the back of my desk chair, and I rummaged in it just enough to be certain my wallet, cellphone, keys, and tissues were in there. There were, of course, more items than those in there, as well. Several crumpled receipts from the grocery store ("thank you, Mrs. Craig, do you need help out with that today?"), a package of gum, a box of dental floss, a notebook, three pens, some loose change, a granola bar, two folded reusable shopping bags, a bookmark advertising the Writers' Guild of Alberta–nominated works for last year, two or three wrapped candies left over from restaurant cheque trays, a nail clipper, and a tube of lip balm were also housed inside the bag, which was probably why there was a groove in my right shoulder.

I looked around the house, checked that windows were closed, drapes were drawn against the morning's promise of heat, appliances were off, and my fly was zipped. I was ready. I slipped on my sandals at the door, locked it behind me, and went out to the back stoop to wait for Denise.

She pulled up, true to her word, within minutes. I had been just about considering heading back in for a cardigan, Edmonton summer mornings being what they were, but she had the top down on her convertible Bug, and the seat warmers on, so I figured I'd be fine.

"You look like a Frenchman in a comedy sketch," Denise said, taking in my stripes and cropped trousers. "All you need is a beret, a bicycle, and a rope of garlic."

"Shoot. I was trying for beat poet."

"I have graded the finest minds of my generation?"

"Something like that. Where are we having breakfast?"

"I was thinking Cora's. I love the fruit designs they make, the lineup shouldn't be too bad on a weekday morning, and chances are pretty slim that any of the university or theatre crowd will be that far out. As far as I can tell, only about seven of them own cars."

I laughed, but had to concede it was true that most of the actors I knew lived close to either downtown or Old Strathcona and seemed to walk or bike everywhere. I suppose that was the way you survived on a salary embedded in the arts in Alberta.

Denise drove down 109 Street with the aplomb of a taxi driver, whisking us around a turn and onto 104 Street and pointed toward Calgary. Cora's was a popular chain that had crept out from Quebec, dazzling morning diners with omelettes, puffy pancakes loaded with fruit, cheery servers, bottomless coffee cups, and sunny signs all over the restaurants. On weekends, it was a good twenty- to thirty-minute wait to get in, but the portions were large and the atmosphere somehow invigorating. There were several Cora's dotted around the outskirts of the city, and one or two in the outlying commuter towns. We were aiming for the one on the southern entrance to Edmonton.

And it wasn't long before we were there. Denise had surmised correctly. There was no lineup on a weekday morning and we were seated efficiently next to a sunny window. Coffee was poured as the menus were delivered to us, so we settled in to read through and gaze at the lovely photos of breakfast offerings.

Breakfast, on the whole, is my favourite sort of meal, and I could cheerfully eat breakfast for every meal of the day: cereal, omelets, sausages, pancakes, eggs Benedict, fruit, porridge—who couldn't make a meal out of that at any hour? I was deliberating between Cora's oatmeal with fruit, and the ham-and-cheese-stuffed French toast when Denise closed her menu decisively. The waitress seemed to have been waiting for such a sign, because she was at our table almost immediately. Denise quickly ordered the Florentine omelet, and I panicked and opted for the April 89 crepe filled with fruit and custard.

The waitress tidied away our menus, poured more coffee and left us for the moment to our own devices.

Denise took a sip of coffee and looked me in the eye. "They think I did it, you know."

"Who does?"

"The police."

"Have they arrested you?"

"Not yet, but I am a 'person of interest.' Did you know that they say that to you directly? I thought it was only for offering as a sop to journalists. But no, I am a person of interest and have been advised not to leave the city without informing Staff Inspector Iain McCorquodale. Randy, I am not certain I can handle this."

"Of course you can. They will figure it out. You are obviously a person of interest because you were romantically tied to the man who was having an affair with the victim. That doesn't mean you are the principal suspect in their eyes. They just can't overlook you, that's all." I had never seen Denise this perturbed. If there hadn't been a collection of condiments and syrup between us, I'd have patted her hand. I was hoping my words were enough to pull her out of her funk.

"I hope you're right about that. But I don't think so. That Detective Gladue looks at me as if I was about to strangle someone in front of her."

"I thought Eleanor was stabbed."

"Whatever. Maybe I branch out."

The waitress arrived with our breakfasts, which could each have fed a family of four. Well, a small family of four. I eschewed her offer of authentic Quebec maple syrup in favour of the sugar-free kind on the table. It wasn't that I was calorie-conscious as much as I was cheap.

Denise, thank goodness, was as hungry as I was, and we didn't talk for about ten minutes. I had demolished half my food before I sat back and took a breather.

"We have a couple of options, as far as I can tell."

"What's that?"

"Either we spend our energy trying to make you a solid alibi for whatever time they figure Eleanor was killed, which I can tell you from experience is really tough to do. Innocent people have a hard time coming up with ironclad alibis, since we seldom think we're going to need to account for our whereabouts. For instance, did you pay attention to what time we walked into this restaurant? Do you know any of the people here, who would be likely to remember you? Did you do anything outstanding that would stick in their memories?"

"The time should show up on the bill, right? And while I seem to be here with a member of a French mime troupe, I could, if you like, stand and recite some of *Henry V* in a stentorian manner. I think they'd likely remember that, no?"

"That's my point. Unless you think you will need an alibi, you never do that sort of thing to call attention to yourself. Well, at least I don't. Maybe people remember you showing up just by being you."

Denise shrugged. She was aware of her looks, even if she

didn't trade on them. "What was the other thing you had in mind?"

"I beg your pardon? You said there were a couple of options."

"Oh right. I got carried away there, imagining how Cora's patrons would take to your rendition of 'St. Crispin's Day.' The other option, as I see it, is we have to find a few more suspects for the police to concentrate on. It worries me that they might focus on you to the detriment of their investigation and not pay attention to other possible murderers."

Denise sat forward. "That sounds good. How do we do that?"

"If past experience is anything to go by, we make a lot of lists and ask a lot of questions."

"Who knows, we might even solve it ourselves!" Denise was getting a little too enchanted with this idea, and I could tell she was channelling Nancy Drew, the part with the titian hair and the shiny roadster. I, on the other hand, thought about Nancy's friends Bess and George trapped down a well, which was the kind of thing that was far more likely to happen when you skipped off looking for desperate people.

On the other hand, Denise energized and optimistic was far more fun to be with than Denise worried and afraid. I mentally promised myself I'd apologize to Steve for unleashing one more girl detective on the city, and doggedly finished my fruit crepe.

We paid up at the till, saying no thanks to a piece of "breakfast fudge," and were soon out at the car. Denise casually asked if I needed anything over at South Edmonton Common, since we were so close anyway, and she could stand to pop into the huge Superstore for some groceries while we were so close. Like any carless person offered transportation near a grocery store, I jumped at the chance. While we were navigating the various curves and overpasses that to a crow would have been a kitty-corner manoeuvre, Denise confessed there were a few other things she needed to pick up.

Two hours and six stores later, we were pointed back to my place with a car full of bags. I had netted a rainbow's worth of peppers, apples, frozen fish fillets, a tub of Greek yoghurt and a large bottle of white vinegar, new running shoes, some yellow file folders, a drawer organizer, and a sundress with a pattern of large daisies sprouting up from the hem. It was a good thing I had a summer gig.

Denise had fared equally well, and while I invited her in to make some lists, she demurred, noting she had to get her frozen stuff home. We side hugged before I climbed out of her car, and she swooshed off as I was still wrestling my purchases through the back door of the apartment.

The pulsing light on my phone informed me I had a message waiting. I put away my groceries and filled the kettle before checking it out. The first message was from Steve, which gave me a twinge of regret for not having been in to speak with him. He was just checking in, though I figured there might be more to it than that. I wondered if Iain was keeping him in the loop about Denise being a person of interest in their investigation.

The next message was from Kieran, wondering if I was planning to attend first run in the park. Or maybe it was an invitation to attend it. One could never be sure with Kieran. To me, statements that he might think of as sounding graciously open had vague tones of imperiousness to them. It was more of a command performance than an invitation. I dutifully marked the date on my calendar so that I wouldn't forget. The run was only four days away, but with everything happening, there was no guarantee I'd remember anything if I didn't write it down.

I made a pot of tea and took it into the living room with me, setting it on the trivet I kept on the coffee table. Somehow, tea in the afternoon always made me feel civilized and British, even though I had realized long ago that whenever those heroines in the three-volume novels were talking about having tea, they were actually eating supper at four, before their sumptuous dinners at eight, like hobbits having two breakfasts. I instead opted for a huge pot of tea in the afternoon, topped off by another huge pot of tea in the evening after dinner proper.

My list making was something Steve had teased me about in the past, but it did a lot to concentrate my mind. Whenever chaos rained down, I grabbed a pencil.

I made a list of everyone who would have had a connection to Eleanor Durant. First off, there was everyone in the Shakespeare company. I limited it to Kieran because he'd been bedding her, Stacey and Louise who had something to gain from her death, David who loved Stacey, Coby the costume designer because he seemed to hate everyone, and Micheline, because I wouldn't have wanted her to feel left out. I wasn't sure Eleanor had rubbed anyone else in the cast the wrong way and would have to do some digging to find out.

Outside the festival cast and crew, Eleanor had relatively few ties to the city. Paul Mather, the writing genius behind *Gopher*

Broke, had originally been from Edmonton, but he and his family spent time between Toronto and Los Angeles these days. Marlon Davies, the elderly actor who played the requisite curmudgeon, lived here, and Eleanor and he had been featured on the front page of the *Journal* when she had first blown into town, but it seemed to me he was off somewhere shooting an ironic indie western this summer. I put a question mark by his name with a note to check that out.

Eleanor's family was from near Edmonton, and that would be another thing to look into. Was that a happy family, or a Chekovian one?

And of course, people who may have been connected to Eleanor from seeing her as she went about her daily habits: shop owners, fellow runners on the trails she frequented, people in her apartment hotel/condo building, frenzied fans.

I now had three lists of people: Shakespeare connections, Edmonton connections, casual connections. Denise was right to be concerned, and I could see why Detective Gladue was paying attention to her. She was linked to Kieran, and therefore connected on the Shakespeare list. She was also linked to casual connections, because Eleanor was known to run a route that Denise frequented. I hadn't thought to ask her if she knew any of the Durants from Spruce Grove and made a note to do so.

On the whole, it did look problematic for Denise. But that was only looking at the situation through one lens. It was possible to shake off the idea of seeing where Denise fit and check where someone else could be found to intersect with Eleanor. And honestly, why would it be necessary to connect more than once? All that would be necessary was a hatred big enough to want her gone.

I shivered. Just thinking about that sort of hatred frightened me. Thinking of it in the close context of my best friend really scared me.

If no one else was going to look for a suspect other than Denise for the crime, it would have to be me. And I was going to have to do it for more than just Denise's sake.

If there was one thing I had learned, the older I got, it was that the evil that could bring itself to kill rarely brought itself to stop once it got going.

14.

I spent the next couple of days at home, putting together plastic tubs full of activities for Shakespeare camp. Amanda, who had been with the company from the beginning, had warned me that the weather was something you could never predict, so I had come up with an organizing principle of rainproofedness. I had tubs full of handouts, erasable pens, and battered copies of plays I'd been scrounging from secondhand stores for the kids to look through for soliloquies and to get them used to the five-act layout of Shakespeare. I had sticky notes and flags for their use in marking readings. I had my precious card games in another tub, along with various scarves and hats I'd picked up from thrift stores, to help them build different characters as they practised their scenes.

I was also laying out my work wardrobe for the three-week stint. I figured I could wash it all on the second Wednesday evening and be ready for another go-round of the same togs, but I didn't want to have to stop too much for general housekeeping during the run of the camp, just in case. Teaching university-age kids for two or three hours a day wears me out. I had a feeling that herding a group of teenagers all day long for what amounted to a half-term summer session course was going to use up every last ounce of energy I had.

Micheline called me every day around 11:00 a.m. I had a feeling I was on her list of chores, making sure I was awake and industrious. I wondered if she had got used to this sort of thing from her stage management work in the past. Did wake-up calls to actors feature as a part of those job specs? She never caught me sleeping, of course, since I was usually up around six and puttering effectively by eight o'clock.

Today's call seemed different. Maybe it was her tone, or perhaps I was just more sensitive about anything dealing with Denise. Micheline was one of those women who respond poorly to beautiful women, as if somehow another's beauty diminished her. Whenever Denise popped by to meet up with Kieran or connect with me, I could sense a stiffening in Micheline that hadn't been there moments before, which of course spoke volumes of what she thought of my looks.

She was listing who was at the tables purchased for the Sterling Awards, an event that would be happening the following Monday at the Mayfield Dinner Theatre. Denise had just the evening before asked me if I would like to attend with her, since she had been sent two tickets with a map of the theatre showing a small table for two near the buffet doors. Kieran had apparently shifted her off as gracefully as possible, which was all right with me. Besides, it wouldn't have been appropriate to have one of the judges sitting with any particular theatre affiliation. Still, I had a feeling it had been a stinging blow to Denise. Kieran had really got under her skin more than most of her beaux.

Micheline was noting that Kieran, she, Louise, and Christian would be sitting with Barb Mah and a couple of other people from the Walterdale musicals.

"We are at table 17," she said, as if that should mean something to me.

"I'm at a table close to the food, that's all I know," I replied. "I doubt Denise and I'll do all that much socializing, of course. It's not the judges anyone will want to talk to."

"There will be a memorial moment for Oren Gentry, of course, but they're talking about adding a moment for Eleanor. Maribeth from the Citadel has taken it upon herself to organize it all, and she's been on at me for photos from rehearsals. We don't have much, so I sent her the headshot Eleanor was using with her resumé. I figure that would be the best thing to use, anyhow, since it was a photo Eleanor approved."

"Absolutely. It would likely have been her choice," I murmured encouragingly. Micheline was winding down.

"Anyhow, we received our keys to the park yesterday, and I give you your choice: either pop by the office here at the Library today, or you can come down to the park tomorrow after 9:00 a.m. I'll be setting up shop in the trailer on site. This year, they are promising the wifi will be strong enough to keep me connected. We shall see."

"Tomorrow is good for me. Is there any place I will be able to store four small plastic tubs down there? Or will I be schlepping this stuff to and fro each day? It won't be easy on a bike."

"Oh heck, I can fit your stuff in under the second desk in the trailer. We're not talking huge rough tote size, are we?"

"No, more like mid-size dishpan."

"Fine, bring them down."

Micheline sounded much jollier by the time she rang off. Of course, when she realized I'd be hauling stuff with the help of Denise and her car, her tune might change a bit. Oh well, I didn't have to wade through that river till tomorrow.

The final thing I had to concentrate on in planning what was starting to seem like a three-week siege was the food I would have on hand. The kids were told to bring a bag lunch, since there was nothing in the park for kiosks or food trucks. In the winter, the building by the skating pond sold hot chocolate, but in the summer months you were on your own. The kids were also bound not to leave the tent compound, since guarding and corralling children was what summer camps were really good for—education and entertainment were enjoyable byproducts. Parents wanted to be certain their darlings were there at the end of the day, preferably worn out enough to eat supper, chat happily about their day, and then fall asleep without fussing. Of course, that was for younger kids. I supposed parents of teens were hoping they were too tired to go hang out in front of convenience stores, brooding and looking for trouble.

So, while ostensibly I had an hour's break for lunch, we were shorthanded down on the site, and it would be up to me to keep an eye on the campers over the lunchtime break. I would need to head out to the Safeway for provisions, or I'd end up gnawing on the stale granola bars that rode in the bottom of my satchel for those just-in-case times.

I smiled at my pile of plastic tubs with their content lists taped to the side. Organization was like catnip for me. I couldn't always get my life to fit into tidy rows and columns, but when it did, an air of calm would slide through my veins, like that hazy sense of ease that starts in your ankles when you're getting anesthetized. Maybe someday I would throw in freelancing and academic pursuits and take up bookkeeping.

I grabbed my keys and backpack stuffed with reusable grocery bags, and pulled the little rolly cart from its place beside the fridge. The daydream of heading into work daily to a tidy office existence lasted till I passed the schoolyard on the way to the grocery store.

Bookkeepers wouldn't have the luxury to do their grocery shopping in the middle of the day, along with the pensioners and stay-at-home moms, who were never in as much of a hurry as the five-o'clock executives dashing in on their way home. Bookkeepers would have to squeeze all their chores into frantic weekends. Bookkeepers would have to tug their forelocks and request time off to visit their dying mothers. Bookkeepers were starting to meld into a Dickensian version of Bob Cratchit in my mind by the time I was passing the Garneau Cultural Centre and crossing the street to cut through the Safeway parking lot.

The best thing about this Safeway was its understanding of its clientele, which was predominantly students and seniors. Kraft Dinner took up half an aisle. Tomato and cream of mushroom soup, which could be used either as soup or as canny sauces for various low-cost recipes, held pride of place in the soup aisle, though you could also find dried soup mixes filled with organic beans and lentils. The butcher on site packed single cutlets and smaller portions, mindful of the older fridges and freezers found in student basement suites in the area, and the smaller appetites of the seniors who also shopped there.

I wonder if that mix of octogenarians and co-eds in the same neighbourhood was what accounted for the pleasantness of Garneau. In other cities, the university areas surrounding campus could get rundown and mangy, as if hanging some Tiebetan prayer flags on your porch was going to make up for the knee-high weeds in the front yard. By contrast, there was a good mixture of house-proud retired folk still in their homes surrounded by well-tended gardens, and several new owners either upgrading the older homes with good bones or razing them and erecting modern edifices in among the beautiful older trees. So, while there were plenty of worn rentals, they were mindful of their permanent neighbours, and the noise and grime quotient was held at bay. Garneau was an utterly pleasant place to live.

I filled my cart with nuts, yoghurts in little tubs, pepperoni sticks, cucumbers, and carrots. I also sprang for some pre-sliced Swiss cheese and processed luncheon meat slices to shove into pitas. I grabbed a dozen eggs and some mayonnaise, thinking it would be nice to mix up a couple of days' worth of egg salad for sandwiches, too. I would be able to store my lunch in the small fridge in Micheline's office trailer, so I didn't have any fear of dosing myself with food poisoning.

I packed my groceries into the rolly cart, which efficiently snapped its two wheels into place and spread to contain five or six snug bags of produce. I'd bought it a few years ago at the Italian Centre, when I got tired of my arms shaking and tingling for hours after hauling groceries five blocks home. I wasn't sure whether the cart made me look like an old European woman or Ramona Beezly delivering papers, but it made it a lot easier to tow my groceries. On the rare occasions that I ventured further afield to shop, I could manoeuvre it onto low-floor buses, some of which would tilt down for me as if I had a baby stroller. I didn't like to ride the bus with the cart, though, since it took up space, and I always felt as if the folks in the first few seats were judging me by whether or not I'd bought marshmallows.

By the time I got home and unpacked everything, it was almost three o'clock. I made myself a pot of tea and helped myself to a pita smeared with peanut butter. My preparation list was complete. I had materials, clothing, provisions. Bring on the maddening crowds. I was ready.

The phone rang as I was channelling my inner Thomas Hardy. I took a swig of too hot tea to clear my palate of peanut butter and picked up the receiver.

"Hello?"

"Randy?" It was Denise.

"Hey! How are you doing? You know, I think I am finally ready for camp to begin. Now I have to figure out what to wear to the Sterlings with you."

"Oh god, haven't you thought about that yet? It's tomorrow night."

"I realize that." I looked up at my calendar on the wall to the side of my desk. There it was, circled in blue. The fanciest night in theatre, on a Monday evening, since that was traditionally the actors' day off.

"That is why I was calling, to talk logistics. I can pick you up at 3:45."

"In the afternoon?"

"The doors open at 4:30, and the meal is at five. I don't want us to be caught in rush-hour traffic getting across the city. Believe me, this is not a room I want to be making an entrance into. I'd rather be there right on time and tucked into our table right away."

"Are you certain you want to go at all?"

"Yes indeed." Her voice was grim. "If I stay away, they'll all say it was because I am feeling guilty. I have to tackle things head-on and live my life as usual. It's just that it takes a lot of energy to keep the Teflon shields up, you know?"

"Oh, I hear you. Okay, I will be ready by 3:30 at the back door."

"Great, see you tomorrow!"

All my contentment at being prepared for every contingency of the next three weeks vanished as I hung up the phone. Tomorrow, I had to go to a gala where Edmonton's prettiest people would all convene in one place. While I already felt like a fringe-hanger, I would be a relative stranger adhering to someone suspected of murdering one of their own.

What the hell could one wear for that occasion?

15.

It took almost the entire day, but after fretting myself to sleep I had come up with a plan. I dashed to the Bay downtown first thing in the morning and returned with a pair of sparkling stockings to wear with my requisite little black dress, which was actually a little brown dress. I added a gold pashmina, two bangles, and slouchy brown ankle boots to the ensemble, and brushed my hair dry with anti-frizz lotion, flattening it out to almost three inches longer than usual. I gave myself a side part and hooked back the fuller side with a gold clip.

I couldn't figure out what to use as a purse to match my ensemble until I remembered a sparkly makeup bag that had come as a freebie with moisturizer I purchased. I used it to haul a spare toothbrush, floss, and toothpaste around with me. I rummaged for it through my satchel, dumping its usual contents onto my desk. All I would need was my keys, cellphone, and some cash to buy drinks with. I intended to toast Denise's hard work seeing all those plays throughout the year.

I took one last look in the mirror on my closet door. Although I was a little thicker in the middle than I wanted to be, on the whole I could still polish up pretty well. I wished Steve could see me. I wished I could see Steve right now.

It was just as well I heard Denise beep her horn just then, before I worked up a good head of self-pity. I checked the stove, even though I hadn't cooked anything hot in three days, grabbed my clutch and shawl, and headed for the back door.

One look at Denise and I wondered why I had even bothered to brush my teeth, let alone coordinate my accessories. She shimmered in peacock blue and green sequins, and her blond hair shone like honey. The convertible roof was up on her creamy little car, probably to protect our hair on the way. I slid in and Denise smiled, which made me feel I'd got the dress code right.

"You look great, Randy. Let's go show the show people how it's done."

Denise steered us out south of the university, following alongside the LRT lines until they ducked under Belgravia Road and we turned onto it toward Fox Drive and the lovely curve of road that took one past the horse stables and on to Fort Edmonton Park. Instead of turning in to the historical interpretive centre, we crested the hill by the statue of shiny silver balls and crossed the river on the Quesnell Bridge, joining the Whitemud Freeway. From that sort of convoluted orienteering you would hardly know that Edmonton was built on a grid system and was fairly straightforward for navigating. The only problem came when trying to get from one side of the river to the other—a river that snaked and curved through the city from the south-west to the northeast, with only eight bridges dotted along at strategic intervals. There were times you had to go quite far out of your way to get back to where you were headed, like a literal reworking of a cryptic Edward Albee statement.

The Mayfield Dinner Theatre was part of a hotel and confer-ence centre located in what was otherwise a cross between retail and light industrial area in the northwest part of the city. At one time it had likely been right on the edge of the city. The way Edmonton was expanding, pretty soon the River Cree Casino on the Enoch Reserve would be in the middle of town.

Dinner theatre had sprung up in the '70s, and at the time it was a vehicle for light-hearted theatrical romps like *Same Time Next Year* or *Under the Yum-Yum Tree*. Local actors would be cast in secondary roles and former television stars would fly in to be the headliner. The halls leading to the theatre area were lined with black-and-white glossy photos of actors who had appeared on *Love Boat* or *M*A*S*H*. Some of them had been great, some not so much, but everyone agreed that the fabulous buffet was what had kept the Mayfield chugging forward into the twenty-first century while so many other dinner theatres had called it quits and folded up the curtains.

And then something interesting happened. The Mayfield stopped relying on faded stars to sell tickets and began to put on smaller musicals, the kind not needing elaborate set changes. They hired local actors, many of them dynamite triple-threat singer/dancer/actors who had been trained at Grant MacEwan's musical theatre program. And before you knew it, people were no longer lining up for the smoked salmon, they were there for the show.

All that said, I was admittedly thinking about the smoked salmon as we entered the tiered theatre. The usher pointed us toward table 121 which, sure enough, was close to the buffet doorway, and I followed Denise along the carpeted aisle. You don't see all that many restaurants with thick broadloom flooring, but I supposed it was better to have to spot clean the occasional spill rather than have falling cutlery clanging during an intense moment in a play.

Denise and I sat down and began surreptitiously to look around the room. Not everyone was here yet, but there was a steady ingress. I could see Jeff Haslam from Teatro la Quindicina talking with James Kirkpatrick, who was nominated for his Don Quixote in a Mayfield production of *Man of la Mancha* that had slayed me last November. I could see Belinda Cornish talking to Marianne Copithorne and Taryn Creighton: now, there were three powerfully talented women. Both of the former two had written award-winning plays. Belinda and Marianne were magnetic actresses who were also incredibly funny, and Marianne and Taryn were directors of renown. Marianne taught at the university and Grant MacEwan when she wasn't darting off to Calgary or Saskatoon, and Taryn ran Black Box Theatre, a pop-up theatre that used found space around the city to present edgy, unconventional works. From what I had gleaned from Denise, Belinda was a Sterling board member and might be co-hosting the evening ahead.

The place was beginning to fill up. Several young things in

tuxes and rhinestones burbled by. Some of the older crowd were already heading for the food line, which Denise and I figured might be a good idea. From what we had heard, the Sterlings ran a tight ship and the show would begin promptly at six. It would be best to have eaten up, so that one's table could be cleared and all noise reduced.

I was deciding between pickled mushrooms and baby corn by choosing both when Denise stiffened beside me and hissed. Gracefully managing to avoid hitting my head on the sneeze hood, I turned to see Sarah Arnold walking into the buffet room on the arm of Kieran. They were laughing in that electrically charged way that indicates they know people are watching them and are pretending they're not putting on a show. You would think theatre people would be better at pulling off that illusion.

"This is going to be awkward," whispered Denise. I knew what she meant. Kieran and she had been almost inseparable since April, and now after three weeks of near radio silence, he appeared with Denise's counterpart in the Drama department, the woman who had in effect introduced them in the first place. And Sarah was dressed for bear. Even in this crowd of extroverts, she stood out. The last time I had seen her had been in mourning black, complete with veil.

This time she was in a crimson lace gown that revealed more than it covered. Long-sleeved and high-necked, the lace was patterned to be tighter where modesty required coverage, but was almost transparently sheer everywhere else. And it wasn't lined in ecru like skaters' costumes. I could see one of the tattoos on her hip clearly through the lace. Her hair, which she usually wore shoulder-length and was a nondescript light brown, had been piled on top of her head and adorned with shiny little ruby dots. And I had thought my shiny tights might be over the top. I could have passed for serving staff compared to Sarah.

Kieran wore a tux the way someone like George Clooney would, easy and tossed off, as if it had just happened to be hanging there when he thought he might want to put something on. I had been watching him work in jean shirts and cargo shorts for the last few weeks, so seeing him all dressed up gave me a more objective view. I could see why Denise had fallen for him. It wasn't the fact that he was gorgeous, which he was, that had likely attracted her. It was that he was so indifferently aware of his own beauty that it must have been a relief for her. She wouldn't be worshipped on a pedestal by Kieran, because he dealt in that sort of coinage every morning when he looked in his own mirror.

It hadn't occurred to me till then that it must have been very restful for Denise to date Kieran and connect with other beautiful people, in the same way sorority sisters connect no matter how many years they've been apart, or family members fall into familiar roles at annual events. It must be nice to be somewhere where you always know your lines and you don't have to spend time either explaining yourself or pretending to be what you're not.

Sarah and Kieran hadn't seen us yet, and Denise made the executive decision to deliberately continue down the buffet line to the hot food, pretending she hadn't spotted them either. I followed her lead, trying not to overload my plate while at the same time offering her a buffer to hide her from their view.

We had just turned from receiving a slab of prime rib on top of everything else on our plates, and were about to make it out of the room back to our table, when Sarah called out.

"Denise! How lovely! I wasn't sure you'd make it!"

The news of Denise's problems must have circulated further than I knew. All the thrumble of people serving themselves from two separate buffet lines went silent. There we were, the centre of attention, and now half of the Edmonton theatre scene knew that I had taken too much smoked salmon. I was not sure what I could do to diffuse the tension short of dropping my plate full of food, and there was no way I was going to do that willingly.

Kieran, whose back had been turned when Sarah spoke, stepped forward and put a hand on her arm. He nodded our way, but I'm not sure he looked Denise in the eye. I sure didn't get any ocular connection.

"Lovely to see you. Enjoy the show. Sarah, shall we?"

They sailed past us, back into the theatre. I noticed that on Sarah's plate there were three olives and a piece of skinless roasted chicken. If that was what it took to fit into a dress like that, I'd settle for my little brown number.

Denise smiled grimly at me as the noise in the buffet room resumed, and we gave them a couple of beats before following into the dining room/audience area.

"Well, if that's the bumpiest it's going to get, we may not need to fasten our seat belts, eh?"

There seemed to be some unwritten law that you didn't schmooze with food in your hand, so we made it back to our table without incident, though I noticed Denise nodding and smiling to a couple of people. On the other hand, I saw no one I knew personally, though I did recognize a good segment of the crowd. Jeff Haslam and Stewart Lemoine were looking dapper at a table for four. Though I didn't remember the names of the other two young actors with them, I did recall seeing them in last year's Teatro la Quindicina productions.

Jim de Felice and his family were seated close to the stage. Both Jim and his daughter were nominated for best director of a Fringe show. Talk about dynasties. I spotted Mark Meer, the mercury-quick improvisational comedian, who was also the voice of Commander Shepherd in *Mass Effect*, an internationally popular video game that was produced here in town. He was sitting with another couple I didn't know, but I suspected that his wife, Belinda Cornish, was now probably backstage, as the programme noted that she had directed the awards evening. Of all the more recently arrived actresses in town, I really liked her. She was originally from England and brought with her a lavish adoration for the language that reminded me of Stephen Fry or Michael Flanders. I'd seen her in previous years at the Shakespeare festival, though this year she hadn't been cast in anything. Perhaps she was busy preparing a Fringe show, as she was also an award-winning playwright. Or who knows, perhaps there had been some sort of falling out with the director?

Maybe she had insights into what it was like to work with Kieran. A conversation with Belinda was something I should look into organizing.

People milled around us, but Denise and I worked our way

through our respective plates of food. Our table was rather well situated, in the first tier up from orchestra level, on the aisle. We had to contend with a table of four in front of us, and it did mean tucking ourselves closer to the table as the elderly foursome made several trips to the buffet. I didn't recognize any of them as actors about town, so I presumed that they were relatives or former high school teachers of some of the nominated. Or maybe they were dyed-in-the-wool theatre fans. These sorts of folk actually existed in Edmonton, after all. Otherwise how could we support all those theatre companies per capita?

Denise set down her cutlery and sat back, allowing one of the fastidious and capable wait staff to swoop in and clear her plate away. I was still cutting up my last bit of Yorkshire pudding to match up with my final taste of prime rib. There was the secret to a long and successful dinner theatre—amazing food. People raved about the Mayfield buffet, and with good reason. It was all fresh, beautifully cooked, and gorgeously presented.

"Do you want to scope out the desserts? We have at least half an hour before the programme begins." Denise pushed back her chair and dropped her napkin into her seat. I tried for the same panache, but the casters on my chair were not quite as fluid as they were on hers. I narrowly avoided sending our water goblets tipping over as I got up. Of course, this would have to be the moment Louise Williams was walking by.

"Ooh, careful there, Randy!" She smiled brightly, but it was the fake sort of smile that grown-ups give to children who are brought along unexpectedly to dinner parties. Louise obviously thought I shouldn't be here. I would have to do my best not to spit unwanted food back onto my plate or interrupt when other people were talking. Like now.

"I haven't seen you in weeks," Louise was chirping brightly to Denise, who was using all her diplomatic wiles not to look grim. "I was thinking you had gone off on sabbatical, or whatever it is you academics call it."

"We call it vacation, Louise, unless it lasts half a year or so."

Louise wasn't one of my favourite people in the company, and it hadn't helped my view of her to see how quickly she had transferred her belongings to what had been Eleanor's area of the dressing room. Although the dressing rooms weren't the roomiest and all the women shared one, it was implied that the first full mirror seat to the right went to the principal character. If it weren't for the magnanimity of Maureen Shannon, who was playing Beatrice/Amelia and was ostensibly the lead, Eleanor would have been second mirror. Kieran had encouraged Maureen to bow to the power of celebrity. However, since Louise had less seniority in the company and was cast only as Hero for the first play, a much lesser role, her assuming the same spot as Eleanor was beginning to rankle Maureen. I had seen it in action the day before and was waiting to see how it played out. Maureen might be pleasant, but there were standards to uphold.

And besides, Louise had rubbed me the wrong way from the first minute I'd met her. I wasn't sure if she reminded me of someone I had disliked in the past—a student who'd bitched about her grades or a classmate who had sneered at something I had said in class—or whether I was merely responding to the aura she cast into the world, a spiky, nasty aura that was set to attack first before someone else could attack you.

How could someone that armoured be a good actress? I wasn't sure what Kieran saw in her. Maybe those offensive defences came down on stage. Or maybe he'd slept with her, too, once upon a time. Or maybe she held a secret on him.

I wouldn't put it past her. Louise had that sneaky attitude to her, as if she would love to let you know she is keeping a secret but wouldn't deign to share anything with you, even if it would help her out.

By the time Denise had shaken Louise and joined me back in the buffet hall, I had loaded up my tiny little dessert plate with a square of coconut torte, a slice of hazelnut truffle cheesecake, a little glass of chocolate mousse, and a skewer of pineapple run through the chocolate fountain.

"Why didn't you grab one of the larger plates?" Denise laughed.

"Other people were taking plates full of cookies," I said defensively.

"That was likely for the whole table for during the show."

"Oh." I hadn't thought of that. Everything I had chosen required a fork, which might clack against the china. Cookies would have been a better choice. Oh well. I would just have to scarf it all down before the lights went out.

I managed.

The show was supposed to begin at 6:30, and within three minutes of that mark, Belinda's cultured voice was heard over the intercom, asking people to take their seats, turn off their cellphones, and prepare themselves to be dazzled. I looked at Denise to share a grin at Belinda's quip, but she was looking toward the stage with the sort of awe and delight I probably demonstrate in the doorway of libraries and stationery stores. Or bakeries.

The theatre really was Denise's first love, and maybe her immersion in Shakespeare was a means to an end. The gypsy life of an actor or playwright isn't for everyone, and Denise was high maintenance when it came to creature comforts. She also had the brains to soar academically, so perhaps her family had nudged her toward academe rather than the arts. Or maybe I was reading too much into her dreamy look toward the stage.

I followed her gaze, snagging just before I got to the dais. Seated at the edge of the stage on the lowest tier of tables was Kieran Frayne.

Maybe it wasn't the stage Denise was really struck on.

16.

The Sterlings were long, but probably not as long as the Tonys or the Oscars. It helped that I had seen quite a few of the shows over the course of the year, so it was more interesting to hear the results of the nominations and see the actors speaking their own words instead of those of the playwright.

Both Marty Chan, whose wife was up for an award in stage management, and Trevor Schmidt, who had two directorial nominations and a design nod, were live-tweeting the show. Morgana Creely, the photographer hired for the Freewill Shakespeare Festival's archival scrapbook, had been covering the room, taking group photos and candids, but was now set up near the lip of the stage to cover the award action.

The new play Sterling went to Stewart Lemoine, who must have a shelf full of them, and Taryn Creighton took the directorial Sterling for her eye-popping and populist *Major Barbara,* staged in an empty warehouse next to an actual soup kitchen, which I recalled loving. I was more than ready to leave, with no desire to attend the after-show dance. I suppose it was lucky for me that Denise and Kieran were on the outs, as she seemed ready to pack it in, too. Of course, if they had been a duo, she likely wouldn't have needed a date to the event in the first place, so it was all academic.

After all the noise and bustle of the evening, Denise didn't bother to turn on the stereo in her car, which was unusual. She normally was trying to school me on some new band or an old favourite. Silence was fine by me, and we drove down the Whitemud Freeway in relative quiet. It wasn't till she was turning onto my street, near the medical sciences buildings, that Denise spoke.

"On the whole, that was less awkward than I had imagined it could be, but it wasn't entirely pleasant."

"I was rooting for Kendra Connor."

"I didn't mean the awards."

"I know. I was just trying to be funny. Sorry. I think you handled yourself magnificently, if you want to know."

Denise pulled into one of the stalls behind the Garneau Cinema, from where it was close enough for me to walk, allowing us to sit in the car and continue our chat.

"I think I can manage it, you know. When I wake up in the morning, as I put on my makeup and button my blouse, I think, I can handle whatever the day is going to throw at me. But every day, more people have heard rumours, or maybe I just run into different folks, and I have to see that look in their eyes, and it's all I can do to stand upright."

"I know exactly what you mean, except that, of course, you know more people than I do."

Denise laughed. I took this as a good sign.

"But it's going to be okay," I continued. "Steve will be back soon, and Iain will stumble across something that doesn't make sense to him. Meanwhile, you make sure you have documented lists of wherever you are, and proof that you are there. It would help if you could travel with a nun and a copy of the day's newspaper at all times, just in case. Alibis R Us, you know!"

Denise laughed again and I knew I could safely leave her to survive the night. It was just all the tomorrows and tomorrows I was worried about. If Detective Gladue was so intent on pinning Eleanor's murder on Denise, the Edmonton theatre community wasn't going to object. Something had to give. Someone had to stand up for Denise, before she broke under the weight of standing alone.

And I supposed that someone was going to have to be me.

Steve wasn't going to like this one bit.

17.

I had already tried to get Myra McCorquodale to intervene for me with her husband, but she wasn't having any of it. I would have to gird my loins and tackle Iain directly. Steve's partner didn't actively dislike me, as far as I knew, but I had the sense that he only tolerated me for Steve's sake. We didn't double-date with Iain and Myra, and even at police events, we didn't hang together all that much.

However, if Jennifer Gladue seemed to see me as just a piece of flotsam drifting between her and Steve, a possibility I had to grudgingly admit was an unproved and ugly bit of jealousy I couldn't prove or quell, Iain was a much better ally to seek out. I left a phone message on his office phone number and then went to shower. It was a Tuesday morning, and I didn't have to be at the park till ten. All that would change next week when the camps began. I was relishing the pace while I could.

I had dressed, cleaned my dresser top (one chore a day keeps the hoarder at bay), eaten a poached egg on toast, and was just beginning to pack up my backpack for my hike to the park when Iain called me back.

"Randy? What can I do for you?" He sounded muted, as if he was speaking near people he didn't want knowing his business. I mentally pushed myself not to whisper back at him. I, after all, could speak up just fine.

"Hey, Iain. Thanks for returning the call. I was hoping to get together with you sometime today. Do you have any time later?"

"I could meet for lunch, if you like."

"I'm going to be down in Hawrelak Park, but if you don't mind driving there, I could meet you outside the theatre compound."

"Sure. Around 11:30 I'll be driving through Timmy's, so I'll pick you up something, too. Head over to a table riverside, before the second turn. I'll find you." He hung up before I could agree, offer to pay for lunch or tweak the plans. Well, maybe that's what it took to climb the ranks in law enforcement. Steve, I knew, was in so many ways an anomaly to the average police detective.

Not having to pack a lunch made things a whole lot easier for me, and pretty soon I was strolling down 84 Avenue, humming "What's New, Buenos Aires" from Evita. I sometimes rode my bike to the park, rolling it down the ridge built in the stairs for such, but the thought of pushing it back up the hill after a full day of work made me choose walking instead. There was a parking lot in the park we could use, except on the weekend when the world triathlon event took place. During the run of the plays, the city had a shuttle bus that ran from the LRT station at the Health Sciences stop to the park, but it was only a twenty-minute walk from my door, which was the best choice of all.

Coming at the amphitheatre from the south end of the park rather than the pathway leading from the parking lot, I could see the backstage area through the chain-link fencing. Green mesh was strung along the inside to allow some privacy from the picnickers and paddleboaters, but if you squinted you could see movement and general activity. I could see a tall, angular fellow I figured must be James Kirkpatrick and a little bustling person I knew had to be Micheline. I strode across the green space and circled around to the side gate near the dummy-locked entrance. I let myself in and popped my backpack into the trailer, which was for the moment empty.

All the top-of-the-hill tents were in place, and the set was shimmering silver in the summer morning light. I had a mad urge to do some yoga there in the quiet calm of the morning, which would have been a great idea if I'd been wearing less constrictive jeans or if I knew any yoga poses. Just then, Micheline appeared from the back of the amphitheatre. She caught sight of me and waved.

"Randy! Good morning! Just the person I was hoping to see." She climbed the slight rise that was the natural amphitheatre of the site and met me near the merchandise tent. "Beautiful morning, no?" She looked around brightly, as if she had created it herself. "Are you hectic busy with things for your camps this morning?"

"I was going to write up the note to the parents and create the name-tag lanyards for the campers, all the stuff to hand out the first day, but I still have time. Why, what did you need me for?"

"Kieran has been riding my ass to get the front-of-house storage out of the green room. Their props table this summer is more complex and he wants things spread out a bit more. So I need to cart all those boxes of programmes and the extra merchandise cartons up to the locking bin in the back of the ladies' washroom."

"Sure, sounds good. Just show me what and where, and I can haul stuff."

"You're a lifesaver. It's not all that heavy, but it's bulky and there is a lot of it. I'm thinking we'll lock it all up in the mesh cage where they store the toilet paper, and just take out one box per show to the trailer."

We had been walking back to the green room beneath the stage as she spoke, and I nodded at Christian Norgaard, who was standing off to the side of the lower walk, having a cigarette. Honestly, for artists whose bodies were their palettes and instruments, actors were notoriously self-destructive. In a world where fewer and fewer people smoked, the only people I knew who maintained the habit were all actors.

Micheline took me through the doors and pointed to the pile of cartons to the right, near the couches. They were nowhere near the props tables, as far as I could see. Micheline must have read my body language, or I was getting telepathic in my middling years, because she hurriedly pointed to the ironing board and sewing machine and said, "Kieran thinks we can move this stuff over where the boxes and bins are stored and enable one more table to go there in their place."

I shrugged and hefted a box of programmes. They were heavy

enough to warrant carrying only one at a time, but compact enough that a short walk up the hill to the indoor washrooms set into the hillside wouldn't be an utter hardship. I could count it as my exercise for the day. Screw yoga.

More and more of the cast arrived for their penultimate rehearsal day as I lugged boxes up the hill. I was on a nodding acquaintance with most of them, so it didn't feel too uncomfortable to keep wandering in and out of the green room where actors of both sexes were in various states of undress. Christian was now playing cribbage with Troy O'Donnell, and Maureen Shannon was standing in her underwear discussing a quick change into fishnet tights during the first act. Aside from the occasional nod, no one paid me any attention.

It was nearly noon by the time I had all the cartons of programmes stacked up on one side of the chain-link cage and the five plastic tubs of touristy merchandise like tee-shirts, travel mugs, and lap blankets stacked on the other. I dusted my hands, used the toilet since I was there, and washed up as thoroughly as possible in the icy cold running water provided. While it was nice not to have to rely on porta-potties in the park, the facilities weren't exactly extravagant.

I walked purposefully to the trailer to retrieve my backpack before Micheline could think up another task for me. While it was true that I had four workdays before the first camp began, I was pretty sure my presence down on the site was making Micheline dream up chores. There were things I still had to prepare for the campers, their parents, and my peace of mind, and it would likely have been a whole lot easier on all of us if I had been allowed to keep working from home. Kieran was one of those micromanaging types, though, who needed to see people at work rather than just the work delivered, so I needed to be on site as much as possible. I was just as happy to print the material here on the festival's paper budget than have to submit claims on top of my grant-fed salary. And it helped to keep my eyes open for Denise's sake, too. Since I was satisfied that she hadn't jealously murdered Eleanor, and I couldn't imagine her death being an anonymous piece of jogging rage, it was likely that someone else here had been the murderer. If the police weren't going to look in this direction, it would have to be me.

I just hoped I didn't look too obvious. Someone here had already killed to get whatever it was they wanted from Eleanor, most likely to get her out of the way. It would be just as easy to kill a second time, I figured. Of course, what did I know? Maybe that sort of thing got harder as the chance of being understood and forgiven got more remote with each compounded sin. Could be, but I didn't think so. I had the sense that bad habits and evil deeds got easier and easier to justify in your mind, the more you practised them. Just like Christian Norgaard smoking outside the green room doors.

Could you get addicted to killing people, though? I guessed that was what serial killers were, when you got right down to it. Addicts. And there was no patch or methadone for that sort of thing.

Just thinking about it made me feel like a sitting duck. I look behind me and all around as I settled myself at one of the picnic tables at the top of the hill. There was just a fence behind me, and I could see anyone coming toward me up the hill from the audience-right seats. People might be able to skulk behind the barbecue tents to the left of me, but they'd have to appear out in the open for at least ten yards before reaching my table. I considered myself as safe as possible.

Besides, the site was buzzing with activity by now. Kieran had called a run-through of all the fight sequences in both plays before a complete run-through of *Much Ado*. The clanging of sabres was ringing from the stage, and Janine the fight choreographer was calling out critiques from the first row of seats.

I could see Micheline talking with Maggie, the volunteer coordinator, who was going through some last-minute changes on her roster. I made a note to speak with her later, since I figured we might need a volunteer or three to man the concession tent on the afternoons the campers would be presenting their work to their invited audience of parents and friends.

I finished off the letter to the parents and hit print, since the site wifi could connect to the printer in the trailer. I would have to haul my laptop inside to run the name tags, though, because I had to feed the dye-cut name cards into the printer by hand. That could wait. The last thing I wanted was to get conscripted again by Micheline.

Finally, I saw her head down toward the stage, where she joined Kieran and a couple of the actors sitting near Janine, who was now putting Dogberry and his kooky deputies through their paces with Conrad and Borachio.

I picked up my laptop and made my way to the trailer.

The name-card paper was in the second drawer I checked

and pretty soon I had my camp's worth of campers printed off. I counted out twenty-two lanyards with plastic casings and headed back out into the warmth of the sunny afternoon to pull apart the tags and create the name tags.

This time I perched at the picnic table directly in front of the management trailer. I could still see Kieran speaking with the collected cast of *Much Ado*, who seemed to be in various elements of costume. A familiar-looking woman wearing black from head to toe, with magpie iridescent hair and a couple of tattoos peeking out from the edges of her tee-shirt neck, was setting up a tripod near the stage. Micheline had sent us all a message about Morgana Creely the photographer being hired to track the process, shoot the actors, and provide as much as possible in the way of promotional material. I wondered if she had been to any of the earlier rehearsals as part of her overview project. Maybe she would be worth talking to. Someone watching with no agenda and a wide-angle lens might be just the sort of person to observe untoward relationships occurring on set. Then I recalled Micheline saying she'd only had Eleanor's headshot glossy for the Sterlings. Maybe Morgana was only on contract for the time we were down in the photogenic park.

I liked the choices of costume. Coby had gone against the blacks for Don Pedro's crew and the browns for the householders that had become so common since Kenneth Branagh's film had solidified them in people's minds. Instead, Beatrice and Hero and their kinswomen were all in rainbow, hippie-flowing garments, giving Antonio's household the feel of a California commune crossed with a Renaissance fair, and Benedick and his bunch coming across as West Point–polished soldier boys. The dichotomy was there, and the eye candy of colour on the stage was intoxicating.

Louise was wearing the headgear that Coby had designed for Eleanor, but as far as I could see, she was still wearing her original costume. I was guessing Eleanor's doublet would need taking out a bit to fit Louise, and Coby was likely letting her stew. Coby just didn't like anyone much, as far as I could tell, but there really was no love lost between him and Louise.

I could see Christian and David talking on the balcony, waiting to work out their swordwork down the staircase. It would be fun to see Janine work with my students, showing them the various ways to telegraph a move in swordplay so that one's partner could counter it easily while at the same time making it look like violent and dangerous fighting. Even capped, the sabres used were plenty dangerous. I wondered if Detective Gladue had thought to have all the swords counted and tested for blood.

Of course, stabbing someone to death with a sword that was nearly a metre long would be a bit much. The likelier weapon would be a knife of some sort. I couldn't imagine someone not being seen carrying a sword in the river valley, either. Mind you, Eleanor might have not been killed where she was found. I wondered if I'd manage to get that information out of Iain over lunch. Thinking about lunch, I checked my watch to see how much time I had before I needed to make my way to the other end of the park to meet him. My stomach was already gurgling a bit, signalling it had to be close to lunchtime.

I couldn't imagine carrying a dead Eleanor up or down the

steps in order to shove her under the stairs. Surely she must have been killed on the stairs themselves, which would indicate that either she had been followed by someone intending to kill her, or she had happened upon her enemy by accident and provoked him or her to stab her with the weapon to hand.

More and more people in Edmonton did seem to carry knives. Every couple of weeks you would read about an altercation happening after the bars had closed or in one of the dodgier areas of town. There had even been a poor young man killed on one of the other staircases to the river valley a few years back, just below the beautiful Macdonald Hotel. He had just been left there on the midway platform, though, not shoved under the stairs out of the way.

I wondered whether or not Eleanor's body being tidied away meant anything psychologically. Could some profiler figure out who had it in for her by how they had left her body? That got me thinking about the Val McDermid books I'd read, where the profilers tended to get so close to the killers that they were often the final target for the serial killers, no matter what sorts of people those killers had originally targeted.

Did we have an incipient serial killer at work here in Edmonton? Maybe it was a killer targeting joggers, and the fact that Eleanor was connected to the theatre world was complete coincidence. Of course, we would have to wait to see if either another actor or another jogger was killed to determine what sort of person the serial killer was targeting. Unless it was another actor who jogged. Which would not be impossible; they were for the most part very body conscious, aside from the smoking.

Theorizing outdoors was giving me a headache. Or maybe it was the sun. I rummaged in my satchel for my sunglasses and glanced at my watch. It was 11:40. I figured I should head over to the end of the park Iain had suggested now, since it would take a bit to walk there, and then a few more minutes to make sure he wasn't already there, and another few to choose a table where he would see me easily from the park ring road.

I waved to Micheline and mimed that I was heading out by walking a two-fingered stick man down my other arm and then pointing out and away. She nodded distractedly and continued her discussion with Tracey down near the lip of the stage.

I shoved the staff gate open far enough to slide through and then slid it back into its fake-locked position. I had to circle around behind the amphitheatre area and cut across the little footbridge across the wetland at the end of the man-made lake that was the central splendour of Hawrelak Park. In the winter, the lake was shovelled off for skating, and one of the park buildings was created as a skate shack complete with a hot chocolate canteen.

In the summer, paddleboats could be rented at one end of the lake, while fountains, ducks, and Canada geese used the rest of the glassy surface. In the past few years, they had de-icked the lake enough to host the Canadian Triathlon swim portion. The event ran toward the end of June and was the bane of the Shakespeare festival, as it ate into one of their rehearsal weekends down in the park. I had seen the crews setting up running lanes in the parking lot when I arrived in the park earlier and could understand why Kieran had been so rude about the triathlon when he talked about it earlier in the season. There really was no place for playgoers to park, and even if we attracted all bicycling patrons or pedestrians, they'd be hard pressed to make it around all the paraphernalia involved in jumping off one's bike and running for the lake.

The paddleboats were in full swing, mostly filled with one parent and one little kid, which tended to make them go around in circles rather than in a straight-ahead trajectory. Kieran and Louise had done a deadly impression at the opening party of Hamlet's soliloquy being punctuated with the call for "Boat Number Seven, please return to dock," and now I could hear that same bored loudhailer voice for myself.

I walked past the paddleboat pond and headed west across the open greensward, where young men played Frisbee with their tee-shirts tucked into the back pockets of their cutoff jeans in some sort of odd mating ritual for the amusement of young women in bikini tops and sweatpants rolled up to the knees and down to the pelvic bones. Feeling like Margaret Mead in Samoa, I trudged along, hoping desperately not to be hit in the head with a Frisbee.

The best thing to do would be to head for the second turn, which Iain had wanted me not to pass, and work my way backward along the ring road. I was about midway along, by a picnic table devoid of trees nearby but with a great view of the river, when Iain drove up. He parked expertly alongside the site and got out, balancing two coffees stacked in a tower and carrying a brown paper bag from Tim Hortons in the other.

I took the top coffee and hauled my leg over the bench on one side of the table. Iain sat on the other side and ceremoniously opened the bag, handing out napkins, wrapped bagels slathered with cream cheese, and two pots of soup.

"They had Italian Wedding Soup, so I thought that would be a good idea," he said as he handed me a soupspoon. Trust Iain to bring soup to a picnic. I smiled, but had to admit he wasn't wrong about it being tasty. Neither of us spoke till half our soup was eaten. I was gnawing on my "everything" bagel when Iain began to speak.

"So, tell me what you want to talk to me about."

"Well, as you probably know, people are treating Denise as if she is some sort of pariah because the scuttlebutt is she is a 'person of interest' in your investigation."

"There are quite a few persons of interest in our investigation," he answered drily.

"I'm sure there are, but no one else in the theatre community seems to be so clearly interesting to you."

"And your point?"

"I'd like to be a character reference for Denise."

"She isn't applying for a job, Randy, she is a person of interest in a murder investigation."

"But she couldn't have done it."

"Because she is of good character?"

"She didn't even know that Kieran was fooling around with Eleanor. How could she have a motive if she didn't know she had a motive?"

"It's difficult to prove a negative, as you well know. She can tell you and she can tell us that she didn't know about her boy-friend's proclivities, but we have a witness who heard her argu-ing with Kieran a week before the murder."

"Who?"

Iain just looked at me.

"Where were they supposed to have been arguing?"

He smiled at me patiently, the way uncles do when you beg them to tell you what is in the biggest birthday present wrapped in the hall. He opened the Tim Hortons bag and handed me my dessert, a Canadian Maple doughnut.

"Okay, I get that you can't tell me anything, but please con-sider other avenues of investigation while you're looking into things. Because I know she couldn't have murdered a woman, in cold premeditation stalking her with a knife and hiding her body and then getting home unseen and then looking me straight in the eye and asking me for help because she has become a person of interest. And if she didn't do it, that means there is still some-one out there who did."

Iain reached for my detritus on the picnic table and packed it all up in the bag, which he crumpled in one hand as he pushed up and away from the picnic table.

"I know you are missing Steve, and I know it's an edgy time for you, caught up in the whole community under the micro-scope there, but let us do our jobs, Randy. We're good at it. You can stop worrying about us getting the wrong man, or woman, or whomever we determine is guilty once our investigation is complete. Okay?"

There wasn't much I could say to that except to nod and

thank him for lunch. And hope that he wasn't whipping off an email to Steve about what a busybody his girlfriend was.

Two fit middle-aged women ran down the road, presumably circling the entire park as part of their exercise routine. Watching them, all happy and healthy, I briefly considered jogging back to the theatre along the road, but on the off-chance that my imaginary serial killer was watching and really was after exercisers, I decided to hold off on sweaty exercise for the time being. To play it safe, I would avoid scene study, too.

The rest of the afternoon was busy but satisfying. I was pretty sure I had everything ready for the camps. Telling Micheline I would see her the following Monday, I headed for the park gates to catch the bus back home. I would have two days and the weekend to mentally prepare to be a bardic camp counsellor.

18.

If I had felt at all relaxed over the four short days, that feeling disappeared in the next week's blur of activity. My camp began, and while there actually were more kids attending who wanted to be there than kids who had been forced into it by their parents, it was an uphill slog to jolly them all into being a working unit, which was required if they were going to manage to get scene work of any value accomplished.

Meanwhile, both *Much Ado About Nothing* and *Othello* had opened, to some acclaim. Micheline had managed to attract a stellar crew of Edmonton glitterati to attend the opening nights of each, and while Liz Nicholls, the long-time theatre critic for the *Edmonton Journal*, had utterly dumped on the comedy, people were coming out to it in droves, probably because of the newsworthy elements of having a purportedly murdered character actually murdered. Louise was shaky in the role, but it wasn't as if she had all that much to do besides look cow-eyed at Christian, cry on cue when he dumped her at the altar, and then spend most of the second act hidden away and claiming to be dead.

Whatever brought people to the amphitheatre, it was the magic of experiencing Shakespeare out in the open, brought into a contemporary feel through the setting and costuming, that made their evenings so wonderful. No one who came to see the Freewill shows went away disappointed. If the rain held off and the mosquitoes didn't get any worse, we were headed for the best year ever in terms of box office and refreshment sales. Micheline had mentioned that she was phoning in a second order of tee-shirts, so merchandise was moving well, too.

Kieran must have been told things were going well with the camps, or else the stress of rehearsal and getting the play up and running had dissipated enough for him to turn back into Mr. Nice Guy. He had come up to me during the lunch break while the kids were spread out around the picnic tables at the top of the hill, hunched over smart phones or laughing together about whatever teenagers laugh about. I sat there hoping it wasn't me he was headed for. Kieran plopped himself down beside me and nodded, pleased with what he was seeing.

"It's a good crowd this year, eh?"

I nodded and finished chewing the huge bite of sandwich I had taken just prior to his arrival. Grace in action.

"Are you finding any budding thespians?"

Finally I could swallow. "There are a few who have the necessary audacity, the class clown sort. I have one or two girls with intensity, but I'm not sure whether that translates to stage presence. We'll see once they get up on their feet with their scenes.

So far we have gone through some games and puzzles on Shakespeare and his times, to get them primed. Janine is coming in this afternoon to give them an hour or so of stage-fighting techniques, which should be worth a laugh."

"Good job, Randy. I've called Louise, David, and Christian in for an hour to run their duo scenes. We've got to get her a bit more comfortable in her roles. However, we can gather in the green room till three, if that gives you enough time with your fighting."

"That should be fine. I need to keep watering the kids or someone will keel over with sunstroke, so we'll be off the stage by three and settling back here for scene work and a crossword puzzle till it's time for them to head out."

"Do you think it's warm enough for sunstroke?"

"This is not the sun of our childhoods, Kieran. I don't trust it not to fry our brains while we're not looking. I get sun rashes now, when I used to just brown up without thinking about it." I reached down to the plastic tub at my feet and hauled out the large bottle of sunscreen I had on hand for those who forgot their own. "My motto is to be prepared for the worst so you can enjoy the best."

Kieran laughed and pushed himself up off the picnic bench.

"You have a point there, Randy. Well, I'd better get my head in the game. If you see Louise or the boys looking lost, let them know I'm in the green room, okay?"

He strolled down the path toward the stage, and then skirted it to the left and disappeared behind the white column marking the edge of the set. You wouldn't know from our exchange that he was mourning a lost love, let alone missing a leading actress, except for perhaps a weariness around the eyes, which someone else could just as easily take for squinting against the sun. If Kieran was missing Eleanor, he was doing a magnificent job of hiding his feelings. Of course, before he was the artistic director of the festival, he had been an actor. Denise had told me about his years in Stratford, which may have been part of his allure, as the Festival there in southern Ontario was a sort of mecca for her.

Had Eleanor ever played Stratford, I wondered. It might be worth finding out how far back her relationship to Kieran had gone. This might not have been a new thing at all. Instead of usurping Denise in Kieran's affections, Eleanor may have been just starting up a new chapter in a long-running serial.

The kids were getting restless and I could see Janine trudging up the hill toward the chain-link gate, so I clapped my hands to get their attention. I gave them a five-minute warning, time to hit the washrooms and pack up their lunch detritus, and meet on the stage.

Janine and I conferred. Some of the actors and stage folk didn't want me hanging around when they took the kids through their paces. Others were far more nervous of the kids than of a full audience and seemed to want me to hover and maintain a sense of authority while they did their thing.

Janine was of the confident type, and she had soon herded the kids into pairs and started her exercises to limber them up, all the better to fling themselves about in pretenses of battle. I walked back up the hill to sort my puzzles out of my files and haul my boxes back to their hideyhole in the trailer. Micheline was at her desk, counting ticket stubs from the evening before and entering the numbers into the columns of her spreadsheet. She was humming, so I assumed beer sales the night before had been good.

As she got to the end of a column and hit enter, she turned and smiled at me.

"Hey Randy, how goes the pied pipering?"

"That's what it feels like, for the most part," I sighed and lowered myself onto the leather couch along one wall of the trailer. The other desk belonged to Maggie, the top of hill/volunteer coordinator, and while she probably wouldn't have minded my using her chair while she wasn't there, the couch looked comfier. "I am not sure how these kids are going to get old and mature enough over the span of the next year to enter university, to tell you the truth."

Micheline had grown kids, so she laughed.

"You'd be surprised at what a difference a year and a grad corsage can make. They'll be running the world in another ten years, you know."

"Heaven help us all."

"Well, I can't see them making a worse mess of it, can you?"

"Oh, you bet I can. These kids can't spell, they don't read, they barely pay attention to politics, and they are so tied up in social media that they have a skewed concept of what is happening in the world."

"What do you mean? Surely they're more aware of politics around the world. We get more information, quicker. Uprisings and protests are shown on Twitter before they get coverage on the news."

"That's part of the trouble, I think. We see so much so quickly that we are getting paranoid about the level of unrest in the world or violence on our streets. I read statistics the other day that crime is actually way down all over the world, but we keep calling for more police presence and more prisons, partly because we are just more paranoid, but partly because we see things so quickly and become so saturated with every story that we begin to think there are killers on every corner."

Micheline thought for a minute and then shrugged. "I see your point, but I think kids are pretty much as focused on things as any generation before them. It's their time to release their sillies before putting on their big-kid pants and getting down to business. They'll do fine." She swivelled her chair around to look straight at me. "Besides, there is a killer on our corner. We don't even have to go online to get paranoid."

She had a point.

19.

I made it home before the rain started.

Ever since the flooding that had sent southern Alberta into a tailspin and created the greatest natural disaster in Canada, strong rainstorms had a sobering and frightening effect on westerners. More and more intersections would turn into small lakes and sinkholes would appear in various spots on previously impermeable roads. It was a combination of water tables rising, the Gulf Stream slowing down and letting major weather patterns sit too long in one place, and elements of our provincial infrastructure having been left unmaintained or upgraded through the glory years of getting us "debt free." It was all probably due to mankind's egregious misuse of the planet and willful human error and we were responsible for it all. I knew we had to take the blame for our voting history, at any rate.

I stood at my kitchen window watching a stream of water run down the middle of the alleyway, whipping small branches along with it. Summer in Edmonton was never predictable. I hoped that this rain would abate in time for people to decide to head to the park for the show tonight. *Othello* would be nice and atmospheric with a darkened sky and glowering clouds. As long as the weather wasn't life threatening, the Shakespeare plays went on. Most of the audience was covered under the high tent, and anyone who had decided to watch from a blanket on the lawn could scramble under cover if need be. The worst thing was a grey day leading up to the show, as it meant the house would be small and the mosquitoes might be plentiful. Of course, Maggie's volunteers in the concession would do a booming business in bug spray.

The rain seemed to be settling in for a while, though it didn't seem as militant as before. I turned on the lamps in my living room and decided to settle in for the evening. I had puzzles to mark for the kids who had turned them in, a slide show of costumes to put the finishing touches on, and the mail to go through.

I made myself a pot of tea and hauled it to the coffee table, along with some apple slices and a pile of crackers. I thought I had a heel of cheese still in the fridge, but I was mistaken, and the remains of the small jar of cheese spread I found pushed to the back was dried out and definitely non-foodlike, so it was now soaking in the sink, prior to recycling the jar. I was loath to break into the sandwich slices and portable goodies, as I needed them for my daily lunches. Somehow, I was going to have to fit in a trip to the grocery store soon. My time was so focused on being down in the park and I was so exhausted at the end of the day that most of my weekly tasks had gone by the wayside. It was a good thing I had planned my outfits for the whole stint of the camps, or I'd be stuck wearing the same grimy jeans for the last three days straight.

I knew a lot of my tiredness had to do with being outside for so much of the day. It was not for nothing that mothers took their children to the park each day to run off their energy; there was nothing like a few hours in the outdoors to make me sleep like a baby. I only hoped the kids under my care were wearing out on a par with me. We had another fortnight to go, and I wasn't sure I could harness all that energy they demonstrated initially.

When I had Friday's material ready, my clothes laid out and the lights off, I dragged myself to bed. It might have been glorified camp counselling, but I was putting as much energy into three full weeks with these teens as I'd require for a spring session intensive course. I felt utterly justified that I was earning my cushy grant.

It was funny to think that Micheline and I had enjoyed such a good chat this afternoon after the edginess she'd demonstrated when I first came on board. There was no doubt she had thought the grant should have gone to someone in the Drama department. I was pretty sure there were another couple or three folks in the cast and crew who had thought the same. Amanda, bless her soul, was just happy the position had been filled and welcomed me with open arms, thrilled she wasn't going to have to handle senior high hormones with her bard.

There wasn't so much a rivalry between the Drama and English departments as there was a détente. Each of them taught courses in play analysis, but there was a definite slant to each. While English could defend itself as being essential to liberal arts and general literacy, Drama had always been an outlier. It had strong support from the Faculty of Education, which needed teachers schooled in theatre arts, but it vied with art history and music appreciation and film studies for the general students looking to fulfill their fine arts credits. In order to keep all the specialized courses for the thoroughbred BFA acting students on the books, it needed to keep its theatre history and overview play analysis courses afloat.

So maybe that whole ages-old rivalry between departments had also fuelled Sarah Arnold's attitude toward Denise. She had been outwardly welcoming and happy to work with her, but really quick to turn on her when the going got tough.

I fell asleep wondering how Denise was feeling and making a mental list on which "call Denise" was at the very top.

20.

Friday went by in a blur, with the kids working feverishly on the monologues they'd be giving for a select audience of Kieran, Coby, Morgana, and Christian the following Monday. And by "select" I meant the adults I could round up. The kids were also eager to find out the casting for their scenes and excited to consider they'd be working on costuming and staging by the end of the next week, in order to present them to their parents and invited friends the following Saturday, prior to the matinee of *Much Ado*. I made sure the weekly paperwork was in to Micheline in plenty of time and clocked out at 4:30, just as several of the actors were drifting in to warm up prior to their six o'clock call.

I was hoping to have a completely untheatrical weekend, but Denise called with tickets to the new Stewart Lemoine play at Teatro la Quindicina, and I couldn't resist. I promised to meet her for dinner first at the Next Act the next day.

That meant I had all of Saturday, till five o'clock, at any rate, to reclaim my life without Shakespeare Camp. I woke to no alarm clock, showered for ten minutes more than necessary, and popped across the hall with my load of laundry before settling in with a breakfast of coffee and eggs. I was still sitting there, with my hair turbaned in a towel, basking in the sunny eastern window, when the ululating ring of the Skype program on my computer sounded. I swivelled around to my desk and grabbed my laptop. It was Steve. It had to be.

"Hey there, Sultan! What is it with women being able to do that with towels? Do you get taught that in gym class or something?"

"No, I think we're born knowing how, you doofus."

"What's shaking?"

"It's Saturday morning and I am trying to figure out why I ever thought running a Shakespeare camp for a group of sixteen-year-olds would be a good idea. What about you?"

"I am *mycket nyfiken men mycket trevligt,*" he responded.

"And that means?"

"I think it works out roughly to 'nosey but nice,'" he laughed. "At any rate, that's what the cleaning women at the train station here called me. I wrote it down phonetically. Sort of fits my idea of you, too, come to think of it. *Nyfiken men trevligt.* We could put that on a tee-shirt for you."

"Very funny. I don't feel all that nosey, personally. I just find answers calming."

Steve laughed again, and then the picture of him froze, making him look a little maniacal as we continued to talk. I didn't have the heart to tell him he was frozen.

I told him I'd had lunch with Iain, because I figured he already knew and I wasn't about to appear to be hiding anything from Steve. There was a bit of a break in the transmission at that point, so I wasn't entirely sure if he said he thought that was a great idea, or not a great idea, but I didn't know that it would make all that much difference to me to find out. I didn't get much face time with Steve and I didn't want to waste it having him repeat himself. The picture component had reanimated itself and he was once more twinkling at me, or rather at my clavicle.

The positioning of the internal cameras on computers always ended up making you look down, since you were focusing on the image beneath the lens on the screen you were watching. I always had a sense that people I spoke with on Skype were being thoughtful and philosophical as a result of entire conversations taking place without their really meeting my eye. There was another concept to fit into the MacLuhan one of the media transmogrifying the message for you.

I pulled myself back into the conversation, hoping my meandering thoughts had been written off as computer freeze.

"So what is up with Denise?" I heard Steve say.

"She's really worried that she's going to get arrested for murder. Whenever she talks to Iain or Detective Gladue, she is given the impression that they're just looking for ways to prove she killed Eleanor, instead of looking for anyone else who may have done it."

"I don't think they would be confiding their process to her, especially if they think she is a person of interest," Steve pointed out. "I am sure they're following all avenues in the investigation."

I shrugged, though he may not have seen that. "I know. And that's what I keep trying to bolster her up with. But this is not a very friendly town to Denise at the moment. Whoever doesn't have a vested interest in making sure they don't get caught probably has an interest in not being targeted with suspicion, anyhow. The drama crowd is probably very thankful that the brunt of the investigation is Denise and not them, especially as they gear up for the Fringe."

"That's a bit cold, isn't it? After all, a woman has died. That has to rank higher than a self-produced show in the old bus barns."

"Those shows make up a large part of some actors' livelihood, and I know for a fact that businesses on Whyte Avenue count Fringe as their mega-sales time of year, even higher than Christmas."

"Okay, point taken. Still, do you think there really is a closing of ranks against Denise?"

"Well, I can sure sense it over at the Shakespeare festival. She is persona non grata, and I'm feeling a little byblow frost, being connected to her. Not that I mind that," I hurried to add. "I'm just worried about her."

I told him about Sarah Arnold's cutting of Denise at the Sterling Awards and how Denise was pretty sure Sarah was going to try to worm her way into being the only person sent to New Orleans for the paper on the *Romeo and Juliet* project the two of them had worked on.

"The thing to ask is, would Sarah have had any sort of motive to kill Eleanor?" queried Steve, effectively cutting my huge conspiracy theory off at the legs. Even I couldn't make a case for someone being killed so another person would be framed, giving a third person all the minor glory of delivering an academic paper.

We finished off the conversation by discussing things I would far rather deal with, like the details of his return. I dutifully wrote down all the numbers of his flights and times of arrival, and promised to get his car from his parkade where I had returned it after delivering him to the airport and to meet him at the airport in four days' time.

We reached that awkward point in Skyping where both of us had said all we wanted to say yet couldn't bear to cut the connection of seeing each other. Finally, Steve said, "Okay, on a count of three…" and we simultaneously hit the disconnect.

In four days he would be home and everything would get worked out. Sunday, Monday, Tuesday, Wednesday; I would count down the days.

21.

Denise and I finished off our burgers and salad and, after chatting with our pleasant waitress, paid up and slid out of the booth at the Next Act. The buzz of patrons was happy but not overly boisterous, and there had been no lineup. That would all change in a few weeks, during Fringe season. Then, there would be a line curling around the alley, and the wait staff would be up to their elbows in action. Families and couples who for the rest of the year never made Old Strathcona part of their shopping circuit would descend on the area to see plays, eat interestingly fried foods, watch street performers, shop the craft tents, and lay out money for psychic readings. There were folks who would also spend their Fringe visits camped in the beer tent areas, after twenty-five years still tickled they could drink outside on an Edmonton street.

But tonight, it was relatively calm. The shopping hours for the boutiques along Whyte Avenue on a Saturday ended at 6:00 p.m., and the weekly Farmers' Market, which would suspend action during the Fringe, had already closed up. The farmers who had driven in for a 5:00 a.m. set-up time were by now well on their way home.

Teatro la Quindicina, one of the theatres that shared the space known as the Varscona Theatre, named for a now razed art deco cinema near the university, ran its season counter to the regular September-to-May offerings of all the other theatres, presuming correctly that its audience was loyal and starving for theatre in the summer months when it was actually a delight to get out at night and line up for a show. They ran three shows prior to the Fringe, one show during the Fringe, and one show in the beginning of October, and that was their season. The artistic partners in the company were then free to take on roles in other theatres or venture to other cities for plum roles.

I loved Stewart's shows. They were always witty, alternating bittersweet with kooky, and the language and erudite hypotheses always had the ability to tickle my funny bone. They were like meringues and I had a hard time describing the plots to anyone, even a week after I'd seen one, except to say, "Go, you'll love it." Teatro always did two classic Lemoines in their season as well as one of his new works and often a play by one of the associates, and had recently added a remount of a classic.

Tonight's offering, *Pith!*, was a play I had seen twice previously, and it was one that actually stuck with me, though the sharper bon mots and structure had fled my memory. The plot entailed a drifter being invited into a wealthy widow's home by her stalwart and plucky maid, who through the course of the evening helps her to overcome her debilitating grief through an elaborate game of parlour charades. Only in the Lemoine world would a drifter be psychologically astute and altruistic. Stewart's universe was populated by troubled aristocrats, prescient teenagers, and Burt Lancaster as Bill Starbuck, the rainmaker. It was a world I wouldn't mind inhabiting, come to that.

Denise and I bought eight red licorice whips each, and although it was general seating and there was plenty of choice, we made our way to our usual seats at the back right of the theatre. There was talk afoot that the whole theatre, which had once been a fire station, was going to be ripped out and a new theatre built in its place. No one was sure when this was going to happen, but every time I came into the cool darkness of this cheerful little space, I felt a tug of pre-nostalgia, already missing what was going to disappear.

The only other theatre in town that made me feel this much at ease yet close to the action was Chautauqua, Oren Gentry's lovely theatre, at one time a cinema, which is what Edmontonians turned into theatres when they ran out of fire stations. The Roxy over in the gallery district was also a former cinema, but it had a longer and narrower audience area.

As far as intimate theatre went, the tiny experimental spaces that Taryn Creighton turned into theatres made for some of the coolest experiences in town. While you could have audiences of only 100 or fewer, it was the ticket to get for wildly inventive and thought-provoking theatre. You let your Black Box subscription lapse at your peril; I'd heard there was a 900-names-long waiting list to get season's tickets.

One thing I loved about Edmonton theatre was that, except

for the Shakespeare plays, which needed a chance in our long summer days of getting dark enough to use some lighting effects in the second act, most performances started at 7:00 or 7:30. That meant that on a given evening, you could see a show, stop for a drink with friends, and still make it home in time to catch the news and go to bed at a decent hour. It fit neatly into one's schedule. And to my way of thinking, that was how it should be— part of the world as you knew it. After all, theatre was built to be disruptive enough on its own, without making it so uncomfortable that people shrank from adjusting their lives to take it in.

We spilled out on to 83 Avenue in time to see the western clouds showing glowing gold undersides in the still bright blue sky. Denise had parked in the lot past the funeral home, so we strolled there, reliving our favourite lines from the show we'd just seen and marvelling at Andrew MacDonald-Smith's physical antics as he became a mute Inca canoist paddling the Amazon.

"When you consider it's a play within a play within a play, it's really quite marvellous." Denise was marking the distinctions with her fingers. "We are watching Pith! In the play, he is a drifter. He pretends to be a counsellor, and they embark on the pretense of a voyage, where he is a fellow traveller. Within that context, as a fellow traveller, he becomes the native guide. And we continue to buy it, because he is thoroughly committed to his role, whatever it happens to be."

"What gets me is that on top of all that, he can sing and dance."

"Oh, he's probably a reasonably good accountant, too," Denise laughed. "From what I can tell, that Teatro crowd just muddles in and takes a turn at doing everything. Jeff runs the subscription base and Leona could probably give courses in period costuming, and then they all troop onto the stage and steal your hearts."

We got into her little car and drove the zigzag pattern across the one-way streets of Old Strathcona toward my house. I got out by the fire hydrant, where Denise pulled up for a moment so that she could continue on track to her place instead getting tied up in my back alley. That was one trouble with the great location of my apartment building. There was never street parking available in front of it.

I let myself in the front door and walked the long, dim, carpet-runnered hallway toward my door near the back of the building. My new locks made for a jumble of keys, but having more than one deadbolt made me feel monumentally safer. I occasionally wondered whether I should alternate leaving one of the locks open, so that any lock pick would lock one as he or she unlocked the others, but I was worried it would screw me up into forgetting to lock any of them.

I flicked on my overhead light and snapped the bolts on the door behind me, then moved to close my blinds and open the air holes in the kitchen window to get a cross-draft going. The temperature was marginally cooler once the sun went down, and soon it would drop several degrees in the evenings, warning us of the months of ice to come. Tonight it was mild and dry, so even though the temperature hadn't gone down much, I wasn't turning into a sweaty, muggy mess. I would be able to sleep under my summer-weight duvet just fine.

I popped the kettle on for a cup of sleepy tea and moved toward my phone, which was blinking messages.

The first one was from Micheline, telling me that two of the parents of my camp kids had been at the show that night and were both raving to Kieran about how much their darlings were getting out of this year's program. I made a mental note to thank Micheline for sharing that. Feedback was so sporadic in the teaching game; you had to feed your ego with scraps.

The second call was from my mother, who wanted to remind me to get a card in the mail for my Aunt Ruth's birthday. I don't think I had ever even known when Aunt Ruth's birthday was, but my mother had taken it upon herself to be sure her sister-in-law was well cossetted by the family she still possessed since her recent widowhood. I made an actual note to myself to go get a card, since I knew I wouldn't remember that task.

The third call was dead air. I had the phone tucked under my chin, writing myself *card for Auntie Ruth* on a pink sticky pad, waiting for the voice mail computer voice to come in and ask if I wanted to erase or reply, knowing that if I tried to erase before then it would just reset and start to play over again, some glitch in my personal voice mail box. Assuming someone had reached a wrong number and had inadvertently listened to my message too long, triggering the answer space, I waited for the program to run its course. It surprised me to hear the click of a phone receiver being set down. I hadn't been listening to dead air.

I had been listening to someone listening. Creepy.

22.

Sunday morning I woke to birds squawking at each other outside my window. The magpie population of Edmonton had exploded this year, and I wasn't sure why. Maybe the coyotes in the ravine were otherwise occupied with bunnies. Or maybe bird flu had carried off more invasive birds, if there were such a thing. Whatever. They were raucously boisterous and as such they were better than an alarm clock.

At first I sat on the side of my bed with a sense of complete disconnect. I wasn't sure what day it was, where I was supposed to be, what was happening. Lord help me if I ever do suffer some cerebral disorder; I have spent enough time daydreaming in the course of my life to have managed a successful part-time job, I am sure. I wiggled my toes and did some shoulder stretches and then remembered that I had to go to the bathroom. I wasn't sure bodily functions counted as memories—or tasks, for that matter—but once I was up and moving and my general ablutions were taken care of, I pieced together the facts that it was my day off, Steve was coming home only three sleeps from now, and Denise had seemed pretty calm and together the night before. Things could be a lot worse.

It wasn't till I was drinking coffee and eating toast with sliced tomato that I recalled the silent phone message. I had tried to see who had called, but the number was listed as Private Listing on my display. Not for the first time, I considered getting rid of my phone altogether.

Over the years, I have had my share of harassing calls and nasty events. It was never fun to be targeted by a stalker, because no matter how much they protested their innocence or even their care for you, eventually the malevolent streak that propelled their actions came out toward you. There was no way I wanted that sort of attention, but from my experience, the police rarely took silent phone calls seriously. Who could blame them? Considering that they were all that stood between the innocent citizenry and knives and guns and road rage and illegal reptiles, it was understandable that a creepy phone call or two would register very low on their radar.

Oh well, I had deadbolts on my door, and Steve would be back Wednesday. I could cope.

Washing up my meagre breakfast detritus, I tried to make a mental list of all the things I needed to get done that day. Sighing, I realized it just wasn't going to work, so I swished out the suds, dried my hands, and went in search of a pen and a pad of paper.

Soon I was working on a three-column list: the household chores for the day, grocery items I needed to pick up, and a list of anyone I could think of in the city who hated either Denise or Eleanor.

Wouldn't it be awful to be killed just as a means of putting the blame on someone else? Not that it was any more acceptable to be killed because you were despised; to be hated so much that someone was willing to step over that line was a little daunting to contemplate. But being collateral damage in someone else's line of detestation would have to hurt, especially someone in the performing arts, where so much was tied into ego and drawing the attention in the room.

I figured that no one hated Denise so much that they bumped off one of the top stars in Canadian television. Denise was by-product, not target. So was there any other reason beyond hatred for someone to kill Eleanor Durant? Was someone threatened by her return to Edmonton? It wasn't as if we had a burgeoning television industry here. But then again, most theatre people in Canada were multi-task-oriented. They would appear in movies, then show up on stage or begin directing a festival theatre. Some augmented their acting salaries with historical interpretive work or national park adventure tours.

Maybe Eleanor was planning to branch out into someone else's territory. But whose? I couldn't imagine Belinda Cornish or Coralee Cairns knifing someone on the river valley stairs because they were concerned there wouldn't be enough roles for actresses over thirty in Edmonton. If that was motive enough, the streets would be flowing with blood from Hollywood to Stratford.

The trouble was, I didn't know enough about Eleanor, and

there was no way either Iain McCorquodale or Jennifer Gladue was going to give me any insights. I was going to have to find someone in the theatre community who actually knew what was happening. Kieran would never gossip. Denise had told me everything she knew, and so had Micheline, I was sure, because that girl wasn't holding back anything.

Who else did I know in the theatre community? There were the folks in the plays down at the Shakespeare Festival, but while I was on a pleasant nodding acquaintance with Amanda, Louise, Christian, and the others, I didn't feel anything like a part of the fold. Sarah Arnold had pretty much cut me dead when she was dissing Denise at the Sterlings, so I could forget about her.

Janine, the fight instructor at the Festival, might be a good person to take for a drink, but she herself was relatively new to the community. I really needed someone with some insight and history.

That's when I thought of the perfect person to call. Taryn Creighton. She was the only director in town with whom I had a slight in, having appeared in her MFA production of Brecht's *Galileo* back when I was doing my MA. The directing students had to cast a wide net for actors, since all the BFA students were caught up in their year-end shows at the same time as the thesis work needed to be presented. I had gone along for auditions, thinking it would be a lark, and it was. I ended up as a gypsy who sang little aphoristic ditties before each scene. No one recognized me behind the makeup and layers of petticoats and shawls, and the show had punctuated my last bit of thesis writing with a bit of fun.

Taryn Creighton was about my age, having been an actor for the same length of time I was a freelance writer, and both of us had done post-secondary degrees in our late thirties. That had provided a nice respite from always being the eldest in the room. She and I had got along quite well, and while we hadn't stayed connected, we spoke when we ran into each other in theatre lobbies and at the Fringe. I never made it to a Black Box opening night, so I rarely saw her at her own productions.

Maybe I could call Taryn in my position as Shakespeare camp leader and take her out for lunch. While talking about elements of theatre for teens, I could also find out if she had any ideas about what Eleanor might have been doing in town that could worry someone enough to erase her from the equation.

Lucky for me there was only one T. Creighton in the phone book, because the only person I could have asked for her contact information was Denise, and she'd have been curious. I didn't want to get her hopes up by saying too much; it was as if she'd reached a sort of equilibrium at the moment and I didn't want to unbalance her. As it was, waiting for the police to decide whether or not to arrest you must be edgy enough.

Taryn sounded a bit diffident on the phone, and it occurred to me that she might not actually remember me, but her voice warmed as we spoke, and as luck would have it, she was free that evening and could meet for supper. She suggested a small El Salvadorean restaurant near her home, and stressing that I was paying, I agreed. I looked the place up on the Internet and jotted down the address. I figured I could walk there from the Grant MacEwan campus downtown.

Somehow, getting that sorted made me feel as if all the lists were doable. I whipped through my household chores and pretty soon my apartment was in shape to last me another week of cleaning inertia. I grabbed my wheelie cart and made my way down 109 Street to the Safeway and stocked up on essentials.

On the way past the City Arts Centre, I heard my name being called. I looked around, and eventually spotted Louise waving madly from across the street. Her light finally turned green and she dashed over.

"Hi! I didn't know you lived near here! I'm just down a couple of blocks toward the Varscona, there," she sang at me. It was as if everything Louise said was directed to the back of the auditorium.

"Really? How do you like it down there?"

"Oh, I love the location for getting places, but I have to sleep with earplugs, it's so noisy at night when the bars close. And you have to watch where you walk in the morning, if you know what I mean." She wrinkled her nose as she nodded knowingly.

I had no idea what she was talking about, unless she meant that people defecated on her sidewalk, so I just smiled and nodded back.

"Are you doing your grocery shopping?"

I would have thought the fact that I was hauling a wheelie cart with bags containing milk and pasta was a pretty obvious clue, but Louise might not read mystery novels. She also could be one of those people who always questioned the obvious, filling the terrifying void of silence between people who had nothing to say to each other.

I smiled and nodded again. "What are you up to? Don't you have shows today?"

"I'm meeting Kieran and Sarah for brunch before the matinee," she burbled, obviously wanting to tell someone. She pointed to the restaurant inset on the corner we were standing on, so I said, "Well, you'd better not keep them waiting," and nodded again at her.

On the whole, I would not want to spend time with work people when I wasn't working. But maybe she just wanted a ride down to the park, or maybe she found Kieran and Sarah a delightful couple and just couldn't get enough of them. Or maybe Kieran had directorial advice for Louise that he didn't want to give her in front of everyone.

That was just me being snide and petty, I was pretty sure. I didn't think, on the whole, that Kieran would bother trying to save anyone else's feelings if he had something to say to make his show better.

While I was on my petty line of thinking, it occurred to me that Louise might want me to know that Kieran and Sarah were being openly social, just to rub it in to Denise by proxy. I decided I really didn't like Louise.

I made it home without any other disruptions and had my groceries put away in time to change and check my various streams of social media before heading off to meet up with Taryn.

My mother was posting pictures of Hawaii on her blog, Denise and our old pal Leo were having a war of wits on Twitter, as usual, and people were starting to send out invites via social media to their Fringe shows. I automatically pressed "Going" to Kate Ryan's show, since I enjoyed anything she and her Leave it to Jane players did. Their mandate was to find lost and forgotten smaller musicals and mount them imaginatively for the Fringe. I had seen all their shows and had never felt like I'd backed the wrong horse.

Before closing my laptop, I googled Taryn Creighton. She had several entries and impressively took up the top fifteen herself. It was only when you got to the second page that you got to a law firm in Wisconsin, an obituary for someone in the last century, and a misspelled page about J.M. Barrie's *Admirable Crichton*.

She had directed all over the country and still did so between seasons of her Black Box Theatre. She had won two Sterlings, been awarded a YWCA Women of Distinction Award, and was apparently on the City of Edmonton's Culture Wall of Fame over in the walkway between the Citadel Theatre and Canada Place.

It made me wonder what the heck I had been doing the last dozen years or so. Everyone I'd been in school with was getting on with their lives. Denise was tenure track, Taryn had conquered the theatre world, Leo was ensconced at Memorial University, Steve had a career track toward eventually becoming Deputy Chief, if he wanted it. And me? I grubbed from one job to the next, missing the career turn time and time again.

I shook off my maudlin thoughts. Once the summer was over, I would again mount an attack of resumés and queries. If I couldn't get enough courses for sessional work to pay the bills, I might check with a temp agency or even send in a job application or two to the municipal or provincial government. I wasn't so sure about the feds. If I got in with them, I had the feeling they'd up and move me about, like they'd done our family when my dad was in the Armed Forces. I had had more than my share of moving cities. Now I just moved paycheques.

It was time to get ready to meet up with Taryn Creighton and paint myself a picture of just what was happening behind the Edmonton theatre scenes.

23.

The walk to the restaurant from where the bus let me off was longer than I had anticipated, and I arrived a bit sweaty and hot. However, it was cool inside the little restaurant, and shade trees kept the sun from beating in the windows. Festive garlands hung from the ceiling, mitigating against the sparseness of the tables and other décor. I pulled off my sunglasses and looked around, spotting Taryn off to the left by the wall. She waved and I waved back, smiling at the woman by the desk near the front of the restaurant.

Taryn stood up and touched my arm, an appropriate equivalent to hugging a friend. We weren't exactly friends, but we did have a history.

"I'm so glad you agreed to meet me," I started, sitting down in a chair that was about two inches too low for the table, making me feel as if I was visiting the principal's office.

"It's been a while," Taryn said, and then suggested we check the menus before we did anything else. "The food is really good, but it takes a while, since they make most everything fresh. I am a sucker for their tortilla soup and tamales, but everything is good."

I opted for Mexican enchiladas, and once our orders were through and water delivered in bright plastic glasses, I started over again.

"I have been trying to figure out how to get a clear picture of anything that may be shaking in the theatre scene, but I need an objective eye and thought of you. I've been working with the Freewill Shakespeare Festival in a teaching capacity for their high school camp, and so I've been tangentially involved in the investigation of the murder of Eleanor Durant." I was looking right at her as I said this, and nothing twitchy seemed to register, so I figured I had been correct in my assessment of Taryn as the perfect person to talk with.

"Another friend of mine, Denise Wolff, has been implicated in the murder, and now there seems to be a stalemate, with all that suspicion hovering over her head and the police not beating any other bushes."

"Maybe she did it?"

I bristled. "No, she didn't. That's not on the table for discussion. At least not this table." I took a deep breath. "The thing is, I figure it all boils down to someone killing Eleanor Durant for a reason the police haven't thought of, because it's a theatre reason. And so I thought maybe you could talk to me about what is happening in the theatre community that might have something to do with Eleanor coming to town and being in the way, or at least in the wrong place at the wrong time."

Just then our food came, and we tacitly agreed to tuck into it before continuing the conversation. I hadn't realized how ravenous I was, but half my enchiladas were gone before I bothered to speak again.

"Did you know Eleanor well enough to know what she was planning after the summer Shakespeare season?"

Taryn smirked. "Oh, I have a pretty good idea what she was planning."

"Really?"

"Yep, I'm pretty sure she was going for Oren Gentry's job."

"The artistic directorship of Chautauqua?"

Taryn nodded. "You bet. Anyone with half a directing chop in a circumference of a thousand miles is salivating over that position. I'm applying, you'd better believe it."

I was curious. "What's so great about Chautauqua Theatre? I mean, I've been to shows there, and support it and all, but what does it have that, say, the Roxy or the Varscona or even the Citadel doesn't have? Why would you leave Black Box for it?"

"That's a good question and probably one I'll have to answer the board if I make the cut for interviews." Taryn nodded thoughtfully. "Obviously, there is a much smaller budget than the Citadel has to work with but about ten times what the Black Box can muster, although money isn't the motivator. It's the mandate for Chautauqua that interests me the most."

The woman came by to clear our plates and I handed her my Visa card.

"Oren had a vision of a Canadian theatre that would run Canadian plays, new and classic. He said that the only way to produce a classic is to remount a production, for the next generation and the one after that to discover. And who does that? We get maybe two new works from outside the province and a *Drowsy Chaperone* and we're grateful for the Canadian content around here, and that's with grants demanding some. Can you imagine what would happen with the big boys if there was no culture vulture watching out for a little national pride?"

"But surely there is a lot going on in local playwrights' work being delivered," I countered. Taryn made some good points, but this was starting to sound like a screed rather than a measured argument. "That has got to count as Canadian content?"

Taryn nodded. "Of course it is, and I'm not trying to diminish it. But we need to keep cycling and recycling our plays, looking for what we have in common with each other, coast to coast, and each other, generation to generation. We need hipsters to watch *The Farm Show*, we need another generation to be terrified by *One Night Stand*, we need rural westerners to watch and understand *Balconville*, and Maritimers to cry over *The Ecstasy of Rita Joe*. There are classics in our repertoire and we need to honour them on the stage and not just in historic overview courses in the English department, if you pardon my meaning."

"And that was what Oren Gentry was doing, right?"

"Yep, and I admired him for it. His recipe was one new work from an Alberta writer, one celebrated new work from away, which usually meant Daniel McIvor, but he was always looking for more, two classic Canadian works, aiming for a comedy and a drama, and the springtime new works reading festival. He didn't bother with the Broadway musical, the Shakespeare, the

Shaw, or the Ibsen. He counted on the Citadel to cover those bases, which you have to admit they do an admirable job of. No, Oren's vision was to be 100 per cent Canadian."

"And it was working," I said.

"No shit, Sherlock. People loved it. I'm glad they were voting with their pocketbooks, because I think Oren had a bit of trouble with his board at first, who were a little nervous of banking it all on Canadian plays everyone had seen before."

"What changed their minds?"

"Well, I guess they began to realize that an entire generation has grown up and had babies of their own since most of those plays were performed. And those babies are going to their own versions of Paperbag Playhouse or Opera in the Schools and participating as magic trees in the forest or bits of furniture for Snow White to dust and getting pulled into the theatre for another generation. That's what? Five generations from Gwen Pharis Ringwood. What are they going to make of *Still Stands the House*? They'll never know if they never see it."

"Well, hell, I'd hire you, Taryn. You sound like you could really dig your teeth into that sort of focus." I had paid up by this time, and we got up from the awkwardly low chairs and moved out into the sunshine.

"If only you were on the board," she laughed. "Did you drive here? No? Would you like a ride? I'm heading over to near Whyte Avenue. Darrin Hagen is doing the music and sound design for our next production and he's got ideas he wants to try out on me this evening."

I gratefully climbed up into her grey SUV. On the front seat was a box of papers, which she transferred to the back seat to give me room. I noticed a lot of gear in the back, including ropes and electrical cables, a cooler, and what appeared to be camping equipment.

"This car ends up being my working office," she said by way of apology for the mess. "One of these days I'm going to book a day and just dung it out. So, where were we? Oh, right. Eleanor and Chautauqua." Taryn pulled out into traffic from the small side street, making a brave left turn without the aid of a light. "I'm sure she saw it as a way to maintain a level of importance in the Canadian theatre scene without resorting to face lifts. It's a sad truth that women in theatre don't get that much respect between the ages of thirty and Betty White. Once you get that old, you're a novelty flavour and, like Jessica Tandy, you can write your ticket. So the trick is to become a director, or even better, artistic director of a theatre, where you don't even have to direct the whole season. You administrate and glad-hand and work the shows you have a yen for and teach a class at one of the universities and hobnob. If you're very clever, you even have a manager who does the grunt work like writing grant proposals and reports to the board. From a distance, it's a grand life."

She gave a laugh that was both cynical and regretful in tone, though I couldn't tell in what measure. We were on the High Level Bridge by this time, and I had to check the flow of conversation to give her directions on how to sidle off at the end of the bridge and let me off in the parking lot behind the Garneau Theatre so that she could manoeuvre back onto 109 Street easily.

Taryn rolled the passenger window down as I got out and

closed the door, so I leaned in to thank her for the ride home. "No worries, and thanks for dinner. I hope you got what you wanted. I'm sure that was why Eleanor came to town, even though she said it was to nurse a sick relative. She had her eye on taking over a theatre, and Oren's was the best bet. I wouldn't have been surprised to hear she'd knocked him over to get her hands on Chautauqua. And then someone else in the running bumped her off. Maybe you need to get the list of people applying for the artistic director role, Randy. Present company excepted, of course." Taryn laughed and drove off, the window rolling up like a curtain coming down at the end of a play.

She knew a good closing line. Of course she did. She was only mistaken in thinking I'd keep her off a list of potential murderers. After all, she had just given me what I finally needed—a good motive for the murder of Eleanor Durant.

And the more I thought about it, as I trudged across the gravel drive to my apartment door, she might have given me another murder to contemplate.

What if Oren Gentry's death hadn't been of natural causes?

24.

I spent the evening sorting through timelines, trying to figure out what had happened when, in order to have things ready for Steve when he got home. I knew better than to give any of this to Iain, as he had plainly told me to keep my oar out. But something had to be done to goose them into looking beyond Denise as a jealous lover. It wasn't that I considered them inept; they were just wrong in this case, and while I couldn't fault their logic, they didn't know Denise the way I did.

I printed off a series of blank calendar months from my computer so that I could map the order of events. While Eleanor had been murdered in late June, I printed off May through July, since that was when Denise, and by extension I, had become involved with the theatre folk.

Denise and Sarah had done their *Romeo and Juliet* co-production in May, but had actually begun the work in April. I printed off another calendar month. I wondered when Denise and Kieran had got together. I remembered that they had been together at the after-party, because that was when he floated the idea that I apply for the teaching grant for Shakespeare camp. I checked my wall calendar and noted the scrawled "Denise: Party: 9 pm," that happened on May 23.

I scribbled in events as best I could, realizing I'd have to clue Denise into the exercise and get her over here with her date book.

I had got the job on May 30, giving me a month to prep prior to the festival and camps getting into full gear. The announcement that Eleanor was cast had come before that, because I recalled Steve saying Denise'd be only three degrees from Kevin Bacon, since Kiefer Sutherland had had a cameo on *Gopher Broke* and had appeared in A Few Good Men with Bacon.

I did a quick search through the archives on the *Edmonton Journal* website and found their full-page spread on Eleanor on April 23. Kieran either wooed her quickly and well, or they had organized it prior to her arrival.

Oren Gentry died on June 12. His funeral took place on the 15th which, given its complexity, was amazing.

Eleanor had died on June 21.

The time frame seemed stretched out and elongated as I sketched in the events across the pages of the year before me. In reality, it felt like they had all taken about fifteen minutes and as if Steve had been in Sweden for months, when in reality he had left only a week before Eleanor died. Mapping things out was a good exercise, but I wasn't sure it was going to mean anything to Steve beyond my getting things straight in the telling.

Taryn said that there would be loads of people vying for

Oren Gentry's job. I wondered if it would be possible to get a list of the candidates. Maybe Denise could find out. Who was I kidding? If Steve thought it was worth having, he'd be able to get the list, no problem.

I wondered if Taryn's throwaway comment about Eleanor killing Oren held any water. It seemed too pat that one killer would kill another, as if the domino effect could sort itself out that way. But what if someone had killed Oren to get the job at Chautauqua, then realized that Eleanor would have a better chance at getting the position and so had to be got rid of as well? Maybe killing Eleanor hadn't been the real focus, which would get Denise off the hook admirably.

And really, that was all that mattered to me. I had read all the theories of closure and heuristics; I knew what Dorothy L. Sayers had said about murder and John Donne had said about death. But Eleanor Durant's death in no way diminished me. It was Denise Wolff being suspected of the murder that tolled my bell.

I spent another couple of hours on my timelines before heeding my body clock's own timeline and heading to bed. Tomorrow was another day amid the teens, and I needed all the rest I could get to keep up with them.

I made a note to call Denise about helping with the timeline before Steve got home on Wednesday, and then another note to myself to go get Steve's car on Tuesday night so I could get out to the airport to pick him up the following morning.

Assured that my life was measured out in sticky notes, I washed my face and went to bed.

My alarm woke me the next morning, getting a jump on the magpies. I washed my hair and got dressed, sorted through the outfits I'd arranged for camp wear, and checked the temperature predictions on the weather website. I was going to bike down to the park today, so I braided my hair nice and flat down my back in order to wedge on my bike helmet, which was barely large enough to fit over my head before a mound of thick hair got stuck to it.

I slathered on the sunscreen, clipped my mosquito-away fan to my waistband, and grabbed my satchel, which I bungeed into my bicycle basket. Give or take a headwind on the hill by Emily Murphy Park, I should be at the amphitheatre in fifteen minutes.

It didn't even take that long. No matter how long I live here, I'll probably never get used to how much the traffic lessens around the university in the summertime. I fairly sailed down Saskatchewan Drive, noting that the earth sciences folks had planted even more specimens in their rock garden, a project I found delightful. I recalled small trays of tiny rocks and minerals we'd have to test for hardness streaking. Here, you had a sense of the mineral the way you might actually find it in nature, huge and old and immovable. Students sat on the rocks to eat their lunch, classes of earth science students combed the field in the fall, and passersby like me got to enjoy their unconformity. I supposed the groundskeepers didn't much care to mow around them, but I wasn't overly fond of grass anyhow, so my sympathies weren't entirely with them.

The slope of Emily Murphy Park Road was enough to make my heart start beating a bit faster. Who needs a roller coaster when you've got our river valley? I made it cautiously through the mini-maze of stop signs and turns to get across the roadways to the Hawrelak Park road, which lay along one of the river's northward meanders before it turned eastward once more. The Mayfair Golf and Country Club was situated at the very expensive bend there, which probably accounted for the mishmash of roadways I'd just manoeuvred. There was a riverside footpath around the back of the club, but I'd never walked it. As beautiful and peaceful as the river valley was, for a woman alone, there were areas where it was just a bit too cut off from the rest of the world for me to feel completely safe.

I noticed a splat of mud on the corner of our banner at the gateway to the park. I figured I'd tell Micheline about it, if seven other people hadn't already done so. She could get someone to head out with a bucket and a brush to clean it up. At least no one had tagged graffiti on it. Kieran was particularly proud of it, as it was new this year. The trademarked shadow bust of Shakespeare was in royal blue at one end of the weatherproofed yellow banner, with the Freewill name and dates in matching blue and "plays for a midsummer's evening" in green italics across the bottom.

I thought it was a great sign, as signs go: Of course, the minute you put something up, someone did their best to make it ugly. I just hoped it wasn't one of my campers. This had been too violent a theatre season, with Eleanor's death, already. Mudslinging could be a gateway weapon.

I forgot about the mud as I neared the amphitheatre. Three of my students were already here, sitting with their backs to the fence next to the gateway, which was still locked. I smiled at them and proceeded to get awkwardly off my bike, as one does when teenagers are watching, aware that I looked like a flowerpot person in my bike helmet.

"Is the gate not open yet?" I asked in an overly cheery voice, to mask the obvious fact that while I was nominally in charge of them, I had no control over the present situation.

"I guess we're early," offered Diana, who was wedged between two gangly boys, Nathan and Ethan, whom I regularly mixed up in my mind. I had to consciously determine what one of them was wearing each day, because both had sloppy brown hair in their eyes and the slouchy way of walking that made one wonder if they'd been reanimated in a mad scientist's laboratory after having been constructed with vacuum hoses.

It turned out that Nathan had the use of his mother's car and had picked the other two up on the way. Likely, because of the freedom it afforded, they had left earlier than usual. Still, it didn't explain why Micheline hadn't been here ahead of everyone, as she usually was, to open the gate and set things up.

I knew the combination to the key safe, of course, and proceeded to get myself and the kids into the enclosure. I returned the key and pulled the gate closed so that it looked locked to the casual observer. The kids seemed amenable, so I set them to work unrolling newsprint onto the picnic tables and stapling it under the table lips. We brought three of the heavy tables together to form one of banquet-hall length and placed the small bins at either end for me.

All the other kids eventually trooped in. I quelled my

discomfort at being the only adult around and explained the rules to the Shakespeare families game. Each team was allowed a copy of the complete works, three of which were mine and two others I'd picked up at secondhand stores. I'm not sure why people think a complete works of anyone is the way to an English major's heart, but two of the copies I handed out to the teenage teams before me had been gifts, one from a great-aunt and the other from a fellow who thought it would be more inventive than flowers and chocolates. Inventive, maybe, but not quite as satisfyingly romantic.

The kids groaned a bit when I started to explain the game, but after a sample round they realized it wasn't quite as easy as they first had thought. They had to strategize on how to collect a full set from a play while at the same time recognizing and remembering who was in what play with whom. This was where the collected works came in. Soon they were shouting out their claims ("Do you have anyone from *As You Like It*?"), shuffling through the cast lists to recognize characters in their own dealt hands ("Quickly, Quickly, where is someone named Quickly?"), and trying to outfox their opponents by bluffing what they might be collecting themselves.

They had started into their second solid game by the time Micheline showed up, a good hour later than usual. She nodded me over to her, away from the kids, who probably didn't notice me anyhow. I had unleashed a crew of Elizabethan card sharks on the world.

"Randy! You made it in okay. Thank goodness. I was pretty sure you had the key safe combo, so I wasn't too worried."

"Heck, I was worried about you. Where have you been?"

She pursed her lips and sighed.

"Where haven't I been? I've been to seven stores looking for Mylar balloons shaped like dragons. You would think, given the hoopla over the *Game of Thrones* on TV and the *Hobbit* movies, that dragons would be everywhere, wouldn't you? I even figured by the end of the search that I would settle for a dinosaur, but nothing!"

It turned out Micheline was designing and stage-managing a Fringe show, which was, from a preparation and production standpoint, just around the corner. She and the various actors in the Shakespeare plays who were involved in the Fringe would have barely two weeks after the Festival ended before the Fringe began in earnest. Some people had been working on their shows since they'd been given the green light the previous November. Others seemed to nervously throw something together the weekend before, or so it would seem.

That wasn't totally fair. In the beginning, maybe, but over the last thirty-odd years, the Edmonton Fringe Festival had grown up and developed into a sure-fire form of entertainment delivery. There were several playwrights and companies one could depend on to deliver a satisfying hour or two of pleasure. It was just as well, too, since ticket prices were now uniformly high. With the Fringe tax, each play cost $15 a ticket. While that was still a far cry from the price of a ticket to a Citadel play, or for that matter a ticket to a hockey game, it added up. And most Fringe plays didn't last longer than about an hour or seventy-five minutes.

I knew people who organized their vacations for the Fringe and counted coup by the number of plays they managed to squeeze in. Others seemed to just congregate in the beer tents, happy to get soaked while watching the passing crowd. Some of them probably didn't even know that there were more than 200 plays being performed in venues all around them.

I wondered if Micheline was going to mention to Kieran that she had spent the morning on Freewill time doing chores for her Fringe project, for which she would also be getting paid, although it would come later as a percentage of the final take. If I knew Micheline, she'd have negotiated a set fee from the actors.

She looked at me with arched eyebrows, silently requesting my collusion. I shrugged and smiled at her. It wasn't my budget. If Kieran wanted company loyalty, he could be around a little more often to run things. Micheline smiled back at me, then bustled off to the trailer to boot up the computer, tally the previous evening's results, and do whatever else she did to keep things ticking over seamlessly.

I turned back to the camp crew, who were still engrossed in the game, but as I had hoped, in a different way. One group was still playing furiously, but two others had segued into examining the cast groupings and determining what each play was about. One girl was even guessing who in a repertory cast would play each character, and making some interesting connections. I'd have to mention her to Denise, who would love to hear about that sort of insight into how Shakespeare had written with specific actors in mind and how that had shaped his storyline.

Since Janine was coming in early, I made them break for

lunch so they'd be fed and watered and settled prior to a vigorous hour-and-a-half of stage fighting. They shuffled the decks back into their colour codes and put things away. I was beginning to like these kids a lot. I didn't think any of them could have muddied the sign.

That made me remember to tell Micheline about the dirty banner. As the kids were now all hauling their lunches out of their backpacks and bags, I left them to go find her in the trailer. I was passing under the trailer window, which Micheline must have opened to catch a breeze, because I could hear her on the phone speaking furiously to someone. I knew she could have a temper on her; like most people in the theatre world, she kept her emotions in her shirt pocket so they'd be handy. But I was glad she'd never spoken to me in the tone she was using now.

I slowed down, mostly because I didn't want to interrupt her and inadvertently become the brunt of her present mood. But, since she couldn't see me under the window, she continued to rant into the receiver.

"I don't care what you thought you saw. No one is going to believe you, so just try spreading that rumour. What I want you to think about is who is going to hire you in the future if you open your mouth and poison things now. Just think about that for a bit before you do anything!"

I stood there, not sure how long to wait before opening the door. Aware that I could be seen by the teens if they happened to be looking this way, I counted five hippopotamuses and then stomped a bit as I walked toward the door. By the time I had hoisted myself up the step and into the trailer, Micheline was composed and working at the computer. She turned toward me with a quizzical smile. You'd have never known she had been spitting venom down the phone line seconds earlier. Who knew that Micheline could be just as effective on stage as behind the scenes?

"Yes?"

"I meant to mention to you that there was a splat of mud on the sign by the gate. I noticed it on my way in. You might want to get someone down there with a mop and some paper towels."

Micheline winced. "Eww. Okay, thanks, Randy. I'll see if I can get Marco or one of his boys to see to it on their way in." Just then the phone rang. Micheline glanced quickly at the caller ID and then held her hand up to me quickly. "Marco? Speak of the devil! Are you still at home? Great. Could you pop a scrub brush and some spray cleaner or something in your car, and clean the banner on your way into the park? Someone tossed some mud on one corner, Randy noticed it on the way in. No, I didn't see it. I'm not sure how thick. Just a roll of paper towels and some water might do it, sure. Whatever, just trying to save you a trip back out to the gate once you're here. Yep. See you."

She turned back to me. "Thanks for letting me know. Was there anything else?"

"Nope. I'm letting the kids eat early because their stage fighting time is moved up this afternoon, so they're on the loose, but aside from that, everything is under control." I smiled at her, and it was probably due more to her distraction than my acting that she didn't notice how uncomfortable I felt.

"Well, you're welcome to sit in here for a while if you like. I have to go to the bathroom, but I think I'll head down to the actors' bathrooms if your kids are on the rampage."

She headed for the door and I made room for her to pass me.

"Thanks. If you don't mind, I'll use the phone and then get back out to monitor the kids."

"Sure thing."

Man, if I hadn't actually heard her myself, I would never have believed that she had been fighting on the phone minutes earlier. I wondered who she'd been speaking with as I dialled Denise's number.

"Hello?"

"It's me, Randy. I'm down at the park, but I'm through at three this afternoon and I was wondering if you wanted to come by my place for supper around five? I've been working on a timeline of sorts and would like your input on when and where various things took place."

"Sure, I guess so," said Denise. "I'll be just finishing up with Belinda around three-thirty. She wanted some help streamlining the template for the Fringe Sterling judges, and since she's probably the only person in the theatre community still talking to me, I couldn't say no."

"She seems like a nice person."

"She's lovely. I'd probably do it even if she wasn't talking to me. Or if everyone was still talking to me. Oh, you know what I mean."

I laughed in spite of the semi-pathetic tinge to Denise's voice.

"Yes, I know what you mean."

"Did you need me to pick up anything for you? Did you need me to pick you up?"

"Nope, I brought my bike, so though I will probably end up pushing it part of the way up the hill, I am mobile."

"Push it up the stairs over in the south corner of the park where no one has to see you grunting," suggested Denise.

"Good idea. Well, I'd better go before my teenagers either stab themselves with sporks or impregnate each other."

Denise rang off and I clicked the stop button without having to fumble for it, as the festival's landline was the same sort of phone I had at home. As I held the handset, it occurred to me that I might be able to figure out who Micheline had been talking to.

I clicked the phone history arrow, and M Katz and his number appeared, Marco the stage crew member who was supposedly coming to wash the sign on his way in. I clicked the arrow one more time and saw C Norgaard.

Micheline had been fighting with Christian Norgaard.

From hearing one side of that very harsh conversation, it sounded like Christian Norgaard had seen something he shouldn't have, or something he figured he could leverage into power. Whatever it was, it didn't sound like he was angling to go directly to the police.

I turned the phone list off and left the trailer. The kids were clearing things up, and I did a silent head count. I was missing two, but they emerged from the bathrooms just as I was about to recount. I announced they had half an hour to work on their group scenes before Janine called them to the stage, and they split into their respective groups eagerly. They were a good group.

I stood surveying the area. Five groups of kids were congregated in various places: two at opposite ends of the long picnic tables, one set in the audience seats, one on the lawn in the sunshine, and one on the lip of the stage. Micheline appeared on the left side of the stage and made her way around the outside of the audience toward the trailer, just as the actors would do later when positioning themselves to enter from the back of the theatre. James, the sound guy, had arrived at some point and was reworking some sound cues from inside the concrete bunker booth at the right rear of the audience.

Squirrels were chasing each other along the pathway, oblivious to my legs in their way. They split and ran behind me and into the shrubs. Birds were singing, or that might have been a sound cue. In the distance, I could hear the loud hailer from the paddleboat dock calling in boat number 5.

It was a beautiful Edmonton summer day in late July. And I would not want to be Christian Norgaard for all the tea in China.

25.

Denise had given me good advice about pushing my bike up the stairs, as one of those handy troughs was built into each side of the staircase to accommodate the tires of a bicycle. This way I looked like a smart cyclist availing myself of a proper portage of sorts rather than an out-of-shape middle-aged woman panting her way up a hill, being passed by real cyclists. Still, it was heavy going, since my bicycle was built for sturdy reliability, not lithe racing speed.

I appeared near the top of the hill at 87 Avenue, by one of the last remaining traffic circles in the city. I pedalled along a bit nervously, close to the right lip of the road. Edmonton was trying more and more to be a bicycle-friendly city, but between belligerent drivers who didn't even like sharing their roads with buses full of socialists, let alone granola-chewing bike riders, and cyclists who ticked people off by either clogging up traffic when they could be using an adjacent bike path or riding on downtown sidewalks not designated for anything more than pedestrians, there were still a few wrinkles to iron out.

For the most part, riding around campus was pretty safe. Cars had to watch out for jaywalking students all over the place, anyhow. But during rush hour one of the roads most frequently used to navigate out of the downtown area toward the Whitemud Freeway and the far west end of town was 114 Street past the university hospital. I decided that discretion was the better part of remaining in one piece; I ducked off 87 Avenue at 116 Street and did the rest of the route home through the mostly pedestrian throughfare of 88 Avenue, past the Students Union Building, Administration, Dentistry-Pharmacy, HUB Mall, the Fine Arts Building, Law, and then the block of student housing originally created for the Universiade Games and expanding through North Garneau at the same rate that kudzu took over the southern states.

I got home, sweaty and self-righteous, and locked my bike into its space in the small shed beside the garbage bins. I just had time to take a shower and start chopping up salad ingredients before Denise came over.

I also had time to mull over what I could possibly say to Christian. He was putting himself in a very vulnerable place if he knew something a murderer didn't want known. On the other hand, he could be the murderer, threatening more people, and if I was to pop up and let him know I knew something, I would be putting myself into that same position I'd just considered for him!

It was a mystery, and not the happy tidy sort that come with scones and lavender eau de toilette. How did one keep Christian safe if he was innocent and remain off his radar if he wasn't?

I decided the best course of action would be to tell Steve all about it once he got home and let him approach Christian.

I had got just about everything ready by the time Denise arrived. She handed me a bottle of pinot grigio and a dark bottle of Chocolate Shop red wine.

"I wasn't sure what you were planning to make, so I erred on the side of excess," she laughed. She kicked off her shoes at the door and followed me into the dining area. I had laid the table with my big salad bowl full of tossed greens taking pride of place. I was on my last flip of the frittata I had been easing along, so I divvied it up in the pan and served Denise straight from the stove. My mother would have disapproved, but it meant one less dish to wash later.

"Oh yum," said Denise, digging in happily, "it's almost breakfast for supper, my favourite kind of meal."

I was pouring us each a glass of white wine as she said that, and my openly quizzical look made her laugh. "Okay, maybe not breakfast completely."

We ate without talking for a bit, and then didn't talk about anything of consequence for a few minutes while I cleared the plates away and Denise refilled our goblets. I wasn't sure if it was because we were tired of the subject or shy of starting in again, but neither of us seemed all that eager to discuss the problem at hand.

"Brad called me this afternoon," Denise said after a brief shared silence.

"Really?" Brad was the chair of the English department. "What about?"

"He wanted to know if I was going to be able to teach this fall, with the 'unresolved issues involving me,' or whether he should consider reassigning my classes." Denise's chin crumpled as she said this, and tears welled up and overflowed her eyelids and rolled down her cheeks. "I thought he was going to offer some sort of solidarity message, like 'we're all behind you,' but he just wanted to see how he could minimize the damage. I have a feeling that if this isn't 'resolved' in time, he's going to suggest I bow out of the roster, just to keep people from whispering in the halls."

"You never know, it could boost enrollment if they all thought you were Lizzie Borden. Brad should be considering that aspect of things. He could definitely prove that English courses had high enrollments and should be immune from the next round of cuts. You could be the hero. People in modern languages and theatre tech would be wooing you to teach for them. Think about it," I rolled on hyperbolically, trying to turn Denise's tears into laughter. "You could singlehandedly save the University of Alberta. Other institutions would be scrambling for their own murder suspects to keep their programs solvent. Brad would be down on his knees, thanking you for your mixing yourself up so handily in 'unresolved issues,' really. I can see it."

Denise was hiccoughing with laughter and dabbing at her eyes with her paper napkin. The danger was over.

"Well, if he's going to be a dick, we'd better get this whole thing resolved as soon as possible," I concluded, pushing back from the table and ushering Denise into the living room, where I had laid out my calendar pages, a couple of pencils, a pile of sticky notes, and my laptop.

For the next couple of hours, we dredged through our memories and email folders to figure out when various things had occurred. Denise could detail her first date with Kieran, but she couldn't recall exactly who had introduced them. She tried to remember whether Sarah, whom she had known from grad school courses, had approached her at the New Year's Eve party or one of the theatre opening nights she had attended as a Sterling judge to consider the cross-departmental *Romeo and Juliet,* but she had the sense of there being a lot of bonhomie and wine glasses surrounding them.

"So it was Sarah's idea to have the double class?" I asked.

"Oh yes, I give her complete credit for the idea," nodded Denise. "I did a lot of the formatting of the lectures, providing the historical and literary context, and made up the charts we use in our presentation as to how much background materials a Drama student would receive about the play as opposed to an English student, and the questionnaire for the students about how comfortable they felt in performance mode, and how much it differed from having to do a group oral presentation in other classes. We were trying to examine the playing field, as we knew it wasn't even; the kids self-select into courses that allow either for quiet absorption with minimal but hopefully some interaction, or totally hands-on extraverted interaction and the promise of audience. If we could minimize the discomfort on one hand, and check the level of background info received on the other, we might be able to make a case for an equality of intellectual wrestling with the same material." She smiled wanly. "We were trying to mend fences and build bridges between the departments. Maybe it was all in our heads, but it seemed there was always such a wall between us, and a territorial fight. That's why we picked *Romeo and Juliet* for our test run, of course. It was always about the 'two houses, both alike in dignity.'"

"Such a cool project," I agreed. "And did it do what you wanted, do you think?"

Denise shrugged. "You know, until Eleanor died, I was thinking it had worked miracles. There was talk of having a shared lecture series in the fall, and we were encouraged to run the shared course again in the spring of next year. The presentation about it was pounced on when we submitted it for Congress, and we were actually invited to present down in New Orleans, so people have been talking about it. But now, I have no idea. Sarah is not someone I feel like calling at the moment, and she certainly hasn't contacted me. For all I know, she's going to take the whole presentation on herself, though how one person at a dais talking about cross-campus collaboration is going to play, I'm not sure."

I tried to get us back onto our goal of timelining events, though privately I figured I would stick Sarah Arnold onto a list of her very own and deliver her to Steve along with Christian's weird phone call. There was a motive in there somewhere, at least to cut Denise out of the research paper and discredit her contribution.

We sorted out Denise's version of when Kieran had first let her know Eleanor was in the mix for playing Hero.

"Everyone was talking about the fact she was in town. I think she'd been down to one of the Die-Nasty live improvised soap opera evenings and charmed the socks off everyone. So Kieran said he should see if he could nab her for the festival. He had made the general announcement of what plays were going to be produced and a list of the actors hired. I guess he hadn't finalized the cast lists, because the next thing you knew he was announcing Eleanor as the headliner."

"Would it have been a good choice?"

"Oh, for sure. Eleanor didn't have the internal gravity to play a Beatrice, but she could have been an adorable Hero. She skewed very young, even more so in person than on TV."

"So you spent quite a bit of time with her?"

"Enough, I guess. I quite liked her, but then I had no idea she was screwing my boyfriend, eh? We met at the party Kieran had for the cast in May, where they unveiled the set and laid out the rehearsal schedule. I liked her, and we even met up to go running a few times after that, but the connection dwindled. Maybe she had a conscience after all and couldn't keep up the pretense one-on-one."

"You went running together? I know you talked to her about trails, but I didn't realize you actually went out together. Tell me you didn't run the Queen Elizabeth Park steps together." No wonder the police were all over Denise for Eleanor's death.

"Of course we did. I showed her two or three circuits that offered hill and stair challenges. I warned her, though, about running alone at certain times of day."

We marked down the May date for the cast party, and for

good measure I marked down the date of the party when I'd met Eleanor, which was a lot closer to the start of the rehearsal process. Kieran certainly believed in a lot of parties to build cast camaraderie.

"So, in your estimation, when do you think Kieran began his affair with Eleanor?" There was a date worth knowing, I figured.

"I haven't the faintest idea," moaned Denise. "I feel so utterly idiotic, not having any intuition about that."

"Was there a date that got broken because he had to do some extra work? Or was he late for anything when you were supposed to meet?" I knew I was pushing Denise close to painful areas, and she'd already cried once this evening. I hated to persist when she was so vulnerable, but I reminded myself that it was precisely because she was so vulnerable that we had to continue.

She shook her head slowly, staring at a corner of my living room but probably not seeing the crammed bookcase, my banjo or the small television that resembled a large computer monitor. She was walking through memories, looking through the good times for the small, irritant pieces of grit that she had ignored or brushed aside at the time. I let her be, silently wondering if I'd ever have the strength to examine that sort of situation.

If I was exposed to the world as naïve and unaware, would I be able to step out of the pain and look objectively at the situation? Would it even be a good thing to do? Or would it be like picking at a scab, not allowing it to heal naturally and in its own time?

Trouble was, Denise didn't have the time to hide away, lick her wounds, and reemerge whole. She had to be one step ahead of the metaphorical gallows if she was going to maintain her liberty, let alone her reputation. I admired my friend her strength of purpose. It didn't surprise me, though. Whatever Denise did, she did beautifully.

A tiny little voice at the back of my brain said words that I might have been submerging for a while. "If she does everything perfectly, could she have pulled off the perfect crime?" I stood up suddenly to silence the doubt and went to put the kettle on for tea while Denise continued to sort through her memories.

"You know, there were a couple of times when he begged off going out after rehearsal, right around the time you started prepping for the camp course. I didn't mind, all in all, because Sarah and I were prepping the abstract for New Orleans, and one evening I had time to drive you out somewhere for Mardi Gras masks."

"I remember that! Let me see, I can even figure out what day that was from emails." I scrolled through my Friends folder to early June and clicked open two or three emails from Denise before I found the one that noted she could take me out to the party store that evening because plans had fallen through and she was free.

Memories of that evening, when we had laughed at the crazy piñatas and Denise had talked me out of buying plastic disposable dishware that looked fancier than my own, flooded back. We had found the domino masks I needed for the scenework the kids would be doing, and I'd also picked up a few of the silly hats that might help them create a character. It had been a good time.

And now, forever more, it was going to be tinged with the knowledge that while we had been out enjoying ourselves, Kieran had been enjoying Eleanor.

Grimly, I put a large asterisk next to the date on my June calendar page. I just hoped this all was going to be useful to Steve, because it was hardly painfree.

We drank green tea and talked in circles for a bit, but nothing else jumped out as important dates to record. I looked at our timeline. It didn't amount to terribly much, but at least I now had a sense of when Eleanor had appeared on the scene, where Denise had intersected with her, and how quickly things had escalated once the rehearsals had begun.

"You know, we should probably put Oren's funeral down on the timeline," I mused, looking at the calendar before me.

"How come?"

"Well, everyone was there, including us. In fact, if Steve and Iain want to know who all the players are in this, all they need to do is to get their hands on the condolence book everyone signed."

"That's not a bad idea," said Denise, and I made a note for Steve. As I was writing a thought hit me and I stopped, mid-scrawl.

"But you know, if we look at Eleanor's death from a lens of getting her out of the way to get Oren's job, what is to stop us from seeing Oren's death as a way to get Oren's job?"

"Randy, are you saying what I think you're saying?"

I nodded. "Yep. I think Oren Gentry may have been murdered."

26.

After another cup of tea, Denise excused herself and went home. I cleared things up and called it a night myself. I was still aching a bit through the shoulders from pushing the bike uphill, and there was just something about spending so much time outdoors through the day that made me tired. I supposed that was why mothers pushed their babies out for walks in the open air; it helped them sleep soundly.

I tossed and turned through the night, though. I might as well have stayed up and done something useful like solving a murder or writing the great Canadian novel. I looked like a sad raccoon the next morning, and even a shower and under-eye concealer couldn't do miracles. I decided to walk to the park, since the simple mechanics of a bicycle seemed like a little too much heavy machinery for me to be handling.

This morning Micheline had beat me to the park with plenty of time. She had coffee brewing in the trailer and was typing away furiously when I popped my head in. I tucked my meagre lunch into the mini-fridge and sat on the couch behind her till she finished her task. There is nothing I hate worse than being interrupted in mid-flow of a thought. I had no desire to inflict that pain on someone else.

Finally, she swivelled around and smiled. "Morning, sunshine! You look like you went a few rounds in a cage match."

"I cannot sleep very well when it's hot, that's all," I shrugged. It hadn't been stifling last night, but it had been muggy and close. We'd likely see rain later tonight. I just hoped it wouldn't keep people away from the play.

"I know what you mean. I had fans running all over my place, trying to make the air move a bit even if it wouldn't cool down. Still, it beats February weather, right?"

I nodded and smiled, though I wasn't all that sure about it. At least with February weather you could put on another sweater or woollier socks. In the summer, there was only so much you could peel. I couldn't imagine how people in sultrier climes did it, especially before the advent of air conditioning.

Micheline was looking at me expectantly, either to say something or remove myself from her lair. I remembered then what I'd been waiting to tell her. Man, I must be really tired.

"I have a bit of a conflict tomorrow morning, but only for an hour or so, and I was wondering if we could get one of the actors to cover off for me with the kids."

"What sort of conflict?"

"Steve, my boyfriend, needs to be picked up at the airport. I figure he can drop me off here on his way home, but I have to get his car out to him, and his flight lands at 9:30 a.m. There's no way I'll be here for ten, and if there is any delay, which there well may be, I might not get here till noon."

"Right. Well, we could call Tony or Louise. You know, if you were to spring about $50 for supplies, I'll bet Louise would do a stage make-up session with them. Why don't you call her?"

"That's a fantastic idea. I don't know why we didn't schedule that into the camp in the first place!"

Micheline flipped the call list over to me and I found and dialled Louise's number. She was amenable and told me she'd pop by the theatre supply shop on her way in today, and we could settle up later on the cost of the greasepaint and sponges.

"She's very good; she used to teach the course at the Banff Centre, you know." Micheline nodded and looked justifiably proud of her suggestion. I hadn't known that about Louise, but was very relieved that things would work out this way, probably even better than originally planned. I could go get Steve, the campers would have a great morning, and I could maybe even manipulate my way into sounding out Louise about possible alibis she might have for the day Eleanor was killed and stuffed under the stairs. After all, stepping into the role of Hero gave Louise one of the more obvious payoffs of anyone who stood to benefit from Eleanor's death.

I felt a bit guilty to be suspecting someone who was doing me such a favour, but I didn't let it bother me overmuch. After all, these were actors we were dealing with. Any one of them could be putting on the performance of their lifetime, all the while leaving Denise out to hang for their crimes.

The kids began to arrive, and I herded them over to the hilltop area we had claimed over the course of the camp. Some of them were asking if we could play the card game today, which was gratifying, but I'd set today out for putting the scenes together so we could determine a running time for our class presentation at the end of the week. I explained to them the slight change in procedure for the next day, and they all looked pretty excited at the thought of playing with makeup—even the boys, which goes to show how useful performers like Eddie Izzard and Gene Simmons can be for naturalizing experiences.

Aside from that, though, the next few days would be working their scenes to get off book and sorting through costuming ideas to get continuity between the scenes. We would be changing the actors for each scene, so there had to be a unifying piece of costume to designate each character. That was one of the things we had to discuss today, because the kids would have to search out and bring their costumes by Thursday for sure. That would give me enough time to raid the Value Village on their behalf, if necessary, before the presentation the following Saturday at noon.

The day went by quickly. I was impressed by the kids' grasp of the language, since some of them had been openly disdainful of what they hadn't understood a week earlier. Being caught up in the excitement of the festival and surrounded by good-looking adults who obviously loved this stuff had rubbed off, as had their exposure to the Bard himself. Whether they liked it or not, we had created twenty-three more theatregoers in what was already a very drama-supportive town. Yay, us.

We wrapped up with each kid taking home a list of things

to search out: white shirts, blue scarves, toques, tweedy vests, denim skirts. I figured that even with variation, audiences would be able to track which person in the scene was Benedick, Leonato, or Beatrice. The fact that they all had to wear masks during the dance scene made things trickier, and the kids would really have to work on how to show the audience who they were while telegraphing which characters were fooled by costume and which ones could spot all the players no matter how they were dressed.

There was a metaphor here for Denise and me, too. People all around us were wearing disguises. Some of the people in disguise were masters at seeing through artifice. Some were missing the disguises of others while dissimulating at the same time. And still others, like me, were caught in the middle of the dancers, not sure who was performing for whom and who was hiding something.

Kieran, who had been working with the sound guy most of the afternoon to see why the mics for *Much Ado* were working so well while the voices of Iago and Othello seemed garbled for people sitting to the sides of the theatre, was walking out around the same time I was and offered me a ride home. He was on his way to dinner, he said, and was going right past my place.

The thought of trudging up the hill in the late afternoon heat, even without my bike, was enough to make me accept gratefully, even if to my mind he was an asshole for cheating on my friend. I didn't have time to consider the slippery slope of the collabo-rator, though, because I realized that this was a good chance to ask Kieran some probing questions about his relationship with

Eleanor without being too overt. Now if only I could figure out how to begin.

Kieran made it easy.

"You know, I think I met you the same day I asked Eleanor to be part of the cast. We were all at that shindig Denise and Sarah were throwing for their students. Glad to know that at least one of the decisions I made that night has turned out to be a good one."

I raised my eyebrows. While I was not immune to praise, Kieran seemed a bit cavalier about the death of his leading lady. He was concentrating on navigating his way out of the park, which was filling up with families heading to picnics and being vacated by Frisbee players and apartment dwellers on their days off. Even at the park speed of 10 kph, you didn't want to be hit by a car.

He continued. "I thought that casting Eleanor would be the answer to getting the average Joe out to the park for the shows. Once you get them there, I really think the magic will win them over, but it's getting them there that's the trick. Who better than a television star from a show that hit the proper demographic?"

He had a point. "Well, *Gopher Broke* was broad spectrum comedy, for sure, but it was still a Canadian show. Do you think the average Albertan, the folks Premier Ralph Klein had called 'Martha and Henry,' would tune in to a Canadian show to begin with? After all, they could be watching *CSI* or *Matlock* reruns."

"Don't you think it's fascinating that our most intentionally grassroots premier picked those names for the people in his rural stronghold? Why do you think he figured those names sounded so right together? Do you think he might have been channelling Martha Henry, one of the great doyennes of Canadian theatre? I think it's way too much of a coincidence."

"Ha! I never thought of that, but you're right. I'll bet it rang a bell for him and rolled off his tongue. So, subliminally, the rural voter is actually a fervent supporter of the Canadian performing arts scene? You see a lot of proof for that assumption?"

Kieran laughed. "Sadly, not that much. But never underestimate the artistic endeavours of small-town Canadians. I've seen great opera librettists come from northern Alberta and mezzo-sopranos from Millet. A soundman in Fort Macleod has won several Emmys. There are towns devoted to producing annual theatrical productions that would rival a Broadway show. And getting back to your question, *Gopher Broke* was a justified hit show. I think it had more viewers per week than *The Beachcombers* ever did, and they only had two other channels to compete with in their day. No, Eleanor would have been an amazing draw."

He pulled up across from my apartment in a no-stopping area, forcing me to hop out quickly.

"Still, the ghoulish draw of associating with a murder scene has done a lot for our box office, too," he grimaced. "See you tomorrow, then!"

"Thanks for the ride." I closed the door and waved him off to the beeping of impatient drivers behind us. I stood there, wondering just how callous Kieran Frayne actually was and how much of it was an act.

Masks. Was everyone wearing one? Maybe it was time I put on a protective mask of my own.

27.

Steve looked great.

He was one of the last people through the customs doors, so there was no huge crowd to watch our reunion hug. It was probably just as well, since I am not that big on public displays of affection. I don't mind holding hands in public, but having to watch strangers explore each other's oral cavities makes my skin crawl.

I had missed my man, though, and it was great to feel his arm wrapped around me. He looked tired, the sort of grey behind the skin that comes from long-distance air travel. Eight-and-a-half-hour flights will do that to you. I grabbed his suitcase trolley and urged him toward the revolving door nearest us.

"Your flight was pretty close to being on time, which is a good thing. I arranged to have someone cover my camp class this morning, just in case, so if you like, we could go somewhere for breakfast. If you don't mind dropping me off at the park before heading home, I can ease into the morning."

"Sounds great. Why don't we stop for dim sum then?"

"Sure, we could hit the Tasty Noodle on the way into town."

Food was one of the greatest things about Edmonton's vast multicultural mosaic. Not that ethnic diversification should be all for my benefit, but honestly, you could find superb cuisine from every corner of the globe here. It was so good that people actually discussed where the best dim sum chefs had been hired. There seemed to be a quiet vying for supremacy, and some crowds went from place to place in the city while others stuck to their tried and true restaurants for their elaborate spread of Chinese delicacies served in steamer stacks from trolleys down the aisles of the restaurants.

I pulled into the parking lot that housed the restaurant and a few other big box stores, and soon we were chowing down on shrimp cakes and sticky rice. With a few cups of Chinese tea and a barbecued pork bun in him, Steve's colour was returning to normal and he looked completely his old self.

I pressed him to tell me about his trip, and he gave me a capsulized version of the findings. One of the things that seemed clear to him was that money invested in LRT routes all over a city that were then patrolled and maintained to a standard that made people respect them, deterred all sorts of crime and road rage.

"The more you increase foot traffic and reliance on public transportation, the less likelihood there is for smash-and-grab crime, which really requires getaway cars and high-chase pursuit. You have people seeing other people on a daily basis, recognizing their neighbours, and rubbing up against humanity. It changes people into more compassionate communities, by default. It's an amazing thing. And if you get people espousing the environmental cause of helping ease the stress on the planet, they all feel good about themselves as well."

"From your mouth to the city planners' ears." I smiled at him. It was nice to see him caught up in a cause. Too often Steve got tossed at cases that had a university connection, just because of his sociology degree. He was so interested in macro- and micro-cosm compatibility, though. This was all right up his alley. I was glad to see that his superiors had seen this potential in him, too. Even if it didn't mean a promotion, it would make for more interesting work for him.

"But now tell me what's been happening here. Is Denise really the prime suspect for the death of that TV actress?"

I filled Steve in as much as possible over dumplings and cocktail buns, and promised him my timelines and lists, which made him smile.

"Of course you've made lists. When in doubt, sketch it out," he teased. I stuck out my tongue and he laughed. "Don't be insulted. Your lists are great. I will bet, without even looking at them, that there will be at least three important items on those lists that Iain and Jennifer should be paying attention to."

My face must have shown something because he cocked his head.

"What? Have you had a set-to with Iain? Or was it Jennifer who put your back up?" His ability to read me was uncanny, and at times, like this one, uncomfortable.

"Jennifer Gladue is not my type, you do know that, right?" Steve teased.

"Does she know that?"

Steve laughed. "Oh, don't worry about that, I'm sure she does. She does come across as a bit aggressive, I realize, but I think it's because she is very goal-oriented. If you ask me, she's got her eye on being the first female Chief of Police for Edmonton."

"That's a lofty goal, don't you think? Don't they mostly hire from outside the force for that sort of role?"

"Don't tell Jennifer that; she'll just tell you it's because no internal candidate has appeared strong enough." Steve shook his head. "Don't underestimate her. She's intelligent and tenacious. You certainly don't want to get in her way or make her an enemy."

"Well, I don't think I've done that. Not yet, anyhow."

Steve waved a waiter over and handed him our bill to tally up, along with his credit card. "Let's get you to work and me to a long shower and a short nap."

"Is that how you are supposed to deal with jet lag in this direction?"

"The best advice I got was to set my watch to Mountain Daylight Time the minute I got on the plane and consider myself already here. So I feel as if I pulled an all-nighter. If I can hose off the travel grime and rest a bit, as if I was having a lazy Sunday, then I should be able to meet you for dinner later, make an early night of it, and be in pretty good shape for work tomorrow."

"I'll believe it when I see it. Do you want me to call you when I get home, or will you set an alarm? I can make us something to eat for about six-thirty, would that be okay?"

"Sounds perfect." Steve got behind the wheel this time and

soon had me at the parking lot in Hawrelak Park. I'd be arriving in plenty of time to help Louise with her stage makeup class.

"I'm not going to hold you to coming over for supper if you're too tired. Just leave me a message if you want to go back to sleep when your alarm rings."

"Will do." He leaned over to kiss me, a proper kiss, not the sort you deliver in front of airport porters and strangers waiting for their grandmas. "I've missed you so much, Randy Craig," he whispered in my ear. I pulled back for air, and just looking at him made me feel safer and easier of mind.

"You have no idea how good it is to have you home," I replied.

28.

The kids loved the stage makeup class, especially some of the tricks Louise had offered on creating realistic black eyes and bruises. It was a good thing she had invested in several tubs of wet wipes, or their parents would have been storming the fence for the person who had beaten up their kids. I had made it back in time for Louise to beetle down the hill to her scene rehearsal with Leonato, Beatrice, and Hero. She waved off my thanks and I promised to settle up with her later.

After lunch, and once the kids were semi-respectable again, I gave them a half hour to do an "Italian run through" of their monologues in groups of three, a trick of rattling off dialogue as quickly as possible to get it memorized in some sort of cerebral muscle memory. The results were such that great bursts of laughter kept erupting from the various groups. It was nice to hear.

They were occupied, so I wandered off to the perimeter of the theatre site well away from the trailer and picnic tables, closer to the paddleboat edge of the lake. I wanted to make a call to Denise, and I didn't particularly care to be overheard by anyone here.

"Did you tell him your theory about Oren?" Denise wanted to know. "I've been giving that one a lot of thought, ever since you brought it up and you know, that puts a whole list of people on notice."

"Like who?"

She must have written them down because she rattled off names like she was reading them from a list. "And the latest two MFA directors to graduate sans theatre, though theirs would have to be the long game, hoping to gain one of the smaller theatres vacated by whoever took over from Oren."

"Holy doodle, that's some cold thinking."

"Murder is a cold business, Randy," Denise said, "to say nothing of theatre. But I came up with a couple of more lists."

She was turning into me, I swear. "Sure, let's hear them."

"Well, if we add in people who might have had it in for Eleanor, and leave Oren as an accident, we could include Stephen Tracey, who plays the taxidermist's son on the show. He lives near here and might have had a hate on for her. He was getting a lot of laughs at the beginning of *Gopher Broke* when he was trying to run a taxi service by taping a cardboard over half the sign on his dad's truck, and now he's barely featured."

"He could have been asking to go light, so he could pursue other things."

"In Canada?"

She had a point.

"Then there is Paul Mather, the writer," she continued. "In fact, he may have killed Oren, too, wanting to move into the sure thing of directing as opposed to television writing."

"Listen to yourself. The most successful Canadian television writer since Paul Haggis wants to come back to Edmonton to run a live theatre in the west end of town?"

"Directing is something they all want to do eventually. It's playing god." Denise sounded strained. She also sounded like she'd been trolling IMDB for whatever faint connection to Eleanor she could find.

"Well," I said, trying to sound supportive, "I'm sure a list like that is going to show the police that there are more ways than one to look at this puzzle."

"It's not a puzzle, Randy," Denise said in a clipped tone. "It's my life they're debating."

"I know. Listen, I have to get back to the kids. Send me that list by email, along with your reasons, so that Steve can have a look at them. I'll be sure he gets them and passes them on to Iain and Jennifer Gladue."

"Thank goodness he's back." Denise heaved a sigh. "Now maybe someone over there will listen to reason."

"Well, we'll see. Better than nothing, though, right?"

We muttered a couple more things to each other, Denise pretending she was calm and collected and me pretending I believed her act.

The kids had already divided themselves into their scene groups and were diving into their rehearsals and planning. I grinned in spite of myself. There was just nothing like the lure of the stage to focus people on a goal. I had a feeling some of the parents coming at the end of the camp to watch our presentation were going to be quite surprised at the evidence of dedication and burgeoning talent.

Louise walked over to debrief me on the morning.

"They were so sweet. And quick to get the concepts, too. It's really all about knowing how the light hits surfaces, stage makeup. It's not that often you get kids who have never even experienced a wrinkle figuring out how to enhance and create one with light and shadow. I was impressed."

"I cannot thank you enough for taking that on for me, Louise. I could have let him come in on the 747 bus link, but I think being met at the airport is one of the best things, and I wanted to be able to do that for him."

"Besides, you missed him! I get it. No problem. I was glad to help."

She strolled off down the hill to the backstage area. I had paid her for the supplies, but I figured I would have to pick up something nice for her as well, like a bottle of wine and a basket of goodies.

The rest of the afternoon went smoothly enough, and I waved off all the kids and got myself out of the park and halfway up Emily Murphy Park Road by 4:30. Passing the Groat Road rush-hour traffic made me grateful for the thousandth time that I didn't have to rely on a car for transportation. Edmonton was getting more and more congested, even with the extensive city bus system. I was hoping Steve's crew's eventual report would highlight the absolute need to continue and expand the LRT system throughout the city. We had spent enough rounds of city councils deciding to shelve the plans for later, all the while supporting developments better left to private investors.

I was hoping Steve would feel awake enough to come over, but I wasn't holding my breath. Somehow, the whole travelling westward jet lag just slammed people. He might be foggy for a good couple of days.

I sure hoped not. I needed him sharp and on his game. And so did Denise.

I needn't have worried. At six-thirty, Steve knocked and then turned the key into my apartment. He looked clean and shiny. If you looked closely, you could see that the skin by his eyes was still a bit drawn and thin, but that would be the only indication he'd been up for more than twenty-two hours straight and covered a good chunk of the globe in one day.

I fed Steve salad chopped full of pea pods, cucumbers, and red peppers along with boxed lettuce greens, and broiled chicken breasts with rosemary and lemon slices. I also made mashed potato pies, a concoction of potato, egg, chopped broccoli and cheese in a ramekin that I had created to approximate the tasty little potato circles you could order in the IKEA restaurants.

He ate with gusto, which is the best compliment a cook can receive.

Later, we sat in the living room with a pitcher of iced tea, looking at photos Steve had downloaded from his camera onto a flash drive. Norway looked gorgeous, as if a crew of people went out and washed the scenery and the streets every evening in anticipation of the next day.

"They have their troubles just like any other place," Steve laughed, "but it really is a wonderful country. And I brought you this." He pulled a small parcel out of his pocket.

I unwrapped the small white paper bag he'd rolled over itself and reached in to find a three-inch statue of a troll on a ribbon.

"He's a *niessen*, a house troll who will keep your abode safe and your milk sweet."

"Well, what would I do without sweet milk, I ask you?"

"There are all sorts of different trolls in Norway who are responsible for various amounts of mischief. This little guy is a protector troll."

"For when you can't be around?"

Steve leaned in and kissed me on the nose. "Exactly."

"He's great. I wonder if he'd moonlight and protect Denise as well."

Steve sighed. "I know you're worried, Randy, but you have to have a little faith."

"I am not so certain. Without you in the picture, there has been a whole lot of focus on Denise. It comes off people in waves whenever we go somewhere. And it's as if they are projecting relief as well as blame, like she's been staked out like the scape-goat for the sins of the theatre community."

"What is this, *Children of the Corn*? The whole theatrical community rose up and sacrificed Eleanor Durant in some sort of arcane river valley ceremony?"

"Eww, no. But wouldn't that be utterly spooky? Now I'm going to have nightmares all night."

"Well, I wish I could stay to keep them at bay, but I really need to conk out for about twelve hours."

"And I have to be down to the park bright and early for the next week and a bit, and then I'm done."

Steve promised to take Iain the lists Denise had made, along with my annotated calendar of events. I promised to focus on my job. We made plans to celebrate his return properly on the following Saturday night, when I'd be finished my gig and he'd be unjetlagged.

"We really have quite a bit of catching up to do, after all," Steve leered, and then laughed when I blushed.

"Oh Randy, I've missed seeing everything you think played out on your face. Hanging around the acting world has done nothing to help you, has it?"

I swatted him. "I'll have you know I'm learning a whole lot of new tricks. It's all about light and shadow."

Steve waggled his eyebrows at me and headed down the hallway to the door. I closed and locked my door and grinned.

It was good to have him home.

29.

The next eight days were a blur of activity. The kids were thrilled to discover how their costumes tied the scenes together. I had brought in my good camera to take a group shot and photos of each scene's groupings, with an eye to emailing them to each camper as a memento of their summer. All five Beatrices insisted on having their picture taken together, which began a run of similar shots. By the time I was done, I realized it was going to take an entire evening to sort out the permutations and combinations of who was in what photo. They weren't going to be anything like Morgana's photos of the real cast, which were being flashed all over social media and on one bus bench, but even in the little viewfinder, they revealed a group of happy kids who knew that they were making magic happen and that they were stronger together than apart.

Their Saturday noon production was favoured by a beautiful sunny day. I had biked down to the park with three clamshells of big bakery-made cookies for the mini-reception after the kids' scenes. They and their guests were all invited to stay for the matinee performance, and Micheline had offered to set up a coffee urn for the parents between times.

The energy and joy were electric, and even if I hadn't been so invested in them, I would have been delighted with the performances. The audience, already prepared to love them, was swept up in the moment and burst to their feet for the curtain call.

Kieran, who had been glad-handing and schmoozing with the parents and students, came up to me with a large cookie in his hand.

"This was fantastic, Randy. Exactly the sort of reputation I want to build for this program. These people are going to be our best ambassadors for the summer Shakespeare."

"The kids were great," I agreed. Kieran went on about his vision for the coming years, bringing in guest lecturers, having concurrent classes when it got bigger, moving toward a year-round weekend program, and my mind turned off a bit. Running a year-round Shakespeare camp for teens wasn't my goal in life. Kieran could dream all he wanted. He'd be finding someone else to run things. Someone who would have to buy decks of my patented Shakespeare cards.

He sensed our conversation waning, and we melded into two other groups of conversations, as one does at fancy, crowded cocktail parties, or in a tented enclosure with seventy-some bemused, proud adults and twenty-five zingingly adrenalined teenagers.

As I met and shook hands with someone's grandmother who had been in Robert Altman's *Nashville* and was so proud her grandchild was following in her footsteps, it occurred to me that Kieran's grandiose plans for the Shakespeare camp weren't consistent with Denise's idea that he would sell his soul to get the artistic directorship of Chautauqua Theatre. He sounded as if he had more than enough high hopes and big plans for the Freewill Festival.

Of course, he could be just hepped up on the moment. I knew the feeling from being a sessional lecturer. No matter what you were teaching, it was your favourite topic in the universe; the course was your absolute dream course and you wanted to teach it forever; the syllabus you'd prepared was the very best reading list you could imagine. You had to gear yourself up into that sort of fervour to make things palatable and desirable for your students. That could be how Kieran operated as well; whatever he was doing at the moment was his ultimate dream.

That could be why it was easy for him to switch-hit with girlfriends, too. I still couldn't imagine him throwing Denise over for Sarah, nor could I imagine him cheating on Denise with Eleanor. But if he was of the "love the one I'm with" persuasion, it made more sense.

I continued to schmooze and congratulate my students. I didn't particularly want to hang around for the matinee performance of the festival, so I was angling my way toward the trailer, where Micheline had let me stash my bag under her desk.

She was in the trailer when I got to it, which was a good thing, because she let me know that my final cheque was missing the vacation pay portion that needed to be determined once the full run of the festival had wrapped up. She said to check for it within a couple of weeks, then she gave me one of those awkward hugs people who don't like each other much seem to think they need to deliver at specific moments, such as extended departure.

I didn't mind Micheline, but she certainly wouldn't be someone I would ask out for lunch if I had to travel to get there. On the whole, while I had enjoyed my experience with the Shakespeare folks, working outside for long periods of the day was my least favourite location. I could handle the youth, since they were barely a year or two younger than the students I taught whenever I got a sessional gig. I could handle the theatre people, for short bursts, although their need to perform and entertain instead of merely converse wore me out. I could even handle the out-of-the-way aspect of getting into and out of the park. However, once you got there, it was either stew with Micheline in the trailer, sit in the green room and be bombarded with young actors wandering about in tights and little else, or be outside.

I hadn't known quite how much a creature of comfort I was till I passed a picnic table on the way out of the park and with a small shiver of delight realized I wouldn't have to sit at another one of them for the rest of the year.

I trudged my way up the big hill so I could walk home via the Windsor Park mini-mart and pick up a litre of skim milk. Steve was coming over for an early supper, so I wouldn't get a chance to head out for a larger grocery shop. I had enough fixings for a warm weather meal, anyhow. I just wanted to get home and put away my thoughts about the summer camp experience and get into gear for the fall.

I was planning to drop a CV off to Grant MacEwan on Monday, popping in to see the Chair of the English department while I was there. From my experience, August was always the scariest month for chairs and deans. The majority of their workforce were academic gypsies, and while a lot of sessionals were married to tenured professors or other professionals with anchoring jobs keeping the family local, others of us could move like the wind and did, leaving planning a fall term a bit of a nightmare. Likewise, last-minute registration and the temptation of more tuition revenue always increased the chances of another class section or two appearing by August 15 and requiring a lecturer at the helm.

A great trick, if you were mobile enough, was to appear like a magical fairy in mid-August, ready to teach an 8:00 a.m. class, able to whip together a syllabus from default, pre-ordered textbooks and not be fussy about sharing an office only for set student office hours. Since I had nothing on the horizon, I was certainly that easy. I was maybe even a bit too eager, hopping in there right off the bat the first week of August.

I had a track record of sorts with MacEwan, though, and I didn't want to leave things too late. The older you get, the less the gypsy life appeals, if it ever really did. More and more, I envied Denise her security. In fact, as long as one overlooked her strong potential for incipient arrest, her life was perfect.

Steve had been at work; I could tell by his collared shirt. Even though it was a short-sleeved madras plaid, it was in muted tones and matched the khakis he'd tucked it into. Normally, on a weekend or day off, he'd be in a tee-shirt and jeans. I wondered if he had to head back to work after supper, but he assured me he was done for the day.

"Iain and Jennifer called me in for a consultation on your calendar listings I shared with them. Jennifer seemed interested, Iain not so much. But you know Iain; he'll come around if you bring him something tangible. Jennifer seems to think in patterns, more like you."

I wasn't sure how I felt about being compared to Jennifer Gladue, even positively. Trying not to dwell on it, I asked Steve if they were looking into Oren Gentry's death.

"That I couldn't tell you, and not even because I shouldn't even if I could. I sketched them a vague concept of theatre hierarchies and the drama scene as you portrayed it to me, and they both sort of nodded. I think they've tuned into quite a bit of that, but the whole 'open job' aspect didn't seem to be news to them."

"Well, I guess that's a good thing. It offers one way in which all suspicion doesn't fall on Denise."

Steve was thoughtful. "Unless they get it into their heads that Denise was so overcome with delight on directing that student production that she wanted to change careers and become an artistic director."

I laughed, as I was supposed to. "As if. You don't just wake up and decide you want to become a director. The base requirement is an MFA, and you need plenty of experience before actors will put their faith in your vision and trust you to guide their performances. It's difficult enough for an actor to shift into becoming a director, though several have done it. They go back to university and when they come out with their MFAs, they're often the best directors because they know just how far they can push their actors."

"Who else wants to direct, besides former actors?"

"Who doesn't? Well, apart from me. Some people just grow up to want to control the vision, just like some musicians grow up knowing that their instrument is an entire symphony and that they are destined to become conductors. Probably some theatre critics would like to be directors; maybe some drama teachers. But I would think that the least likely person would be a university prof. Too much investment in solitary research, too much introversion. So no, I think you're probably more likely to have Liz Nicholls, the critic from the *Edmonton Journal*, want to become the new artistic director of Chautauqua Theatre than Denise."

"Would Liz Nicholls be up to wielding a knife on a beloved Canadian actress?"

"Excuse me, have you read her reviews?"

"A literal knife."

"Oh, well, in that case, no. Although she is wiry enough to drag a body somewhere, I think."

"To be frank with you, knowing my fellow cops, I think it's going to stretch their imaginations a bit too far to try to incorporate a death from natural causes into a murder investigation. When working a murder case, the object is to simplify the strands of the evidence, not to exacerbate the issue by bringing in more angles."

I sighed. "Do you think it's beyond the realm of possibility that someone murdered both Oren Gentry and Eleanor Durant in order to become the new artistic director of Chautauqua The-atre?" I sat back, a bit deflated. "Oh. Now that I hear it out loud, even I think it's a bit far-fetched."

Steve nodded at me. "See what I mean? It's a hard sell. But you know I will do what I can to make them question the feasi-bility of it being Denise."

"I know."

We sat there quietly for a bit. There wasn't much to say, and we were in that weird lull that happens when someone has been away, living a life with different patterns. There is a point at which the descriptions of the new world stop and the one left behind is tired of hearing about it, and weary of catching the traveller up on what has transpired in their absence. So, without a shared month between us, Steve and I were forging ahead to make some more connected memories.

With any luck, the new memories wouldn't contain any dead bodies.

30.

A couple of weeks went by.

I got my resumé in to MacEwan, cleaned my apartment in a way I hadn't been able to since the Shakespeare gig had begun, went to a couple of movies with Steve, and spoke to Denise on the phone pretty much every day.

She was preoccupied. While she was going through the motions of getting syllabi together for the fall, her heart didn't seem to be in it. When you're worrying you might be trying to make bail that fall, laying down the laws about plagiarism sort of pales in relative importance. Don't forget to cite your sources. Don't even think about stabbing people and stuffing them under the stairs.

I had done one positive thing to help. Under the guise of finding out if she had any Fringe recommendations, I had called up Taryn Creighton again. I tried to insert enough breadth to the conversation so that I could determine if she jogged or had been anywhere near the Queen Elizabeth steps during the time Eleanor had been killed.

It made for an awkward conversation, and I came away with only two bits of information. Taryn was a climber, not a jogger, and I should try to take in Belinda Cornish's play about Wallis Simpson's first marriage.

I had been hoping to eliminate Taryn completely from the list of suspects, since I liked her, but because I like Denise even more, I was relieved to see more than one name on the list.

Denise had suggested that Kieran was planning to apply for Oren's vacated position, too. While I hadn't sensed that from any of my dealings with him, I was willing to believe her. She knew him more intimately, after all.

So, we had three names: Denise, Taryn, and Kieran. Two of them knew Eleanor. Two of them were directors. Two of them were women. This was like one of those logic puzzles.

It occurred to me that I had turned it into a puzzle. I plumbed my emotions and realized I couldn't summon up much sadness for the death of Eleanor. I just hadn't known her well enough to really care. While I did care about Denise, I couldn't in my heart of hearts believe that an innocent person would be incarcerated, even though I knew it did happen from time to time. So, I was treating this like a logic game. If not Denise, then who?

Games like this are paradoxically always easier when there are more characters involved on the grid. I needed more suspects. And so did the police. If I could just give them a few more names, maybe they'd get motivated to look beyond Denise. That kind of opening was all I really needed.

I have great faith in the Edmonton Police Force. I just wanted them to keep on keeping on in this case, rather than settling for the answer they thought they already had.

So, more suspects. Denise had given me more names, directors of theatre companies even smaller than Black Box, and freshly minted MFAs. I wasn't so sure about the new recruits. I had a feeling they were probably still idealistic and egotistical to think that they could create something from nothing.

A couple of the actors from the Freewill Shakespeare Festival, like Christian, might be contenders for my list, too. They might not have the credentials, but they didn't lack for ego, as far as I could see.

Steve dutifully took my thoughts to Iain, but I could tell from his lack of enthusiasm that Iain wasn't receiving any of my offered help with good grace. I couldn't let that stop me, though.

One nice thing was that because Steve wasn't working the case, I felt I could discuss it with him. Not that we discussed it much. He was busy with his write-up on the Scandanavian trip, to deliver the group's findings in early September. We were still dealing with a bit of a barrier, but at least I didn't have to worry about imagining a budding relationship between him and Detective Gladue. Whatever free time he had, Steve spent with me.

I was glad, because pretty soon my free time was going to be taken up with teaching again, if there was any justice. I had the last couple of weeks of August to play, Fringe and relax, and then, if the gods and chair of the English department were smiling, I would be assigned enough classes to pay rent and feel like a contributing citizen of the world come September.

I looked again at my list of suspects, all except Denise predicated on wanting a solid position in their field of endeavour. Maybe I could knock off one of the full-time lecturers and guarantee me some courses. If I timed it right and, say, pushed one of them over the railing of the High Level Bridge on August 25, then my curriculum vitae could look like the answer to a department head's prayer.

What was I even thinking?

I looked at my suspect list again, this time with a more realistic eye. No one killed for something as pedestrian as a paycheque, did they?

But maybe being artistic director was more than a paycheque. Maybe it fulfilled a dream. A dream worth killing for.

31.

As soon as the Shakespeare festival wraps up, with the Teatro la Quindicina's season already in full swing, everything starts to gear up for the Fringe Festival. Started more than thirty years ago by the musings of a director who had become enamoured of the unjuried mayhem that was the Edinburgh Fringe Festival, the Edmonton Fringe had sprung up so successfully that it had sparked a whole circuit of Fringe festivals across the continent. Nowadays, a canny company could start in Orlando, Florida, work their way up the eastern seaboard and skip across Canada from Fringe to Fringe, ending on Vancouver Island along with the good weather.

Edmonton's Fringe was centred in Old Strathcona, a neighbourhood that was rediscovered at about the same time as the Fringe began. The Edmonton Transit bus barns were being evacuated, and into them moved a Saturday farmers' market and several theatre spaces. Beside the market in a former fire hall was Walterdale Theatre, a long-running amateur theatre company, and across the way was the Varscona Theatre, home of several small professional theatre companies. The Varscona had also been a newer former fire hall. If you vacated a largish space in Edmonton for more than five minutes, it was likely to turn into a theatre.

Several former movie theatres were now live theatre spaces, as was the movie space in the Citadel Theatre complex. Another couple of spaces had eventually turned into nightclubs, but for the most part, Edmontonians out for an evening seemed to want to see others strut their stuff.

Our Fringe had a special theme for its advertising every year, based on old movie or book titles or popular culture memes, ever since the second year's poster was unveiled as "The Return of the Fringe." The entire neighbourhood had embraced the festival, which brought the whole city to Old Strathcona. Several boutiques and bistros survived the entire year on what they made in two weeks' worth of Fringe sales. Until it had burned down in 2002, Uncle Albert's, the popular old pancake restaurant that had long stood on the corner of Whyte Avenue and the Calgary Trail, proudly displayed framed Fringe posters along its walls. The career waitresses, who looked like they should all be named Flo and Wanda, had been very up-to-date on which shows to see.

More than just theatre happens around Whyte Avenue, of course. Every Saturday, people are lured there after their visit to the Strathcona Farmers' Market or their shuffle through one of the nearby antique malls.

There is an annual art walk, when painters set up outdoor

mini-galleries all along the sidewalks of six or seven blocks. In between admittedly bizarre purple portraits of celebrities, you can snaffle prints and small acrylics while meeting the artist at the same time.

Pop-up designer stores happen on Whyte more often than anywhere else, and at Christmas, several stores reach back into nostalgia and produce animated story windows worth braving a cold trek to smile at.

But it's the Fringe that brings the party to the neighbourhood, and there's no arguing with that. The ten-day event makes driving crazy and parking almost impossible, but if you don't mind a bit of a crowd, being at the Fringe can satisfy your craving for mini-doughnuts and walking on hot tarmac without having to deal with carnies. The people are a mixture of theatregoers, hipsters, teens hanging out, older guys who like drinking beer outdoors, families enjoying the sun and buskers, and a couple of creepy old clowns who make balloon animals and suggestive remarks.

I braved the crowds to get through to the second beer tent, tucked in the shade behind the Arts Barns. That was where Denise said she'd be. It was where the CBC drive-home show broadcast from, but they didn't start till 3:00 p.m., so we had figured it would be a safe bet as a rendezvous.

We were planning to see the Teatro show running during the Fringe, which we had seasons' tickets to, anyhow, and then risk a couple of unknowns. It was still early enough in the festival to pick a show and grab a ticket. Once the reviewers began to publish their starred summaries, though, there would be a run on remaining tickets to the high-buzz shows.

It was getting pricier each year to experiment. When the Fringe had first begun, and even twenty years ago when I began attending it, tickets were in the neighbourhood of $4 to $8 apiece, and the shows ran half an hour to ninety minutes. You would line up for tickets as soon as the line for the previous show at the venue was let in. It was arduous, but some of the best parts of the adventure came from chatting in line with the friends you'd arrived with or the new friends you'd meet.

Now, the Fringe was more organized, more expensive, and a little more regimented. It was also expanding all over the city. There were various "bring your own venue" shows, some even downtown across the river. I couldn't imagine any of those did as much business as the ones located within roaming distance of Gazebo Park in the centre of the action.

I found Denise poring over her Fringe program. She had flagged several pages, and by the time I got back to the table with two pints of Big Rock Warthog Ale, she had flagged at least three more. Being questioned in a murder investigation, losing her boyfriend, and being shunned by local actors and drama academics didn't seem to dim Denise's love of theatre. She looked up at me with the excitement of kids in toy stores.

"Okay, so there is a Coriolanus from Winnipeg that runs eighty minutes in the Orange Hall, a kabuki version of *Streetcar Named Desire* that sounds interesting, something called *Much Ado Ron Ron*, and *The School of Night* who improvise a complete Shakespearian drama with suggestions from the audience, including a sonnet extemporized on the spot. I've read about these guys; they're supposed to be amazingly quick-witted."

"What are our times like?"

"We could manage the kabuki, which is around the corner here at the Cosmopolitan Music Society in an hour, then go to Stewart Lemoine's play at 3:00 as planned, and as soon as we get out of there, join the line to get back in for *The School of Night*."

"Deal. Let's go get tickets as soon as we finish these beers."

Denise sat back on her rickety plastic folding chair. She was wearing sunglasses, so I couldn't see the stress lines around her eyes, but she was doing a pretty good job of looking relaxed and at ease. Anyone who didn't know her well wouldn't notice the way her shoulders were a bit drawn and how her middle finger and thumb were meeting to tap out a continuous beat without the aid of a castanet.

It worried me to see her this way, and I was hoping the shows might take her mind off things, but surrounded as we were by the Edmonton theatre crowd, it wasn't going to be easy. Maybe it would be better just to take the bull by the horns.

"Have you heard anything more from the police?" I asked.

Denise's fingers stopped their tarantella. "No, have you?"

"Steve said he was trying to draw Iain and Detective Gladue a wider picture of possibilities, but he wasn't holding out much hope." Denise slumped a bit, but you'd only notice it if you were really looking. "I think we need to flush the killer out somehow, because if what we think is correct, there is going to be no resolution till you're arrested and tried, and then we'll never be able to prove that whoever is the next artistic director of Chautauqua is the killer."

"How do you think we could flush them out?"

"We need to have another director step forward as a contender for the job."

"But we've already got at least three in the running."

"Kieran and Taryn, yes. Who else?"

"Well, there are the boys from the Cement Productions, and the fellow who's been directing the touring shows for the schools."

"Are you sure about those names or are you just imagining them as contenders?"

"More the latter, I guess," sniffed Denise. "But what does it matter? There could be a dozen strong contenders. Any one of them might be the killer."

"That can't be true. First of all, you eliminate the people who lack the senior level of validity. The board of Chautauqua is not going to hand over the reins to someone wet behind the ears. They need a strong and capable person to keep Oren Gentry's vision going. And they need something more than that, given he was such a persona in the community. I mean, doesn't he even have a park named after him?"

"It's a small green space with a bench, between diverging roads."

"It's still a big deal."

"All right. So you are saying the Cement boys don't have the gravitas. So we're back to Kieran and Taryn."

"And I cannot imagine Taryn killing anyone."

"Why? Because you went to school with her? Listen, I was far more intimate than that with Kieran, and you don't see me pulling him off the list. Fair is fair."

"I take your point. But really, don't we just naturally gravitate to men for violent crime? I don't think it's misplaced, either. After all, Kieran is a big lad. He could cart Eleanor up the stairs easily enough, even though she'd be a dead weight."

"Why do they call it dead weight? Are you really heavier the minute you're dead? Maybe they could scare anorexics straight with that sort of campaign. Stay alive, or you'll end up really heavy!"

"You're getting off topic," I said, putting on my schoolmarm voice. "Anyhow, we should go line up for tickets if we're going to do this right."

Denise hoisted herself up off her chair and stacked our plastic cups for the bussing person to gather. "You're right. After you, my dear Alphonse."

We wended our way out of the beer tent and south to the entrance of the main office of Fringe Theatre Adventures. The cattle pen ropes were set out to deal with a longer line than the one we were joining, so Denise held up the rope halfway along and I scrunched under. She followed and we walked the rest of the line to stand behind about ten people waiting to buy tickets.

It might be less bohemian and more expensive, but the central ticket sale concept was much handier. We picked up the kabuki Tennessee Williams but were informed the School of Night tickets would have to be purchased at the Varscona, as they were also a Bring Your Own Venue group. So, on the spur of the moment, Denise got us tickets for the silly-sounding *Much Ado Ron Ron* the following Tuesday evening at seven.

"It's worth a laugh," she said. "And it will be a good way for you to bury your summer's work."

"Deal," I said. I counted out $30 to hand to her, since she was putting all the tickets onto her credit card. I'd have to walk past a bank machine on the way home. Even in this age of plastic debit and credit cards, I didn't feel right if I didn't have at least forty bucks in cash to cover whatever might happen. My mother called it "mad money," enough to get you a cab home in an emergency.

"We should be able to buy the School of Night tickets when we pick up our Lemoine/Teatro tickets," said Denise, as we left the Fringe box office. "Okay, which is the quickest route to the Cosmopolitan Music Society?"

We went back the way we had come, circling the beer tent and picking our way along the gravel path near where the historic streetcar tracks came to their terminus. Coming toward us from the other direction were Louise and Sarah. Since it would be utterly awkward to just walk past each other without speaking, and because Louise either didn't have any idea of the chasm between Sarah and Denise or was possibly happy to stir things up, we stopped to exchange pleasantries, which amounted to agreement that the weather was great and discussion of how many plays each of us was seeing. Sarah was a Sterling judge for the Fringe shows and heading to her twenty-seventh play. Louise was appearing in a David Belke remount that didn't start till Wednesday, so she was catching as many shows as she could in the meantime and recommended a one-man show called *The Quilted Panda*. I responded that we were Fringing like crazy today and catching another show on Tuesday evening. Denise just stood there, looking pained and beautiful, like Grace Kelly in *The Country Wife.* Sarah broke the awkward silence with a bright, "Well, gotta dash," and we continued on to the Cosmopolitan Music Society.

The building we were after was the home of several levels of amateur orchestras, the place where school band geeks found each other again and wannabe clarinetists earned their chops. I had only ever been inside for Fringe shows or to meander through an annual hipster craft fair that took place near Christmas. I had bought my mother a trivet made to look like an Etch-a-sketch once. She had been bemused. The tie with a photo of a moose on it had pleased my father much more, I thought.

The kabuki company spent quite a bit of time establishing the concept of Blanche and Stella being sisters, which I guess made sense; without words, it might have been awkward in the later scenes. They also ran the action linearly, running through Blanche's petty, tragic life and then sending her along to Stella, instead of letting us discover her backstory through an unlayering of her lies and subterfuges.

As a result, it was more as if we were watching a white-faced version of the Three Little Pigs minus one. The weak pig finds refuge in the home of the stronger pig, and then the wolf huffs and puffs and blows the weaker pig out. Denise laughed the first big honest laugh I'd heard from her in ages at my interpretation as we hurried up Gateway Boulevard to get to the Varscona Theatre.

"That is too funny, and better than they deserve," she said, wiping tears from her eyes as we rounded the corner by the farmers' market. "Sometimes things just shouldn't be meddled with."

We had no trouble getting tickets to the School of Night improvised Shakespeare along with our season's tickets to *The Sparkling Glissando,* Stewart Lemoine's latest play. We got into line, and Denise left me briefly to hold our places while she popped over to buy a plate of green onion cakes and a bag of kettle corn.

"The specific food groups of the Fringe are now covered," she said, offering me half the green onion cake. We ate ravenously, tying up the rest of the kettle corn and putting it into Denise's purse. I squeezed anti-bacterial wash on our hands, and Denise pulled out our tickets as the line began to move.

The play, like all Lemoine confections, was a delight. Whimsy, intricate wordplay, a few bittersweet reflections on the world, and one or two outrageous leaps of faith all tossed into a hopper and dressed in fabulous forties costumes.

I went to the washroom while Denise lined up again for the improv show. There were three narrow stalls in a room intended for one spacious experience. I wedged myself into the centre stall as soon as the door came open. In the next stall, I heard a cellphone ring.

A voice I almost recognized answered the call, which I had to imagine was an embarrassing situation. I think I'd have let it go to voicemail, given the circumstances. What if someone flushed?

"She's here, I saw her in the back row," said the voice in the next stall. "I can't believe the gall." There was a pause. "Well, not yet, but they will."

I wanted to hear more, but the woman on the other side of me flushed and I realized that I was holding up a substantial line of people who had lineups aplenty to get to. I flushed and got out to do a bit of a dance with another woman washing her hands. The person on the phone was still in her stall, though no longer talking. I couldn't stand there waiting for her to emerge, it was too small a space.

I went out to meet Denise, who was well back in the line to get into the next show. As I joined her, the line began to snake along. With all the movement, I had to abandon my attempts to see who was emerging from the washroom door.

I hadn't quite recognized the voice, but it made me edgy all the same. I knew I wasn't being paranoid. We had been sitting in the back row. The woman had been discussing Denise.

32.

I am never certain if it's the English accent or the British school
and broadcasting system that makes for a richer use of language, but I tend to think people with British accents seem more
well-educated. Even when I tune into *Coronation Street*, with
its blue-collar, working-class characters, their ability to say, "I'm
a trifle flummoxed by this" rather than "I don't get it" makes
me think more highly of their inability to manage whatever has
presented itself. This is, I believe, why British émigrés manage to
snag good North Americans jobs, PBS is clogged with English
television shows, and Hugh Grant movies rule at the romantic
box office.

Or maybe it just has something to do with Hugh Grant.

Whatever the case, there was no denying that the three
young men of *The School of Night* were intensely clever, weaving
an improvised plot around a model of a five-act revenge tragedy,
sending up tropes and Shakespearian standards as they went.
They provided a double whammy, educating at the same time

as they parodied. Their audiences were going to leave having learned enough about Shakespeare to laugh knowingly with the rest of us as the School of Night sent him up.

"Oh, that was just what we needed," laughed Denise, as we emerged to a still sunny but slightly more adult Fringe. As the evening began, the fire acts became pronounced among the buskers and more couples on dates could be seen in the milling crowds. We made our way out to the west and toward the parking lot where Denise was parked.

It was slow going, but Denise dodged in and around the one-way streets of Old Strathcona and emerged onto 109 Street just long enough to get in the left lane and turn toward the university. She let me out in front of my building, reminding me that we had a date for Tuesday.

"Shall I pick you up? It will be over at the College St. Jean, not the Fringe proper," she reminded me.

"That would probably be best. It's a bit of a jog to get there, though I could get a bus along Whyte Avenue and walk down after."

"No, I'll come get you, say at five."

"Great!" I waved her off and then went into my apartment. There was a light blinking on my phone machine.

I pressed the button and Kieran's voice came into my house.

"Randy, I was wondering if I could talk to you. Privately? It's sort of a delicate matter." He went on to offer a couple of times when we could meet, and suggested the Three Bananas Café down in Winston Churchill Square, which to my way of thinking was probably the least private place I could imagine, in view from all angles, but on the other hand, you'd certainly see anyone approaching you.

I didn't particularly feel like talking to him so soon after spending time with Denise, so I emailed to say that his suggestion of Monday at 2:00 p.m. at the Three Bananas would be fine.

So, I was looking forward to meeting a potential murderer on Monday, a suspected murderer on Tuesday and, with any luck, hearing from the chair of the English department by Wednesday. There was a sort of symmetry there, if you looked at it just so.

Though it was only about eight o'clock on a summer Saturday night, I felt too stimulated to even watch TV. I sent a chatty email to my mom and dad, telling them about the Fringe shows, another less chatty one to Steve, floating the idea of going out to brunch the next day, and then went to wash up and get ready for bed.

I was scrubbing the smut of the day from my skin with my favourite washcloth when I thought about what I had said to Denise about Kieran being strong enough to carry a dead weight up all those stairs. Why did he have to be carrying Eleanor's body up the stairs at all?

He could just as easily have been carting her body down the stairs. It's just that someone might have been more likely to see him at it. But maybe they'd think she was drunk, not dead. Who was going to notice a fellow and a seemingly intoxicated girl leaving the Old Strathcona area? Especially if he timed it for when all the bars let out and the drunks shouted and slurred their way through the otherwise beautiful neighbourhood? For the first time, I wondered what exactly Eleanor had been wearing when they found her. Maybe she hadn't been in obvious running gear at all.

Maybe we had been looking at it all wrong. And if that was askew, what else wasn't I seeing?

I brushed my hair and braided it loosely so it wouldn't wake me up in the night by creeping into my mouth or strangling me, and pulled on a cotton nightie. August evenings weren't quite cooling off yet, so one had to do one's best to make do.

Having set my bedding just so, to afford a yank of the duvet when I eventually would want the cover, I lay there with my body ready for sleep and my mind racing. There was one death or maybe two to solve, and way too many suspects if one were to consider desiring a plum job the reason for murder. Aside from Bob Baker, who would probably be artistic director of the Citadel Theatre for another twenty years, any director in town would leap over their granny for the Chautauqua job. And in Edmonton, that meant a slew of people.

It wasn't sheep, but I fell asleep counting theatres in Edmonton.

33.

The night's sleep had done nothing for me and I woke up
feeling rumpled and headachey. A long shower, which usually could sort me out, only helped to make clear what the trouble really was. I was feeling sidelined while the world swirled
around me. Denise was in trouble, even though things moved
so politely and slowly from the police end of things.

The theatre community was in flux, however much they
seemed to believe that the police were honing in on the right
person. Well, all but one of them was thinking that. I was positive the killer was somewhere in the theatre community. It was
too ludicrous to imagine that Eleanor had been the victim of a
random mugging gone wrong. While we did have sporadic elements of non-targeted violence in the city, it was usually associated with hockey season.

Most violent acts in Edmonton, including once when someone aimed a small plane into a suburban bungalow, had a specific person in mind. The murderer had been stabbing Eleanor

Durant and stuffing her under the Queen Elizabeth stairs, not just some redheaded jogger.

Someone had wanted Oren Gentry dead. That was something I could get Steve to poke around in, I was hoping. Fifty-four-year-old men didn't have heart attacks as a regular occurrence. Or did they? Who knew how stressful running a mid-level western Canadian theatre could be? Who could I ask? Kieran? Not likely. He was my top suspect.

I had to admit, he was mostly on top of my list because of the shameful way he had treated Denise, taking up with Eleanor behind her back and Sarah so quickly after breaking it off with my best friend. Kieran was a certifiable asshole, but that didn't necessarily translate to killer. It would be nice to lock him up, anyhow.

As if the universe was bugging my thoughts, my email pinged and I discovered that Kieran was weaseling out of our Monday meeting at the Three Bananas. Just when I'd had my mouth set for one of their designer café au laits. Whatever he'd wanted to discuss with me couldn't have been all that important after all. Well, at least it meant I would definitely not be asking him anything about Oren Gentry.

I'd cleaned away the breakfast mess on autopilot and set about getting ready for some more thoughtful work. Valerie had kindly back-channelled me the default list of texts that had been purchased for freshman English classes at Grant MacEwan, and I planned to scan the tables of contents to rough out a sample syllabus, just in case I did get hired at the last minute.

Luckily, everything was online these days. I found the

anthology listed on the Pearson website, clicked onto the "look inside" button, and flipped through to the table of contents. I always used to start with the Shakespeare and the play offerings. It was how I tended to choose anthologies, although of course I'd be stuck with this one for my first term.

You could supplement poetry and short stories if you had to, but plays were pricey and the Shakespeare was the cornerstone to the course. Most high school students had read *Romeo and Juliet*, *Julius Caesar,* and *Hamlet*. Woe betide you if you made them read something twice, so I was glad to see that *The Tempest* was the Shakespeare of choice in this collection. *A Glass Menagerie* would do nicely as the modern offering, too. Both plays had characters the students' age and were on the surface simple enough for freshmen to grasp their linear plots.

I was halfway through a list of poems I'd stick into the opening section on poetry when the phone rang. Having to drag myself out of the mindset of term architect made me realize how much I missed the classroom atmosphere. I hauled myself up off the loveseat, where I had been hunched over my laptop much of the morning. Creaking myself upright, I reached for the phone. It was Steve, wanting to know if I had lunch plans.

I looked up at my yellow wall clock. It was already past eleven. On cue, my stomach rumbled.

"I'd love some lunch," I said. He said he'd be five minutes, which gave me enough time to close my computer and grab my bag. True to his word, he was pulling up outside the back of my building just as I was coming out the door.

"Where do you feel like going?"

"I have no preconceived yearnings," I admitted. There are times when anything would be good, and the first thing you hear is just what you've been longing for.

"How about mac and cheese?"

"Blue Plate Diner mac and cheese?"

"Is there any other?"

In no time, we were ensconced in the eclectic little restaurant in the midst of the trendy stretch of 104 Street, just north of Jasper Avenue. There had to be a warehouse full of chrome and Formica tables to kit out so many restaurants in this particular style. Granted, several of the tables seemed to be distressed old wooden jobs, too. It was a noisy place, and no place to hold a business meeting or reunion of any sort, because you could hardly hear yourself think, let alone hold a conversation, but the food was delicious and relatively quick.

Steve and I both ordered the macaroni and cheese without bothering to look at the menus and sat back to look around. The place was two-thirds full, and the noise levels were bearable. A mother and daughter shared a table near us; four young girls with shopping bags around their feet were obviously taking a retail therapy break; two hipsters in skinny jeans and plaid shirts with bow ties were laughing together in the far corner; and in the middle of the restaurant were a couple of familiar faces. Just as I was figuring out that they were Christian and Janine from the Shakespeare troupe, Louise walked into the restaurant. After a quick look around the room, she spied their table in the middle and joined them.

"That's funny," I said, as quietly as possible, given the acoustics.

"What?" asked Steve.

"What's a table full of actors doing so far from the Fringe? You would think that every one of them would be either part of a show or busy supporting friends. At the very least you'd think they'd be on the other side of the river, hanging out in a restaurant in Old Strathcona instead of downtown."

"Maybe they're hiding out from the theatre crowd."

"In the very middle of a popular restaurant?" I was dubious.

"Well, as you say, they're far from the epicentre of theatre in Edmonton at the moment. They could be avoiding someone they know for sure is at the Fringe."

"Possibly. Or maybe they just live around here. There are loads of lofts and condos in the area now." I liked this street a lot, and if I could afford to buy a condo, it would be around here, for sure.

"Do you think actors can afford downtown prices?"

"I never presume to know what people can or can't afford, or what level of debt they're comfortable living in." I shook my head. "There have been students in my classes who would mention their vacation plans or accommodations in their journal entries sometimes, and I'd think hey, I am really in the wrong business."

"Okay, so imagine they live nearby. Is there any reason why that particular trio shouldn't be together?"

I shrugged. "It's not a clear fit. Louise is at least fifteen years older than Christian, so I don't think there's anything romantic going on there. Janine is a fight coordinator, so more connected to the stage management and techie ends of things than the acting. Plus, I'm pretty sure she's gay, so there's nothing between her and Christian, either. I think Louise and Kieran had a thing going a few years back, making her ostensibly hetero. So, truth to tell, unless they all discovered a mutual love of anime while they were working at the Shakespeare festival, I am not sure why they'd be together."

"Isn't Christian a director as well as an actor?"

I looked at Steve. "You've been talking to Iain and Jennifer Gladue, haven't you?"

He dipped his head and grinned. "Well, I couldn't let you have all the fun. I've cleared away some of the Scandinavian transit report material and offered my services to them as a third-party sounding board. We were discussing things yesterday, and they could use the help." He took a bite of the divine mac and cheese that had just been served to us in big white bowls, three types of cheese melting together and sending up fumes of delight.

I was blowing on a steaming forkful of noodles and cheese, ready to take a bite.

"So you know what this means, right?" Steve looked at me, with a "don't shoot the messenger" look. "I'm not going to be able to discuss the case with you from here on in."

I chewed the mouthful of comfort food, wondering if Steve had deliberately chosen this restaurant to divert me from his announcement. "That's okay; at least I know there will be someone on the team who doesn't immediately believe that Denise is capable of murder."

"That's true." Steve took another bite of his mac and cheese.

"But don't forget that I can believe that anyone is capable of murder."

"Even me?" I batted my eyelashes at him in my best Clara Bow manner.

Steve cocked his head and smiled. "Oh, I would never underestimate you in any way, Randy."

We let the noise of the restaurant overtake our conversation and devoted ourselves to the bowls of noodles and cheese. The place had filled up by now, and from where we sat I could no longer see Louise, Christian, and Janine. I was glad to hear Steve was going to be part of the investigation. But really, what on earth had he meant by his all-encompassing statements?

Could he really believe Denise was guilty of murder? Was nobody listening to reason?

Of course, what could possibly be reasonable about murder?

34.

Denise was relieved to hear Steve was joining the investigation, as I knew she would be. The strain of being suspect number one was wearing on her, and she took the news as evidence of someone being on her side. Someone of value to the cause, that was, because I am sure she knew I was on her side.

I didn't let her in on his last couple of statements, since I figured she needed all the optimism she could find.

We were on our way to the French campus of the University, College St. Jean. Years earlier it had been a private French boys' school run by priests and nuns. Eventually, they had combined with l'Academie Assomption, a private French girls' school adjacent to a convent in the inner city, and become a francophone separate school called J.H. Picard. The old girls' school had been various things and was currently a social services centre. The boys' school had evolved into a French-language campus satellite of the University of Alberta. Set as it was in the heart of the francophone district of the city, it became a hub for the French community. While outsiders thought French in Canada was relegated to Quebec, and most Canadians considered only Quebec, New Brunswick, and parts of Manitoba to be bilingual centres, there was actually a strong and vibrant Franco-Albertain presence, especially from Edmonton northward. It really shouldn't come as a surprise to anyone with even a vague understanding of Canadian history. If you followed the rivers of the fur trade settlements, you saw the entwined histories of French, Scottish, Irish, Cree, and Métis peoples, like the colourfully woven sashes called "flèches," which voyageurs had once worn and many Métis associations had adopted as their talisman.

Denise had made us reservations across the street in the Café Bicyclette for a quick meal before our Fringe play. I was settling for a salad with warm goat cheese, because I really wanted to save room for their cinnamon brioche, which I'd spotted on the counter on the way to our table. Denise was tucking into duck with lemon sauce and wild rice.

"So, guess who else has applied for the artistic director position?" Denise smirked, so I knew it wasn't going to be good news.

"Who?"

"Sarah." Denise tore her roll apart with a twist that made me feel as if she was picturing Sarah's head and shoulders coming apart between her hands.

"Sarah Arnold? I didn't know she wanted to leave academe."

Denise shook her head. "In theatre, academe is rarely something you want to be in if you can actually get your hands on a professional gig. There are a very few people who are driven to become professors of drama, and the ones who do see it as a vocation usually have a pretty healthy professional life alongside their teaching." She held her hand out and counted a few people off, mentioning a couple of names I knew, like Tom Peacocke and Jim De Felice. "Aside from them, and they're spread right across the country, everyone else is either a sessional augmenting a professional career, or a wannabe."

"Okay, so Sarah Arnold is now on our list of suspects."

Denise smiled grimly. That allocation seemed to make her happy. I wondered who else had dismissed her from their lives in the last few weeks and how much more of this she was going to be able to take. Denise had always had a healthy sense of her own worth, based on the proof that whatever she set her mind to, she excelled at. Now, though, she was being categorized as a murderer in the minds of people who didn't know her well, or people who had envied her seemingly effortless success. They obviously hadn't seen all the work and discipline Denise had infused her life with.

Well, I had seen it and I wasn't going to desert her.

In the way of great homonymic delight, my dessert arrived just as that thought went through my head, and I tucked into my brioche with small cooing noises that Denise felt honour bound to point out.

"You're making your amorous food noises again," she said, folding her thick linen napkin and placing it beside her plate on which remained a radish rose, a small smattering of wild rice, and three clean bones. The waiter came and whisked it away, refilling our water glasses and gazing admiringly at Denise.

"This is so good, would you like a taste?" Denise made a small moue and negative motion with her hand, which was fine by me. I finished it off with a bit of a flourish, and we called for the cheque. Within minutes we were on our way across the street to the theatre in the north basement of College St. Jean. There was already a lineup, but we had our tickets and weren't worried about seating.

"What have you heard about this show?" I asked Denise. From what I could tell, we'd just picked it because of the funny Shakespearean pun. I wasn't even sure if it was locally produced or not.

Denise shrugged. "The program says it's the third Fringe appearance for the Underwater Underwear Alliance, whose mandate is to rethink classics from the viewpoint of a modern, localized telling." She turned over the brochure in her hand. "There are glowing quotes here for *Lady Windermere's Fanboy* from Colin Maclean, and Liz Nicholls seems to have loved *A Doll's Houseplant,* which sounds as if it was about angst and the inability to form relationships."

"Shoot, I was hoping this was going to be funny. Don't tell me we are in for an ironic vision of twenty-first-century dating."

"Supposedly an old poster of Shaun Cassidy makes an appearance like Marley's ghost. So you know that's going to be good." Denise grinned. I laughed. No matter what, Fringe shows were entertaining. This one was longer than most at ninety minutes, and it had already given us some diverting value through the write-ups and bizarre promotional blurb in their photocopied program.

At 6:20, the doors opened and we filed into the theatre, which was quite steeply raked. We settled ourselves in the middle of row G, supposedly the sweet spot of any theatre, and watched with interest as the entire house filled. Already, five days into the ten-day festival, word of mouth was creating hits of various shows, and it seemed as if this was one of them. I felt quite proud of our having chosen it blindly, as if somehow that proved we had our finger on the zeitgeist of Edmonton culture.

Soon the lights dimmed and the curtains opened on a thirty-something woman with a suitcase being shown into a bedroom by an older woman. "It's your cousin's old room, but I'm sure you'll be comfortable till you get back on your feet, dear." Sure enough, over the twin bed was a poster of Shaun Cassidy, looking all blond bangs and teeth.

As soon as the aunt left the stage, Beatrice flopped back on the bed, obviously finding herself at the very frayed end of her rope.

Denise leaned over to me and whispered, "I feel a song coming on." Lucky for me, the sudden swelling music of accordion and penny whistle masked my bark of laughter, and Beatrice, the independent thinker who in this version had a real feminist slant, indeed broke into a song about getting out of her relationship with Ben in order to be independent but having to swallow her pride and crawl back to her family and feeling like a fifth wheel while they were planning her cousin's wedding. As songs went, it was fine. As Fringe songs went, it was quite lovely.

The play then went on, bouncing between Beatrice's wounded sensibilities at her aunt and uncle treating her as if she was a teenager just because she was single and staying in her cousin's old room, and her prickly nostalgia for her life with Ben. Meanwhile, the actual play was somehow woven in, through an amateur performance that her uncle's friends were rehearsing.

There was one amusing point where, short-handed, two men carried on an entire scene, shifting and grabbing and taking off hats to denote other characters. It was a rip-off of the most recent stage version of *The 39 Steps,* but it worked well in this context too. Beatrice was reconnected with her old beau, mostly so that her aunt and uncle could get her out of the house; her cousin, who was missing, returned and all was happy and bright. The whole cast came out for their curtain call, which turned into a sock hop of twisting to "Da doo ron ron."

Denise and I found ourselves humming the tune all the way to the car. "What an earworm," Denise laughed. "Well, it makes a break from 'Longfellow Serenade,' which is what usually gets stuck in my brain."

"For me, it's Burton Cummings's 'My Own Way to Rock.'" We drove along Whyte Avenue, enduring the congestion created by the Fringe crowds at 104 Street. I had forgotten to bring my sunglasses, so instead of squinting into the western sky ahead, I turned my head and watched the people on the sidewalk. It was like a Fringe play all its own. There were people seated at small tables in front of restaurants and ice cream parlours, with crowds flowing past them, and groups massed at the corners, while others manoeuvred their way around the corners through the narrow spaces of light.

Earnest young actors attempting to drum up audiences for

their shows were pressing playbills on passersby. Girls with messy knots of hair piled on the tops of their heads strolled along, wearing shorts and vests over thin tee-shirts. Young men in red trousers or long shorts or skinny jeans and high-top runners were everywhere, arm in arm, or walking backwards while conversing excitedly with groups of friends.

There was altogether too much humanity there for my sense of serenity. Denise, on the other hand, took it all in stride and drove at ease from one red light to the next, till we had eased our way past 107 Street and the last of the Fringe venues. "Do you feel like coffee and dessert somewhere?" she asked.

There was nothing to drag me home. Everything I was doing at the moment was completely on spec, hoping it would lead to work in the fall. Why not?

We pulled into the High Level Diner parking lot, and had to wait only a few minutes for the people in front of us to be seated and another table to be cleared. Soon we were pulling apart hot cinnamon rolls and drinking lovely brewed decaf, discussing the variety of ways one could revisit Shakespeare without being disloyal to the plot or dismissive of the intent.

"Try to imagine any other playwright who has had so many modernizations of his plays and not had them just disintegrate under the machinations," Denise marvelled, shaking her head admiringly.

"Well, I saw a version of *Uncle Vanya* set in the Canadian prairies," I countered, but it was true, there were not many examples I could think of. I supposed *Lysistrata* had been done a few ways, just updating it to determine whatever war the women didn't want the men fighting, and I could count three variations of *Madama Butterfly*, but there was nothing like Shakespeare for being set to music, done in jackboots, performed with multiple versions of the same character or in lime green afro wigs.

Denise lit up when she talked Shakespeare, and it was a pleasure to enter into the game. I could see why she was consistently nominated lecturer of the year; her students couldn't help but be caught up in her enthusiasm.

A small voice in the back of my mind asked, "Could that fervour become murderous in the right circumstance?" Luckily, Denise had her head down, concentrated on buttering a piece of her cinnamon bun. I took a swig of my coffee and tamped down the voice of doubt. If I didn't believe in Denise, who would?

We stood by her car talking, till I suggested she come in for tea. She checked her watch and said she had to head home. I waved her out of the parking lot and trundled across the alleyway to my apartment building.

I kicked off my sandals, locked the door, and headed directly for my bedroom and through to the washroom. My clock radio's red buttons said 9:38. I was tired and decided to crawl into bed. I left my clothes in a pile between the door to the washroom and the end of my bed and swiped a washcloth over my face. My nightshirt was hanging on the bathroom door.

I was asleep probably within ten minutes of getting home. Middle age, what a pathetic comedown. I slept till 9:00 a.m. and probably would have slept longer if it hadn't been for the phone ringing insistently.

35.

"Hello?" The sleep frog in my throat was all too obvious. I coughed up a bit of phlegm, and then muttered, "Excuse me?" because I hadn't heard a thing being said on the other end of the line.

"Randy, are you all right?" It was Steve. I coughed into a tissue I'd managed to snag and sat down hard on the loveseat. The air coming in through the window screens behind me was already midday hot. I leaned forward and twisted to check the clock on the wall to be sure it was really as early as I had thought. Sure enough. Nine o'clock.

"One of the few pleasures of the underemployed would be a certain allowance to sleep in from time to time," I growled into the phone. I hated the phone before 10:30 on principle; being woken up by the telephone never boded well.

"I needed to talk to you right away. Do you have any idea where Denise was last night, say between six and midnight?"

"Easy answer, yes. She was with me. We went to a Fringe play

280

and then to the Diner for cinnamon buns. She headed home just after 9:30. Why?"

"There has been another murder, and I was hoping you'd be able to fill in some of the timelines."

"Have you talked to Denise?"

"We haven't been able to locate her as yet." That was odd. Denise, though fully employed, was enjoying the same schedule I was for the next couple of weeks until classes began. She should have been home, luxuriating in not having to mark a pile of essays. Of course, if I knew Denise, she would have been up at the crack of dawn jogging or swimming or learning Italian.

"Who is dead?"

"They haven't released the name of the victim yet," said Steve, in that formal way he had of talking that told me he was calling from his desk at work and there were folks milling about nearby.

"If I were to guess someone in the theatre community, would I be in the ball park?"

"Home run."

"Good lord. If they keep this up, we're going to lose our status as a theatre city. Wait. Have you checked people from Calgary for all this?"

"I think the situations speak to a knowledge of the city," said Steve drily. "Look, sorry to wake you up, but if you hear from Denise, please tell her we're looking for her, okay? If she could call Iain or Jennifer or me, it would be a very good thing."

"Sure, I'll tell her if I hear from her," I said, and found myself looking at the phone receiver, Steve having hung up rather abruptly.

Who had been murdered? Where? And why would the first assumption be to pin this one on Denise? Could it be another person vying for the Chautauqua job? Or was that a blind alley that Denise and I had been running up?

It was too late to try to regain whatever dreams I'd been having, so I headed for the shower to commit entirely to the day.

I was dressed and presentable within twenty minutes. When you hit a certain age, it becomes just a matter of brushing your teeth, slathering on some sunscreening moisturizer, and if you intend to impress, mascara. Add another four minutes to brush and braid your hair, and you can be ready for action. Of course, folks in the theatre community probably spent a bit more time on their looks, though I had seen several actresses on the street or in the supermarket looking very drab in comparison to their onstage personas, so maybe they liked to play it low-key if they didn't have to hit the boards.

I called Denise, mostly just to have it done. I didn't doubt Steve when he said they couldn't reach her. She still wasn't picking up. I sent her a quick text message from my cellphone: "Where are you? It's important you call Steve."

Then I called Steve back. He sounded very curt, a signal that he was feeling some sort of pressure at that end. I asked if anyone had driven to Denise's condo.

"Not that she might not be out jogging or something, but it is sort of worrisome, if you've been trying to reach her for a while this morning."

"I'll see if we can get a car out there, thanks. Sorry, Randy, things are exploding here, I can't talk now." I said I understood and agreed to text him if there was anything I needed him to know.

So there I was, fully awake in a town where a murder had just happened, and radio silence from both my best friend and my boyfriend. How was I going to learn anything?

I pulled my laptop toward me and opened it, wondering if there might be a hint of whatever had happened to pull Steve into cop land so thoroughly. Having cancelled my newspaper subscription in response to a particularly odious columnist, I now had to rely on social media for my current affairs fixes.

The story was everywhere. I scrolled past two entries of cats sitting in boxes and tortoises wearing knitted dinosaur cozies, and found the *Edmonton Journal*'s link to their news article about a body found on the Fringe grounds. There wasn't much in the article, and a vagueness as to where the body had been found that was odd. Were they protecting the festival from a surge of ghouls or abandonment by the squeamish? Or were the police withholding the information?

I scrolled down the site until I saw a weird posting by John Ullyat, an actor in town and co-owner with his remarkable wife Annie Dugan, of Firefly Theatre, an aerial-focused circus act troupe.

JOHN: For the record, Annie and I were not involved in any way with what some people have called "performance art in questionable taste." We are performing on the side of Old Strathcona High School at 2 pm

for the next four days. Please come see us
there.

That was odd. I scrolled further back, like a fast-action
archaeologist dusting away the layer of time accrued while I was
sleeping. There were posts linking to reviews of various Fringe
shows, more cats, several rude but funny phrases attached to
Victorian-looking silhouettes, and then a few interesting posts
from around 10:30 the night before.

- There are police all over the Fringe.
- Did you guys see the body in the tower
at Walterdale? I swear it was a body.
- That was probably Firefly Theatre you
saw. I saw them being flies on the wall
yesterday.
- This was a body inside the thing on the
top.
- The cupola?
- Firefly Theatre was in the cupola of
Walterdale?
- There are police near Walterdale. Was
someone getting feisty in the beer tent?
- Sirens ruined our final song. #fringefail
- Anyone know why there are so many cops
around?

No wonder John Ullyat had been responding. From what
I could piece together, a body had been observed hanging in
the bell tower of the Walterdale Theatre, which was smack dab
in the middle of the Fringe site, and while various people had

written it off as an insensitive theatre piece, the police had been summoned and now a murder investigation was underway.

I wondered who it had been. It wouldn't be easy to get into the Walterdale, either. It was a real theatre, set up with a lobby and a box office and off-limit backstage areas. Anyone prowling around would be noticed by the folks slated for Fringe performances there.

So maybe it was someone from one of those shows. I padded into my dining room/office to get my Fringe program. The subtitle was always, "you can't tell the players without a program," but as I flipped through to the Walterdale site, I realized you couldn't tell the players even with a program. All that was listed in the thumbnail sketches was the title of the play, the running time, the name of the company and where they were from, and a two- or three-line teaser about the plot. I noted that all seven plays slated for that venue were from the Edmonton area.

I made a list of the plays and paid attention especially to the running list from last night. While we had been at College St. Jean at the Shakespeare pastiche, people had been watching *Zombies on Parade, Naughty Marietta,* and something called *The Penis Dialogues.* The musical probably had the largest cast, which would mean a whole lot of people wandering about backstage between 8:00 and 9:30. That might work to the murderer's advantage, if they were part of the company or known to the company. On the other hand, the smaller shows—and I couldn't imagine a thirty-five-minute and a forty-five-minute show being too big—would have fewer people backstage to notice someone taking a dead body up the bell tower or marching someone up there to kill them.

I looked at my scribbling on the legal pad on my lap. Jennifer Gladue was probably up to speed on all of this, so why was I even bothering? It didn't sound as if Steve was in any position to have me talk things over with him, either. What did I think I was doing?

I was trying to help my friend—that is what I was doing. And if I knew where she was and who it was she was supposed to have killed, I might be able to help her a lot more.

There was a knock at the door and I jumped, in spite of myself. I looked through the peephole, wondering which of my neighbours it could be, since we all now kept the outer doors firmly locked.

It wasn't a neighbour. It was Detective Gladue.

I opened the door, hoping that Iain or Steve was just outside the fish-eye lens of the peephole, but no, it was just her, looking trim and capable in light-weight grey trousers, a grey and cream tee-shirt with a scoop neck that showed a few freckles and some collarbone but no cleavage, and a cream poplin blazer over top, the sleeves pushed up to her elbows.

"Ms. Craig, I was wondering if I could come in and get your statement from your time with your friend Denise Wolff yesterday?"

"Sure, Detective Gladue, right? Come on in. Can I get you a cup of tea?" I hated the fact that she was entering my apartment. I invited very few people into my sanctuary and tried to avoid letting in anyone I didn't particularly care for. My personality, what there was of it, was on my walls and book-shelves, and I felt invaded and on display with this competent but utterly dismissive woman in my living room. My skin crawled a bit as I felt her look around the room, judging me through my belongings.

Of course, I had very few belongings. I'd been far more choosy about what I accrued now, since the break-in. In comparison to what I had previously hoarded, my apartment was absolutely Spartan. After getting her a cup and pouring her some tea from the pot on the coffee table, I sat back. Let her judge.

"Detective Browning told me he has spoken with you about your knowledge of where your friend Denise Wolff was yesterday." Detective Gladue was taking a formal approach.

"Yes, he did. And I told him that she and I had been together from just before suppertime till about 9:30. We had dinner, went to a Fringe show over at the College St. Jean venue, drove back to the High Level Diner, and then Denise went home, as far as I know."

As she was writing down what I said, I looked at the scribbles on the notepad in front of me. Maybe she wasn't as icy as I had presumed, and perhaps she would appreciate whatever thoughts I had about the situation.

"I was piecing together what must be happening after Steve called, and I figure it must have something to do with people seeing someone hanging in the bell tower of the Walterdale Theatre," I offered. Detective Gladue's head shot up quizzically.

Perhaps I shouldn't be oversharing with this hunting dog of a woman, I thought, but I'd already opened the barn door. "It's all over the Internet. I have no idea who is dead, but I went through the Fringe program to see what shows were in the theatre last night. They're all groups from Edmonton, if that helps at all."

I handed her the program, opened to the Walterdale venue page. She took it and nodded. "We got this from the Fringe management folks, along with a list of the people attached to each production."

"I was thinking," I volunteered a bit tentatively, "that the operetta, Naughty Marietta, would likely have the most people backstage and onstage. I wasn't sure if that would be a good or a bad thing."

Jennifer Gladue looked at me, and I think it was at that moment that we turned a corner. Maybe she saw in me some innate intelligence she could appreciate, and could tell I was, in general, on her side. Maybe I saw, for the first time, that she really wouldn't be Steve's type, since I got the sense that, as hard-working and clever as she might be, she really didn't have much of a sense of humour.

Whatever it was, she made a decision. "I have a list of all the people from each production at the Walterdale over the time period the coroner's preliminary report has given us. Would you be able to take a look at it for me and see if you could fill me in on any connections between people you might notice?"

I shrugged and smiled. "I would do that, sure. I don't know if I'll be all that much help to you. I know my way a bit around the theatre scene here in town, but I'm not overly familiar with the younger layer of actors."

"Any help will be appreciated." She pulled a few pieces of

paper out of her sleek grey Coach bag. They were printed emails with cast lists on each one, mailed to her from Fringe Theatre Adventures, the management that oversaw the festival.

I scanned the lists. I had heard of the writer/actor of the zombie show but didn't know much about him. The parody of the Eve Ensler *Vagina Monologues* was created by two fellows newly graduated from Grant MacEwan, and one of their names sounded familiar; he might have been in a freshman English class I'd taught as a sessional a few years ago. Most of my former students were like that, just sort of vague memories, like the shadows left by atomic devastation. A person was here, it has been noted, but that was all. I didn't feel guilty about it; I knew their names while class was in session and I got their papers marked and back to them within a two-class time frame. What more did they want from me?

I looked at the third page, which listed the cast and crew from *Naughty Marietta*, an operetta from the thirties. Marie/ Marietta was being played by Kendra Connor, and War- rington, her saviour/suitor, was Jesse Gervais. I noticed that Micheline was stage-managing it. This must be the show she'd been prepping for during the run of the Shakespeare festival.

"Micheline was the managing director for the Shakespeare festival, during which time Eleanor was killed," I shrugged. "That's the only connection that leaps out at me." Detective Gla- due nodded.

"Yep, that popped up for us as well. She was on her head- set the entire time, supposedly to the fellow in the lighting and sound booth, but she was backstage, near the door that leads to the bell tower."

"So someone really was hanged in the bell tower?"

Detective Gladue looked as if she was warring with herself, which I appreciated as a sign of her humanity. Steve often looked like that while talking to me, and it occurred to me that my curiosity about elements of his job might really wear on him. I promised myself I would try to keep out of his work and offer him a respite from all that from here on in. Just as soon as Denise was out of trouble, that was.

I was so busy promising myself I was going to become June Cleaver that I didn't hear Detective Gladue say something. She was looking at me expectantly, the sort of look you can't just fudge with a non-committal response like "sure" or "maybe" or "if you like that sort of thing." I begged her pardon and asked her to repeat herself.

"I said, it might be better to say he was found hanging, if that clears anything up."

"Eww," was my mature response. Then what she said resonated. "You said HE. Can you tell me who it was?"

Jennifer looked around my tiny apartment holding just the two of us, as if she expected to see Staff Sergeant Keller standing by the mock fireplace. "I don't suppose it will hurt. The name will be made public by the end of the day, anyhow. It was an actor/director named Christian Norgaard. He was in the Shakespeare plays this year, too. Did you know him?"

"Christian?" I was shocked, mostly because we had just seen him downtown at dinner, and there is nothing weirder than having someone you've just seen bursting with life turn up dead the next day or so. "Was he directing the show?"

Jennifer shook her head, and I recollected having seen another name I didn't recognize on the list she had shown me. In fact, come to think of it, Christian's name hadn't been there at all.

"So what was he even doing in the Walterdale?"

Jennifer shrugged. "Twenty-thousand-dollar question there, eclipsed only by 'Who would stab him and then string him up to swing in the bell tower for the entire Fringe-going public and their children to witness?'"

I was struck by the ugliness of the image and the passion with which Detective Gladue spoke of the families who would have witnessed it. She was definitely growing on me.

"If it is any consolation, it sounds as if most of the folks on the Internet think it was an aerial stunt, like when John Ullyatt hangs off the wall as a human fly." Jennifer shook her head, a comment on either the gullibility of the general public or the wackiness of theatre people.

Her humanity was probably why I decided on the spur of the moment to share my suppositions with her, which Steve would probably kick me for. I wasn't supposed to get on the radar with his boss Keller, and so anything I ever mentioned to Steve he managed to weave into the context of something he would arrive at on his own. The trouble was, this wasn't Steve's case and Denise was still in trouble.

"You know, this makes two directors dead."

"Two actors, you mean."

"Well, technically both Eleanor and Christian had some directing chops and plenty of ambition in that vein, to hear talk. The thing is, there is a job hanging on the horizon, at Chautauqua Theatre, due to the sudden death of Oren Gentry."

Even Jennifer Gladue had heard of him. "But he had a heart attack, right? And a big funeral?"

"He was fifty-five. What if it wasn't a natural heart attack? What if this is all about getting hold of that artistic directorship?"

"People killing for a job?"

"This is a theatre town. And it's a great training centre for directors. The university churns out two MFA directors a year. The statistics don't have to get very complex to show there are more directors than solid jobs. Just think how many people are directing Fringe shows, just keeping their hand in, feeding their desires."

"So someone murdered Oren Gentry for his job? Why not Bob Baker?"

"Baker doesn't need theatre, he has the Citadel, the biggest of them all. Oren Gentry dies, leaving the way open for someone with ambition. Then along comes Eleanor Durant, who may have an inside track. She dies, once again clearing the way. And miraculously, it can be blamed on the spurned English prof, keeping the spotlight off anyone in the drama sector. However, something happens and Christian looks like he may have a chance at the job, so Christian has to die."

"This sounds like the plot from a Simon Brett novel," Jennifer scoffed, shaking her head.

"You read Simon Brett?" I asked, delightedly distracted.

"All the Charles Paris novels, and *After Henry*, but I haven't much liked those Mrs. Pargeter ones," she said. "I've sort of moved off him and onto Denise Mina and Christopher Brookmyre. I like the British mysteries the best. They're like mini-vacations."

"Busman's holidays for you, though," I said. Jennifer smiled and suddenly she looked utterly human and like someone I could befriend, even if her loyalty to great mystery writers was in question.

"I bet most cops read crime fiction of one type or another." I thought of Steve and his shelves of Walter Mosley and James Lee Burke. Jennifer Gladue was probably right. I wondered what sort of crime novels Iain McCorquodale read and if I would ever get up the nerve to ask him.

"Okay, so it sounds far-fetched," I admitted. "But it makes a certain amount of sense. Unless there is someone who just doesn't like actors or actors wanting to become directors roaming the city, what other rationale could there be?"

"This is all doing a pretty good job of discrediting your friend Denise. Is there anyone who wants to see harm come to her?"

"I can't imagine who, but on the whole this last murder, if you folks determine it is indeed the same hand that killed both Christian and Eleanor, should exonerate Denise, because I was with her the whole time in question and therefore she has a cast-iron alibi."

"But who knew that?"

I shrugged. "Anyone who saw us together at the Cité Francophone for dinner, or the College St. Jean at the play, or the High Level Diner after can vouch for us."

Jennifer Gladue was shaking her head. "No, that's not what I meant. If we think along the lines that someone was trying to pin their crimes on Denise, which seemed to be working, so why not continue? Why would they kill someone at the Fringe? Because they figured Denise was going to be in the vicinity. So, someone had to think that Denise would be at the Fringe last night."

"And we were Fringing last night, just not at the main site." I shook my head slowly. "You are saying that Christian was killed at the Fringe because the killer wanted to frame Denise for this murder, and the killer therefore believed that Denise would be at *Naughty Marietta.*" Jennifer nodded.

"Or in the vicinity. This whole Bring Your Own Venue isn't something a lot of people have wrapped their minds around. If someone overheard Denise say she was Fringing on Tuesday night, they wouldn't necessarily think to question where. When you think Fringe, you think the epicentre, which is 83 Avenue, right by the Walterdale Theatre. And the minute they heard Tuesday, the plan was activated."

"Man, that's cold."

"That's reality. So," Jennifer Gladue leaned in. "Who knew you would be Fringing on Tuesday?"

I tried to think before I said anything. This wasn't Steve I was talking to; for all I knew, anything I said to Jennifer would come back at me in a courtroom.

"We hadn't even planned to come back on Tuesday; that was sort of a spur-of-the-moment decision while we were buying tickets on the weekend. So, the ticket seller would have known, but I don't think either of us knew her. And besides, she would have known our venue destination." Jennifer was nodding along, as if she was coaxing a child on skates to venture closer to her. "We ran into Louise Williams and Sarah Arnold after we'd bought the tickets, so maybe we chatted about what we were going to see, or whether we were doing a lot of Fringing, that sort of thing. Things are awkward between Denise and Sarah at the moment, so I really don't recall just what was said. I was mostly looking for a way to politely get us away without looking like we were ingoring them. Oh," I said, suddenly remembering the ugly phone call I'd overheard in the washroom of the Varscona Theatre, "there was something that you might want to know." I explained how I couldn't tell who had been speaking on the phone, but that it was obvious to me that she had been talking about Denise, which proved to me at least that someone was keeping tabs on Denise at the Fringe.

Jennifer nodded. "You could be right. It could be someone tailing you two, overhearing 'Tuesday' and going on that. Or it could be absolute coincidence that you and Denise were Fringing the night Christian Norgaard was killed. It may also be completed unrelated to the death of Eleanor Durant, although they were found within a half-mile radius of each other."

I stared at her. She was right. The Queen Elizabeth stairs were only about four blocks from the epicentre of the Fringe, but I never thought of my city in that way. The river valley occupied a different area of my mind, the part that managed nature and exercise. Old Strathcona was housed in the theatre/bistro/great stationery shops section of my pre-frontal cortex. But really, they were so close. I wondered who in the theatre community lived in close proximity. Then it occurred to me, who didn't? The Old Strathcona neighbourhood from Whyte Avenue to the river valley, the Queen Alexandra area on the other side of Whyte Avenue, the Mill Creek section, and even the Richie area on the other side of 99 Street were teeming with artistic types. Heck, even Steve lived along Saskatchewan Drive, the meandering lovely road along the top southern edge of the river valley. About the only shining light that came out of that realization was that one person I knew didn't live in that area: Denise.

Jennifer had poured herself another cup of tea and let me think, which I appreciated. She was really growing on me. Of course, she might be thinking it was some sort of mind game to make me confess, but since I had nothing to confess, I wasn't too worried about that.

"You know, if whoever it is only makes a move when he or she thinks it will damage Denise, what would happen if we were to take Denise out of the equation?"

"What do you mean?"

"Well, if the object of the exercise was simply to frame Denise for murder, wouldn't it be simpler to kill people who had something to do with Denise? Granted, I can see how Eleanor might be connected, since she was having an affair with Kieran, but Christian? I don't see any connection to Denise, unless he too was having an affair with Kieran."

Jennifer smiled drily. "Not that we're aware of."

"Right. So, the minute you put Christian into the equation, you lose Denise as being logical for the murder. She was just supposed to be in the vicinity and already under suspicion, right?"

"I'm not quite sure where you're going with this."

"It gets even clearer if we do add Oren Gentry's death into the mix. The object of killing each of these people is that they stand in the way between the killer and a desired element, the job of artistic director at Chautauqua Theatre. So, if we accept that the killer seems to be acting only behind the screen of Denise's convenient movements, how about we take that camouflage away and have him or her try to make a move in the open?"

"And how do we get rid of Denise?"

"We could get her to go out of town for a week or so, as a break before classes start."

"The Edmonton Police Service frowns upon letting suspects in murder investigations leave town for short vacations," said Jennifer.

"But you know she didn't do it!"

"The murderer shouldn't know that, though, right?" She had me. Pulling Denise out of the mix that way would smack of some sort of police sting. Maybe putting pressure on the other end would be a better idea, anyhow.

"Well, what about upping the ante on the job search for the theatre? Maybe you could approach the board and see if they could make an announcement that they had a short list, or would be coming to a decision very soon. The stakes would get higher, and the time shorter."

"And what do you suggest we do? Just sit in dark corners near the short-listed candidates and wait for someone to pop them off? This is sounding like *Who is Killing the Great Chefs of Europe?*"

"Oh did you read that book? I remember just loving it."

"No, I only saw the movie. I'm a big George Segal fan."

I stared at her. "George Segal? It's the twenty-first century; who is a George Segal fan?"

Jennifer shrugged. "He reminds me of my father."

I shook off the idea of George Segal Gladue and tried to get back to the thread of the conversation. "No, this isn't a farce. I really think, as motives go, this is pretty clear."

"No one kills for a job."

"No? I hear people all the time saying exactly that, 'I'd kill for that job.'"

"Yes, but you work in academe."

She had me there. If even a quarter of the sessionals and adjunct lecturers who supposedly made up two-thirds of the teaching workforce in universities and colleges across the continent actually followed through on their muttered comments about tenure-tracked fulltime staff, there would be a blood bath and the ivory towers would drip red.

So, if it wasn't in order to land Oren's job, why were Eleanor and Christian killed? What else did they have in common besides the fact that they were both actors with aspirations to direct?

Just then my cellphone buzzed twice. I glanced at my text messages, one from Denise and another from Steve, both telling me that she had been at the screening of one of the Metropolitan at the Movies operas. So, she hadn't been jogging, she'd just been out getting some aria. Fine, I could stop worrying about where she was and get back to worrying about who was trying to frame her for murder.

"Was that Denise?"

Jennifer was reading my mind. Maybe all cops could. I was going to really have to watch myself while jaywalking.

"Yeah, just checking in."

"Fine. Well, back to what we were talking about, Eleanor and Christian do not have all that much in common, but they were connected to the Shakespeare festival, they both attended Victoria School for the Arts when they were younger, they both lived in the Old Strathcona area, and if their resumés are to be believed, they both played Viola in productions of *Twelfth Night*?"

I nodded wearily. "Yes, I remember that. A couple of years ago, Cement Theatre did an all-male Shakespeare, to demonstrate how it would have been presented in Elizabethan times. There was a bit of a gripe about it in the editorial section of a couple of papers, the main issue being there are not enough roles for women in theatre to begin with, and by doing an all-male production, even if historically accurate, you denied at least three actresses work. I wasn't sure what side of that argument I was on, because it was really interesting. I guess, if it had been a student production and scores of professional actresses weren't losing work over it, I'd have been totally happy with the experiment."

"Okay, so two Violas are killed. I wonder if that is the link." Jennifer held up her hand to ward off my incredulity. "I just wanted to let you know how ludicrous other people are going to think your purported motive for these murders will sound."

"Really? I think you need to push the situation. At least find out if they already have a short list for the position." I knew I was pleading, but when was I going to get another chance? Steve wasn't going to discuss the case with me, and Iain sure as shooting was not going to be listening. Right here, right now was Denise's best chance to have the police reopen their eyes to seeing the situation without her in the middle of the bull's eye.

Jennifer Gladue stood, and with a questioning nod of her head, took her tea mug into the kitchen and set it in the sink. Returning to my tiny living room, she towered, so I stood up to look her in the eye.

"We are going to follow every lead and take all tips and suggestions as seriously as they deserve to be taken. And that means I will bring up the artistic directorship as a possible motive. I will suggest we take a look at their short list. But that's as much as I can promise you, and I want to underline to you how inadvisable it would be to poke around in this situation yourself, either you or Denise Wolff." For a moment, the cop carapace fell away, and once more I saw the woman I had just started to get to know. "You do not want to get in the way of this murderer, Randy. This person knows their way around a knife. Norgaard's body barely bled after being strung up, but he was stabbed beforehand."

And with that she left me to clean up the rest of the tea stuff.

While I was picking things up, I noticed she had left behind the three cast and crew lists of the shows running at the

Walterdale. I set them on the kitchen table, not sure whether I should just toss them in the recycle or whether she might come back to retrieve them.

Maybe she had brought them for me. What did that mean? It's not like she couldn't get more if she needed them. Maybe they weren't actually important to her investigation. Under the principle of erring on the side of caution, I left them there till I could talk to Steve and find out if they'd be needed.

I putzed around a bit, made myself a peanut butter-and-banana sandwich, hummed a requisite Elvis tune in honour of his favourite concoction, and sat down at the kitchen table.

Unless there is someone around to talk to, I need to read while I eat. As my parents could attest, this is a habit refined over years; way back, I wasn't all that keen on interacting with others even if they were around. I usually kept a book or a magazine tucked by the wall end of the table, right next to my little basket of condiments, but I'd just finished my latest book and hadn't yet started another.

I pulled what was at hand toward me, Jennifer Gladue's cast lists. As I ate my sandwich, I pored over the names and positions of all the people. There were several I could put a name to, but more I didn't know at all.

I went through the zombie show first and realized I had taught one of the leads at Grant MacEwan. I was happy to see she was pursuing her dream of being part of the theatre scene by playing a character named Legless Lucy. I wasn't sure whether this character was supposed to be a drunk or extremely truncated. I didn't recognize any other names on the list.

It was a different story with the operetta cast and crew list. Aside from Micheline as stage director, and Kendra Conner and Jesse Gervais in the leads, there were only two other actors I knew of by name, and neither of them had been involved with the Shakespeare festival, so I didn't feel guilty about neglecting to point them out to Gladue. It wasn't as if I was so caught up in the theatre scene that I knew every name. She should be taking this list to someone like Trevor Schmidt or Taryn or even Kieran to identify the players.

As I ran my finger down the list on the page, it snagged on one name: M. Creely, Set Designer. I wondered how many M. Creelys there were in Edmonton, because I'd bet anything that was Morgana Creely the photographer. I had no idea she was into set design, but I supposed that a photographer's eye was every bit as artistic in setting a stage for a static vision as a stage designer's had to be for designing the backdrop for a show. I picked up a pencil and drew an arrow with a little star and a question mark next to her name, intending to mention to Steve to tell Jennifer Gladue that there had been another person connected to the Walterdale show and backstage from the Shakespeare circle, albeit tangentially. I doubted that Morgana had been down at the festival site more than three days, total.

Of course, if she was expanding from photographer to set designer, who was to say she wasn't hoping to hang out her shingle as an artistic director? I wondered if Jennifer Gladue was going to take my theory seriously and check into Oren Gentry's death. It would take a police requisition to reopen that file, and I wondered if anything could be done, as I knew from having seen the urn on the stage that there was nothing remaining of Gentry to test for unknown poisons that would simulate a heart attack.

I had the feeling Jennifer had just been putting me in my place, milking me for whatever I might possibly know and placating me with the pretense of taking what I said seriously. Denise was still her main suspect, I felt, and who knows, maybe the timelines would show that my best friend could have stabbed and hanged a six-foot-tall actor in a relatively public place a few minutes before picking me up for dinner and a play. Or maybe she'd done it while pretending to use the ladies' room in the restaurant.

I pushed the papers away, frustrated that no one was stepping up to help us. Secreting Denise away would work to lure out the killer, I knew it would. Why couldn't Jennifer Gladue see that?

I stopped, frozen, my hand still flat on the table. There was something that would work even better.

36.

Denise wasn't hard to convince, which probably spoke more to her level of despair and frustration than to the solidity of my plan.

We were making ourselves as visible as possible in the Next Act restaurant, which was no hardship because I adored their burgers and side salads. While Denise picked her way through a meal-sized salad, I laid out the bones of the plan that had struck me.

"I was trying to explain to the detective how your being out of the limelight would make things more problematic for whoever is responsible for all of this, but really, we need you to be even more visible." I waved my strawberry and pea sprout–laden fork at her for emphasis. "You need to announce that you are applying for Oren Gentry's job."

Denise looked shocked for a moment, and then cocked her head to the side. "My qualifications match Sarah's, I suppose. Won't this play into the hands of the person trying to frame me for the murders, though?"

"Well, you're already being framed as the slighted woman, though I am not sure why you'd supposedly kill Christian, unless you suspected him of an affair with Kieran as well." Denise laughed abruptly.

"Not likely. Kieran may have been a swinger but it wasn't both ways. Christian would not have been his type."

"Okay then, so we make whoever is doing this see you as less of a scapegoat to tie all the blame to, and more of a rival to eliminate on the way."

"But we are going to figure out a way to be a target without being killed in the fallout, right?"

"Of course, right. We will be ready for anything, because we'll be expecting it. And you won't be on your own. I am going to be with you the whole time, starting now. The minute we start this, anything could happen."

"And what's to stop whoever it is from killing us both?"

"We are quick and clever and anticipating an attack, which is at least one less attribute than the other victims probably had."

"And we're going to tell Steve?"

"We can't do that. I mean, I will let him know where I am and all that, if he asks, but I can't detail what we're about to do. For one thing, he'd try to stop us, because it could be construed as impeding a police investigation, and he'd also pooh-pooh our ideas, which would make us second-guess ourselves. The thing is, if we're going to do this, it has to be totally focused or else no one is going to buy it."

"Yes, we are going to be giving the performance of our lives, to an audience of professional performers. The hardest audience of all," Denise shook her head. "I'm not sure I'm even up to it. Maybe the reason I went the academic route to Shakespeare was my innate knowledge that I couldn't make it on the stage."

"Or maybe it was your profound and complex appreciation for the plays that transcended the need to hear the words out loud?"

Denise smiled. "You're right. It could be that." She took a sip of her pint. "Okay, so how do you see your plan unfolding?"

"My theory is, you submit your application and resumé, and we seed the message to a few different people. It shouldn't take long before everyone in the theatre community hears about it. After all, they're mostly all still congregating for Fringe shows, and the week of shows chosen to be held over will continue to bring people here all next week. Once people know, someone is going to come looking for you."

"But several people could come looking for me, to congratulate me, to talk me out of it, to just wonder why I want to change careers midstream. How will we know which one is the murderer?"

I laughed in spite of myself. "Well, I think the knife will be the giveaway."

Denise laughed, too. I suppose you couldn't really get Shakespeare without an appreciation of the darker sort of humour. "Yes, I can see that. I was hoping, though, for a bit more lead."

"That's the best I've got. We bait him, lure him, and catch him, then we turn him over to the police, and you get your life back."

"Would that it were so easy." Denise lifted her glass in a mock toast. "Here's to foiling evildoers."

I raised my glass to clink it with hers. "To quote Hamlet, and who doesn't, 'The play's the thing wherein I'll catch the conscience of the king!'"

"Don't forget, he also kills an old man by mistake, drives his girlfriend to suicide, has his two best friends killed in his place, and brings about the end of home rule to his kingdom. I wouldn't be so quick to model myself on the great Dane."

"If you don't want to do it, just tell me now."

"I didn't say that."

"Because I think it's the only way we can find this killer."

"Well, there is another way, but I might be in jail long before it happens."

"What's that?"

Denise looked grim. "We just sit back and arrest whoever ends up in the Chautauqua job."

"If killing all the competition is their way of getting the position, who will be left to buy tickets?"

"Okay, I'm in. Where do we start?"

"First off, you send your resumé in to Chautauqua. Then we mention it to everyone we run into. What are you doing?"

Denise was clicking a few things on her iPhone, which she'd pulled from her small purse. "I've got a current CV. Give me a few minutes and I can whomp up a cover letter and we can send it from here."

I left her to compose her letter on the tiny screen and went to use the lavatory. It was a small one, and bit of squish to get past the sink to the two stalls, but I was on my own in there, so the problem was averted. The polished silver of the stall walls was nice and kept graffiti to a minimum, which was just as well, since it was usually either the religious, the mundane or the profane in Edmonton washrooms. Clever people were saving their bon mots for Twitter these days.

I washed up and returned to our booth. On the way, I noted that the place had filled up with some people I recognized. Three or four of the actors from Stewart Lemoine's play were in the large booth in the corner. Louise and Micheline were sitting at the bar together. The fellow who had been Benedick in the silly Shakespeare we'd seen was sitting with John Kirkpatrick at one of the tall tables. Everyone came to the Next Act. Eleanor's and Christian's murderer was probably here right now.

That thought made me shiver as I slid in to the booth across from Denise.

She looked up at me, raised an eyebrow, and hit a button on the screen of her phone.

"I just sent my application for artistic director to Chautauqua Theatre. I hope you know what we're doing now."

So did I.

37.

We managed to chat with Louise and Micheline on our way to the till without making it look too targeted. I thought John Kirkpatrick also overheard Louise's incredulous "You're applying?" So there were two streams of information heading out. We walked through the Fringe site to maximize our visibility and see if we could find anyone else to inform.

That's the thing about Edmonton. You can't go anywhere without running into at least three people you know, and this was no exception. We chatted briefly with Jim de Felice, who was buying a green onion cake before heading to a one-man show by a fellow from Victoria that was said to be a hit of the Fringe. He wished Denise all the best in applying for the job, saying the "expansion of thought" might be a good thing for the theatre, which was really big of him, seeing as how he'd taught most of the directors in this town.

We talked with Belinda Cornish and Ron Pederson, who were coming out of the doors of the Fringe offices. I was effusive to Belinda about her performance while Ron and Denise spoke. He had been one of her students, it turned out, when he was first at the university.

"A first-rate mind, you know," Denise confided as we walked away. "He'd have made a great academic if he hadn't figured out how funny he was."

I laughed. "I wonder if he thinks he's missing anything?"

"Oh, I doubt it. There is a certain level of performer exhibitionist in all teaching academics. Otherwise, you'd move into a pure research stream and it wouldn't be difficult. The university certainly can stick another sessional lecturer in front of a class more easily than they can attract research grant monies."

"You mean you don't have to teach if you don't want to?"

"If you brought an endowed chair with you, you could write your own ticket," Denise said. "The point I was trying to make, though, is that most people do want to teach. They are performers. They hop and skip and trill and persuade their students to love the material they love. Because, by creating more acolytes and devotees, they assure themselves that theirs is a useful endeavour, that they have not wasted their lives writing esoteric articles about Herrick or Fowles or Shaw."

"And you think there's a chance they have?"

"Have what?"

"Wasted their lives?"

"Oh, there's a great chance we're all going the wrong direction, Randy. We could be in a great galactic experiment, running mazes against other worlds, rising and falling in relation to the reagents and parameters of the gods."

"Who's sounding like Hamlet now?"

She laughed. "You're right. No need to get philosophical when someone could be trying to kill you. A much better idea is to just get your runners laced."

By this time we were close to the parking lot where Denise had left the car, so we left the Fringe site and headed for my apartment. We had decided that if we were going to be serious about being vigilant, we needed to maintain a connected front. We might be independent and strong twenty-first-century women, but we weren't idiots. This was no time to be alone. I was going to pack up a few days' worth of clothes and stay over with Denise at her place.

I left a message for Steve, who wasn't picking up his phone, telling him I'd be at Denise's and contactable by cellphone. Denise watered my paltry violets while I tossed some underwear, makeup, a couple of tee-shirts, sweatpants, and another pair of jeans into a duffle bag. I grabbed a hoodie from the back of the bedroom door, my laptop, my cellphone and computer cords, and the book by my bed. I checked the date on the milk in the fridge and figured it would be okay. One quick glance at the window locks, and I was ready to head out.

Denise suggested stopping for groceries on our way to her place. "After all, if we're under siege, we don't want to be running out of muesli." Maybe it was a reaction to the stress we were under, or just the word "muesli," but I got a fit of the giggles as we entered the grocery store's gaping doors. I was dabbing at my eyes with a fuzzy tissue from my pocket and walked right into someone coming out the other way.

"Excuse me." I heard exasperation and annoyance in the voice. "Randy?" I cleared my eyes and looked directly into the face of Taryn Creighton.

"Taryn! I am so sorry. I really need to look where I'm going, because I'm not that coordinated even when I am operating on all cylinders. Are you okay?"

"No worries. I wasn't watching oncoming traffic either. Hello." She spoke with her head cocked to one side and I recalled my manners.

"Taryn, this is Denise. Denise Wolff, Taryn Creighton. Taryn and I met in a research methodologies class back in our first year of grad studies."

Denise smiled and gave a small salute, since Taryn's hands full of bags meant shaking hands was a no go. "I recall that class as being the only thing that got me through my bibliography."

"Yes, it was good for that," Taryn nodded. "And you're the Shakespeare specialist now, correct?"

Denise nodded and I jumped in. "Taryn is the artistic director of Black Box, and teaches scene work over at Grant MacEwan, too."

"Right. I have seen your work and really enjoyed it," Denise chimed in.

Taryn smiled awkwardly, the way you do when you have a hard time receiving compliments. "Well, there's ice cream at the bottom of one of these, so I should be going. Nice to see you, Randy, and to meet you, Denise."

We waved as she left, and Denise said, "We should have mentioned my application to her, too."

"I was thinking the same thing, but how do you just fit that into a conversation without being too obvious?"

Denise was putting apples into a plastic bag after examining each one to be sure it would be a perfect prop for a remake of Snow White. "I know."

"Oh well, she's bound to hear about it pretty quickly, as networked into the theatre scene as she is. She already knew who you were."

"This is a small town posing as a big city. Everyone has heard of everyone."

"Ha, even the city is an actor. I wonder if Edmonton would like to direct someday."

We tried to stave off the tension by shopping as if we were planning an extended slumber party, which I guess we were. Over a base of good-for-you stuff, like apples, bananas, grapes, a large yam, and a bag of broccoli went a tray of croissants, a bag of cheese pretzels, two tubes of liverwurst, three bags of rice cakes, a block of cheddar and a small wheel of brie, a carton of orange juice, a dozen eggs, two tubs of greek yoghurt with honey, a frozen lasagna and, indeed, a box of muesli.

"That should do us for a bit." Denise smiled at our purchases piled on the conveyor belt. I offered to help pay, but she refused to let me on the grounds that as it stood, she was the more likely to have steady work in the fall. That sort of hurt. After all, for all we knew, she was going to be locked away wearing an orange jumpsuit this fall, and she still had better likelihood of employment. I really had to get cracking on finding a full-time gig, preferably one with benefits and a pension.

At any rate, I could help schlep things to the car, so I loaded up with bags on the end of either arm, leaving Denise just the bag with eggs and pastries. We drove west out of the parking lot towards Belgravia, the genteel neighbourhood in which Denise had purchased a condo on the day she received tenure.

Belgravia was just south of the university's west end, and as such, it was filled with overflow professors who couldn't find a house in Windsor Park. It bordered the river valley on one end and the LRT on the other, and ended at the erstwhile University Farm, which was now turning into South Campus. The folks of Belgravia had attempted to prevent the LRT from coming so close to their neighbourhood, either because it would bring riff-raff to their streets or lure their children downtown to dens of iniquity, but instead it just increased the value of their proper-ties, which was just as well, because it became very inconvenient for them to enter or exit their neighbourhood. Still, with a mix of single properties, high-level condos, one elementary school, and a church tucked in among mature trees and landscaped gar-dens, it seemed like a very restful place to come home to.

Denise's condo was along a curvy road that wound its way through the north part of the neighbourhood. While it looked like a classy four-storey walk up from the front, it was actually a series of fourplexes with underground parking. Each unit was made up of two storeys with a central staircase and an elevator from the parkade. Denise had the top two floors on the west end of the line, giving her kitchen a tree-house effect from its win-dow. From her bedroom on the upper floor she could see over the treetops all the way to the river valley, which curved south at that point before heading west again past Fort Edmonton and further toward Devon, and southwesterly on towards Abraham Lake and its source.

I sat at her breakfast bar while she unpacked our siege supplies, twirling lazily between her southern view from the living room, all dappled sunlight through leaves mixed with a prism or two she had hung in the window, and her kitchen view to the west.

"This really is a lovely home you have made here."

"Thank you, Randy. I know it's not as funky bohemian as yours, but I find it so peaceful. 'One touch of nature makes the whole world kin,' as Willie would say. Even in the winter, it feels like a bower in here, because those spruce trees across the way are so rich and green against all the white."

"And I like the fact that you're up off the main floor. We can sit here safely and not be surprised by whoever comes looking for you."

"Oh, it's a very secure building. I do feel very safe here."

"Good. Because we've already started the ball rolling. If we're correct, a murderer is going to come looking for you."

"What if we're wrong, though? Won't my declaring I want the job of artistic director suddenly give the police the motive they were missing for all the crimes they are considering me for?"

I stopped and looked at her. "Oh god. You think? No, they wouldn't think that because you will have me to tell them it was my idea."

"And you think they'll believe you all of a sudden about that when they haven't given your other testimonials as to my character all that much credence? I don't know, Randy," Denise leaned her face on her hands, looking pensive and tense, "this may have not been such a good idea."

"Okay, you tell me what to do and I will do it. Either we continue as we've been going, and I send out a couple of emails about how you've applied for this job, and isn't it exciting, or we send a couple of quickie emails to people like Louise to say that it was all a joke or performance art or something, and you didn't mean it, and we sit here and eat all the croissants."

"Oh, I think we should have a girls' night anyhow, and what the heck. Let's leave what we've done so far and not push it any further. I've put in the application, we've told a couple of people; let's see how efficient the machine really is. I should get a few phone calls in the next day or so to confirm the rumours. We can take it from there. God knows nothing else is happening to get me off the hook."

I got out my laptop and sent a quick email to Steve, giving him the gist of what we were doing, just to avoid the scenario that Denise had painted of adding grist to the police theories that she was their culprit. I then posted a couple of messages into the social networking ether, saying how proud I was of my friend Denise and her decision to tackle new challenges. We figured that coy messages like that would add fuel to whatever curiosity there might be out there, and that gossip from Louise would likely end up with more traction as a result.

It wasn't as if I had all that many followers, but most of the folks from the summer's adventure in Shakespeare were on my list, as well as a select few from academe with crossovers. Linda from the Black Widows must have been online simultaneously to my post, because she obligingly retweeted it to her thousand-plus followers with a YGG, meaning, I hoped, You Go, Girl, not the airport code for an aerodrome on Saltspring Island.

So it was out there, the rumour. And we were in here. And now all we needed to do was wait.

38.

Although the sun set earlier every day in August, in Edmonton that still factored out to being light out until around 9:45 p.m., and the long exposure of sunshine seemed to make the day stretch out very long and languorous. Denise and I busied ourselves cutting up the fruit we'd bought into bite-sized pieces and creating a fabulous salad onto which we dolloped Greek yoghurt. Eating out of serving bowls, we sat on her expansive leather sofa and watched several episodes of *Gilmore Girls,* Denise's secret vice. I had never seen the program, so while the loquacious single mother and her precocious daughter drank coffee and nattered sixteen to the dozen, Denise was keeping up a running commentary about who was in love with whom, why Rory's friend couldn't tell her mother she was playing in a band, the original pact of Friday night dinners Lorelei had agreed to in order to have her snarky parents pay for her daughter's education, and that Kurt was really quite a comic genius.

I was meanwhile falling in love with the magical town the

show was set in and wishing for a world where everyone could find a job that would keep them in glorious veranda-clad Victorian houses and surrounded by eccentric but loyal friends. It seemed like a dream come true, and I could understand why Denise would be so taken with it. All of the mother's former loves still seemed to be pleasant and friendly, which was how Denise's world worked, too. It made me wonder what Denise's relationship with her family was like.

Since it seemed to take her mind off being the focus of both a police investigation and a murderer's target, I let her play video historian, showing me one or two episodes of each season, explaining jumps in the situation for the two lead characters, which seemed to change only in terms of Rory's school levels. We opened a bottle of wine, pulled out the cheese and rice cakes, and were well into season four by the time we noticed the sun had set. We had nothing to do the next day except watch more television, so we decided to call it a night.

Denise cleared away the evidence of our feasting and I helped her load her dishwasher. By eleven, we were both brushed and flossed and tucked in bed. Somehow, it seemed safer not to close the bedroom doors. Even though I couldn't see Denise from my vantage in her guest bedroom, I could hear her clearly as she called "Good night, Randy."

I was pretty sure that even by Edmonton rumour-mill standards, one day was too short a time for anything much to get going, so I was pretty easy about going to sleep. That thought, along with the amazingly comfortable pillows Denise had invested in for her guests, put me out pretty quickly. Or maybe it was the wine. Anyhow, I didn't recall tossing about much before I didn't recall anything.

When the noise came, it took me a minute or two to get my bearings.

The alarm clock wasn't in the right place for my instinctive check, and as I searched the room for a digitized light, I realized I wasn't at home in my bed. The cylinders spun into place; at the same moment I figured out I was in Denise's guest room, I read on the bedside clock that it was 3:04 a.m.

The lump in my stomach made me certain that whatever sound had woken me was real. I slid out of bed as noiselessly as possible, thanking Denise's keen foresight to have thick carpeting on the second floor of her condo.

As I reached the door of my bedroom, so did Denise. I could see her clearly, thanks to the nightlight plugged into a low outlet in the hall. Looking willowy and anachronistically Victorian in a long, white cotton nightgown, she had a finger to her lips and was pointing downstairs. She had her cellphone in the other hand, clicking it to silent. She handed it to me, and mouthed "Steve." I nodded, input his number into her contacts, and began to text him, letting him know the basics, that we were in Denise's condo and had heard a noise downstairs, and the address.

Craning for another sound, we stood at the top of the stairs, as I shielded the gleam of the cellphone's face so as not to give away our presence. Steve texted back almost immediately, making me thankful for the first time that my boyfriend was such a light sleeper.

"Lock yourselves in Denise's ensuite NOW." I showed her

the text, and she nodded and led me back across the hall and into the bathroom that lay beyond her walk-through closet. She closed and locked the door as quietly as possible and then, for good measure, reached over to pull a towel off the rack and place it at the bottom of the door before turning on the light.

I texted Steve back. "We are in the bathroom. Now what?"

"Now you wait till we get there."

I held the phone for Denise to read and she nodded. We didn't talk; we barely moved. I looked around surreptitiously for anything we could use as a weapon against an attack, but aside from a decorative plunger and a metal rod that held back-up toilet rolls, there wasn't much. I pointed at them both, and Denise grimly smiled as she removed the rolls and stacked them on the toilet tank. She handed me the plunger, which was chrome-handled and looked as if it had never been used for the purpose for which it had been bought. She gripped the toilet roll holder, and the two of us stood there in silence, wondering what sort of person was creeping about on the floor below, whether they'd managed to climb the stairs without our hearing, and whether even now they were on the other side of the door to our crowded little sanctuary.

Denise's phone lit up again. Steve was texting to find out if there was a silent way to get into the condo. His universal fob could get him into the front door or the car park, apparently.

Denise quickly texted him back with the information that a spare key to the condo was in a magnetized box under the back bumper of her little cream Volkswagen Bug. Somehow, just knowing Steve was in the building made us feel better. Even though we stood there gripping hands and listening quietly, neither of us seemed quite as tense as we had been just moments earlier.

All of a sudden, a great many noises seemed to happen at once, so that it was hard later to figure out what had happened first and what next. We heard sirens coming down the street, a strange popping noise, and then a knock on the bathroom door followed by Steve's voice saying, "Randy? Denise? You can unlock the door, it's me, Steve."

We opened the door to find him standing there in his leather jacket with a pyjama top tucked into his jeans. The lights were on in Denise's bedroom and in the hall beyond. What was most odd was that the drapes along one side of the bedroom window seemed to have been sucked out through the open hole, and the screen was leaning against the wall below. We were four floors up. Surely no one had left through that window.

Most frightening was that whether or not he had left that way, someone had disarranged Denise's window treatment, meaning whoever had been in the condo had indeed been right outside the bathroom door. If they hadn't disturbed our sleep with the original noise, they'd have made it right up to her bedside undetected.

That thought must have occurred to Denise at the same moment, because she sank on to the cedar chest at the end of her bed, still clutching the toilet roll holder. The sirens had stopped, though flashing red and blue and white lights were coming in the window.

Jennifer Gladue entered the bedroom. Idly, I wondered how

many people were in Denise's condo at the moment. Steve left my side, after squeezing my shoulders, to confer with her. I edged over to sit with Denise.

After several minutes, both of them came to talk to us. Diplomatically, they crouched down to speak at our level. One good thing had come from this scare, I thought. The police were treating Denise as a victim rather than a suspect now.

"There is a bit of a mess downstairs, but nothing that can't be put right. Thing is, we'd like the scene of crime folks to come and give it a lookover, and they're on their way. I know it's late, but how would you like to get dressed and come down to let them know what is the same and what looks different to you?" Steve sounded as gentle as if he was speaking to a child, and I wondered just how spooked we appeared.

Denise nodded, and while I went with Steve to the guest room, Jennifer Gladue offered to stand guard while Denise changed, because no one could touch a doorknob to close the doors till the fingerprint guys came with their messy powder.

Pretty soon we were all downstairs and Denise was making coffee for a collection of people, including two very taciturn scene-of-crime people who were most interested in the French doors to Denise's balcony.

"So we thought it would create enough flux to draw out the murderer if I announced I was in the running for the artistic directorship," Denise explained to Jennifer Gladue, who was stirring sugar into her coffee at the breakfast bar next to Iain McCorquodale, who was drinking his black and disapprovingly. Steve was leaning against the stainless steel range, smiling slightly in the way he had when he was being particularly indulgent.

"Let me guess, this was Randy's idea, right?"

I glowered at him. "Well, it seems to have worked, hasn't it?"

"It almost worked too well, don't you think? You two came within a hair's breath of being victims four and five."

"Or five and six," I countered.

"What?"

"She thinks Oren Gentry, the former artistic director, was the first victim," Jennifer Gladue offered. Steve's head swivelled over to her.

"You knew about this?"

"I had no idea of the decoy plans. I knew about Randy's theories of someone killing the great directors of Edmonton."

Iain grinned suddenly. "I loved that movie," he shared. Jennifer nodded her agreement. Steve shook his head in exasperation and was going to say something he'd probably regret, but right then the scene-of-crime fellows came back downstairs and announced that they were finished. Steve saw them to the door. It took him a few minutes to return, which Jennifer and Iain filled by talking about George Segal movies.

"What made the noise that woke us up?" I asked Denise, who had been busy with a scene-of-crime girl taking notes of everything she said and taking pictures to correspond with whatever she'd written.

"The concrete gnome on my deck. I had moved it to the corner of the mat I have out there, to force down the curl that's been happening. I guess it was masked by a shadow, so whoever broke in climbed over the side of the balcony and tipped it over on the way to the French doors."

"You have a gnome on your balcony?"

"It's from my parents' garden. When my folks downsized a few years ago, they asked me to come and take whatever I wanted from my childhood. I took that tea wagon there and the bedside lamps in the room you're using and the garden gnome. I used to love them when I was little, and I was surprised later in life when I realized how kitschy they were considered to be. My mother, who has really exquisite taste, had an ironic streak in her that was capable of seeding her garden with gnomes. I kept it to remind myself that people have hidden depths, I guess."

"Well, good thing you did. That gnome probably saved our lives."

Steve came back into the suite and gestured for us to join him in the living room. Denise and Jennifer and I sat on the couch, Iain leaned against the mantel and Steve sat in an overstuffed chair in the corner, close to the now firmly closed French doors.

"Consensus is that the intruder or intruders climbed up the side of the building to the balcony and came in through the French doors, which really should have been locked. They then proceeded to explore the main floor, mostly Denise's den. You confirmed with the scene-of-crime people that papers on your desk seemed a bit out of place, and there are smudges on your keyboard rather than finger prints, indicating someone wearing gloves woke up your computer, attempted a few possible passwords, and then gave up.

"Nothing in the kitchen has been touched, from which we

can assume they came already armed with whatever weaponry they intended to use. There are clear finger and palm prints from both of you on various drawers, and no overlay smudging. Now, possibly you made a noise at this point, luring them upstairs, but if they weren't armed, the default would have been to pick up a handy knife along the way." Steve looked grim. "So, we can assume that whoever stood outside the ensuite door, wearing a men's size 8.5 athletic shoe, had his or her own knife."

Denise shuddered. Steve went on.

"Either the noise of me entering the suite or the sirens were enough to spook the intruder, who chose to depart via the bedroom window. The curtains were used as a rope, allowing for a lesser drop back to the balcony below and then down the way he'd come up."

"But that's two storeys down, even at the balcony level. That's a heck of a drop."

Steve nodded at me. "And it's a heck of a climb, but not impossible. There are slight markings on the ridge of railing, and Denise stated she hadn't hung a window box there. We're assuming it was a grappling hook tossed up to the balcony with a pretty accomplished hand."

"So you look for a theatre director who is a mountain climber," I offered, more than a little excitedly. "Or an aerialist."

"Or anyone who came up through the ranks of stage tech," said Denise wearily. "Most of the stage crew in Shakespeare's time were former sailors, used to riggings and rope climbing. That's why it's considered unlucky to whistle in a theatre. Sailors used a complex system of whistles to determine which sail to raise or lower, and whistling backstage could get you a sandbag landing on your head as the backdrop for the next scene went shooting past you up into the rafters."

"Well, we may be able to confirm it is a person from the the-atre world who is responsible, given the evidence of rope and cable knowledge," offered Jennifer Gladue.

"Surely we already know it's a person from the theatre world," I said.

"Motive would indicate that," Jennifer nodded, "but we have to establish evidence to back up that motive or we have nothing."

"Oh, right." The best part of hearing her talk that way, espe-cially in front of Steve and Iain, was the way it showed she was thinking of someone other than Denise. Well, I guessed by now all three of them had erased Denise from their list of suspects, which was our primary goal.

Now, to stay alive till they caught the real culprit.

It was as if Steve was reading my mind.

"You may have managed to prove to us that we need to be broadening the scope of our investigation, but I cannot stress enough how problematic you've made things. Now, in addi-tion to looking for a killer, we are obliged to protect you against another crime. And, even though the speed with which you summoned aid might spook the murderer into assuming your whole announcement was a set-up, they may not be able to leave that alone. So, your help in this case is officially not required. Is that understood? No more sleuthing. No more innuendo. No more cryptic announcements. You, Denise, will officially with-draw your application tomorrow. You, Randy, will contact every person you spoke with, and make up some way to tell them you were wrong, and Denise is not applying." He looked as fierce as he could, which was hard, because he was by nature good-hearted, but he almost managed to get a Staff Sergeant Keller-in-a-good-mood look to him. "And then you are going to stay here, with an hourly patrol, until we get to the bottom of things."

"But that could be days," I said.

"Weren't you planning for days?" Steve smiled grimly.

"Trust us, Randy," said Jennifer, a bit milder than Steve. "We do know what we're doing."

And after that, they were gone. Denise gathered up the coffee mugs, and I got out her spray cleaner and some paper towels from under the sink to tackle the fingerprint powder near the doorknobs and along the bannister up the stairs. The sun was almost up, anyhow, and we were too wired to sleep.

By 7:30, everything was set to rights and we were back in front of the television, eating big bowls of muesli and longing to be living alongside Lorelei and Rory in Starr's Hollow, where no one broke into your home and tried to kill you.

39.

Even when a place is two storeys tall, beautifully appointed and comfortable, with two bathrooms, wifi, a full pantry, and good company, if you cannot choose to come and go, it is a prison. Denise had completed all three of her syllabi and called the bookstore to ensure that her book orders were stocked. She'd organized her first week's lecture notes, created a new PowerPoint for her third-year Shakespeare class, and sorted out the seminar for the honours group she had agreed to oversee.

I had managed to get Valerie to email me the timetable for Grant MacEwan and sorted out a mythical syllabus for both a Monday/Wednesday/Friday fifty-minute class and a Tuesday/ Thursday eighty-minute class, just in case I was tapped to teach. I was checking my voicemail obsessively, for news either from the chair of the English department or from Steve to tell us they had caught the killer. So far there was no word from either. Steve called at around seven o'clock each evening to give us an update on where they were, and Denise kept a running timer on when the police cruiser went by.

"My neighbours must think someone dreadful has moved into the block," she said.

"Either that or they are all sending commendations down to City Hall for upping the police presence in their community. Never underestimate the calming effect a cruiser can have on the average citizen."

"Does that make me a shifty character, then? Do you think I was a criminal in a former life and this is residual resonances of those attitudes?"

"Ha! If you were a criminal in a former life, it would have been an Iago or a MacHeath, you're that complex a thinker. No, I don't think you're venal in your thinking. I think you're over-thinking, that's all."

"God, I wish I could go out for a walk."

"Me too."

"Why don't you ask Steve tonight if he thinks it would be a bad idea."

"If he thought it was a good idea, he'd have let us go out ages ago."

"Are you sure? Maybe he's just telling us to stay put so he doesn't have to worry about us fidgeting with his investigation anymore. It might just be more convenient for him to have us shelved for the nonce."

I halfway agreed with Denise. It had been three days. Security installers had come and gone. We were off the map, according to the social media sites. Denise was no longer a contender for the crown, so whatever lists the murderer was checking no longer had her name on them. Hell, we'd already been menaced; maybe that was enough. Now that we knew our place and had acquiesced to not pursuing the gold ring of artistic directorship, life would be fine.

"What I don't get is how whoever is doing this doesn't see that by landing the role of the heir to Oren Gentry, they automatically set themselves up as the killer. They may as well be signing a confession as a contract with the Chautauqua board."

She had a point.

"Well, maybe they're banking on the fact that people won't connect the dots."

"We did."

"Then maybe we're not out of the woods yet."

"Okay, so no walk." Denise slid open the door of her entertainment console. "Have you ever seen *Joan of Arcadia*?"

Another day slid by, and the frustrations the television teen was having with talking to god in various forms mirrored our own. When the intercom rang announcing Detective Gladue, Denise leapt to put the kettle on. We were honestly that delighted to have company and a change in the pattern.

We settled her into a corner of Denise's loveseat and perched, expectant, wanting to know anything we could about what was happening in the outside world. Jennifer Gladue was obviously revelling in being the centre of attention, even with a captive audience.

"I thought I should pop by and update you on what is going on. Steve said he was going to come by later this evening, Randy, but things are getting a little kooky at work. Maybe it's the weather, or just the end of a season making the cranks want to catch up on things, but we're getting loads of fights on Whyte Avenue and complaints about noise levels and neighbours. It's eating into the regular policing, if you see what I mean."

I did. Having been so long with Steve, I had come to appreciate just how much we take our police force for granted. Most people in town never have any interaction with the police at all, unless they slide into another car on Gateway Boulevard or find their patio window shattered and their laptop gone. But the Edmonton Police Service are there, keeping the pot on simmer when it wants to boil over, walking the beat, smiling, nodding, riding bikes and Segways, watching, reacting quickly, and smoothing things back down, driving the streets, only occasionally turning on the lights and the sirens and setting nerves a-jitter. So, I could believe Jennifer when she spoke of crazy season. Behaviour, like the weather, came in waves, and if they couldn't quite explain it, the police could certainly sense it, and usually better than the rest of us. It was their job to keep their finger on the pulse of the city, and their job to make sure the city took its vitamins.

Although she had once dated a reporter, Denise had certainly spent enough time with Steve and me to develop a more muted sense of police procedure and attitude. I could tell she was slightly in awe of Jennifer Gladue, which probably had a lot to do with the detective's visible holster under her thick, cotton-weave blazer. It was probably a taser and not a handgun she was armed with, but I could understand her desire to feel self-reliant and protected. In fact, it made me feel more protected just having her there with her weapon under her armpit, like a chick tucked under a hen's wing.

"We have been questioning everyone connected to the Shakespeare festival who was also involved with a Fringe show this year, and especially those with directing credits on their resumés."

"We need an Edmonton theatrical Venn diagram," Denise mused, and Jennifer and I laughed.

"That's it exactly. Our suspect base is where the intersects happen."

"Has anything been done about seeing whether Oren Gentry was murdered or not?" I pushed, trying not to sound like the crazy conspiracy theory lady.

"I've put it on the board, but as he was cremated, there is no exhumation possibility. I am waiting to get the autopsy notes, or medical notes if there was no autopsy." She reacted to my raised eyebrows. "If someone has a pre-existing condition and they die, seemingly of that known cause, there would be little reason to consider it a suspicious death. We don't autopsy everyone, you know. The provincial medical examiner would end up with a pre-existing condition of her own."

So we could only hope that someone had been suspicious or at least thorough in their notes prior to Gentry's death. I was sure he was the reason and the start of all this, and I wasn't going to let it go easily.

Denise offered Jennifer more tea and said casually, as she was pouring, "You don't have any idea how much longer we're going to have to stay put, do you?"

"We don't have everything back from the lab vis-à-vis foot-print analysis, etc., but we're pretty confident that whoever was in your condo the other night was the same person who strung Christian Norgaard up in the Walterdale cupola and hid Eleanor Durant's body under the Queen Elizabeth stairs. We're hoping we can count on you to remain here, under general surveillance, as a safety measure, for at least another day or so." She stood up, putting her teacup carefully back on one of Denise's coasters showing pictures of the Stratford Festival. "Well, I had better get back to it. Thanks for your time."

We watched her walk down the front path to the cruiser she had parked in front of Denise's building. Time. We had nothing but time.

40.

We watched three episodes of the second season of *Joan of Arcadia* before calling it a night. Steve hadn't been able to come by, but he had called around nine, mostly to check up on us, but being deliberately chatty about the mundanities of his day to set me at ease. Denise and I had made popcorn for supper, neither of us feeling up to much more.

When we were ready for bed, all scrubbed up and teeth brushed, we stood in our pajamas at our respective bedroom doors for a few minutes, not quite wanting to break off into solitude.

"Oh this is silly, isn't it?" Denise laughed, a bit forced. "Imagine two grown women afraid to go to bed."

"Well, it's not without cause."

"But we're being watched by the police and there are alarms on all the windows now, which I will probably be setting off accidentally for years to come."

"You're right. We are safe. Sweet dreams." I turned to go into the guest bedroom.

"Same to you, Randy. And thanks for being here with me."

"Any time, Denise." After all, that's what friends were for.

Despite our shared fretfulness, it didn't take me long to fall asleep. I had taken a couple of painkillers to stave off a headache that all that television had induced, and the pills probably added to the soporific for me.

I might have caught two or three hours' sleep before being woken by a noise in the hall. My heart was beating like a tambourine somewhere in the region of my clavicle. I convinced my body to move quietly out from under the covers, though all I wanted to do was freeze where I was, listening for another sound.

There was nothing to grab by way of a weapon, so I took one of Denise's thick pillows as a possible shield against the killer's knife-wielding skills. I crept to the door of my bedroom, and put my hand on the doorknob.

It was like gearing up to pull off a bandage. I took a deep breath and yanked the door open. By the glow of the hall nightlight I could see a figure creeping toward the stairs. The noise I had made stopped the movement and the figure turned toward me.

"Denise! What the hell are you doing?"

"Oh Randy. I'm so sorry to wake you. I was hoping I could go and be back without anyone being the wiser."

"Go where? I don't get it. We're supposed to be staying here to avoid being killed. Why would you want to go out in the middle of the night, dressed all in black? You look like a cat burglar."

Denise looked abashed. "I was thinking about what Jennifer Gladue said about who they were targeting, and it occurred to me that Kieran is all of those things. He is a director, involved with both the Freewill Festival and the Fringe, and he is very much into physical activity. We were talking about going skiing in the mountains this winter over the Christmas break, and maybe doing some ice climbing in the Maligne Canyon."

"So he's outdoorsy. That doesn't explain why you're sneaking out in the middle of the night. The police have just barely got over the idea that you are their prime suspect and here you go, playing right into the hands of whoever is trying to frame or kill you."

"But I was thinking I could be there and back before dawn."

"Dawn comes pretty damn early these days." I had to go to the bathroom, but I couldn't risk turning my back on Denise while she was set on doing something foolish. "Where were you planning to be back from?"

"Kieran's back shed."

"Okay, so I really have to go to the washroom. Promise me you will not go anywhere without me." Denise brightened in spite of herself. I pulled the door closed, hoping she'd honour the promise. To keep her there, I kept talking through the door. "What is in Kieran's back shed?"

"That's what I was hoping to find out. I was lying there, thinking about what Detective Gladue had been saying to us, and thinking about him and his skiing and ice climbing, and the whole thought of climbing gear is what I landed on."

I washed my hands and swiped them on a towel before rejoining my friend the second-storey gal in the hallway.

"So you think that Kieran's climbing ropes are how he got Eleanor into position under the river valley stairs and hoisted Christian into the bell tower?"

"For all I know, they're how he got onto my balcony the other night. And he would know where to find me. He has actually been here, which I can't say for every other director in town."

Once again, she had a point.

"Okay, give me five minutes to get dressed. I'm coming with you."

Steve was going to kill me, but that was only if we didn't end up dead first. I slipped into socks, a pair of jeans, a bra, and a sweatshirt. The nights were just starting to cool down a bit from the heat of the days, and although we'd been stuck inside for three days, we had spent enough time on Denise's balcony to gauge a slight chill in the weather.

Denise was wearing her running shoes, but I grabbed my walking sandals. I hadn't really packed for breaking and entering when we'd planned my extended sleepover. In fact, we were just lucky my sweatshirt was plain and dark-hued, and not my World of Science souvenir glow-in-the-dark constellations map.

Denise popped her keys and a small flashlight from her kitchen drawer into a thin leather fanny pack. I grabbed my phone, setting it on silent, thinking it would be useful as either a way to call for help or to take photos of incriminating evidence we discovered in Kieran's back shed. If we ever got to his shed.

I whispered to Denise as we went down the stairs to her

underground parking stall, "If the police have the place under surveillance, what makes you think they'll not notice us driving away?"

"They have been coming around on the hour. I don't think there is anything happening out there right now, at 2:18. We can head out the parkade door, and left down the alley, drive through the next alley and be out on University Avenue within a block. Mostly, traffic goes in and out either on 76 Avenue to the east, or at the light right across from the Aberhart Clinic to the north. Very few people pay attention to the first Saskatchewan Drive entrance ever since they closed Keillor Road and the LRT tied things up at the other end. It just doesn't pay to cut through Belgravia anymore."

I shrugged. She sounded like she'd thought things through, and that was enough for me. My friend was one of the top scholars in her field. If she had set her mind to this problem, she had dealt with all the potential pitfalls and possibilities. In fact, that was the reason I had always known without a doubt that Denise was innocent of the crimes, even when the police were considering her their prime suspect. If Denise *had* been the killer, not only would no suspicion have fallen on her, but all the murders would have looked like accidents.

As we drove down a back alley completely free of police vehicles, I realized that the first death was indeed still looking like an accident. I glanced at my friend, so determined in her actions, which at present included driving down a narrow alley with only running lights on. This was no time to doubt her morality. Denise was no killer.

She flipped the lights on when we got to the end of the second alley. Another turn and we were making a left out onto University Avenue.

"Doesn't Kieran live over in Old Strathcona?"

"He's in Mill Creek, but I figured we would take the scenic route."

"It's almost three in the morning, what's to see?"

"Trust me, Randy." And sure enough, once we were down the hill by Hawrelak Park, where I had spent so much of the earlier part of the summer, we crossed the bridge and beetled along the northside of the North Saskatchewan River and down River Valley Road toward the baseball stadium. Denise turned right onto the Macdonald Expressway and crossed the river again before turning right up the hill by the Old Timers' Cabin. I had counted perhaps three lights, and with Denise's luck, they had all been green. Had she used the south-side route, there would have been at least fifteen intersections with streetlights.

"At this time of night there's much less traffic, unless you are out on a weekend, but yes, if you try for the arterial routes through or around this city, you can mange pretty well."

I let Denise talk, mostly to keep us both from fretting about what we were about to do. She drove two blocks further than Kieran's street and turned left into a leafy, dark avenue.

We found a place to park a block and a half away. She and I walked quietly back the two blocks, turning down the alleyway behind Kieran's house. After three or four lots, Denise shook her head and led me back to the mouth of the alley.

"All the fences are high, and I can't figure out which is his house. We're going to have to go around to the street side and count from the corner." We walked to the other side of the road, which was the side without streetlights, and counted seven buildings till Denise nodded and pointed at the tall house with the huge veranda. It looked well kept, but older than the houses on either side. Since this was a desirable neighbourhood, with access to a ravine park and five minutes away from either downtown or Old Strathcona, a lot of people had been buying up older houses and razing them to erect modern megahomes in their stead. Most had incorporated elements of the neighbourhood into their designs, so it could have been a lot worse than it was.

Kieran's house was painted in dark colours; maybe it was even black. All cats look black in the dark, as my grandmother used to say, which was some sort of sexual aphorism that I never wanted to get into with her. There were no lights showing from the front. There were no lights on in any of the houses, but of course, at three in the morning that wasn't terribly surprising. Edmonton had never been accused of being the city that never slept.

We doubled back to the alley and walked in, counting to eight. There was a two-car garage taking up most of the access to the yard and a six-foot gate filling in the rest of the space to the left of the garage. Even in the dark, the fence boards looked darker than their neighbours'. Denise looked at me and shrugged before reaching for the latch on the gate.

The hinges were well oiled and made no sound as we let ourselves into Kieran Frayne's backyard. "The shed is on the other side of the garage," Denise whispered into my ear. We crept forward along the dark path beside the garage, me hoping that Kieran didn't have an outdoor security system, or a dog. As we rounded the corner, no motion detector lights came on, so we picked our way past the jardinières that lined Kieran's brick-covered yard. The man had no grass at all. I doubted we'd be tripping over a lawn mower in his shed.

Denise got to the shed first, but I managed to grab her shoulder before she touched the hasp on the door. I motioned to her to pull her sleeve down over her hand. She smiled grimly and did so. The door wasn't locked, mostly I guessed because who would assume there was a narrow building wedged in between the garage and the neighbour's fence? The shed was tucked back two feet from the edge of the garage, so from most of the yard it would be invisible. I wondered how Denise had known it was there.

She turned to me and held her finger over her lips, the universal sign of "you're too stupid to realize we need to be quiet now." Reaching into her fanny pack—which she must have bought for her trail running, because there was no way Denise would keep something that was no longer in style just for sentimental reasons—she pulled out her penlight. It was a surprisingly wide and powerful beam.

The first thing we saw inside was Kieran's ten-speed bike. Or maybe it was a fifteen-speed; I couldn't tell. My bike was a single-speed with the brake in the pedals A skateboard was leaned up against the wall between the studs, and some high-tech snowshoes were in the next section of studs. Cross-country skis and their downhill cousins were tucked back-to-back between large brad nails that appeared to have been pounded in deliberately for them. A scuffed pair of polymer-and-clamps speedskates hung from another nail.

Denise knelt near a red bag and unzipped it to reveal its contents. "Here's his climbing gear." She sat back on her heels to let me see inside the bag. There were various shiny metal pieces with one sharp end and a hole at the other, a short-handled pickaxe, a belt or harness of some sort, a helmet that looked like fibreglass cladding on a Styrofoam bucket, and a bunch of carabiners and hooks.

"Where are the ropes?"

"That's a very good question," Denise whispered.

I took pictures of the bag's contents, the bag in situ, and the length of the shed, hoping the flash of my camera wouldn't alert anyone to our whereabouts. Finally, I tapped Denise on the arm. She was poking about at the far end of the shed in a jumble of old lawn chairs and a frayed umbrella.

"We need to get out of here." She nodded. We made our way carefully past Kieran's tidy sporting equipment and out of the shed. The space and relative brightness of the outdoors made navigating the backyard a breeze. Pretty soon we were heading down the alley and back toward Denise's car.

On the way home we stayed on the south side. Denise drove Whyte Avenue till it meshed with University Drive and then replicated her earlier route back to her condo. By mutual agreement, we decided sleep was out of the question. Although Kieran's shed had been almost unnaturally tidy, I showered quickly to remove any possible residual cobwebs while Denise put on coffee. When I came into the living room in my sweats and a towel turbaned on my head, she excused herself to wash up.

I drank coffee and uploaded the photos I'd taken on my phone to my laptop. The flash had done a good job of brightening the scene, showing more in the split-second captures than we had managed with a concentrated flashlight source. I was right. Kieran was an amazing housekeeper. Make that shed-keeper. Everything was in its place. Everything was clean and tidy. There was no dirt on the floor to show up footprints, which was lucky for us, because we hadn't even thought about that when we'd sneaked in.

There was a shot of half of Denise's face in one photo, which was something we didn't need to have as evidence. I scanned it for any other useful data, but it was mostly of the far end of the shed, where the junky stuff was stashed. I pulled the photo over to the recycle bin on my laptop and clicked on the next photo. The bag of climbing gear, open on the floor of the shed, looked even larger and emptier as I thought about the missing ingredient of ropes. I wondered if they were now in the evidence room at the southside police station, or still hanging in the bell tower of the Walterdale Theatre. Or maybe they were somewhere else, for a perfectly valid reason. For all I knew, climbers didn't store their ropes with their clamps and hooks.

I looked at the other pictures, and Denise came and sat beside me, eager to find something useful from our dangerous foray.

"He's awfully organized."

I nodded. "I've never seen such a tidy shed. Is his house the same?"

"His pantry looks like a store display. And everything is where it needs to be. There is a second shampoo bottle behind the one presently being used. The recycle bin is under the mail table in the hall, and his chequebook, stamps, and extra envelopes are in a drawer there, in case he wants to send a donation to a charity that has written him."

"Wow, what sort of mind does it take to be that organized?" I wondered.

Denise shrugged. "He directs two plays simultaneously each summer and is constantly looking ahead for the next winter projects to tide him over between seasons. To survive in that context, you'd need to be organized."

I gazed at the photos. Everything was in its place in Kieran's world. Everything except his ropes.

41.

The phone rang, startling us both. It was barely 6:00 a.m. Denise unfolded herself from the couch and went to grab her cordless phone at the kitchen island. "Yes?" She listened for a moment and then handed me the phone.

It was Steve. "I tried your cellphone, but you weren't picking up so I chanced waking you both up." I had plugged my phone into its charger after depleting most of its reserves taking photos.

"That's okay, we were awake."

"Well, you may be off the hook and out of purdah soon."

"Why, what's happened?"

"Cars were called to Kieran Frayne's house an hour ago. Apparently there was a break-in. I'll let you know as soon as I know anything more. I'm not sure whether it was Frayne who called it in, or his house-sitter, or what."

"Uh …"

"What? Randy, I don't like the sound of that."

"What sort of a break-in are we talking about?"

"Side door smashed in, main floor trashed, some things probably stolen, but it's unclear, because of the mess. You know the drill. Why?"

"I think you need to come over here."

"Why?"

"It's something I'd rather not say on the phone." Steve muttered a few choice words, but I chose to ignore them. He would be even angrier when he heard what we had to say.

"Okay, I can be there in an hour. Put on the coffee."

I pressed the red button on Denise's phone and handed it back to her.

"We're in so much trouble. Kieran's house was broken into tonight. Maybe while we were in the shed."

Denise paled. "They're going to think it was us, aren't they?"

"I am not sure what will happen. We have to tell Steve we were there. But since we didn't see anything happening in the house, we're not much good as witnesses. So, we just have to figure out how not to be fingered for the break-in. Why did someone break into his house tonight of all nights? We have been sitting here on ice for four days and nothing has happened out there. The one night we do something stupid, and bam." I looked at Denise and she looked at me.

"Someone is watching us," we said in unison and looked out into the sunrise-lit, tree-filled window. Out there, someone knew exactly what we were up to and how to manipulate the information to our detriment.

True to his word, Steve was there within the hour. I had

347

changed from my sweats into clothing a little more armour-clad: a tee-shirt, cardigan, and jeans. I needed to feel my strongest, because I had a feeling this was going to be a dressing-down like I'd never seen before.

Denise volunteered to start. She told the story, stressing how it had been her idea, and that I had gone along only to help and protect her. Steve's eyebrows arched almost into his hairline as she explained the drive through two sets of back alleys to get out of the neighbourhood, and he put his head in his hands as she described sneaking into Kieran's back garden and rifling through his sports equipment shed.

"It never occurred to you that this is exactly why I asked you to stay locked away?" he said finally. "Whoever is using you as the scapegoat for his or her crimes obviously has you under surveillance. You were just playing into their hands."

"But how could we know they would be robbing Kieran's house at the same time?"

"I doubt if they planned to. Your being there was all the opportunity they needed. We'll probably discover there was nothing stolen from Frayne's house at all. It was just done to implicate you once more."

"That's going to an awful lot of trouble, though."

"Murder is an awful lot of trouble."

"But Kieran wasn't murdered, right?"

"Lucky for you. What the heck were you looking for, anyhow?"

I opened up my laptop. "We have pictures."

"I don't think I want to see them. I shouldn't even know about them." Steve still sounded mad, angrier than I'd ever heard him.

"Look, we're not going to lie about going over there, so you might as well see the pictures, right?" I opened up the file I'd emailed to myself from my phone. Steve sat down heavily beside me on the couch. I wiggled closer to him to let Denise sit on the other side of me, and felt him solid and resistant against me. I wondered if I'd pushed him too far this time.

"Here is the shed." I pointed to the screen.

"Which wasn't locked," Denise interjected.

"Right, so even if we 'entered,' we didn't actually 'break,'" I said. "I hope you can persuade Keller of that finer point." I clicked through to the next photo. "Denise had a flashlight and these are taken with the camera flash, so it looks really bright, but you know, as sheds go, you could eat off the floor. Kieran is compulsively neat about his stuff. I hope they didn't do too much damage to the inside of his house. I have a feeling that untidiness hurts him."

"Maybe whoever did it knew that." Denise nodded. "Going for the worst they could do to him."

Steve looked skeptical. "Someone who has been murdering folks suddenly starts punishing others by disarranging their houses? It doesn't totally compute."

I continued to click through the pictures, which were amazingly good for having been taken by a phone camera under less than perfect conditions.

"And that is his gear for ice climbing." Denise was narrating the photos to Steve as I clicked through.

I stared at the photo of Kieran's climbing gear sans ropes. I had captured a bit of Denise's feet as well. Her shoes were tidy in the shot, lined up evenly, just like Kieran's would be.

"Hang on," I said, and clicked backward to the beginning of the file. There was his bike and his skateboard and his snowshoes and his skis, but where were any boots or shoes for these sports? "His shoes and boots are missing, too."

"What do you mean?" they asked in unison, and then laughed a bit across my head. I was too caught up in my discovery to care.

"See? All the equipment except the shoes or the ropes or a sleeping bag or anything fabric. I bet you his ropes weren't used on any of the victims. I'll bet you they're inside the house, somewhere a mouse couldn't chew on them. That may be why this shed is so preternaturally clean. Kieran might have had an infestation of mice." I sat back, proud of my deductions.

Steve smiled at me for the first time since he got there. "Not bad, Nancy Drew, but you're forgetting one thing."

"What's that?"

"The house has been ransacked, so unless we find climbing ropes hanging neatly above a whole shelf of sports shoes, we're not going to be able to prove your theory. And if the ropes are gone, this break-in will only serve to cloud whoever might have used them last. I'm not totally sure you can determine ownership from a rope, no matter how great your forensic team is."

"I think the worst thing here is that someone is watching and following us," said Denise, as we veered off from what for her was the real topic. "Do you think they are sitting out there right now, listening in to our conversation with one of those spy microphones? Or have they bugged my condo?"

All the talk of bugs and mice was beginning to make my skin crawl.

"It could be even easier than that." Steve shrugged. "They could be monitoring the GPS on your phone and just watching when you made a move."

"So I drove down all those back alleys for nothing?"

"I wouldn't call it nothing," Steve said drily. "You did manage to avoid the police drive-through from calling in anything of interest. But yeah, it's way easier to keep track of someone these days. Everything is potentially programmed to connect and communicate with everything else. Your phone could talk to your fridge to determine whether you need to stop and get milk on your way home. Your GPS that helps you find your destination transforms you into a flashing blip on the great map of the electronic world. It just depends who is keeping track of that map."

"Who do you think it is?" I asked.

"Well, I know we have the capacity. I'm just wondering if someone else does, too."

Even with all the coffee we'd been ingesting, I was suddenly wildly sleepy. I gave an enormous yawn and Steve laughed. "Right on time. The adrenalin is wearing off. I predict the two of you are going to need a nap for a few hours right about now. Should I come back later?" Denise, who had been politely hiding her yawns behind her hand, smiled and nodded.

Steve promised to increase the number of drive-by patrols, then left to report our having been at the crime scene without being involved. We agreed that he would call around 7:00 p.m.

to make sure we'd woken up in good time. I didn't want to lose an entire day or sleep too long and then throw off my rhythms entirely.

Even with everything going on, I didn't recall any crazy dreams when I woke up, spot on at 6:00 p.m. All I knew was that I was ravenously hungry. I pulled on the jeans I had left at the end of the bed and shuffled to the guest bathroom to splash water on my face and run my toothbrush over my tongue. I then headed downstairs to her kitchen area.

Denise was already there, cracking eggs for an omelette. "Breakfast for supper okay?"

I nodded happily and went to man the toast station. Soon we were digging into a hearty meal. We tried to keep the conversation light until we were smearing jam on our last bits of toast, with general comments on how weird it was to have a long nap in the middle of the day, but a full sleep seemed proper, and how circadian rhythms could affect one's mental capabilities, and whether we liked apple butter more than ginger marmalade.

We couldn't keep off the topic forever, though. It was like when your tongue can't help going back to explore the sore tooth.

"Who do you think could be tracking us?"

"Tracking me, you mean. Randy, I am so sorry I got you into this."

"Don't be. You're my friend. Of course I am in it."

"I wonder if things are ever going to feel ordinary again, once this is all over."

"I'm betting they'll sort themselves out once the killer is caught."

"You don't suppose they'll get away with it, do you?"

I shook my head. "Steve and Iain are so committed to their task. They're like bloodhounds who never give up the trail."

"The trouble is the trail keeps leading back to me." Denise moaned a little.

This was the closest she'd come to self-pity throughout this whole ordeal, so I knew things were getting to her. Heck, they'd be getting to me by now, too. She really was amazing, sailing through all this with grace and dignity, if you could overlook her scrabbling through a shed in the dark, though even that she had done with a certain decorum.

It occurred to me that the ordeal really had been hard on Denise, with the police suspecting her and the murderer seeming to frame her deliberately. I stared into the far upper corner of Denise's kitchen where the ash cupboards met the wall.

"Randy? What is it?"

"What is what?"

"You've got that look, where you're cooking something up."

I refocused on her face across the table.

"I was just thinking, what if we've got this all wrong? What if the murders haven't been about getting the Chautauqua job, except maybe incidentally? What if it's all been about targeting and discrediting you?"

Denise stared at me.

"Think about it. Right from the start, you've been set up as the prime suspect. Someone had to be doing that deliberately. It couldn't be a complete coincidence."

"It is hard to believe that someone has a vendetta against me. And I have no idea why someone would hate me that much, either."

"Maybe they don't hate you, but they want you out of the way."

"Why not just kill me instead of Eleanor and Christian, then?"

"I guess because they needed Eleanor and Christian dead anyhow. But a big part of the plan is to destroy your career or get you out of the way for some reason. The trick is to figuring out what the reason would be."

"Yes, that would help enormously. Or we could just hope for the police to catch a crazed killer and give me my life back."

"We could figure this out by a process of elimination. After all, we have some parameters. It has to be someone who knows you. For something to be this personal, I would say it was a person you knew, too, not just a disgruntled student from a few years back."

"Someone I know. You need me to make a list of all the people I know? Hell, Randy, I teach more than a hundred students a term. Where do we start?"

"We start with the people here in town, the ones who want something you have."

"What do I have that anyone would want?"

"Well, you have this gorgeous condo, and you have a great job, and you had a cool boyfriend."

"Who is now conveniently Sarah's boyfriend."

"Think about that."

"Sarah? You think Sarah killed everyone just so that she would break up Kieran and me? Why didn't she just go after him right away, when we were at that party last spring?"

"I don't know! I'm not a psychologist, sorting out the impulses that impel people to do what they do. I am just trying to figure out the patterns that make sense and come to a logical conclusion. Sarah is a contender, you have to admit."

"So if we think Sarah wanted to deliberately frame me, what about everyone else we've been suspecting? Like Kieran himself? And Taryn; you can't tell me you haven't been suspecting her. I could tell when we ran into her at the Safeway."

"Well you have to admit, she'd be a great director for Chautauqua."

"That doesn't mean she'd kill to get there."

"No, but you have to consider the possibilities."

"Okay, so we have people who hate me, people who climb for sport, people who know their way around a backstage, and people who dislike actors. Who else should we put on the list?"

"I think there is someone who is on all those lists, or most of them, and when we figure out who that is, we'll know who our killer is."

42.

By the time Steve called we had cleared the dishes and got out pencils, pads of paper, and our laptops. It was back to planning central, and we couldn't have been more serious. If they'd had us at Bletchley Park in the '40s, with the concentration we were focusing on the task, they'd have cracked the Enigma Code in a week.

We didn't have a week. We had no idea when the killer was going to strike again, if the target was someone unsuspecting, or if it was us. I was hoping we'd raised the stakes enough for whoever was out there to take another crack at us, since we were on edge enough to be up for a fight. Not that I wanted a knife at my throat. My innards did a cold little shimmy when I thought of that.

Denise was playing with Taryn and Kieran on her list. I had Micheline and Louise and Sarah on mine, but I kept getting the feeling I was missing something. Or someone. There was somebody I'd been talking with this summer who fit all our criteria.

If only I could figure out who it was, tell the police, and get them removed from wherever they were skulking in the shadows, driving me out of my mind with fear.

I tried to visualize the overlying logic. Eleanor was killed and Denise was implicated because they had met previously on running trails and because Denise was thought to be jealous of Eleanor having an affair with Kieran, whom Denise was seeing. The only way for the killer to deliberately implicate Denise would be to know Denise and Eleanor had met while running. Either that, or the killer would have to know that Denise ran, and somehow compel Eleanor to running some of Denise's chosen routes in order to create a "chance" meeting. Now I was getting really convoluted. Surely it was a matter of opportunity. The killer saw that they had met and used that as a convenient blind for his or her own actions. That explanation seemed most likely.

Kieran would have known they had met, since either woman might have talked about the other to him. Micheline might have known about the affair, but would she have known that Denise and Eleanor had met? Maybe Eleanor had mentioned a running partner to her? The same would be true of Louise; it could have come up as greenroom chat—where she ran and wasn't she nervous of running alone, and who she ran with. Eyebrows would be raised, and Eleanor might even enjoy the cachet of running with her lover's girlfriend. Maybe that was what Eleanor had sought, the danger of being found out on various levels.

It made me think less of Eleanor, even though I had been raised to try not to pile resentments on dead people who could no longer defend themselves or make things right. In affairs where a third party is involved, I have a worse time with the woman who cheats, knowing she is hurting another woman in the process. I am not sure why I believe there should be a universal sisterhood, wherein every woman keeps an eye out for every other woman. Goodness knows I'd been disabused of that concept more than enough times. Women were no more and no less collegial or supportive to each other than men were. And some, I had to admit, seemed to want to see other women fail in pathways where they themselves had succeeded, perhaps to make their own journey appear to be that much more amazing.

So, yes, Eleanor may well have bragged subtly that she was cuckolding the woman she was running with. It was a very Shakespearian thing to do, all in all.

Which left me with Kieran, Micheline, and Louise all likely aware of the connections between Eleanor and Denise. I wasn't sure whether I could make the same case for Taryn, but she was on Denise's list, anyhow.

When I moved the parameters to Christian's murder, things got murkier. For one thing, there was no connection between Christian and Denise that I could think of. The only links I could make took me back to who knew that Denise and I would be Fringing that evening. If they wanted to implicate Denise, murdering him at a time she might be conveniently wandering by was icing on the cake. As far as I could tell, everyone could have known about it. We had run into Louise and Sarah just after buying our tickets. We had seen other people in the beer tent who might have spoken with the suspects.

I looked at my paper, which had lines drawn to Denise and to each other all over, till it looked like some macabre spider web with my best friend in the middle of it. The pattern had to be there somewhere.

Or it could be someone else entirely, whom we weren't factoring in as important. Someone who was always there, whom we didn't see.

My pencil broke in my hand, causing Denise to look up. She raised her eyebrows slightly.

"You're cut off the coffee."

"I don't care, I want a glass of water, anyhow." I pushed away from the table and walked around the kitchen island to help myself. I rinsed my coffee cup in the water I was running to get it cold and then stuck one of Denise's heavy crystal tumblers under the stream. I opened the dishwasher just enough to pull out the upper tray and slide the coffee cup in. Denise was right. I didn't need anything more in the way of stimulants at the moment.

I drank my water leaning against the counter, looking toward the dining and living area of Denise's condo and out the window to the balcony and the trees beyond. Denise sat at the table, scribbling something on her legal pad from material she was dredging up on the Internet, like a Chekovian character as the curtains open, working away prior to the scene's action.

And that's when it all shifted for me. Denise sitting in her living area, as if she was on a stage, with the audience sitting somewhere out beyond the windows made me rethink the whole concept and the timing of things.

"Denise?"

She looked up, distracted. Deep into her research, and this work being so vital to her own livelihood, my interruption better be worth it, her look told me. I thought it was.

"Can you tell me again what Kieran's annual schedule is like?"

"What do you mean?"

"I remember you telling me about how organized he has to be when we were talking about how freakishly neat he is. So, what is his schedule like?"

She sat back in her chair. "Well, he is the artistic director of a summer festival, and he directs two plays within that context. He also directs at least two other productions here in town or in Calgary over the winter season, and sometimes he takes on teaching duties for a directing class at the university, though not so much these days. They tend to dole those out pretty sparingly."

"Okay, so he is obviously busy in rehearsal from the end of May for the Shakespeare in the park plays."

"That's right. He rehearses the comedy first for three weeks and gets it up on its feet, and then starts the tragedy for the next three weeks, with a weekly run-through of the comedy. Then for the month of July, he is running the festival, being on site for notes and polish, there to help with any sound problems, interviews with the press, that sort of thing. They do a post-mortem for the board of directors in early August, and then he usually takes a break, unless he has an early fall production with the Mayfield or the Vertigo in Calgary or somewhere else. Usually though, if he directs, it's the January production for one of those theatres." She frowned, trying to sort things out chronologically. "He has to be at a monthly board meeting for the Festival, and

I think he sits on the Edmonton Arts Council, which is a two-year commitment. Those are each one evening a month."

"So he wouldn't go out of town in, say, February or March?"

"No way. That would be when he was working with the set designer to create a dual-purpose set for the plays chosen, and he'd be auditioning and casting."

"And when did you two meet and start dating?"

"We met at a party for the first English/Drama *Romeo and Juliet* reading, the one that kicked off the spring session project, which was March 15."

"Beware the Ides of March," I muttered.

Denise laughed. "Indeed. I remember it for that reason. We were joking that we should have been performing Julius Caesar."

"And you hit it off immediately and started dating right away."

"Pretty much. Kieran is a force to be reckoned with. Well, you know. He can be very charming."

"So, when you met, Kieran had already cast both plays for the following summer's plays."

"Yes, he would have had to."

"So, he had already hired Eleanor Durant before he met you."

"What are you implying?"

"I'm thinking that maybe he started seeing Eleanor back in February, then decided he was going to frame her for his murder of Oren Gentry, under the idea she was aiming for his job as well. So, back in February, he had to find someone to be framed for her murder, as well."

"So you are saying he deliberately chatted me up and began dating me just to frame me for murder? Wow, can you be a little more demoralizing? Was my being hired in the English department just some weird affirmative action ploy? Do you think I'm adopted?"

"I don't mean to imply that you have to worry about people falling for you legitimately, silly. But think about the timing of things. And the way all of this has been crafted, like some weird version of *Othello* mixed with *Macbeth*, where everyone is jealous, and everyone assumes someone else is plotting, and the focus is on the wrong person at all times. We don't argue that you were set up, right?"

"I guess." I could tell she was still smarting from the thought of being dated strategically.

"And someone has known every minute of the day where you were, what you do, what running routes you take. I'll bet he even hired me in order to pump me for information about you and your whereabouts."

"Did he?"

"Did he what?"

"Did he pump you for information about my whereabouts?" Denise was being deliberately obstreperous, probably in order to prove she couldn't have been set up so blatantly without her knowledge. I tried to think about what she was asking. Had Kieran asked anything that smacked of probing?

I couldn't think of anything, but then again I was sort of inured to Denise's paramours asking me questions about her on occasion in order to come up with the perfect Christmas gift or the most romantic outing. Maybe Kieran had done a bit of that, back in the spring. We'd talked a lot over the course of working the Shakespeare festival.

"You know, if you're going to be hurt about being wooed in order to be framed, just think about me. I was supposedly hired for my expertise and creativity. If I'm right about this tack, then all that was hooey and I was hired just so he could keep a better eye on you." I frowned. That did hurt. I guessed I should cut Denise some slack.

Denise stretched back in her chair and pulled her hair into a ponytail at the top of her head with both hands, scrunching her fingers into her hair, fighting for clarity. "Well, if we accept that premise, then the rest of the events have to fit. Could Kieran have killed Oren and Eleanor and Christian? Was it physically possible for him to be there to kill them? We'll have to sort through everyone's timetables. God, it feels like a Freeman Wills Crofts mystery with railway timetables clogging up everything."

"Wasn't that Dorothy Sayers?"

"She did only one, as I recall, to twit him. He was very popular in his day."

"I didn't know you read that sort of thing."

"Normally I don't, but I was tracing references to and effects of Thomas Bowdler's *Family Shakespeare*, and came upon Croft in my grad days. His novels were so calming and predictable that I used them to put me to sleep at night. I have a soft spot for timetable mysteries, I guess."

"Well, whatever the case, we have Kieran capable of killing Eleanor, trussing up her body and getting her down the hillside to stuff her under the stairs. We know he climbs."

"But his ropes are missing."

"So he says. Maybe he was actually in his house last night—was it just last night?—and saw us checking out the sports shed, and so he trashed his own place to cast more suspicion on us and cover up the fact that his climbing ropes were missing."

"And what about Christian?"

"I can't think of anyone more likely to be let backstage than Kieran, can you? He knows everyone in the theatre community. He could have just said he was looking for Christian, gone back, killed him, strung him up the bell tower and strolled out to the front of house. It would be easy enough to say he couldn't find him and 'would you tell him I've called round?' No one would have batted an eye."

"Did that happen?"

"Did what happen?"

"Did Kieran tell the front of house that he was looking for Christian and then announce that he couldn't find him? Is that in the police file?"

"How should I know? I've been here with you. I am just trying to point out how easy it would be for Kieran to move among the folks in any theatre. People would know him on sight, some would be in awe of him, others would be wanting to curry favour to be thought of for roles, others would have worked with him previously and be on friendly terms. He could walk anywhere. You talk about Golden Age mysteries—Kieran is Father Brown's proverbial letter carrier. Like Chesterton pointed out, no one notices him because he is supposed to be there."

Denise pursed her lips, ready to say something, and then stalled. She was thinking hard. "Okay, so he had the means, and he had the motive—if the motive is indeed wanting Oren Gentry's job. So, are we thinking he killed Oren, too?"

"It's got to be pretty easy to stage a heart attack with someone who trusts you enough to let you get close to their tea or food or whatever. Kieran and Oren could have been dining together for any number of reasons. Who knows, maybe he stuck foxglove in his salad?"

"I don't think I'd even know what foxglove looked like."

"I barely know what arugula looks like. Those boxed salads are so full of assorted, somewhat bitter, leaves that I think we might occasionally be eating nettles."

"Okay, but what about breaking into my place the other night? Could that have been Kieran?"

"We know he has climbing gear, and we know he was familiar with where you lived. Why couldn't it have been him?"

Denise's face crumpled. "Because I thought he was a good person. We were intimate. I don't drop defences for just anyone. There is some scrutiny involved. And now you're telling me I've been used, and fooled, and duped, and nearly killed by someone I'd thought was trustworthy enough to see me naked. That's why I'm fighting this."

"I know. This is not easy, and it's a lot to parse. You have to get over the idea that it was somehow a weakness that he managed to fool you, though. He is a great director, and before he was a great director, he was a fabulous actor. He can set a scene and have hundreds of people at a time believe the sky is orange and pigs can fly through it. He turned the full forces of his talent onto you, Denise. You didn't have a chance."

"And like Othello, I was looking only for truth, as I had told no lies. That is how he managed. Why would I second-guess someone like Kieran asking me out? I've had a fair share of attractive, high-powered men in my life. He played on my vanity and I never saw it coming."

"No, he played on your convenience. It was despicable, but certainly no more despicable than murdering the competition to get what he wanted. There is a measure of sociopathy in his makeup."

"I was reading about how there are more psychopaths walking about among us than you'd think, that a lot of charismatic, manipulative people like politicians and directors and CEOs score pretty high on the psychopath test."

"Yes, you don't have to be sadistically cruel to be a psychopath. You could score very high on narcissism or manipulation or lack of empathy."

"You would need empathy to be a great actor, though, I should think."

"Maybe. Sometimes I think you just need great observation. Think about Ripley."

"Sigourney Weaver?"

"No, from the Patricia Highsmith novels. He's a chameleon, able to just fit into any world he wants to get into, but he has no empathy or remorse or kindness."

Denise sat forward and put her forearms on the table, and looked, just for a moment, like a sphinx. "I can't take this. We have got to call Steve and toss this all at him."

"You're right. But how do we frame it so he'll take us seriously?

At the moment, I'm a little worried about having worn out my welcome with him. He seemed pretty angry at us for sneaking out."

"He'll be even more ticked off at us if we just sit here and let ourselves get killed by a mad director."

I shrugged and picked up my cellphone to text Steve. Just then it rang, which startled us both into shocked laughter.

"Hello?"

"Randy? What's funny?"

"Nothing, I was just about to text you. What's up?"

"We just got a message from a patrol car in the area who spotted a plate we have on our list. I'm calling to tell you not to open the door to anyone. What were you about to send me?"

"We've been sorting through our collective memories and thoughts, and we want you to think seriously about Kieran Frayne as a suspect. We're thinking he started dating Denise as a ploy to frame her for murders he was intending to commit."

"As cold as that sounds, it's something we're taking seriously. It's Frayne who is in your vicinity. I'll notify Jennifer and then I'm coming over. Don't open your door to anyone. We have access and can let ourselves in. Do you hear me?"

"I hear you. What are we supposed to do? I don't want to hole up in a bathroom again."

"Get your backs to a wall, stay away from the windows, and keep your phones with you. Someone will be right there."

I hung up the phone. Just hearing part of my conversation had made Denise stand up and hover, ready for fight or flight. "Steve says Kieran has been spotted in the neighbourhood.

We're to stay away from the windows and keep our backs to a wall. Steve's coming, but I figure it will take him at least fifteen minutes."

Denise ran to the kitchen island and brought out two sheathed knives. She took them to the living area and slid them down the narrow crevice between the cushions and armrests on either side of the leather sofa. She turned off the kitchen light and lit a pole lamp close to the window, drawing the curtains across the sliding glass window to the balcony.

"He won't be able to see us moving about with the lamp casting the light to the curtains, like a scrim."

"Ha, fight theatre with theatre. I like it."

I pocketed my cellphone and took up position on the sofa. Denise's front access required a call up to the suite. She placed her cell on the coffee table and watched it obsessively, willing it not to ring.

"What will I say if he calls?"

"You are within your rights to make him stew. After all, he dropped you when you were considered a suspect and took up with one of your colleagues almost immediately. You could be stinging from that. He doesn't need to know you suspect him of murder."

"This could all be coincidence. Kieran might be driving through the neighbourhood to get somewhere innocuous, or to deke around traffic near the University Drive intersection. He might not be the murderer at all."

"And maybe I'm Thomas Pynchon."

We sat in Denise's beautiful condo on her quiet street waiting for god knows what. I was just hoping Steve would get there before we got a phone buzz from the lobby or a grappling hook on the balcony.

Denise reached across the space between us and grabbed my hand to squeeze it. I squeezed back with all the reassurance I could put into my fingers. It occurred to me that we had never held hands before. How could that be? We had been friends since grad school, through thick and thin. Why was it that friends didn't touch? My images of friendship had been forged on Anne Shirley and her bosom friend, Diana Barry, walking arm in arm down the flowered lane. Instead of that simple affection, modern life had brought us smart lunches and air kisses. I held my kindred spirit's hand and waited for a murderer to come and find us.

A noise came from the hall. Our grip on each other's hand tightened, even though I figured it had to be Steve, as he'd said he had access. He'd made good time.

The key scraped in the lock and the knob turned. I realized I'd been holding my breath, since it came out in a snort of fear. Steve could have knocked first. I was about to tell him off for scaring us like that when the door opened.

And there stood Kieran Frayne, smiling with sardonic charm.

"Well, well, it looks as if I might be expected. Is the coffee on?"

43.

"How the hell did you get a key to my condo?" Denise sputtered. The anticipatory fear we'd been feeling was manifesting itself in anger. I just hoped she didn't forget to factor in the fact that she was talking to a double or triple murderer.

"The key was simple, love. I filched your keys out of your bag one brunch and left you for a few minutes to grab something at Canadian Tire, remember? The extra fob I found in a drawer when I was rootling around for a corkscrew. I suppose you forgot to tell the police you had two designated parking stalls in this glorious building, and they didn't think to ask. I've had these since May."

Something was bothering me.

"But if you had the keys, why did you climb up the balcony to get in at Denise the other night?"

Kieran smiled, the same smile he'd used on me all summer down at the park, but now I saw it for the patronizing sneer it really was. "Stage dressing, I'm afraid. I just brought the grappling hook and scraped the edging there so that you wouldn't twig to the fact I had my own entry to your little nest. Of course, it made for an easy exit later on from your bedroom window. You did call in the marines that night, didn't you?" He shook his head, tsk tsk tsk, as if we were somehow lesser beings to have called the police when we heard an intruder.

He was still standing in the doorway, but he took a step in, making both of us tense up even more. Who the heck knew that was even possible?

I found my hand sneaking down beside me into the break between the cushion and the armrest, where Denise had stored a knife for me. I could barely carve a turkey. How could I possibly protect myself from an agile man who had already proved he could fatally wield a knife?

My phone, which was at my left side, was even more inviting, but I was aware that Kieran was paying attention to our every move. Denise must have looked as if she was about to reach for her phone, because he put up a hand to warn her. She pulled her arm back. I tried to relax my hand, letting the fingers play across the screen. I hoped I was hitting the right app, starting the dictation taping feature I'd thought might come in useful for listmaking while walking.

"No, I think this time is for the three of us to talk, before anyone else joins us. Don't you think it would be nice to clear the air a bit? I couldn't come out and chat when you were tiptoeing about in my back garden, so I thought this might be a good time."

"What do we have to talk about?" Denise really was being brave. I am not sure I could have spoken just then.

"Oh, all sorts of things. What you were doing in my shed, why you made the announcement you were applying for the directing position, and just what you are playing at."

"What I'm playing at? Why don't we start with what you're playing at, Kieran? Are you so monomaniacal that your killing people is running second to my sneaking into your shed?"

He waved his hand airily. This time there was a knife in it.

"I thought that was a given to the conversation, Ducks. Of course I have been going after what I wanted, and what I wanted certainly wasn't staging two plays a summer in the vagaries of Edmonton weather on a budget that is decimated by three days of rain and bad houses." He leaned against the kitchen island, still between us and the front door.

"Oren was remarkably trusting, and he really did have a faulty ticker, so a few doses of my father's old digitalis pills just pushed him over the edge. I actually was down in Calgary the weekend he succumbed to his heart attack. It couldn't have played out any better. It was as if it was slated to be. And then that tiresome Eleanor announces that she intends to stay in Edmonton and fill Oren's position. As if.

"I'd just managed to talk her into doing the summer plays, thinking it would bring a whole other demographic out to the park, the sort who need name recognition before they shell out for a ticket. I suppose it could have been worse, of course. She could have been unreachable when she pulled that number. As it was, we were very closely connected." He sneered again, and I put out a hand to Denise's arm, willing her not to rise to the bait. "Pity Christian saw, or thought he saw something. I hope no one ever thinks he was a serious contender for Oren's job."

"And you dated me only to create a patsy for your crimes?" She couldn't help herself. I didn't blame her, but I didn't want Kieran having the upper hand. He was already picking his fingernails with the tip of his very lethal-looking blade.

"Is that what this is all about? Getting back at me for using you so egregiously? Or is it that your ego has been bruised because you're not used to someone playing you? Tell me, my beautiful Denise, what really bothers you? Being framed for murder? Or not really being universally adored?"

He was toying with her. Any minute now she was going to get up and run at him, goaded by his taunts. Then he would kill her, and I would be next.

Something shook loose in me. Maybe it was the thought of being alone with a murderer that had me panicked, but there was no way I was going to let Denise get killed. I stood up.

Kieran's eyebrows went up.

"How do you feel about getting played, Kieran? Or haven't you clued in even now?"

"Clued into what, Randy?"

"We've been on to you since the spring. Why else do you think I agreed to take on the camp job? Do you honestly think it was so fulfilling to spend my time with teenagers? Denise suspected you were up to something ever since Oren Gentry's funeral, so she and I devised this means of keeping track of you."

I was babbling, making it up as I went along, but all I had to do was keep him off balance until Steve and his gang arrived.

"We took our suspicions to the police the minute Eleanor was killed and we've been working closely with Detective Gladue ever since. It was she who suggested we promote Denise as a replacement for Gentry, to force your hand. In fact, this is all being recorded for use against you in the trial, since she was pretty sure you'd show up. We've been a step ahead of you all the way, Kieran. You haven't been playing Denise at all. She's been playing you. That was the one dicey bit of the whole plan. How were we going to get people to believe that someone like Denise would actually be interested in someone like you?"

Kieran's face lost its veneer and I finally saw the real man; a snarling, hateful, spitting face glared back at me. I wasn't sure whether it was his pride at being in control of the production that bothered him the most or the thought that Denise was somehow slumming by dating him, but whatever I'd said, I'd hit the mark. He stepped toward me, and although I tried to hold my ground, I instinctively backed away from the monster with a knife in his hand.

Denise used the time he was focused on me to surreptitiously ease her phone into her hand. She must have hit 911, because both Kieran and I heard the tinny voice of the emergency response, "911 Emergency, how may I direct your call?"

Kieran laughed. "You think the cavalry is going to come riding in, in time to save you? Hello! Man with knife!"

Suddenly Denise was standing beside her sofa, bright orange knife in her hand. I hadn't seen her go for it, and I didn't trust her to do much more than julienne with it, but at least she wasn't cowering. Meanwhile, Kieran had me backed up almost to the drapery. Maybe I could somehow wrap myself in the material and avoid the worst of the knife thrusts. Maybe I could kick the knife out of his hand. Maybe I could lie down and pretend I was dead. I wasn't sure that ploy would even work on black bears, let alone madmen with knives.

I snorted a giggle, in spite of myself, bringing Kieran's unwanted focus right back onto me.

"You find this amusing, Randy?"

"I sure as hell don't, so I don't know why she would. Drop the knife, Frayne."

Jennifer Gladue and two uniformed officers stood in the doorway, guns drawn.

Kieran froze, and then with exaggerated precision leaned down and placed the knife on the floor. He raised his hands and turned to face the music. But before he broke eye contact with me, he winked.

I shuddered and slid to the floor, my legs giving way.

Kieran was marched out of the building to a waiting car. Jennifer had to call in the situation to Steve and Iain McCorquodale before she was able to fully concentrate on either Denise or me.

Both of us were jellied, unable to do much more than shiver, laugh, and occasionally cry a bit. That's what trauma really does. No sitting wrapped in Red Cross blankets on the edge of ambulances and drinking sugared tea for us. Maybe that just happened in movies like *Mrs. Miniver* or *National Treasure*. Instead, we huddled together, too spent by nerves to function.

The younger officer asked us to make a statement, but Jennifer waved him off for the moment and told him to make some coffee. By the time the pot was full, both Iain and Steve had joined us. Denise went to the washroom, and on the way back she brought a couple of shawls for us, so in effect we created the movie scene for ourselves.

"We'll take brief statements now and then I would suggest, for your peace of mind, that you call in a locksmith, Denise."

Denise smiled at Jennifer, and I knew she was striking the right balance of calm assurance and matter-of-factness that would bring her back from whatever abyss she'd glimpsed in those last scary minutes with Kieran.

"Tomorrow is soon enough for a more comprehensive report. If you could come down to the station in the morning, we can manage that there." Denise nodded and so did I.

Steve smiled at Jennifer approvingly. Her take-charge attitude was working. "So, after we get the basics down, I can drive Randy home, unless you would rather stay here one more night?" I looked at Denise, who shook her head.

"I'll be fine and I know you'd like to get back to your own world." She hugged me. "Thank you so much, Randy, for everything."

"What do you mean?"

"Standing up to him there, making up all that crazy plot, saying I was playing him instead of the other way around. I am sure that is what saved our lives."

"I was trying to buy us time."

"You set him off balance, and that was what kept us alive. I am sure of it. For the first time in his twisted trip to landing Oren's job, he wasn't in charge."

I smiled. Maybe I had done something clever. It was nice to think my brilliant friend thought so, anyhow.

We went through the making and signing of statements while Jennifer briefed Steve and Iain. They sent someone down to the underground garage to impound the car that Kieran had driven in with the spare entry fob. With any luck, they'd find traces of Eleanor in the trunk or Christian on some tackle. It would be nice to have physical evidence to shore up our statements of Kieran's preening over the murders.

"Don't worry, he's not going to talk his way out of this. We have everything he said to you on tape," Steve assured me. He drove me back to my cozy little apartment with no view to speak of, which would probably fit entirely into the floor space of Denise's bedroom suite. Even so, I was utterly content to turn the key in the door and come home.

Steve had to deal with a mountain of paperwork at the station but promised to be back before long. With Kieran in custody, I had nothing to worry about and waved him off at the door, feeling remarkably calm.

I'd played at being a Shakespeare expert for the teens in the park. I'd played at setting up Denise as a director for consideration in the Chautauqua job. I'd even played at having the upper hand over a psychopath in the performance of my life. Now it was time to come home, take off the greasepaint, and go back to being myself. Randy Craig.

On my way in, I had retrieved two or three days of mail stuffed into my little brass mailbox. I set my bag down by the door and kicked off my shoes. I looked at the mail. The top two envelopes were come-ons for magazine subscriptions and a third was a letter from my mother, which I would read with pleasure once I'd made some tea. The fourth envelope was from the English department of Grant MacEwan University.

Maybe I was really going back to being my old self after all.

Acknowledgments

I love the theatre community in Edmonton, which is very strong. Beginning with high school programs, summer courses in Drumheller, Artstrek, the Banff Centre, and of course the great BFA/MFA programs at the University of Alberta and the Musical Theatre program at Grant MacEwan, a love of theatre is there for the asking. Couple that with a vital amateur theatre community, great dinner theatres, the mighty Fringe Festival, the flagship Citadel Theatre, Teatro la Quindicina, Workshop West, Theatre Network, Northern Light Theatre, Catalyst Theatre, Rapid Fire Theatre, Firefly Theatre, Concrete Theatre, Shadow Theatre, and the wonderful Freewill Shakespeare Festival—Edmonton is truly blessed.

I want to acknowledge all the folks from the theatre community over the years who have inspired, supported, and befriended me, and who helped with the research for this book: Millard Foster, Tom Peacocke, Jim de Felice, Diane Bessai, Marianne Copithorne, Conni Massing, Mark Meer, Belinda Cornish,

Chris Craddock, Georgina Kravetz, Ben Henderson, the late Bill Meilen, Larry Reese, Tanya Ryga, Maggie Baird, John Wright, Stewart Lemoine, Jeff Haslam, Trevor Schmidt, Darrin Hagan, Timothy Anderson, and Barbara Reese. I would also like to thank Teresa Goldie for bidding on a name for the book as part of a fundraiser for the Freewill Shakespeare Festival (I asked her if she would mind if Christian Norgaard was cast as a suspect or a victim or a smoker, and she replied, "Anything except a Tory!")

I want to thank my great love and husband, Randy Williams, for being my ideal reader, staunch supporter, great promoter, and best friend. Between his devotion, the support of Edmonton booksellers, and the obvious great taste of our book-buying public, the renaissance of local writers of which I am happy to share the wave has made the last several years of quiet, early weekend mornings seem all that much more worthwhile.

While many elements of this novel are based on fact (we DO have a load of theatres in this town), I fabricated some of the other bits. For instance, I played a bit fast and loose with the way the Freewill Shakespeare Festival operates. Yes, they produce two great plays a summer, and they do run a Shakespeare camp for teens, and they are located down in the lovely Hawrelak Park in July (curtain Tuesday through Sundays at 8:00 p.m., matinees on Saturday and Sunday at 2:00 p.m., comedy on odd dates, tragedy on even dates). But their artistic and managing directors are both totally above suspicion in all their actions, and the festival could never afford to lure a big-name actor into their season, because they make their magic for us all on a relative shoestring. So, if you are reading this book and happen to own an airline or a bank or got crazy rich inventing an app for generating cat memes, why not become their corporate sponsor and see what they could do without having to annually worry as they bring us the Bard?

I would also like to thank the publishing team at Turnstone, Jamis Paulson, Sharon Caseburg, and Sara Harms, who make being a Ravenstone author such an enviable position.

I hope you enjoy this book ... and I hope you are using a theatre ticket stub for a bookmark.

Janice

Sticks & Stones
by Janice MacDonald

How dangerous can words be? The University of Alberta's English Department is caught up in a maelstrom of poison-pen letters, graffiti and misogyny. Part-time sessional lecturer Miranda Craig seems to be both target and investigator, wreaking havoc on her new-found relationship with one of Edmonton's Finest.

One of Randy's star students, a divorced mother of two, has her threatening letter published in the newspaper and is found soon after, victim of a brutal murder followed to the gory letter of the published note. Randy must delve into Gwen's life and preserve her own to solve this mystery.

Spellbinding ...
> —W.P Kinsella

...intelligent, thought-provoking and entertaining.
> —Anna Babineau,
> *The Lethbridge Herald*

This is one of those books that begs to be finished at 3 a.m. of the same day."
> —Matthew Stepanic,
> editor of *Glass Buffalo Magazine*

Sticks & Stones / $14.95
ISBN: 9780888012562
Ravenstone

The Monitor
by Janice MacDonald

You're being watched. Randy Craig is now working part-time at Edmonton's Grant MacEwan College and struggling to make ends meet. That is, until she takes an evening job monitoring a chat room called Babel for an employer she knows only as Chatgod. Soon, Randy realizes that a killer is brokering hits through Babel and may be operating in Edmonton. Randy doesn't know whom she can trust, but the killer is on to her, and now she must figure out where the psychopath is, all the while staying one IP address ahead of becoming the next victim.

[Janice MacDonald] has managed to convey the inherent spookiness ... that a social cyberspace can invoke.

—Howard Rheingold

The Monitor / $10.99
ISBN: 9780888012845
Ravenstone

Hang Down Your Head
by Janice MacDonald

Some folks have a talent for finding trouble, no matter how good they try to be, especially Randy Craig. Maybe she shouldn't date a cop. Maybe she should have turned down the job at the Folkways Collection library—a job that became a nightmare when a rich benefactor's belligerent heir turned up dead.

Randy tried to be good—honest!—but now she's a prime suspect with a motive and no alibi in sight.

The Edmonton Folk Music Festival, the city itself and the fascinating politics of funding research in the arts lend a rich texture to this engaging mystery with the twisty end. If you enjoy folk music, you're in for an extra treat. Once again, Randy Craig is a down-to-earth, funny and realistic amateur sleuth: it's good to reconnect with her.

—Mary Jane Maffini, author of
The Busy Woman's Guide to Murder

I have been a performer at the Edmonton Folk Festival for 20 years. I always knew there were a lot of characters there, but until reading Janice's book, I never thought of the festival itself as a character, and a fine place for a murder mystery!

—James Keelaghan

Hang Down Your Head / $16.00
ISBN: 9780888013866
Ravenstone

Condemned to Repeat
by Janice MacDonald

For anyone other than Randy Craig, a contract to do archival research and web development for Alberta's famed Rutherford House should have been a quiet gig. But when she discovers an unsolved mystery linked to Rutherford House in the Alberta Archives and the bodies begin to pile up, Randy can't help but wonder if her modern-day troubles are linked to the intrigues of the past.

Condemned to Repeat *is a compelling tale of secrets from the past colliding with the present, along with a heavy dose of history and travelogue. Plus a murder or two. Not to be missed!*

—Linda Wiken, Mystery Maven Canada blogger,
author, and former bookstore owner

Does for historic sites what she did for music festivals: strews corpses and intrigues in trademark MacDonald style, with giggles and gusto.

—Candas Jane Dorsey, author of
A Paradigm of Earth

Edmontonians in particular will enjoy following the genial Randy Craig through buildings and districts that are as familiar to them as their neighbours, and yet now imprinted with murder and mystery.

—Tom Long, Public Interpretation Coordinator,
Fort Edmonton Park

Condemned to Repeat / $16.00
ISBN: 9780888014153
Ravenstone

Janice MacDonald's Randy Craig Mysteries were the first detective series to be set in Edmonton, Alberta, where Janice lives and works. Having written her master's thesis on detective fiction, she became for many years the *Edmonton Journal* mystery reviewer and an on-air expert for the Canadian television series *Booked*. She worked for almost two decades at the University of Alberta and Grant MacEwan College, teaching English literature, communications, play analysis, creative writing, and extension courses in detective fiction.

Janice has also had a long love affair with the stage. She wrote the music and lyrics for two touring historical musicals for Studio North Theatre : *Northsong* and *Making Tracks*. She was lured away from finishing her MFA in playwriting by the chance to write and produce radio for CKUA, CBC Alberta, and ACCESS. She is a board member of the Freewill Shakespeare Festival. When she was younger, she wanted to be Ethel Merman. When she was really young, she wanted to be an elevator operator.